THE BOOK OF
PANDÆMÓNIUM

The Book of Nevermore is a work of fiction. Names, characters, places, and incidents are the products of the author's imagination or are used fictitiously. Any resemblance to actual events, locales, or persons, living or dead, is entirely coincidental.

Typesetting and Cover Design by FormattingExperts.com

THE BOOK OF PANDÆMÓNIUM

APÓCRYFA

THE KINGDOM REPUBLIC OF NEVERMORE

unmapped

KARAQUIOK VALLEY

BARBATHOR MOUNSTAINS

SHRUUMOTH FOREST

here be monsters

MAOLGON

TROISACK MOUNSTAINS

CANTLGRYM CASTLE

VOIUM

MANTLGRYM

OVIEDOM

KOURII MARSHES

BOGGORN

THORNWOOD FOREST

CASTLE COVADONGAR

TOLGRYM

CANTABRYN

ONIS

unmapped

CHAPTER ONE
AS THE CROWNS FALL

Based on *Leyta's Journals*, cc bastica 100; *Annals of Syago*, cc bastica 90;
Scars of the Martyrs, cc bastica 1011;
The Dark Fortress of Mephorash, cc bastica x;

5th of Novumbre, 246

Tying a cloak over her nightgown, Leyta ran down the stairs from her quarters in a midnight's hurry, wishing she'd taken a nap during the day. Through the castle tower's window slits, she could hear the church bells tolling assault. Until an archdynast was named, an attack on the castle was her responsibility as the castle's archkeeper and a respected dynast. Once out in the castle bailey, she saw the gigantic beast in the foggy night air. A great ozor from the mountains, with black fur that paled and faded around the snout. Its fangs bore down on the wall. But instead of normal claws, this beast had large anthropoid hands. This was a feldinal, the term given to rare, vastly oversized monsters that usually had some form of strange aberration from their typical breed.[1] The standing bulk of the beast must've been at least sixty feet tall, enough for it to reach and climb over the wall.

Leyta ran to the middle of the courtyard, adding lightning to her fellow soldiers' attacks. Its thick hide absorbed the projectiles.

It threw what it held in its hands, but which darkness hid, the objects hitting soldiers around her. Two more landed in front of her—bodies. A blackbird and a long deceased soldier with Cantlgrym armor, both lifeless. Rotting skin clung to the soldier's bones, a sword still strongly in his grip. He was so decayed, she couldn't recognize him. They limped toward her through the fog and mud, the smell of rot overwhelming.

---

1   *Moonspell Hell Light de Lostregos*

Staff in hand, she entered the Vision and saw a dark courtyard tinged with green fear. An attack by a lifeless-throwing feldinal at midnight would do that to even a trained garrison of soldiers. She pushed red anger into the ground, causing rocks and mud to upheave onto the blackbird lifeless, half-burying it. With a surge of hate, she moved the rest of the dirt to cover its thrashing beak, burying it completely and stopping its animation. The soldier lifeless shambled over the jutting rocks, sword leading the way. She backed away, recalling painful memories to spawn anger and, with it, trip up the soldier in the dirt. Noticing priestesses bringing out a large pale of water, Leyta pushed hate into the water, and darkfire immediately arced out to consume the lifeless and freeze him to the ground.

Turning to the titanic beast cresting the wall, Leyta hurried to the group of dynasts nearby. "Dynasts, fire together on its head on three," she shouted. All around, the castle torches flared as she and her dynast students pushed their anger into the flames. The flames swirled around the monster's head, and it gave a deafening roar before crashing down into the courtyard mud. Leyta barely got out of the way, but mud was flung up all over her.

Ignoring the flames still licking at its head, it rolled and began to thrash as soldiers climbed atop it, attacking more vulnerable areas. Qosku, the young Unakan monk and close friend of Leyta's, also jumped atop the monster, swinging an axe into the beast's neck. Leyta watched in panic as the beast shook off the boy and rose, and shouted to the other dynasts for more darkfire. It was easier to produce than regular fire as it derived from moisture and coldness, which fell in abundance.

Black flames licked the sides of the beast, frosting it over in a deeper and deeper freeze. This slowed it but not enough for a monster accustomed to the cold. They pushed the darkflames to swirl around its head just as one of its furry hands lashed out toward Leyta. She tried to back away, but the fingers closed around her then tightened. She clawed at it furiously, choking on her screams as the pressure built around her rib cage.

Just when she felt like every bone inside her would snap if she didn't get away, its hold loosened. Syago's shining sword, the legendary Alexandre, blazed in the night air as the new Holy Knight of Nevermore brought it down on the beast's arm. The Holy Judgment Sword, Leyta knew, had powers that increased its speed and sharp edge which Syago was training to maneuver.

Syago had no issue in that moment, though. He hacked at its arm like mad, the powerful holy blade severing through. Qosku and Count Toriacus's son, Andras, also stabbed it with spears, punctuating Syago's strikes. *But no, it'd already stopped moving.*

Confusion muted cheers as everyone realized what Leyta just had—the beast had stopped moving, though none had delivered anything close to a killing blow. Feldinals often exhibited suffering in their tempestuous existence but they rarely just died. As everyone edged closer to examine their conquest, the fur began to ripple and bulge, and everyone backed away as white bulbs burst out of its face, spraying blood and eye-goop everywhere.

Leyta's eyes widened, and she quickly pulled a rag from her belt to cover her face. Everyone backed away.

The monster had been sick with fungi spores.

As everyone nearby drew their own handkerchiefs or tunics up to their faces, more stems with white bulbs on the end tore through the hide, splaying blood. They rose up, the bulbs opening into an enchanting, if bloody, cap, reaching toward the moon above. All was silent and eerie as the parasite towered over them, like a lord over his conquered domain. Leyta lifted the rag from her mouth to yell, "Let's bring fire to its spore shooters before it gets us too." They needed to be rid of it before it could do the same to them.

The dynasts began setting fire to the mushroom caps while the archemists prepared to break down the body before darkemorg turned it, too, into a lifeless. *Well at least they won't have to go hunting for a couple days, though strange meat this be.*[2]

Later that day, the tallest tower of Castle Cantlgrym held a crucial meeting.[3] The once private room of Castellan Alkant supported a round table of his associates, though three empty chairs waited in vain for Annaruth, Alkant, and the traitor Davagis. Balgor pulled them away from the table without a word.

Now, nearly a month after that bleakest night whence they'd lost Castellan Alkant, Annaruth, and three soldiers,[4] to the seneschal's betrayal for the Cult of the Razhod, they would decide on the next Castellan

2 The placing of this story isn't trustworthy. A fungus attack wouldn't have happened in the middle of darkemorg season.

3 See *La Epica Eluveitia de Sepultura*, 33

4 It was four. Six including the two masters.

of Castle Cantlgrym. The Razhod cult was still an impending threat but not an immediate one. As far as everyone could determine, the cult had no army or any of their old powers, only thieves and assassins, all of them fanatics led by the vagrant Kask. They'd killed six people since their first appearance at Castle Cantlgrym, not counting what their grimshade servants had done. The Royal Chaos had stirred a rebellion that was becoming a full civil war. Both enemies frightened Leyta, but she pretended strength and calmness as always.

They'd been talking about the two deceased as everyone came in and took their seats. A jug of spiced wine was passed around, filling goblets. With all ready, Bishopess Yanet led a group prayer. *"Our Mother, who art in Heaven, hallowed by the mystery of thy name. Thy kingdom come, thy will be done here on Gierra as it is in Heaven. Give us this day our daily bread and forgive us our evil as we forgive the evil done unto us. Lead us not within temptation but deliver us from hell. Amen."* They made the sign of the sun cross, and silence descended where Alkant would've began the meeting.

"Well somebody say something important," Virgow, the Unakan veteran warrior, said. "I'm not here for the mourning."

"Right, I'll cut to it then," Seumas said, turning slowly in his seat to Leyta. Even bent over with age, she admired his commanding if curmudgeonly presence. "It should be you."

"Me?" Leyta asked, surprised. But none said anything to the contrary. "Why not you? Or Balgor? It can't be me."

"The ones who would've taken the position are now dead or betraying," Balgor said, stroking his braided beard. "I can't, I'm not native to here, not viewed as a leader, not truly a dynast, and am needed for the errands." It was true. Balgor was Fomorion, cycloptic and massive. Still, anyone else at the table was a better choice than her. They were all far more experienced, more suited to ruling a military university for The Kingdom Republic of Nevermore.

Virgow nodded. "We're all necessary in our places. You've been archkeeper long enough."

"I'm too young," Leyta countered. The odd fluttering knot her stomach drove her thoughts. "What about Roza?" Gretal Roza wasn't a dynast, but that hadn't been an obstacle for past leaders so long as another stood as archdynast.

"No," Roza said flatly.

"No? Why no?" Leyta pressed after a pause.

"I have my reasons." Roza clasped her hands on the table, gaze fixed on the lantern at the center of the table.

Even if Leyta ended up being archdynast, that didn't necessarily mean she had to be Castellan. But they were supposed to be the same person which meant not Roza.[5] "No is all you need to hear for the time being."

"I can't either," Seumas said as her eyes settled on him. "I teach dyne and arithmetic just fine, but that's not good enough. Poor health and insufficient respect from the youths that way. You know it. Could you imagine me as an archdynast? As the next Black King of Castle Cantlgrym? Perhaps ten years ago but not now." A Black Queen to replace the old Black King, Master Alkant. The crown reference, of course, was purely symbolic. Just as bishopesses were rulers of the Church in Gierra, so too were dynasts to be rulers of hell, priests of non-ecclesiastical justice.[6] It would elevate her to the highest position of the order, yet still under Church authority.

"I'm too young and disliked by many." Even as she said this, she disagreed. She wondered why she was truly objecting. "I'm too inexperienced for the mantle and crown."

"Come now, child." Roza smiled warmly. "You don't give yourself nearly enough credit. You've been archkeeper for, what, three years now? And a dynast for nigh on six." Leyta opened her mouth to object, but Roza cut her off with a dismissive wave. "Or two months if you insist on the technicality. You care for it like your own child. You led the keepers through the captivity and the escape under the enemies. You fought in the Battle of Tolgrym Part of you must want this. It would be good for you. And you're only half a year younger than the recorded youngest Castellan archdynast. Time for a new record, I think."

Leyta's face felt hot, and she resisted the urge to hide her embarrassment. Roza was right: she did want this. But there was also a queasy disquiet in her that made her afraid. Seventeen years, nearly eighteen; she was so young for this. Running the castle, leading an army, leading the call of

---

5 Ibid, 34

6 In fact, Black King or Queen was out of use for a time during the reigns of kings, who didn't like even the symbolic hint of competition. Then it was Black Archon or some such lesser ruler status. The use here indicates a resurgence in the absence of monarchs.

hope while her people faced an impending civil war with Mantlgrym. Not to mention the shadowy cult of fanatics seeking to revive the long dead coven of the Razhod. The weight of it felt vast, crushing. She looked at all their faces, hardly believing their confidence in her. "You've made up your minds already, haven't you?"

They each nodded solemnly. Balgor smiled faintly, and his single large eye twinkled. "Great things are in store for you, Leyti. Don't fight it. I've seen too many women turn down higher opportunities because of a little fear. And for certain you won't be able to play with the little ones as much anymore, but since you'll be in charge of the schedules, I'm sure you can arrange a class or two with them." She hadn't thought of that, but it was a fleeting worry in the cognitive deluge.

"It is the will of the Holy Sanator," Bishopess Yanet said. "The Lady Deova Bondua has prepared you to be the Minister of Hell, for you've always been faithful to the sacred knowledge." She wagged a warning finger at Leyta, though her kind smile softened the warning. "As long as you hold true to those teachings, She will aid you and we, the prelatas, will counsel and support you."

Leyta's fingers played with the designs of her scepter absentmindedly as she thought about their arguments. They each made good points. Still, doubt gnawed at her. "Being archkeeper worked only because Alkant was behind me. And I did terrible in the battles."

"Unacceptable." Roza shook her head. "If we as women don't give ourselves credit for what we've done or can do, then who will?"

"Whining," Virgow growled. "Knock it off and go to work."

"We'll be here to help you," Balgor added in a more positive tone, stroking his thick braided hair. "You can count each of us as your second in command. And if you come to find you still don't like it, you can look for a replacement. Not even our old, stern Alkant would blame you. But we need you to try, and I think your conscience won't permit you to say no either."[7]

Her conscience spoke a slightly different truth. She'd not just done poorly in the battles, but when the bandit troupe, the Royal Chaos, had taken her captive, she'd lost control and burned her friend Gabriol, and almost several others, alive. In the ensuing chaos, she hadn't reported what she'd

7   *I'm watching you*

done. True, she'd demonstrated the ability to maintain control against the lifeless and malwolves, but it still gnawed at her. Of course she'd also kept secret her witnessing of an Asturion soldier killing a Kimoc, but it was Gabriol's face that haunted her nightmares. Her own loss of control, and the consequences of it, was a dark secret she couldn't afford if she truly went through with this. Syago, the only one who really knew, would have to keep it quiet.

She needed to protect herself, protect her dignity and freedom. But she knew that what she wanted was to protect her people. Especially the children. If she did this, Leyta knew she had to do it fully, and not let anyone take it from her, nor abuse their trust.

Taking strength from their words, she started, "If you'll all support me..." She didn't know if she could do this, but she'd have to try. Powerful figures in history always made the pieces fit in times of crisis. "I will do it."

But how will everyone else take it? Not good, she knew. The counts and barons might sneer at her and threaten to dispute her election, but the castle always maintained its authority. As for those keeping at the castle, she'd have to please their wealthy families to maintain the income and the flow of keepers. She'd been their equal, or just above them as archkeeper, and never a well-liked one at that. It wouldn't go down easy even with the ones that liked her. *At least Syago will favor me, and everyone likes him. I just need to not let them push me around, or oust me.*

If she was doing this, she was going to hold it to the end.

Syago sat on the steps that led up the main tower. Leyta had invited him to her meeting, but he refused. He'd only just decided to wait there for the announcement, as a show of support to her. Though she didn't say it, Syago knew Alexandre served the only reason she'd invited him, and the only reason Balgor had conferred with him, though the Fomorion didn't admit it either.[8]

He pulled Alexandre from its sheath, remembering how much he'd wanted the soulsword to choose him. He ran his hand over the hilt, the

---

8   See *Thy Light, Therion!*, 33

crossguard made to look like angel wings. A well crafted claymore, its power lessened the weight and balance closer to a hand and a half sword. Its power also protected the blade from damage and rust, such that the only faint scars on it had come from other similarly bonded weapons in its old battles with the Razhod. Syago tightened the leather wrapped around the handle, which prevented wear on his hand.

He supposed it wasn't really the sword that he wanted so much as everything that went with it. The glory. The legacy. His dream had been to continue in his father's footsteps, to *be* his father. And even though he'd always secretly anticipated the heroic fame that having the Judgment Sword would bring him, Syago also wanted to genuinely do good. Now that he had it, though—the sword *and* the fame—the attention felt uncomfortable. He was now respected merely for being chosen by the sword. A worthy enough reason, he supposed, but his humbling, frustrating, and confusing journey to that point had given him mixed feelings. Still, he felt a reverence for the holy relic his family had wielded for centuries. However, he couldn't forget that it hadn't chosen him first. And it almost felt disrespectful to Milemeron, who did draw it before him and fell soon after. He'd expected gossip about its choosing to spread, but likely due to the travails of Tolgrym, it hadn't. Of course, Andras knew of what had happened to his brother and the awkwardness between them was only now beginning to fade half a month later.

Syago wondered if the sword had chosen Milemeron first because of his noble blood, while Syago was the first of his line with pagan blood and dark skin. But whenever he pressed Alexandre on it, the spirit of the sword either gave no response or rebuked him for questioning its holy choices.

He'd gotten to know the spirit bound to the blade quite well through his training sessions, and even moments as this one, just sitting here. It communicated thoughts and sentiments of loyalty, honesty, and purity. Syago understood that if he stepped out of line, it would let him know or abandon him. There was a measure of self-righteousness and judgment from the sword, like having an extra conscience, one that could physically burn him.

Wielding it had also proven problematic, nearly killing him multiple times. He adapted quickly to its heft and size, but the enhanced speed and edge proved a challenge. After intensive training, he was substantially better, but many of his fellow keepers could still beat him, whereas with a regular sword he would be top of the class. A fact that had stolen the wind out of both theirs and his excitement for it. The sword had powers that he needed to get used to and centuries of battle experience that differed from his own.

Two minds, one warrior. Apparently not a good combination. Somehow he needed to earn respect independent of the sword, while also bonding with it. Until he achieved both, the legacy he'd dreamed of, and was now expected to embody, would remain just that—a dream.

The door opening jolted him out of his thoughts. Sword at his hip, he stood to meet the council as they filed down the stairs. Leyta descended first, looking as beautiful as ever in a dark green dress, and as tired, too. He wondered how this new mantle would affect their semi-courtship. She looked at him, her mouth opening and then closing, releasing only silence.

"Congratulations?" he ventured.

"You knew?!" She tried to look scandalized, but the smile betrayed it. "And you didn't tell me."

"Well, maybe I was threatened into secrecy."

She laughed, and Roza eyed her curiously as she walked past.

"We all agree," Roza said as the others emptied the stairs around Leyta, "including her after a few beatings. Leyta is to be the next Castellan and archdynast."

Syago bowed. "It is well deserved."

"We'll announce in the ceremonial dinner tonight," Balgor said to her. "I recommend a speech with extensive thought and preparation, including for the worst. Hoping for the best, as always. Following the dinner we'll anoint you with the mantle."

At that, everyone left, leaving Syago and Leyta on the stairs. An awkward tension filled the space between them. Without looking directly at him, she said, "Do you think I can do this?"

The question, or rather the sheer vulnerability of someone he knew to be headstrong, caught him off-guard. "Yes," he replied. "It'll be a challenge, but you'll rise to meet it. We all will. Somehow."

"Can you—will you endorse me?"

"Endorse you?" Syago asked, his gaze snapping to hers. He tempered his cringe when he saw insecurity in her eyes.

"I mean, publicly support me." Her eyes bore into his intensely, and he fought the urge to shift his weight back. "Only—well, some won't like this. And we really need a strong front as we're also likely going to war soon. So it would really help if you just say a few positive words about me as the new master at the supper tonight. A quick speech."

"Endorse you," he said again in slight disbelief, now hating the words. "I have always supported you. But making me a political tool?"

"No, not a tool," she countered. "I just need someone the people respect to back me and keep my mistakes quiet. People admire you. They would follow me willingly if you told them to..."

What mistakes? Like asking him to sponsor her? He shook his head. "I'm no leader, I've no wealth or influence. The only thing about me is I have a weapon nobody else does. You're asking for a political endorsement not from me, but from a sword. One that barely listens to me and almost got me killed."

"You can refuse," she said, an edge of anger in her eyes that mirrored his. "But I've supported you. And I need your help. This is how you can help me."

Without waiting for a response, she turned and stomped away from him, her dress whirling around her. Syago clenched and unclenched the sword handle. Its displeasure at his anger only irritated him. He breathed deep, knowing he was overreacting to what he would've considered an honor not long ago. His frustration with Alexandre was getting to him.

The news of Leyta's new position managed to stay secret until evening meal. Syago spent time in his quarters reading, or trying to read. He had a hard time focusing his thoughts away from what he might or might not do at the ceremony. Prayer brought no greater help.

That evening, Syago entered the great hall and took a seat between Andras and Qosku. The latter attempted conversation with Andras but struggled with the language, being new to the region. As the food took its place in front of them, Syago once more thought to himself that Qosku seemed the most genuine person he'd ever known. A thought that influenced his decision.

A bell rang, and the crowd quieted as all turned toward the masters table. "Tonight," Roza began in raised voice, "after much thought and discussion, we masters of Castle Cantlgrym have settled on our new Castellan. May we all come to respect, support, and follow the lead of... Mastra Leyta de Bovua Trastamuir la Eliot!"

She and the other masters clapped loudly, though the keepers were slower to join in. Leyta rose from her place at the bench to take the Castellan's chair at the head table. Roza clasped the mantle around her shoulders, a simple silver-embroidered black cloak. Roza then handed her the Castellan's chalice, to drink of the master's wine. Applause returned as she drank.

"Thank you," Leyta said as the applause died down. "I didn't seek it. I'm not sure I want it. But with—"

"Then do us a favor," a call came from the students. "And turn it down!"

"I—"

"You're younger than me," said another, this time Syago recognized Fernandeon, the privileged imbecile that always spoke his poorly formed mind. "Get off—"

"ENOUGH!" Balgor's voice boomed across the hall. Syago turned to see him towering above his seat. "Leyta is Castellan, and she'll be great for it. If you don't want it, you can leave."

"That'll be cleaning duties for the interruption," snapped Roza. "Don't cut your Castellan off again, understood?"

Silence filled the room. Leyta cleared her throat and continued, "I understand there's disappointment. I'm always willing to hear out your concerns, if you bring them. I will work with each of you to continue—to improve upon what Master Alkant accomplished here. He was an inspiration to me. I have the help of these great masters behind me, I ask also for yours as we learn and fight together."

At that last sentence, she glanced at Syago, which only agitated him further, but he'd already made his decision. Rising from his seat, he cleared his throat. "Let me be the first keeper to congratulate Castellan Leyta on her new position. I've worked, studied, and fought beside Leyta. I can vouch for her integrity and qualifications."

Someone nearby muttered, "Tcha 'cause you're friends with her. Want to get up her dress."

"I also do not tolerate such disrespect," he barked before the masters could. "You got a problem, you come to me, and we'll work it out my way." He paused to glare at the crowd. "Now shut your slop traps and try listening for once."

"Thank you, Syago," Leyta said before continuing. "Expect everything to continue as usual. We will adapt new rules as needed to what promises to be a trying time. With your patience and cooperation, we can make the future brighter."

At that, everyone turned to their food, chewing in between grumbles and stares.

Still moody, Syago finished his cider quickly, then talked Qosku into giving him his. Following supper, they marched solemnly to the chapel to anoint Leyta as archdynast and master of the castle.[9][10] Candles illuminated the space, all the way up to the chapel's high vaulted ceiling. Bishopess Yanet stood behind the altar, the sun wheel cross, while Katti led the congregation in an old chant. Leyta, in a Black Gown Syago heard was quickly designed specifically for her ascendancy, knelt before the steps, then prostrated herself on the fresh woven bed of rushes on the floor. A black quilt was laid over her, covering her completely with silver embroidery of the dynast pentagram in the middle and leviathan sulphur crosses in the corners, winged serpents entwining the edges.

Katti ended the chorus and the bishopess began the prayer, "Our Mother, Lightmaker and Sanator, I invoke your blessing now for one of thy dark servants. In thy name we plea, elevate this dynast to be Mastra Castellan of this domain named Castle Cantlgrym. With thy authority, I dub her the Black Queen of this region of damnation in Nevermore, toward thy glory. That the safety and salvation of humanity may be achieved, their justice served, the hells edged out, and thy will be done, on Gierra as it is in the Heavens. And furthermore, I ask that you strengthen her hand, keep her true, as she leads war against nature, and now our fellow man in the present conflicts. Thus we pray in thy holy name, amen and amen."

The quilt was lifted by the attendants, hanging above Leyta then falling behind her as a backdrop when she rose. The congregation stood, and when Syago could finally see around to the altar, Leyta's calmness surprised him. White powder covered her face with black around the eyes. A black pouch full of animal blood and organs was placed on the altar cloth, a symbol of the evil the archdynast must dominate so that others don't have to. Leyta held the knife high over her head. *So they agreed to it after all?* Syago mused, thinking of the storm Katti had raised about this ceremony being too pagan.

---

9   See also *The Schiltron of Magodeoz*, 36-66

10   But Cavalera's bigger influence could be found in the likes of *Satyricona*

"Holy Sanator," Bishopess Yanet's voice boomed through the chapel. "Bless this blade. Accept this sacrifice. Crown thy servant archdynast."

"Bishopess of the Heavens," Leyta shouted. "It is blessed, and the responsibilities I do accept."

Leyta plunged the blade down. The cut was precise, oozing out blood all over the cloth and onto Leyta's hands. She cut again, to bleed out on the other side. She squoze the bag empty, then took up the glistening cat's heart that fell out. She bit into the heart, then picked up the other organs and put them in a censer. The bowl was lit on fire, which in turn lit the quilt. Leyta turned to face the congregation, blood dripping from her hands. She was glorious, unflinching and regal, her black gown standing out starkly against the inferno. The bloody cloth was draped over her as a cape and Syago found himself falling to his knees in awe, the rest of the congregation following. He gazed at the Black Queen and thought, *How could I have ever wavered in my obedience of her? Truly she is called of Deova to lead the defeat of the enemies and I have to help her do it.*

He drew Alexandre, who buzzed at the events taking place, proud and excited, fearful and wary all at once. Making the sign of fealty, Syago planted the sword in front of him and bowed his head.

"Mastra Leyta," Bishopess Yanet called. "Are you our master here?!"

"I AM!"

"Congregation, IS SHE YOUR MASTER HERE?!"

"SHE IS!"

"Then all proclaim and celebrate it with the hosanna shout."

"HOSANNA! HOSANNA! HOSANNA, TO THE MOON AND SUN, OUR LADY HIGH!"[11]

"Blessed be!" Leyta answered and raised her scepter and extinguished all candles in the chapel, ushering in darkness as its master.[12] She led the march outside, the moon providing just enough faint light through the stained glass windows for the final procession, to celebrate in modest music and dancing.[13]

---

11 A celebratory chant by Batushka in *Dark Fortress of Mephorash*, 66

12 *Ibid*, 35

13 See also *Keltian Keltibeerian*, 36

CHAPTER TWO
THE VENGEANCE PACT

Based on *The Hunter's Parchments*, cc bastica 220;[14]
Scars of the Martyrs, cc bastica 1011;
The Dark Fortress of Mephorash, cc bastica x;

5th of Novumbre, 246

On the floor of Thornwood, beasts and monsters hid and slept whilst lifeless wandered. There were far fewer lifeless now after the Battle of Tolgrym, and most creeped around the small town. But many had followed the Kimoc back to their hanging village of Quoak, waiting nightly in the fog for something to fall into their decaying claws. Up in the thick and gnarled bramble branches, bugs chirped and fled pursuing bats, which in turn fled owls. The cannibalistic wild devoured itself.

Quoak's woshiks housed families, settling down for the night under painted canvasses on furs and wooden seats. Lil'iek and her sister Qio'iek prepared dinner jointly. The two women put the chopped meat onto the corn flatbreads where the dead meat wiggled weakly, harmlessly, followed by beans, mashed calabas, and some fresh thornleaf. The sweet smell filled the room with anticipation even for the distracted children.

Squeezing juice into a shell, Qio'iek looked at Lil'iek conspiratorially. "So sister, how long will you wait until you seek a new husband?"

"Qio!" Lil'iek scolded.

"Oh, don't tell me you've not already thought about it." She smiled mischievously. "I know you too well. It's almost a new moon since, none will

---

14 Here the source account, begun by Fal'iek, is continued intermittently by Lil'iek and Tek'ouk. Lil'iek's contributions are most sparse, but not for lack of ability to read or write. My guess is she learned in Tolgrym as a young girl where she also picked up the Asturion tongue. Tek'ouk learned his from briefly living at Castle Cantlgrym where he also became a dynast. His notes are more studious.

blame you for requesting a new one now. You need one."

Lil'iek said nothing. It was true. All of it. But she still hurt inside. She'd just gotten Fal'iek back after a month alone, made love to him once, fought beside him even and won a great victory, then lost him as the shadow creatures surprised them both. Dishonorable, it'd gone so far as to mock her with a creepy leer before fleeing. Lil'iek had only burned his belongings the night before, freeing his spirit, but placing his bones in the family vase. "It is hard to think about my thirst for love when I still thirst for blood."

Qio'iek responded nothing to that.

Lil'iek had sacrificed for her children, for husband, for tribe. Now they owed her this. She would pursue justice. And if the eternals of the forest were good to her, her plan would bring love as well.

Around the small fire, the family ate a rare feast in celebration. It'd been a great harvest, the grim'iik sighting earlier that day meant that Quoak was safe, and their two oldest children had begun a new stage in their training.

"Mour'iek, you know that's not how we eat," Lil'iek chided her youngest, who also was becoming more independent. A willful boy that knew what he wanted. Lil'iek scooped up the spilled food, dumped the dirtied parts into the fire, and put the rest back into the scrunched flatbread that Mour'iek held to his messy face. Eyeing him to make sure he watched, she demonstrated, "Slower, like this. And bite, then chew." She smiled at his clumsy imitation, drinking in his joyful face.

Not an hour later, she approached the Quoarn'riik, the council of chieftains. She stopped and breathed deep before entering their woshik. Eight of the ten Quoarn'riik sat in the large canvas covering, a brazier burning in the center. Each had traditional face paint in addition to their tattoos and wore feathered headdresses, complex emblems of tribal authority and spiritual power. The elders regarded her with sympathy, as she'd expected. Their authority was given to them not only by tribe ancestors and patron spirits of the forest, but also by the women of the tribe. Even the most distant of them would heed her. Even aside from that, all would listen because of the loss of Fal'iek, her husband and their greatest champion. She'd no doubt that if he'd aged more, he'd have become a Quoarn'riik, although he'd always denied it.

"My elders of Quoak," she greeted, bowing and sitting. "I come with petition."

A pall of silence fell in anticipation of what came next. She forced her hands to stop wringing; she could fight monsters as one of the best, but speaking in front of groups challenged her. "I ask for your permission and aid in gaining justice for the loss of my husband."[15]

"Your husband's murderer will not be easily found or claimed," Quoarn'riik Wiq'olk said after a careful pause. "Are you sure the need is worth it? What of your family here?"

"I remind you that the loss is not mine alone," she said. "But also that of the whole tribe, of the whole land. He was our greatest warrior, warchief, and diplomat. In killing him, they insulted and wounded us all..." She trailed off under their uncomfortable gazes. Pitying. No, she didn't do this for them, she did it for herself. She, who always sacrificed for others but never demanded anything for herself. "It did afflict us all, and we'd be cowards to let it go. But more than that, far more, I do ask it for myself. I demand it as my right. The great wolves didn't kill any of ours during the battle and the grim'iik has passed over our village; all are signs of their favor and protection.[16] My children will be safe here with my family as I seek justice for them—in addition to what the enemy owes me personally."

"But the justice you speak of is a thing of the paleman. We ask for reciprocal reparations, not vengeance."

"Reciprocal reparations work for other Kimoc, but it has earned us nothing from the paleman except more abuse still. These shadowed ones can satisfy me by reciprocating the lives of those responsible."

Her voice quavered slightly as did her hands. She tightened them, daring the Quoarn'riik with her eyes to deny the request. They shifted under her gaze before Link'ouk spoke. "We'll consider it over the next two days. May we have that time?"

She nodded, then stepped back for the next person.

Tek'ouk unwound the bandages around his leg-stump. The ache had dulled but still kept him up at night. Occasionally puss and blood would leak out.

---

15 See *Sol Sistere de Selbst* by Himetuks Himi'n

16 Each eternal Great One will appear in the forms of their creatures, in Kimoc myth.

Maybe if it wasn't so golking hard to keep from bumping other objects, I might actually heal. Of truth, it was much better than its freshness of over a moon ago. His mother-in-law waved smoke over it, chanting in a low voice, then brushed it with feathers soaked in thorn nectar. He echoed her prayer, trying to not curse the motherwood at the same time, knowing the real blame lie with the Asturions who'd infected it.

When she finished, he drank and wrapped a clean cloth around fresh leaves on the stump. Grunting as he rose to his feet, or foot and wooden crutch, he hobbled outside. Though he knew it a foolish idea, he wanted to catch the rest of the Quoarn'riik meeting. Soon they'd pressure him into making a decision. Leave or accept the embrace of Mamak Yoaom in blood sacrifice. Having married into the Quoak tribe through his now long deceased wife, he'd considered going back to Koah, where he was from. But he knew Koah would no more accept an amputee than Quoak would.

He made it halfway across the rickety bridge when its wobbling moved his crutch into a crack in the wood. Rickety now that he was on one leg and a stick. Before, nothing was even remotely difficult or scary. Now, everything was a life-threatening obstacle course. After pulling on his crutch for a minute, and refusing to call for help, he got free and almost toppled over the railing. He began to move again when Lil'iek appeared at the end of the bridge. "Oh, hello." He regretted the awkward greeting immediately, it was only the surprise. "I was just on my way to see the Quoarn'riik."

"Oh, I believe they're almost done," she said, looking off in that direction. "I was just coming to visit you."

A pause. "Um, all right." He started to turn back, but found turning around too daunting on the narrow bridge. "Just a moment to get back in." He started going backwards then cursed under his breath as he nearly fell and said, "Hold on, I need to finish crossing first." He hoped that didn't give away how much the bridge was starting to frustrate him, or make him nervous.

Her brow furrowed with concerned eyes. "I can help—"

"No," he said, wishing he'd not responded so quickly to the expected question. "I need to get used to this. Just, with time and practice." She nodded, wringing her hands. Getting to her was a relief, but stinging in the awkwardness of having to turn back and do it again. Finally inside the clan woshik, they sat on rugs drinking tea from shells. He stretched his arms and stump. Although his arms had developed the muscles necessary for this, they still ached after a long day. She watched him over the shell she drank from. He could only assume she was thinking of Fal'iek. Other than Lil'iek, Tek'ouk was the one who'd spend the most time with him.

"I miss his dry humor the most," Tek'ouk began.

Confusion flashed in her eyes. "Oh, yes. He always knew how to make me and the children laugh even in the darkest times."

He grunted. So she wasn't here to talk about Fal'iek as he'd assumed. Thankfully, she ended the pause.

"I was thinking of what he'd told me before he died. To enjoy the moment while you have it and then move on and not grieve long."

"Wise words. He was very wise, in his own way." He then wondered what she thought of Fal'iek's unbelief now, his forsaking of the traditions. If she thought he was among the lifeless now or captured by some spirit creature, or perhaps a Great One had rescued him out of sympathy and put him into a mewil'shyuuks.

She looked at her tea, then up at the woshik canvas. "I had a realization today that I've always sacrificed for others and never asked anything for myself. There are a number of things I yearned for but could never get because Fal'iek was always out on patrol. Like the chance to hunt and fight out in the wild... and to feel his love."

She looked at him directly. "Tek'ouk, I want to marry you."

He choked on his tea, coughing and spitting it back into the shell. She kept looking at him. "What? Marry me?"

She nodded.

"Wh—have you—Are you serious?" She nodded again. He continued, "I don't think you've thought this through. Have you seen me—you just saw what kind of use I'd be as a husband. I can barely get around, I'll probably have to leave the village."

Her brow furrowed. "What *are* you going to do?"

"Well, I *want* to find a way to live here and even go out hunting. I want to make a crutch that'd let me do that, turn it into a weapon or a scepter or something so that I'm not as vulnerable. But that will take time and still be a hindrance, wanting and succeeding are two different things. Either way, I can't support you. I already don't know about supporting my two sons."

"Then let me support you. Be a father to our children while I go out and get justice."

18

"Justice?"

"Yes, I asked the Quoarn'riik for blood in exchange for the blood of my husband. I want a vengeance pact, or justice restored to me." The inscrutable intensity in her gaze did... something to him.

It struck him then how beautiful she was. About his age and already a friend, he could enjoy marrying her.

Shaking himself from his thoughts, he said, "You asked to go hunt these shadowmen?"

Determination crossed her face. "I *will* go. I framed it to them as a question, but since my children are being looked after by Qio'iek, I don't need to ask. I am going. I am owed recompense by right. If not through contrition, which is unlikely, I will have their heads to burn or drink from or throw in the ocean as I see fit. Their blood is mine."

And that was why he hesitated, she frightened him. She was gentle and kind; Fal'iek had called her his wildflower in confidence. The first time Tek'ouk had met her, she'd been carving up an animal for dinner, her arms covered in blood, but she still smiled, not minding the mess, as Fal'iek introduced them. She wasn't really authoritative, just passionate and unpredictable. Intense. Fierce. Wild. The most ferocious female warrior of Quoak, which was already known for such among the forest peoples, now demanded both vengeance and love. "I'm confused, you want to marry me *before* you go on a mad quest for revenge over your last husband. Sorry if this is rude, but shouldn't you mourn him first?"

But she was not offended. "Tek, I've been mourning my husband ever since we married. He was rarely home and took many risks in the wild as you know, having all the fun without me. I slept alone, thinking he was dead for the two moons before he returned the last time. Yes, I miss him and am sorry he is gone, but now I'm ready to take his advice to heart and life. Enjoy the moment, grieve briefly, then move on. And there's no other man I desire more than the handsome, wise, and kind, if self-pitying, man I see before me, crippled leg included.

"Our children are of an age to take care of themselves with some adult guidance. They understand loss and renewal. They understand how to help you and are helped by other family." She moved closer, sitting next to him. Dim firelight glinted off of her inscrutable dark eyes, making her brown skin and black hair gleam softly. "I would wed you then go on to avenge my lost love and your friend. I may be gone long, but not as long as Fal'iek was from me, and you'll have the aid of my family in the meantime, who'll be a reason for the Quoarn'riik to allow you to stay."

"And if I end up having to leave the village forever?"

"I may yet come with you or we'll figure something else out." She shrugged and smiled for the first time in the conversation, thick lips that he wanted to kiss. "I don't need the decade of mourning my dead spouse that you've taken for yours. Or am I not desirable enough for you?"

"Oh no, you—" He shook his head. "I just need some time to think about it."

She sighed and rose to her feet. "A decade and counting then."

He snorted. "Maybe I was just waiting for you this whole time and can't believe it's finally here?" She raised an eyebrow at him. "Okay no, but it sounded like the right thing to say."

A wan smile crossed her face as she moved to exit the woshik. "Well, don't make it true of me. I was hoping to bed you tonight, but I suppose I can make do by myself until you come around." He shook his head again, this time in disbelief, as she left, calling out behind her, "Don't take too long."

The following night Tek'ouk stood before the Quoarn'riik. He'd not expected how bad it would be. Having to lean on his crutch didn't help his case, and the aches would only get worse.

"Respected Quoarn'riik and observers all," he began. "A petition was made yesterday by Lil'iek to obtain justice by vengeance or substantive contrition by the enemy who slew our noble Fal'iek. I support her claim," he paused, cleared his throat while the surge of whispers died down. "And I request permission to lead the Roah'riik in aiding her on this vengeance pact."

Gasps and whispers flew around the circle again. Lil'iek's gaze fixed on him and for once he read interest. Quoarn'riik Link'ouk, Tek'ouk's father-in-law, held up a hand for quiet then asked, "You would lead them? How, in your condition, could you do this?"

"If I can make it around up here, I can down there. Of course I may need help on occasion, but don't forget that I am a dynast and accomplished archer and blowdart shooter. I'm not so vulnerable. I also know the land and the conflict better than most here or there."

"The conflict?" Wiq'olk frowned. "You're not proposing to go after the Royal Chaos in Mantlgrym, are you? Fal'iek fell to the shadowmen, who are separate."

"That they are, but until we locate them, we'll go after the carnival group. They were, after all, complicit in his death, having provoked the attack in the first place, and assaulted him directly. And I'm fairly certain it was them that desecrated our graves. Once we get a lead on where else to hunt the shadowmen, we'll break off—" A look from Lil'iek caught his eyes. "Excuse me, I believe Lil'iek seeks the Chaos's blood as well as that of the shadowmen. So we'll slay them, then the shadows."

Some scoffed but he continued on before the dismissal could grow. "I agreed with you before. It is an Asturion conflict and none of our affair. We need none of their problems. I pushed Fal'iek to stop hunting them and stay here. But he was right, wasn't he? Did not their conflict come to us anyways? Did we not find safety with the paleman who, I remind you, didn't betray us as we'd expected them to?"

"That is not certain," Wiq'olk said. "There were suspicious deaths, we just don't have proof of it. But who would doubt it?"

"What of your children, then?" Link'ouk asked. "Both you and she are widows now. And you'll make more by taking warriors with you."

He looked at Lil'iek. "I would merge our families that our children and relatives may care for each other in these trying times."

"You wish to marry her?" Link'ouk asked in the stunned silence.

"I do. Or, at least make the promise until Fal'iek be avenged and we return." Though all eyes in the circle wavered between him and her, he could only feel hers as they danced at him.

"You push many new changes at us," Quoarn'riik Qil'koh said, stroking his chin as he looked at the others. "What if you don't succeed, or lose men?"

"I understand I'm a liability here. The palemen have killed and exiled us and now let their problems spill over onto us. I'm asking you to uphold the pride we've been hiding inside ourselves. We can do that without losing ourselves to it."

"We will converse on this and give our judgment within the hour," Qil'koh said.

Tek'ouk nodded and rotated on his crutch to leave the circle when Lil'iek walked up to him and stopped him with a kiss. Deep, wet, and warm, full of thrill. Everyone cheered around them. She broke away, eyes shining into his. "Thank you."

It was later announced that they accepted. Tek'ouk would lead five Roah'riik in aiding Lil'iek. But Link'ouk approached him after, resting a hand on his shoulder and speaking close. "Tek, we have a special condition we didn't want to make public."

He didn't like the sound of this. "Oh?"

"Remember your allies in the fight are also your enemies. Undermine the Asturions. Maneuver the conflict to divide them or cost them resources and men. It won't get us our lands back, but—"

"You want me to betray our allies? This isn't what I had in mind when I brought up fighting for our pride."

"Tek, I only ask the same we did in Tolgrym." Tek'ouk's stomach churned. They'd made a tentative plan, withheld from most, including Fal'iek, to allow Tolgrym to fall to the lifeless. They'd suspected that Tolgrym had similar plans against them. He'd been angry and bitter then and so had agreed, but later regretted it. He remembered the night's battle well, both sides eyeing each other in distrust, never turning their backs to the other. But none had ever acted, overwhelmed enough by the fight itself.[17]

"Link'ouk, that was different. Even if some were betrayed, most of them actually kept their word this time. And attempting to do so might undermine our peace, give them reason to come after us."

"I'm only saying to do it as you're able without taking severe repercussions. When good opportunities present themselves, don't lose them. I may be able to get you more men for this too. Remember, this is Mantlgrym, the same place that took your leg, and the war is something they're already doing to themselves. So is that agreeable then?"

He had a point. As far as Tek'ouk was concerned, that whole city could burn down. He looked hard into the soft eyes of Link'ouk and nodded.

Several nights later, the village gathered for the Woag'mook ceremony that would send off Lil'iek and her Roah'riik escort. Nine Roah'riik sat behind Tek'ouk, who knelt in front, his stump resting painfully on a small fur roll. In front of him sat Lil'iek, as gorgeous as ever with fans of feathers spreading out from her beaded dress. Her black and white face paint resembled a weeping skull. Quoarn'riik Link'ouk emptied a bowl of flower petals on her, their gentle grace belying the venomous danger they'd held. Flutes stopped and drums began the sacred rhythm. The Roah'riik rose, chanting,

---

17 The veracity of this is in dispute. Tek'ouk later blamed himself for many Asturion deaths, but there's been a tendency to blame the Kimoc too much for reacting to incidents out of their control.

dancing. Tek'ouk rose with the aid of his children, who then retreated to the sides. The hellhunters danced in a circle around Lil'iek. Or rather the nine danced while Tek'ouk made an awkward semblance of dancing, blood rushing to his face at how ridiculous his half-movements felt. Yet he preferred it over the shame of sitting out the important ceremony. The dancing slowed, the chanting becoming more of a moan. Someone handed him the mummified head of Fal'iek. Reverently, he passed it to Lil'iek.

She held it gently, raising it to her forehead. Tears streamed down her face, and she whispered something to it, to him. She pressed her lips gently to the leather covering of the mouth, then held it up and shouted, "My beloved husband now deceased, my lover and father of my children, I now begin my promise to avenge you and seek justice. I will have recompense or I will have submission and pain. This is my right, my need, which I also do on behalf of our children and our people. With my faithful pledge, you may pass in peace along the river of stars in the sky to rest with the eternals in the World Above."

So she does believe he gained passage, in spite of his forfeiting the traditions, Tek'ouk thought with amusement. He wanted to believe it certainly, but if all the shamans said otherwise, who was he to disagree? However, wouldn't she have a greater knowledge of his path than they? In either case, he looked forward to learning more of this fascinating woman.

He shouted out, "And we of Quoak hear and support her pledge. We will aid her in this endeavor."

A unified call from the rest affirmed it.

She spoke again to the head. "My love, they hear my pledge and agree to it. They'll support and aid me in this endeavor."

The Quoarn'riik, fully painted and wearing dresses of feather and bone, closed in. Each smoked the insight leaves and drank of the sacred root. In unified chant, they prayed to the mighty spirits, the Great Ones, the eternals.

"The Great Ones hear you and grant your blessing," Chtoam'luk boomed, "so ask."

"Our Motherwood Yoaom, Queen of Thorns," she yelled. "Great Kit'ohte'vaakiik, Lord of the Skies. Great Paksitm'yaguah, Lord of the Land. Great Yacumama, Lord of the Waters. Great Luio'kuuh, Lord of the Beneath. Eternal lords of all Children of the Forest, we ask for your blessing and aid in avenging our fallen champion who was dishonorably murdered. Care for him and care for us as we seek justice and assert the pride and power of our blood."

The priests, chieftains bearing painted skulls of each creature, resounded in unison, "They hear you and grant your blessing so long as proper tribute is given. The insult on you, brave daughter, insulted them as well. They'll accept no mere recompense, only death."

Lil'iek shrieked, "GREAT ONES, I SWEAR TO YOU THAT I WILL DRINK THEIR BLOOD FROM THEIR SKULLS!"

All of Quoak exploded in triumphal joy as the Quoarn'riik spoke the Great Ones' affirmation. Lil'iek lowered Fal'iek's head and returned it to Tek'ouk. Chills swept his body. He was stunned at the harsh turn the ceremony took, and how it energized the village. Once the ceremony calmed, they dispersed in silence to prepare for departure on the morrow.

CHAPTER THREE
THE INSIDE WAR

Based on *Leyta's Journals*, cc bastica 109;
Scars of the Martyrs, cc bastica 1026;

15th of Novumbre, 246

Negotiations with the Royal Chaos, who still held the capital, Mantlgrym, began with a missive directing them to cease the seditious activities in order to receive a measure of mercy. The group of rebels, led by so called King and Queen, responded with a letter that had been so soaked in blood, the ink had become illegible. Unsure what to do about this, Count Gallegom sent another, reiterating his demands with a warning against foolish charades. This second response was too much ink, words scratched all over the parchment without any sense.[18] The Court of Voium agreed to send a messenger. The Royal Chaos responded with his severed hand frozen into a rude gesture. This concluded what the Asturions had hoped to avoid, that the enemy was delaying in spite of being cut off from all towns and allies. Cut off except for the flying demon, the agony called Knave, who seeded dissension with Jester in the other towns.[19]

The contingent arrived from Castle Cantlgrym in Voium the day of the worst incident. Leyta didn't see it, but heard various accounts of Knave gliding above the city in broad daylight. People stared at the strange abomination, not really thinking to shoot it down until it finally pounced, goring the grandchild and heir of Count Cantarchar of Voium. The violence so shocked the people that they all but demanded the count make war on the Chaos

18 And *Schiltron of Magodeoz*, 36

19 See *La Epica Eluveitia de Sepultura*, 73

to protect them. And of course the count didn't need convincing. But Leyta was not encouraged by the mobs storming the streets in protest. Such rage struck her more as a fire in danger of burning out of control. The realm was becoming full of mobs, each justified by the existence of the other.

Hours later she paced the hallway of the Court of Voium. Her home in times past was still recovering from the tragedy wrought on it months prior, of losing a portion of its population to being murdered or kidnapped by the grimshades. The academic city had since been turned into a military bunker. Syago and a few leaders from other towns—counts, barons, and bishopesses—also waited in the hall with her. Even though she had been unsure whether she was the best fit as Castellan and archdynast, now that she had been given the position, she felt determined to keep it. She had but few advantages here in winning the confidence of the other leaders of Nevermore. Her stomach churned.

She went to a small window and peered out on the yelling that had caught her ear. A man and woman were both pilloried in front of the court for heresy. The signs above ready Heresy and Blasphemy and she guessed based on their accents that the woman was a noble, one who'd likely gone too far, and the man a peasant, one who could no longer be ignored. Both switched between loud sermonizing, cursing bypassers, and begging for food. Leyta'd initially been surprised they weren't executed as usual but then surmised that humiliation might prove a more effective punishment than execution, which could make them martyrs. A show for law in the time of the mob.

The door to the court chamber opened, and Esquire Tomas stepped out. "All right, we're ready. Please come in and find a seat worthy of you."

Leyta nodded to Syago, and he followed her without word. She sensed something bothered him and hoped that he could get over it for the meeting. He'd supported her, yes, but he had grown more distant, from everyone. She made a mental note to ask him directly about it later.

Voium's court chamber, a rectangular room meant to seat ten, had sixteen trickle in. It was stuffy and uncomfortable, something Leyta was used to in Cantlgrym but sensed Gallegom wasn't. The Count of Mantlgrym was a large and very proper man, accustomed to having control of a large and powerful city. He had only barely escaped when Mantlgrym was commandeered by the Royal Chaos troupe and their mob. The councilors, most of them counts, held their chairs and slid them closer together to add room for the chairs lugged in by Tomas.

Wordlessly, Syago pulled out the last aisle chair and offered it to Leyta. She moved to take it and Gallegom interrupted, "But Syago, Holy Knight, you're our honored guest as was your father."

Syago smiled faintly, fakely. "A true knight serves all people and especially his liege lady. I will be fine against the wall."[20] Leyta took the seat, and Syago took the one behind her. A captain of Maolgon took the other wall seat.

Following a prayer from Bishopess Anta, Gallegom cleared his throat. "Now, we're grateful to Lord Cantarchar for granting us refuge here, and our sympathies for his recent loss. All here have now lost someone to this madness." He nodded at his contemporary, who, in his dour moment of grief, didn't begrudge Gallegom taking charge of the court in his own domain. Leyta didn't normally like Cantarchar, but empathized with him now.

Captain Alfonsor, a hard old man who led Mantlgrym's army and unofficially all of Nevermore's military might,[21] nodded at what Gallegom had said. "I have plans to take back the city, which we'll discuss last."

"We still don't have our powers back from the blinding ritual that hit us under the True Night," Archamand Bartolina, the emissary and general of the summoner enclave of Bokhor, said in a thick accent. "And we have no leads on what to do, but we're not afraid. Our entire village is trained enough for competent battle. But I did want to ask Mastra Leyta about what exactly the Razhod cult took from them." The woman's stern ebony face turned to Leyta.

Leyta stumbled out a response about old documents and maps, mostly related to ancient history. "We're not certain of their importance yet beyond their religious nostalgia, though we do know that rather than simply steal them, Davagis and Kask wanted to force them from us as a demonstration of their power. I could glean nothing about their future strategy and, aside from a gruesome murder in a chapel, the two have disappeared." She paused. "I wonder a similar thing about the Royal Chaos. They have the city but must not be content with it. What's their next move? Their activity outside Mantlgrym has been sporadic, so what are they preparing for?"

---

20 ibid, 93

21 ibid, 37

Countess Catalana, a portly woman from Maolgon, attending in behalf of her ailing husband, cleared her throat. "We are certain that they're searching for something. We've seen that white demon flying around the plains and mountains near Maolgon, only to return to the city with nothing. This is in addition to the havoc they're trying to wreak in our city, but we're holding strong. But what they're after in the hills is beyond me."

"Scouting out the canyon Kimoc then?" Count Toriacus of Tolgrym supplied, but she denied it. He continued, "What other allies might they acquire if not the pagans? We've not seen them our way since we pushed them out of the eastern woods."

Gallegom chortled. "What does it matter to us if that thing wastes its time getting lost?"

"It will matter to us," Catalana began, eyes sharp, "if it's a buildup to something that will hit us the way it hit you. I don't wish to fall to the same errors you did."

Before he could retort, there was a knock at the door and Tomas's head poked in. "Pardon my interruption, but it appears the Kimoc are at the gates requesting entry, and to join the meeting."

A stunned silence fell on the room. Cantarchar asked, "What? Which tribe?"

"Quoak, my lord. I'm not sure how they knew about it, though I suspect the guards let it slip as the reason why you couldn't address them directly at the gate."

"How convenient," he drawled. "Let them inside. We'll discuss letting them into the meeting." Tomas nodded and retreated.

"What could they want?" Gallegom asked.

"Revenge and justice," Leyta said. "They lost an important figure in Fal'iek at Tolgrym. So I'd guess they want to participate in our civil war."

"And how do we know this isn't another one of their tricks?" Cantarchar said.

"Perhaps we don't," Toriacus began. "But it might not matter if we can use them all the same." All eyes fixated on him with renewed interest, except for Leyta, who didn't like the direction this was going. "We had a plan to trap them against the enemy at Tolgrym, killing two birds with one arrow. But the main fight overwhelmed us. Perhaps we can implement the plan now; a siege will be slower going after all. Even without it, we could use their help, so we make them help extra."

This gave Leyta a flashback to the soldier kicking a Kimoc into Jester's firebomb. *That was planned?* "What exactly are you thinking?" Captain Alfonsor asked.

"Of course it'll depend on what they want to do and how, exactly. But I won't mind edging them out to the front lines, testing them in a wall assault, and so forth. We'll need to talk to them first before we can set up a plan."

"We'd be betraying an ally," Leyta countered, hiding the nervousness in her voice.

Everyone stared at her, then burst into laughter. "Oh my lady," Gallegom said, though Leyta thought he'd almost said *child.* "They've never been our ally, Fal'iek notwithstanding. Even when we fought side by side against a common enemy, it was always temporary. The understanding has been mutual. But Count Toriacus is right, let's bring them in."

Leyta was still not having it. "Regardless, I'm not betraying them." *Let them know you are strong, because you are.*

"Neither am I," Syago declared behind her.

Encouraged, she continued, "Nor will we be complicit in this. We're no longer at war with the Kimoc, even tacitly."

The room fell quiet. Captain Alfonsor interjected, "Why don't you let us veterans plan the strategies, my lady. Doing anything else will make you vulnerable to their tricks, but I wouldn't expect you to know that."

"You wouldn't?" Leyta fought to keep her voice steady. "Why not?"

Gallegom sighed. "I was going to wait until after the meeting, but now's as good a time as any. We're installing Baron Ourense at Cantlgrym to lead there." The baron's surprised expression told it was news to him too.

"No," Leyta said. "You're not."

Tension swelled in the room like heat. Originally the king would've decided and even then it'd been a source of contention, like appointing bishops. Since the fall of the royalty there'd been times the counts had chosen the castellan when the Razhod had slain all the masters, or when an ambitious count installed his brother over their own divided ambitions. But it was supposed to be the masters' decision. Leyta realized her hand subconsciously gripped her scepter. She fought the urge to use it, to make them listen, make them see that she wasn't a helpless girl.

"You're pushing your luck here, miss," said Gallegom. "We've always left you at the castle to yourselves but I've half a mind to correct the mistake that made you the new leader. You can step down to a mastra of high status, a better fit for you."

"I'm just as qualified as any of you to lead. I have battle experience with the enemy, more than most of you—no, more than all of you. I have the support of my people, more than most of you. And I have an extensive education relevant to what's before us. So why am I not qualified in your eyes?"

A pause added weight to her points.

"You're too young," said Alfonsor, his eyes betraying a sharpness his tone kept out. "As are most of your keepers."

"Syago is a year younger than me, but you like him enough to invite to your table. Baron Ourense is only a few months older than I. So it can't be my age." She heard Syago shift behind her and thought remorsefully how she'd just used him again to make a point. "Is it because I'm a woman?"

"Don't be absurd," said Gallegom. "Bartolina and Anta are here in good faith, Catalana as well. All salient women, well accepted." They also glared at her.

"Well accepted because they do whatever you tell them to. No, it's not that I'm a woman, your problem isn't even that I'm a woman in power, it's that I don't stay where you put me. I'm not a woman who listens to you, the men." She fought to hide the trembling in her hands and voice. Why was she trembling? She berated herself.

At the silence, Toriacus cleared his throat. "Perhaps we're getting off topic here. The advantages of using the Kimoc are multitudinous, no less the weakening of their foothold in the forest, but another edge in the war for us."

"Count Toriacus is right," said Gallegom, turning to Leyta. "And not. We will let you keep the Castellanship if you sufficiently aid us in undermining the Kimoc. Easier given the trust you've earned of them. If you don't, we'll withhold funding and recruits." Money and men they did have authority over, and thus leverage with her.

The stares of the court conveyed unanimous agreement.[22]

"And if I refuse to aid you?" Syago asked.

"Then you'll refuse your liege lady, or lord," Gallegom said quietly, eyeing her. "And your kingdom... for pagans."

Leyta turned and met Syago's eyes. Hard and angry, she knew he'd oppose

---

22 It's not clear from the evidence how much plotting against them was done, nor how complicit any were. One thing is clear, however, they would not have mentioned it here had there been none of it. Cavalera had sympathies for the Kimoc, but he was mastozon. It also explains the blood that flows later on.

the treachery even more than she. She wasn't afraid to be extra firm, or even harsh, with the Kimoc, but he wouldn't like even that.

They told the esquire to bring in the Quoakans. When Tek'ouk hobbled in on a crutch, everyone stifled a gasp. Even Leyta, who knew of what had happened, was surprised to see him here. Behind him stood Lil'iek and Mour'ikik. The shadows of the gloomy room on their dark skin, with their pagan dress and fearless gazes, did nothing to enhance their trustworthiness. The three stood at the end of the hall, evaluating the court that evaluated them.

A chair was placed behind Tek'ouk, but he didn't take it, instead straightening further, the other two hanging just behind. "We want war," he began, "as do you, against them. We've come for justice and to protect our people."

"And you shall have it," Cantarchar said. "But on our terms, as it is our war and our people you'll be fighting."

"We demand the heads of their leaders," Tek'ouk said. "Of this Royal Chaos and the cult. We desire nothing of your rebellious citizens."

Gallegom cleared his throat. "The leaders of both have stolen from and betrayed us. Murdered ours more than yours. Their heads belong to us. But we'll let you help, assuming you actually help us this time rather than lead them to us."

Tek'ouk's hard eyes swept the court. "Interesting. Some of you ignore what the rest of you apparently have forgotten, but in the old war, while you Asturions were defending your crown against the Crimson Coven, we were left to deal with the aftermath as devils slipped through your fingers and attacked us. We paid a high price for your struggle."

To the surprise of all, Leyta retorted before anyone else could, "Then you ought to be glad for not facing the Razhod directly. Some of us lost everything to them." *Some of us lost our families and legacies.*

"Except that we did that as well," Lil'iek responded moving out of the shadows. "Me, him, and my late husband fought them. Or have you forgotten that along with the treaties we signed?"

A heavy silence fell. Syago cleared his throat. "I think a contest of who lost most to the old war isn't going to help us right now."

Tek'ouk's gaze fell back on Gallegom. "We don't want to merely help. Or we might offer the same kind of *help* you've given us in times past. Perhaps we'll just go to Mantlgrym and start taking what's ours without waiting for your opinions on it."

Gallegom snorted. Before he could open his mouth, Toriacus said, "Perhaps we can cut a deal. Three fourths to one, due to the size ratio of the armies participating. Or both share in the executions, made together."

Leyta looked between the men, wishing her own bargaining power wasn't hanging by a thread. "Agreed," Lil'iek announced. Her companions nodded. *So she's driving this? Interesting.*

After discussing the supplies and defenses some more, Gallegom said, "I'll just cut to it then. We've two enemies at our doors, and we know next to nothing about them. Both seem formidable and have already cost us dearly, but I think we can take them with Captain Alfonsor's plan."

"As you know," Alfonsor started, "the troupe is using the land and our own people to fight for them. A tactic that has worked so far but reveals they haven't the muscle themselves to do it all. For one, I'm hopeful about reports that their bard clown is dead. My best estimate is that they're now realizing they're way in over their heads, they regret doing this, they'll try a few more tricks then run away with their tails between their legs after we give them a good beating."

"Is Jester dead or wounded?" Leyta asked, looking at Lil'iek. "I thought he was wounded?"

"I gave him a serious wound," she said, her thick accent making her voice grave. "He could be dead, but we should not bet on it."

"What of the shadowmen?" Tek'ouk said. "Or anything with the cult?"

"We've got very little," Alfonsor said. "And nothing of serious note. I'm not concerned. They come off as more scary than that charade of royal actors but they're a small deluded cult of fanatics that can't let go of their dead heroes. They've neither the quantity nor the quality of their predecessors the Razhod. The only leg up they have is the grimshades, or whatever those shadow creatures are. We've no idea where these cultists are, but we'll find them soon enough or take them as they come."

"What's the state of your recovering village, Warchief?" Gallegom asked.

Leyta hardly knew Tek'ouk but she recognized irritation as it flashed across his face. "Well enough for us to come out here. But I believe you're vastly underestimating both enemies. The Razhod cult has demonstrated the same will that their idols perpetrated, and shown similar capabilities. Sure they're not commanding spirits to kill us or blighting our lands, but they've blinded the summoners, they've assassinated leaders in Cantlgrym, they've already taken countless relics, and are poised to do more. We can't let it get as bad as it was."

"We know well how bad those days were, the scars are still here," Gallegom said quietly. "But don't mistake that war for this one. If the Razhod were back, or even coming back in any way, I'm certain we would know by now. We'd recognize that hell once it came."

"No, you wouldn't," Tek'ouk countered gently. "Of this group you know nothing; none of us do. So they didn't come in like their leaders used to, but they slipped in and conquered in a way clearly meant to show they can do more. They couldn't use the Crimson Covenant, so instead they brought in these shadowmen creatures. We can hope that they're nothing, but we must prepare for the worst, which means hunting them now. We have to consider that this following has learned from their old masters."

"And what do you propose we do?" Gallegom asked. "We've no idea where the cult is hiding. Should it please you to run around shouting for the cult to come out and fight, then be our guest, but we won't run with you."

The sides glared at each other. Leyta felt wary of the cult because of the castle betrayal but agreed the Royal Chaos rebellion was the bigger and more immediate threat, so she hesitated to say anything. She cleared her throat and said, "I also believe the Royal Chaos is being underesti- mated, and the Countess's report makes that clearer. You say they tried to force dissension in our ranks because of the insufficiency of their own forces. No, they started with dissension by seeding absurd ideas of liberty. Recruitment for a world of anarchy is their goal. I stayed with them as prisoner for training. They want *us*, not money or land or any of that. And they've succeeded, ignoring that will only allow them to take more."

"Our Quoarn'riik responded," Tek'ouk said. "They conceded the concerns the Chaos incited in our people, and reformed."

"Hah," Gallegom chortled. "Then you've buckled to the enemy."

"An enemy we repelled?" Tek'ouk retorted gently. "And need I remind you again of your riots versus our lack of them? We learned from your mistakes. It's time you do too."

"Didn't I hear something about a personal vendetta," Alfonsor said, but the slight flush in his cheeks gave away the deflection. "That one had a miserable childhood and now seeks revenge on us? That's not a cause like you describe."

Having not heard the tale, the others looked at him confused. Leyta addressed their questioning looks. "Jester told me he was on *The Nascendante* when the Dark Sage was slain," she said. "The explosion that sunk it left his face badly scarred and blinding him, and that much I can say is true, I saw it. He also said that Cantlgrym rejected him as did all the cities before he found King's group. If it's true, it only adds more appeal for the people."

Gallegom huffed, furious. "Are you suggesting that these attacks are somehow our fault? That we deserve this?!"

"It's their fault for assaulting us, and our fault for provoking them," Toriacus stated flatly. "It's not one or the other."

"Is it possible to reclaim Mantlgrym without military assault?" Bishopess Anta asked.

"I see no other way," Milemeron said. "Even more clever maneuvers would require fighting at some point."

"Then I ask why it's even necessary?" Anta's eyes moved to each of the other leaders. "Many of our own people on both sides would die, and by attacking we'd be giving them the fuel to the fires of their rebellion. If we let the rebellion run its course, they'll grow tired of the new conditions and realize they need us. Their anger is unsustainable."

"Fair points, Mother Anta," Alfonsor said. "But it is a key place strategically in a time of two enemies. Furthermore, we can't let the disease of this rebellion spread. It is already happening in Cantabryn and Maolgon. We must communicate strength and intolerance for this injustice. Nor can we let the people think we've abandoned them to the wolves."

Why do I feel like this room is just another mob? Leyta thought. *Maybe it's mobs all around.*

"Perhaps we could offer our people a way out first," Leyta said, inching forward in her seat. "We can send a delegation appealing to their common sense, asking them to surrender. Maybe we'll admit the need for some judicial review. Offer a few pardons. And offer a city under better conditions than those present."

"No pardons," Gallegom said. "Or at least not for those convicted of the attacks that happened. We must show strength against this or it'll come back."

"Strength means doing what's hardest," Leyta said, hoping to convince him of something more workable. "Which in this case is overcoming such bitterness. We can't convict the entire city, so focus only on those leading in the rebellion. Promise the rest an effective clemency for giving up the primary malefactors."

"That's a lot of promises to make," said Alfonsor. "But so long as it appears that we're sincere and realistic, I suppose an offering won't hurt. We'll cut off supplies and escape routes to add leverage."

"My voice will help as well," Syago added. Leyta had almost forgotten he was there. She knew he must be thinking that the requested betrayals will be avoided best with a quick surrender.

At that, Gallegom actually looked optimistic. "We'll leave it to you then," he said with a nod to Leyta. "Even if not all of them listen, we only need enough of them to weaken the opposition."

Leyta didn't doubt that he hoped she would fail, and she resolved not to. Perhaps his optimism was less the idea of weakening the rebellion and more the potential of weakening her.

CHAPTER FOUR
HIDDEN MONSTERS

Based on *Writings of Qosku*, cc bastica 126;
Scars of the Martyrs, cc bastica 1027;
The Nordvargor Testaments, cc bastica 886;

17th–18th of Novumbre, 246

Qosku stood in the empty belltower of the Cathedral de Saint Casilda, armed and armored. Ears trained for the slightest warning, he peeked through the hole of a large stained-glass window. People filled the town square below. On a large wooden platform stood a hooded figure and six naked older men, their skin shining with sweat in the pale daylight. Discomfort pushed Qosku's gaze away from them, but he gathered from the yells and thrown objects, mostly food, that these despised were about to die mainly for being rich. And the peculiarity of these mostly poorer people throwing still-good food at their targets while the city was already running low on stores struck him as a failing more endemic than accidental to the rebellion's situation.

The mob had targeted wealthy aristocrats, but not all aristocrats had suffered. Some had sold off their wealth to pacify the crowds. But most had been looted and taken before they could make any kind of offer.[23]

Above him, the tower bells tolled justice. He considered his options. Directed not to intervene, he hid only as a spy, sent by Leyta. Only she, Andras, and Syago knew he was here. An easy secret to keep, he believed; most people didn't think of his existence at all.

Just as well for him, he preferred living outside of the minds of others who'd never understand. He'd told himself that. It was certain, however,

---

23 See *Losnin Liberado Kani*, 23 especially the section on Saqra's Cult

that the special assignment made him feel important, he finally belonged even if at a distance.

He'd seen executions like these before, though less brutal. Less mocking. For the Unaka, executions were a rigid formality sanctioned by ceremony. For their colonist lords, it was a lesson. But this was entertainment and more so here than before the rebellion. The understanding that he couldn't save them even if he'd tried outweighed his desire to. Too many prisoners, too defenseless, in front of too many angry people. He'd accomplish more on the strategy Leyta had discussed. Sneak into the city, gather information to send back to her.

Cheering brought his attention back around. He shifted to a different window, this one boarded up, to see what brought the new ruckus. On a roof-top stood King and Queen in their unmistakable regal costumes, masks and all. Their voices boomed across the square, though he only caught parts of the speech. "Having fun," "bring down the oppressors," "they're coming but we'll stop them," and "end the tyranny" were the only parts he understood. They seemed content to merely keep the fires stoked. *But for what?*

Then the song began. He heard, or rather felt, Jester's singing better than the speeches because of the dynal power carrying it. He sensed it vibrate, first small and gentle, through the boards and into his body, a surge of wrathful sentiments. It grew stronger, building up energy in that subtle way he knew worked best on an unthinking crowd. The song of anger held no sway on him at first, as he was trained to resist it. But it grew mighty, filling his being. He grabbed the boards to brace his mind against its pull. It pushed on him to act on the rage, to burst out of that room and fight. Not even to save the prisoners, but to beat on the malignant crowd and punish their stupidity.

He saw more items thrown at the prisoners. Three dropped to their knees. The executioner trembled, also unable to contain his rage. He let loose his sword, swinging at their necks. Qosku, now sweating, could only barely see the heads fall among the foods being thrown. Blood splashed and flowed with vegetable splatter and fruit smear. The crowd roared, and the song hit a resounding vibrato that brought Qosku to his knees and tears to his eyes. Hands trembling, jaw clenching, he wondered if maybe Jester knew he was here and was targeting him, trying to bring him out, or if he really was just this powerful.

When the song tapered off, Qosku gasped in relief. After wiping his face, he stood and saw the crowds dispersing, shouting for a celebration.

He picked up his crossbow and knapsack and made his way closer to the western gatehouse of the city wall, navigating the rooftops with care. He jumped between each by pushing anger into his legs, using hate to increase his speed and sorrow to heal when landing too hard. It wasn't far to the edge of town, and he sat atop one of the larger buildings near the wall. The dynfist way, Takanaku, taught balance, so he funneled joy through his body, though meager it was. Still, it energized. He pulled out a strip of parchment and wrote, in lettered Unaka—to disguise the meaning from undesired eyes—of the executions and their foreknowledge of the siege. He then tied it, tightly wrapped, to a bolt and waited for the guards on the outer wall to pass. He cranked the crossbow then shot it high and far, where Leyta's scouts could claim it outside the city.

As he brought the crossbow down, he noticed a parchment that was nailed to the parapet. He tore it off, then darted back to a nearby roof to read it.

> *Humanity has got you by the throat*
> *Haste! The Court of Fools is taking requests*
> *And pay no toll to fear, just jump the moat*
> *A call to order, granting of bequests.*
> *Enter your name in justice lottery*
> *Win or lose, it's all the same to power*
> *Census of the benighted foddery*
> *In Civilization's finest hour*
> *She's a collective with claim on your head*
> *The sum of its parts, you paid for it all*
> *A belonging true even when you're dead*
> *Claim on it all the way up to the fall*
> *We live with each other, little misfit*
> *Wise up, we're all yours now, so deal with it*

Qosku scratched his head, guessing it was more of Jester's rebellion propaganda. Or could it be the resistance? Seeing it both ways, he folded and pocketed it. *Maybe my Asturion is worse than I thought, guess that'll be another text for study.*[24]

Later that day, under a light snow, Qosku caught a glimpse of the demon Knave flying over the city. He almost missed the white creature against

---

24 The poem has sparked interesting debates between Cid de Iago and Coluim de Bodica.

the gray skies but some blackbirds flew out of its way with shrieks and caws. Instead of going on another futile pursuit of it, he decided to examine where it had come from. Following its trajectory back, he saw a small church, its stained glass window broken open at the point of its arch. He went to it, considering the wisdom of entering the dark place alone. But if the agony was gone, what was there to fear?

Spiked mace in hand, he slipped inside. The attic had the bell and rope, and a trapdoor leading down into the chapel proper. He paused for a moment in the lighted area. Against the slanting walls, in the shadows, he saw what looked like the silhouettes of children. His skin prickled and his heart ran cold as he slowly approached them. When his eyes adjusted, he froze. Only the children's heads sat there—eyes staring blankly, mouths hanging agape—on small spikes carved out of coat stands.

All along the attic walls were more and more heads of boys and girls. They looked alike, though all Asturions looked the same to Qosku. The pit in his stomach grew when he recalled the human head of the demon, a little girl's just like these.

That face also reminded him of his twin sister Chaska, now dead by Qosku's hand. Or so he believed, he wasn't sure what had happened with her, if it had been an illusion or not. He didn't think he'd ever know. But this demon would not play a similar trick on him and the children it captured. Not if Qosku could stop it.

He heard the fluttering of feathered wings just outside and quickly backed into the shadows behind one of the racks of heads. The agony looked like a winter cat from the mountains, but hairless and white, and now with the head of a black-haired human boy instead of blonde girl as before. Smaller than he if one discounted the wingspan, the demon prowled lightly into the room, carrying a young girl, held up by the collar, in its little human mouth. Qosku prepared for a surprise attack but stopped when he noted the girl was already dead. There was no blood, but plague marks ran along her skin. A small thump as it dropped her to the floor made him shiver, nearly knocking a stand of heads over. But the demon didn't notice, instead hunching its back in pain, yowling and whimpering. Its claws scratched at the floorboards and the muscles along its bony body convulsed, a very physical suffering. *What is happening here?*

It sat up on its haunches, bony tail twitching from side to side, the curved blade on the end of it scraping loudly across the floor. Qosku could clearly see its face, where mucus caked its boy eyes and snot poured out of the mouth. It would've been a pretty face if not for all that. The jaw clenched and the boy head whimpered. Qosku stood in paralyzed horror as blood began trickling out of the eyes and nose. Its forepaws reached up. The wet tearing sound of a head being ripped from its neck pulled him out of his stupor, and he edged around toward the window. This moment of rare vulnerability for the fiend would've been the perfect opportunity to attack it, but Qosku was too terrified and repulsed to even entertain the thought. Its painful yowling and childish whimpering were cut off as the head was removed. But it was the wet sound of the tailblade whipping into the dead girl's neck that caused him to jump and run toward the window. His frantic haste to get out knocked over two stands, the heads rolling off. Yet his panic drew no attention from the headless agony as it prepared a new crown to wear.

Outside the light snow continued to descend gently on all things, and Qosku ran along the slick rooftops back to his hideout.

On returning to the cathedral, he heard the doors open and the crowds push in. Someone approached the belltower. He quickly grabbed his things and slipped out a window to stand on a precipice. They'd set fire to the church in their first riot, that day when the Royal Chaos took over the city. But shortly after starting the fire, they'd realized they needed the building and put it out. If not for religious functions, then for storage or meetings. Though it now appeared they planned to maintain some form of religion. Religious mantras floated up to his ears, with impassioned sermons surrounding topics of freedom. Realizing they wouldn't be leaving for some time, Qosku sighed and climbed up to a roof to look for another place to spend the night. He ended up in the old round theater, now in poor repair, where he'd first met and dueled Syago. When night came, he dreamt in memory again.

The day he'd finally decided to leave Chuqi'kirau, Qosku knelt among his peers, on the great ceremonial plateau overlooking the valley. At the center stood Baron Kondapac, the village kuraka, in fancy Asturion clothing, pronouncing judgment on a criminal.

The iron weapon of the executioner was expertly made, but Qosku had no admiration for it. Since being old enough to witness executions, Qosku'd grown sick of them. He studied the art of fair fighting. Although this man's actions fully justified the procedure, he hated watching.

Kondapac hummed a hymn along with the others, eyes fixed at places other than the top of the waka altar. Most in attendance whispered in Unakan to the old eternals following praises to the new. Asturion soldiers and priestesses stood nearby, supervising. Kondapac pounded his staff on the stone. "Today we come to dishonor the actions of a brother to death. We ask Deova and Her Saints to accept our pledge and free us of his blight."

Qosku heard the kids behind him snickering. The wind hid it from the kuraka, but Qosku couldn't ignore it. He made a shushing sound. The disrespect bothered him, he didn't like the ceremony either but only the more reason to be appropriate. They giggled even louder again. He turned saying, "Quiet. Be respect—" He cut off when he saw who it was.

Akualchac and his goon friends. Akualchac's angular face grinned. "Shut it, wart."

Qosku turned, hoping it would end at that. The voices continued, "Hey, how many warts are on your tiny?"

He blushed, thinking of his crooked sexuality. The wrongness of his body. He prayed and focused on the ceremony.

The other goons burst out laughing, a couple other kids shushed them. Most seemed too bored to care. "Well," he pressed, poking Qosku in the back. "Is it worse on the backside or front?"

"Lemme 'lone. I'm trying to pay attention," Qosku said, swatting the hand away without taking his eyes off the altar. His face flushed and tears surfaced, held back by his focus.

They quieted down for a few moments, and Qosku thought it finished until something warm settled on his woolen tunic; a small cup from behind dumped chicha on him. "Oh whoa," said Akualchac. "That's disgusting. Qosku just wrecked himself."

"He splurged all over his tunic," said another, shoving him in the back. "Qosku messed himself! Qosku messed himself!"

Everyone in the area, starting with the girls in front of him, joined in the chant, laughing at the sight of Qosku's tunic as he tried to brush off what he hoped was just chicha. He was vaguely aware of the display of blood occurring on the altar as more and more joined in his disruption. They continued, and he shouted, "No, I didn't! He lies, I didn't."

Tears streamed his face as they ignored his protest. Anger fueling his limbs, he grabbed Akualchac and threw him to the side, in between rows of the laughing girls, who now looked frightened. Laughter stopped. Akualchac rolled onto his back, a stunned expression on his face. At once, a priestess grabbed Qosku by the shoulder and led him out. Another priestess walked down to the group of kids. He wondered maybe if he told her that he was really a girl trapped in a boy's body, she'd understand. Instead, once further down the path, the prelata slapped him hard in the face once, then a second time.

Qosku jolted awake, arms up to fight back. Realizing it was only a dream, he curled up in his corner of the theater wardrobe and looked out the broken window to the full moon glaring at him through the clouds. He pulled the tiny blanket back over him, grateful that the nightmare had ended where it had. Though, he was still a girl in a boy's body, a painful disappointment that only faded by subduing it, and never vanished completely.

Rustling on an adjoining roof drew his attention. For a moment, he didn't see anything in the darkness, then the silhouette of a large head popped up. Qosku guessed a thief breaking into a house or scavenging trash. The head turned, and he saw shining teeth and glimmering eyes. Qosku stood. Whatever it was, it wasn't human.

The creature jumped off a wall and onto the roof opposing his as he backed away. With glittering eyes and teeth, it leered at him in the moonlight. It was nearly twice his size, and from the way it moved, Qosku already knew he couldn't outrun it. It looked like an ozor of the Apugakas, but more slim and limber, and with a shorter snout.

What are you, and how did you get into the city?

Rising up on its hind legs, its claws extended, the creature roared. Qosku didn't move. It sprung at him suddenly, and Qosku caught both its arms. They fell, smashing through the floor into the room below. Qosku struggled to keep its powerful arms at bay, but its heavier body dominated him. It snapped at him furiously and tried to pin him to the floor. Using dyne to augment his speed, Qosku reversed the pin and trapped its belly under his knee. Yet all the anger and hate he pushed into his limbs for greater strength wasn't enough. It roared and threw him across the room.

He crashed through several stage props and immediately rolled to a crouch, looking for the beast. Hearing movement on the left, he jumped and kicked, hitting it in the face even as it grabbed his leg and slammed him down to the floor.

Wind knocked out of him, Qosku barely had time to scramble backward as claws swiped toward him. Snarling, the thing lunged, biting into his leg with its foamy mouth.

Stifling a scream, he punched it in the side of the head before it could tear flesh away. It winced and released him, but before Qosku could catch his breath, it picked him up and tossed him out the window.

He landed in a pile of old floor rushes, one story down. Crawling out of the pile, Qosku sat against the wall to regain himself. The cuts from the claws were fine, but the bite on his leg burned. He had a sinking feeling that this was a very bad thing.

A wave of nausea fell over him as he tried to push himself to his feet. He sat back down. He could try and make it back to his bag on the roof, but his new friend might be waiting. Of one thing he was certain, he couldn't be down in the streets in plain sight at coming dawn. He would have to find a place to hide.

He crawled down the alley to a back door and tried to pry it open, but pain lanced up his leg and he retched. The bite was now starting to feel numb. A new sense of urgency set in as he realized the danger of infection or venom. He had some healing skill, but nothing this powerful. To even attempt it, he'd have to be in a position to pray in peace for a long time. He had some supplies in his bag, but he doubted that'd work on this either. He had to leave the city as soon as possible, get to the camp, to Leyta.

But he couldn't leave his bag.

He punched the door handle and broke it open, taking another opportunity to vomit, ignoring the lance that shot up through his dead leg. He crawled to a small staircase and listened. He looked up. Quiet, no attacks, good enough. If he didn't move, he was dead anyways. He crawled up, his legs dragging like the dead weight that they were. Head swimming, he fought against the urge to black out. Halfway up, he stopped to vomit the last he had, then continued, impossible without sentiments providing the energy he needed. Determination flooded him. He slowed at the sound of scratching above him. Hopefully just rats.

Arms at their limits, he reached a room on the second floor, either storage or dressing, and lay gasping for breath. There was no way he could make it to his bag, let alone out of the city, in this condition. A sinking feeling overcame him as he realized infections don't work this fast, but poisons do. All his effort had probably sped up the circulation of whatever was in his blood.

He sighed, wondering why he even tried to continue in the first place. He didn't have much to live for. Always depressed, hating himself and his memories. Hating his body and desires. Bad dreams almost every night, often regurgitating memories. Most of the time, he survived for its own sake. Survival as a goal is fine so long as the challenge and the victory is worth it. But his past held so much misery and loss, and all he saw in his future was suffering, made worse now with an infection he knew nothing about and had no way to treat. Not for the first time did he consider letting his miserable life end early for the relief it promised.

But Chaska would not have accepted this surrender. She wanted him powerful, because it made her, his twin sister, also powerful. And he remembered his commitments; Leyta and everyone else needed him. He couldn't let this beat him. He knew he couldn't give up on his redemption for what he'd done to Chaska either. Caving to this would be akin to caving to the bullies who'd started his exile. Those enemies who were once his friends.

These realizations made him refuse to bow to anything that didn't give him a minimum of respect. Feeling this new determination, he used the last of his physical strength to push himself up toward another staircase, but as he grabbed it, the nausea took over and he prayed to avoid blacking out.

Can't do the stairs, but that balcony enclosure would be a good hiding place for the night, the best I can hope for. He slid over to it, more of an open compartment than a balcony, and closed the curtain behind him. Rotted and worn, much as he felt, it accepted his body. As he settled in, his muscles twitched, tightened, skin itching. He sensed movement somewhere inside him. Something gravely unnatural. A change? He looked at his trembling, almost spasmodic, hand, wondering what was happening to him. He tried to pray again, to stop the infection, but darkness swallowed his conscious experience.

CHAPTER FIVE

BECOME

Based on *Leyta's Journals*, cc bastica 145;
Scars of the Martyrs, cc bastica 1026;
The Nordvargor Testaments, cc bastica 886;

18th of Novumbre, 246

Leyta stood between Syago and Andras, her two armored captains, atop a grassy mound a hundred spans from Mantlgrym's west gate.[25] They'd arrived hours earlier, and it was now past midnight.

Leyta regretted that it had taken so long to get to the siege. The lackluster response allowed the enemy to prepare. A full moon illuminated the wall in front. The gate was relatively small in comparison to the stretch of wall. Several spans behind them, the rest of her troops set up camp under the light snowfall. Already the camp barriers, spiked fences set up over ditches dug with dyne, lined the perimeter. They were sufficiently prepared to cut off supply and escape routes while keeping themselves clear of lifeless and other natural threats.

Hopefully this darkemorg season will keep monster attacks low, and the siege short. She didn't know the people of Mantlgrym to be so irrational. She planned to have some of her troops plead to their families in Mantlgrym to change. If no acceptance came by dawn the following day, her troops would assault the wall.

Katti and Constantin conducted a mass nearby. The Quoak tribe set up camp just south of them, making her uneasy about what she might have to do and how it would affect the following power struggles. Half a month into her ascension and she'd begun to understand that the challenges to her position would never cease and began to regret accepting it even as the naysayers made her want to prove them wrong.

"Maybe twenty spans ahead," Syago said. "We could do the family plea, our bards behind them and soldiers around—"

"It's better if the soldiers are behind," Andras cut in. "Surrounding them will look too much like we're forcing them. If we put them out there, it will show confidence and genuineness on the part of the children."[26]

"I agree with that," Leyta said. "Soldiers behind, hold off on all our elementists. Anything to avoid making it look contrived will be the best push we can make. If Jester's song comes on, then ours will too."

"If they're still executing people, as Qosku's message claimed," Andras said, "they won't persuade easy, if at all."

"It's the clown," Syago said. "King and Queen may run the show, but that bard's singing is the power behind the movement. We should have Qosku focus on him, find him, his secrets, or just take him down."

"No, it's too risky, and this has enough value," Leyta said. "Besides, we also have minstrels. More than they, Tongu being only the strongest. I doubt it'll be necessary though, if they concede. If not, then..."

"We—" Syago cut off and stepped forward, drawing Alexandre. It glowed faintly in the dark. Leyta tilted her head, wondering what had caught his attention. Then she heard it as well. Something coming toward them from the wall. Shambling and noisy, not like a hunt or a charge.

Andras drew his sword. "Step back, m'lady."

In an instant, it was in front of them, swinging a large clawed arm. The two warriors jumped back as it growled painfully and reached for Syago, who kicked it in its furry face. As Syago prepared to cut it down, Leyta called for a halt. Hands out, she stepped forward, confident both Andras and Syago were at the ready.

"Pleeeze... helllp meee!" It wheezed in a hoarse voice as it rose up on long forearms. The eeriness of a talking animal chilled her.

"Fomorion!" Andras and Syago said together. Leyta took an involuntary step back.

"Or a werebeast," Andras speculated after a moment.

"HELLLP... MEEE!" it howled, somehow recognizable.

"No," Leyta said, eyeing its torn clothes. "It's Qosku!"

"What?!" Syago said. "Can't be. He'd never..." Syago trailed off as he evidently saw what Leyta had.

26 wait

"Pick him up," Leyta commanded. "Carefully, and bring him to my tent. Don't let anyone see. Hurry."

They did so, each putting a shoulder under its arms, hesitantly at first, and raising him up. It didn't fight, or try to hurt them as she knew they secretly feared. It, he, did groan and drag his feet. She went ahead and gave orders that cleared the path to her tent.

Once in the tent, they hoisted him onto the table in the middle. "Get Katti. And an apothecary. Quickly," she barked to Andras, who ran out.

The lamplight revealed the extent of the damage to their friend. Both Syago and Leyta muttered "ozor," and indeed he looked like an infant of the mountain beasts. Black fur covered his body, which remained slightly bigger than the Qosku they had known. Thick arms almost broke his gauntlet straps, and his larger-than-normal hands were clawed. He was also wet from... sweating? She shivered but felt relief at the lack of blood. This was a full moon, the worst night, so the transformation was full, though it didn't look it, if her readings had been true. All she knew was lore documented methodically by old priests. Leyta guessed, then, that he'd just been bit and the infection hadn't fully taken over. She knew so little about the curse—er disease—and hoped Katti or whichever apothecary who came could do more.

Qosku gasped and writhed on the table until Syago and Leyta grabbed his arms to hold him down. He shrieked with inhuman agony, "WHAT'S HAPPENING TO ME?!"

"Qosku, your leg... did something bite you?" Leyta asked as Katti swept into the tent carrying a bag, followed by a young boy with another, larger bag. The apothecary? He'd be the first boy apothecary she'd ever seen. Andras followed them in.

"Yesz," Qosku coughed. Katti surveyed him in deep concern. "Augh, help me. What's happening to me?"

"What's already happened, I'm afraid." Katti wrung her hands. "You're on the tail end of your first werebeast transformation. It should be over in a few minutes when the sun rises."

"Is there anything you can do to stop it?" Leyta asked. "Or preemptively weaken it? He can do some self-healing through his training too."

Katti shook her head. "Nothing I can do now. But Deova Bondua is mighty. I will pray." Placing a sun cross on his chest, and her hands on either side of it, she muttered a prayer. Leyta felt a tinge of admiration at the woman's bravery. All the old superstitions cropped up in Leyta's mind, and she could read them on both Andras's and Syago's faces. It was said that miasma rose off a werebeast's skin and infected people, or their future children. That touching one made the beast worse, brought it out more, or gave him your taste. She realized she wasn't sure if she did or didn't believe any of them. They knew so little, and it took a mental fortitude just to stay in the room with him.[27]

The apothecary boy pulled a vial from his sack. "If I'd gotten you in the first hours, maybe I could've done more, but now it's treatment only. This should help with the pain," he said, uncorking it. "Won't hurt at least. Drink."

He poured some onto the clenched fangs of the werebeast. Some appeared to go down, the rest blew out in a cough. As soon as Katti said "amen," Qosku went limp. Still breathing, he now slept. Was that from the prayer or the drink?

Visibly relieved, Syago and Andras backed away, brushing their hands off on their armor.

"What do we do?" Andras asked, paling as though sick.

"We get him to a safe place," Syago said, face drawn and eyes pained. "He'll want solitude."

Head swimming with the implications of this, Leyta sat down on a wooden bench. Most werebeasts were exiled on infection. Kicked outside the walls and never seen again. Some were quietly put out of their misery, sometimes discreetly sometimes publicly with church denouncement. But she'd heard rumors of wealthier families that could afford to make it work. They'd build a chamber that it'd go in at night, or just when the moon was strongest and the man was less... man. Then they'd release the person during the day, keeping the transformation secret from all but their closest. As Castellan, she had some means, but not like that. Her family had some money, but none they'd put to Qosku even if they could. She was all that stood between a monster that may or may not be out of control and a people with dangerous superstitions in time of civil war. A year ago, she might've just exiled him. But now he was a close friend and a hero of the republic. And being leader had given her new perspective on her charges. Slowly transitioning back to human, his body looked most unappealing now. In between the form of a magnificent, if frightening, beast and an adorable Unakan warrior. He looked scrawny and deathly ill. A mixture of pity and love moved her to protect him.

"He'll be my bodyguard." The words were out before she even knew what she said. The others stared at her in disbelief, but she decided it was right. He'd be close to her, and she could ensure safety and secrecy. "We'll make plans, he's well trained and can get a handle on it. We can do this. He's one of our best. We have to support him."

"Leyta," Syago began. "I care about him too. We're friends. But this won't work. For him *or* for anyone else."

"If anyone finds out..." Andras trailed off, darker implications obvious to all.

"I know it's a long shot," Leyta said quietly, looking at Qosku's sleeping form. Most of the hair already shed off; his arms were noticeably shorter. "But I have to try. For him. And for me.

"We'll protect him," she said, moving her eyes over each of them. "As best we can." They all nodded, including Syago, who walked over to Qosku and placed Alexandre on him. Everyone looked at him curiously.

"The sword can heal," Syago grumbled. "Or so the legends say."

No changes took place, so he sheathed it and walked out of the tent. Andras looked uncertain whether he should stay and protect her or leave. She told him to guard at the door, a noticeable relief to him. Katti continued to pray, lacing religious symbols along the bed, and the apothecary filed through his supplies. He looked young, about the same age as Qosku, but seemed to know what he was doing. He noticed her watching, and she asked, "What's your name?"

"I'm Lügos de Roberochester... or Lüg as everyone calls me. Uh, my lady," he said. "I'll tend to him throughout the day, in between any wounded. I might be able to relieve some of the pain if naught else."

"Thank you, report to me on the progress."

Hours later that morning, Leyta stood again with Syago and Andras, and this time with their lead minstrel, Tongunabiagüs, and a battalion at her back.[28] Winds blew and dark gray clouds spanned the skies above, not the sunlit dawn she'd hoped for but they took what was given. Tek'ouk hobbled up to them and, after a brief hug with Syago, greeted Leyta, "Bright is the morning, Mastra Leyta."

---

28 *See Schiltron of Magodeoz, 34-55*

"The morning shines, warchief." She nodded to him, then to Lil'iek behind him. "How fares your army? How've you accustomed to open field warfare?"

Tek'ouk smiled. "The Roah'riik are accustomed to battle everywhere, m'lady. Now what are your plans for the plea deal?"

Leyta waved her hand at the group behind her. "The troops from Mantlgrym and the Holy Knight of Nevermore are going to use what influence they have with the good people of Mantlgrym to avoid civil war."

She saw Syago smile faintly and the young troops fiddled with their hands anxiously. Tongu turned from singing to comedy for them, easing their tension. The Bard of Voium was a large man with a thick red beard and booming voice, a warm smile ever on his face. Though he lacked his usual costume of brightly colored motley and face paint, he still cracked their frowns into laughs. She didn't like peddling them in this way. But these things needed to happen.

Andras called out that the other camps were ready, and Leyta turned to the group. "Time to move!"

The seven kids, all of them younger than her, walked solemnly to the head of the marked spot. Guards lined the wall, and civilians continued to appear at the top, drawn more by curiosity and concern than any need or push.

The troops finally stood together on the mound with Katti who, as lead priestess, would lead the diplomacy. Leyta whispered a prayer to Deova. The first child went forward and, with the aid of the bard's dyne to amplify her voice, announced her name, her family that were in the city, hopefully still alive, and her plea for reunion. The second made a courageous demand for them to overthrow the destroyers that resided therein. He called it their responsibility. The third talked about true change and pure revolutions that could come on conditions of surrender.

The fourth, a boy, was interrupted by movement and noise on the wall. He faltered in his words. Soldiers beside Leyta tensed, ready to defend them from a volley of arrows. Leyta hoped the clatter of activity was toward surrender, but the haunting mantra of the Bard of Sorrow signified otherwise. The unseen presence wasn't overpowering; its true audience was those on the wall, who began throwing objects down below. Soldiers rushed forward but slowed as the objects dropped before the emissaries. Burnt body parts and bloody heads thumped to the ground in front of the group. Horrified screams rent the air and they backed away from the wall. She went from sickly numb to trembling with rage.

"Fall back," she called and looked around. Virgow, who'd joined Leyta as her siege advisor while Balgor and Roza minded the castle in her absence, stood with both hands on his cane and his crossbow strapped to his back, unfazed.

But Syago and Andras looked to her. "Syago, inform the other camps to begin attack now. This disgrace is an outrage. The people, as far as I'm concerned, have lost their minds to that damned troupe."

"Breathe Leyta," Virgow muttered low enough for only her to hear. "They're trying to provoke you into a hasty reaction. Don't let them move you."

"No," she corrected loudly. "We prepare to attack at dusk when our advantage is greater." She nodded to the captains, hiding her deep breath. They peeled their eyes away from the wall and ran to their duties. Virgow's hard Unakan face looked at the dismembered pieces on the ground, his eye-patch leaving him difficult to read. He grunted, and resumed his post with the archers and crossbowmen. She loosened her grip on her scepter, forcing herself to resist the desire to immediately fire on the wall herself.

Someone called her name, and she turned to see Lil'iek running up to her. "What are you doing?" Lil'iek asked. Virgow hobbled back to Leyta's side.

"Protecting ourselves," she replied. "They've shown that they are in full thrall of this mindswept rebellion. They're lost."

"I agree," Lil'iek said. Tek'ouk limped up beside her, expression grim and steady, calming. "But why aren't you moving up to attack now? It's either that or have the other armies go first."

"To prepare," she said. "I'm not letting them goad me, I'll not be their fool to play or walk into their trap."

"But the preparations are theirs to make," said Tek'ouk. "You're already prepared and can only lose ground. Stop waiting and attack."

Annoyed that he was telling her what to do with her army, Leyta said, "This is the strategy. Are you going to fulfill it or not?"

"This strategy," Tek'ouk said, as if talking to a child, "is giving *them* time. Our entire army needs to shift with the wind and assault now."

"Do you think I don't want to?!" she said. "I know what I'm doing. Go run your own army and stop telling me how to run mine. We're allies, not fellow commanders."

"It will only be the worse for you," he said, with infuriating tranquility. "I'm only trying to help you from losing your own goal."

"Stop patronizing me," she snapped. "I can do this!"

Tek'ouk stared at her but said nothing. "Leyta," Virgow said quietly. "Lower your scepter."

She realized she'd been pointing it at Tek'ouk to emphasize her words, a dangerous and forbidden gesture. Shocked, she lowered it and whirled away to hide the color in her cheeks. Luckily, both Tek'ouk and Lil'iek didn't push it, also walking away.

Virgow moved closer to her. "I'll back you in front of others, but in person I give it straight. Real power starts at having more self-control than your enemies. You're a dynast, you should know better than to react on emotion." With that, he returned to his post.

Now frustrated with herself as well, she weighed both Tek'ouk's and Virgow's words, and her options, resolving to think more on her self-restraint as a dynast later. She considered that maybe she'd overreacted and she should listen to those who had more experience. At the same time, she felt fully justified in her reactions. Attack now or attack later, both had veterans pushing toward one or another. She looked up to see people gathering along the walltop. Mostly archers, crossbowmen, and elementists with a few shieldmen as protection. Perhaps Tek'ouk had been right, though of course she couldn't admit it.

Behind her, she saw her troops already holding defensive lines. Pride sparked in her on witnessing the perfect timing and formation of her small battalion. A spark that perished quickly to their shouts. She turned back to the wall to see dark objects arcing toward the various battalions. They'd repurposed the warmachines used to fight monstrous feldinals to catapult refuse.

So waiting is no longer an option anyway.

The wall dynasts waved their staves and the refuse caught fire.

She reacted on pure instinct, entering the Vision and seeing all in shades of sentiments. The projectile came toward them in a red fury, and she raised her staff, augmenting that rage with her own. The refuse exploded, spraying flaming pieces over her soldiers. Realizing the mistake, she quickly shifted focus to the air, tinged green from tense anxiety. She threw all of her fear into it, fear of the battle now on her shoulders, and created a burst of wind that directed the flaming pieces back to the wall. The other dynasts followed her lead and the fallout faded to ash between the armies.

As those on the wall released a flurry of arrows, one thumped into her gambeson, cutting her leg. She yelped, falling to her knees, and panic set in as she saw her own vulnerability. But before she could do anything, Andras and, to her surprise, Qosku were lifting her up.

Syago appeared from behind, raising his shield, his sword swinging as more arrows raced toward them. His shield caught only a few arrows and bolts, but Alexandre did draw attention from her long enough for Qosku and Andras to help her move behind the front line. Qosku stopped suddenly, an arrow appearing in his hand. She realized in amazement that he'd caught it. She also noted Tongu's powerful voice washing over the camp, a song of courage. Renewed by this, the soldiers prepared to charge the gate. She took comfort that her army worked so well even when caught off guard.

She stood up in spite of the pain and walked further behind her battalion while leaning on Qosku as Andras fell in line to give commands to the other shieldmen. There, she took charge of her people and commanded them into assault position.[29]

29 Deaths listed in *We Paid It All* by Bartolome de Sart.

CHAPTER SIX
The Wild and Its Ways

Based on *The Hunter's Parchments*, cc bastica 220;
The Dark Fortress of Mephorash, cc bastica xx;

18th of Novumbre, 246

After Leyta had lowered her staff from him, Tek'ouk turned away, deciding that she'd be the best one to keep close. If he could pit this impulsive, inexperienced leader against the others or lean on her for protection when things came to with them, then it would be victory enough. Hobbling after Lil'iek, he asked, "Why did you suggest she let the others go first? We want them hurt, do we not?"

"Them," she waved at the other armies' direction. "Not her and Syago, I like and trust her more than the others. Well, I did until she stuck her scepter in your face. Maybe they were right about her." Lil'iek fell into step beside him. "A dynast like that is dangerous. We should keep our distance."

"No, I think keeping close is better." He kept his eyes on the stony path as they neared their own camp, placing the crutch awkwardly between grassy rocks but keeping pace. "At a distance she can lose control or do something stupid, close we can monitor and influence."

"Then let me handle it next time," she said. "No use in you getting blasted because you angered her."

"I don't need protection," he snapped, then noticed others at the camp watching them. "Sorry, but no, I can handle it. Dynast to dynast."[30]

She nodded, recognizing his need to stand for himself.

"How long should we wait to join the assault?" Mour'ikik asked.

---

30 See *Sol Sistere de Selbst* by Himetuks Himi'n

Tek'ouk leaned on his scepter-crutch. "We're not starting our own attack, as we don't want to draw attention, but we can support the attacks of Cantlgrym." He called orders to Yarok and Ka'shuar'iik for updates from Count Cantarchar.

This was unnecessary, however, as firebombs and arrows rained down, and his people erected their deflection barriers. Not having metal shields like Leyta's camp, his Roah'riik warriors used a set of daemog hide canvas, which was fire resistant, with wooden shields beneath.[31] Most objects fell short. The flaming missiles bounced off of three of the seven canvases to smolder on the ground. The arrows did better against them, sticking in, but the canvases held. Several darts came close to Tek'ouk as he was unable to move and dodge like the others. He considered pulling back but didn't want to admit the need to. Instead he commanded an offensive response. However, their volley hit the ramparts too weak.

Tek'ouk had spoken true that the Roah'riik could fight anywhere, but they still were much better in their forest.

Mour'ikik pointed out that Cantarchar's Voium camp wasn't firing back at the city, just staying out of range. Yarok and Ka'shuar'iik arrived from there, panting from the run.

"Cantarchar said we provoked them," Ka'shuar'iik said. "He claims we share responsibility with Leyta for messing it up."

"Leyta erred in her reaction," Tek'ouk said. "But she hardly ruined what was already doomed. They're just trying to cast the blame on her, and us as well."

"I pushed them for a back-up plan," Yarok said. "But Captain Alfonsor said attacking at night was the back-up plan. They also don't want to lose people when it's safer to engage with night's darkness as their cover. So they're going to be *generous* enough to attack passively. Since we can't wait until tomorrow, we should respond now."

"Wonderful," Lil'iek muttered. "All this will do is force the enemy to focus on us. So much for the *alliance*."

"What are we going to do?" Yarok asked. "We can't let them treat us this way."

Tek'ouk looked at Leyta's camp, defending well against the heat for now, then around at his men. He had a mind to also deal with Cantarchar's camp but not directly. "What do you want to do?"

---

31 See also *Gybiaaw Blackbraid: Born of Winter*, 6

He asked them out of respect for their custom of collective leadership. He didn't need to, they admired him enough to follow, but their lives were on the line in a fight that wasn't really theirs.

For a moment, nobody said anything. Only the din of fire bombs and arrows meeting frantic defenses answered his question.

"Let's fight," Ka'shuar'iik said nervously, in a rare vocal moment for the young warrior. "Assault the wall with Leyta's battalion. Maybe it'll convince them we're good allies to work with instead of mistreat."

"We can't survive an assault like this just by sitting here anyway," Yarok added. "We either move back and lose ground or press in. And we only have to last until dusk when the others join in. I, for one, am tired of sitting and waiting, I want the blood we came for."

Tek'ouk felt a thrill at the boldness he'd hoped to inspire back in Quoak. His eyes met with Yarok's. The man was the only he knew more passionate and vengeful than Lil'iek, and also one of the few who knew of the side plan to undermine the palemen allies. Tek'ouk nodded. "Call for advance on the wall, with care. We need to be closer to the wall for better shots. Then we can work on climbing the wall while Leyta tries to break through. But carefully, I don't want to spill our own blood for this." As Lil'iek led some off to attempt the wall, Tek'ouk halted Yarok. "Wait, you and... Lolish'ith, come with me."

He pointed to the daemog skulls, and they brought them to the top of a mound. They each grasped the skulls to enter the minds of the nearby herds while the other Roah'riik attacked the wall. They didn't need to move them all, just enough to lead the herd into attacking Cantarchar's barriers, a veiled retaliation. A sporadic abuse to the fence wouldn't accomplish much, but coordinated ramming and burning of a single section would. Through the connection, they splintered the fences as they passed and rammed into the wall, spitting flame. It didn't take long before enough of the troops rallied to drive off the herd, but the damage was already done.

Next Tek'ouk pointed at the sky, and they switched to quervosk skulls. Beneath the ceiling of gray clouds flew numerous blackbirds, waiting to scavenge fleshy battle remains. The three helltamers each took the quervosk skulls from around their necks. The opening of their own minds to the vile appetites of the blackbirds had them clenching jaws against the salivating effects.

Using focused thoughts, they moved the avian scavengers to fly in sync toward the walltop. A few at first, then as a large flock, they swooped down screeching. The push got easier as more birds went, flock mindset driving them together more than the Roah'riik.

Some on the wall fired with dyne and arrow at the birds, most tried to duck away, and many got hit by the unexpected assault. As the chaos spread, Lil'iek gave orders for other Roah'riik to work the birds. The exchange of arrows, rocks, and fire bombs continued, and birds dived once more. But Tek'ouk only barely noticed these things, and more through the birds' eyes than his own. He did see that Leyta had also taken advantage of their distraction and made progress toward the wall. As far as he could determine, both camps held some wounded but none fallen.

Then King and Queen mounted the parapet.

They'd known the Chaos leaders would emerge eventually. The two commanded the wall forces and unleashed their powers, blazing fire from Queen and cold darkfire from King. Tek'ouk called for a united charge against the walls. Bird skulls were held high and the carnal push went out.

The dark flock of birds swooped down on the Chaos leaders in unified swarm. There were so many of them, like a black cloud spearing down. But to Tek'ouk's horror, Queen turned and, in one great blaze, incinerated the flock as they came at her. Hundreds of the large blackbirds perishing as they dove into her blaze. Their clawing hunger was replaced by knives of fear and pain in the connected Roah'riik minds, searing hot images flashing as gurow after gurow died until the hellhunters broke and fell to the ground, trembling and clutching the skulls. When Tek'ouk snapped out of the daze, he saw Lil'iek sitting over him and wiping foam from his mouth. He sat up to examine the others, who were also recovering.

"Is everyone all right?" he shouted. "Recover and regroup."

All but Lolish'ith came out of their convulsions fine. The older veteran lay on his back, spasms done, but his eyes were still glazed over and his mouth was salivating. As several tried to wake him, even administered herbs and prayers, his only response was to raise a hand to claw at the air. They put him on a cot beneath the barrier. "Well, at least he's not dead," Lil'iek muttered. A rare sentiment, Tek'ouk thought, but with some gratitude as a similar thing could be said of him, whom many would've preferred dead instead of crippled. He returned his attention to the wall. "We'll make offerings for him to the eternals."

King and Queen stood between elementists, but higher, probably on top of a box, and tore at the ground below with their dyne. The power of those blasts awed him. He hadn't seen its strength since the Razhod. Flames leaped up on the grass in front of the group, and in front of that, darkfire crackled as the dirt frosted over.

King's amplified voice rang out, "This is not necessary. You could join us in peaceful coalition on condition that you not break up our society by turning our children against us. The people have made their choice. You've only to respect that."

"You mustn't fight," added Queen. "We would welcome you as honored guests in our resplendent halls should you display proper manners."

"You may surrender," said King, "To the Order of Disorder. Or you may continue to break yourselves against our walls of liberty and truth. And judgment's darkfire halt you, hell's flame lay waste the malefactors to the one free society."

In between the two leaders appeared Jester's hooded head, bobbing about and lobbing exploding vials over the parapet. Tek'ouk could hear Jester singing but Tongu, who sang closer, had the greater impact on him, a fact he wasn't sure he appreciated.

His own barrier blocked the fire bursts, but the canvas could only take so much and everything else was either wood or bone, the edges already smoldering. He then saw Lil'iek's arrow catch Queen's arm, but instead of leaving to get it treated a soldier held it up so she could continue using her fire. He felt a strange admiration for her toughness.

"It's time to pull back," he commanded, looking back at Lolish'ith, still ailing in the tent, then to the other armies. *Time they took losses for us.* "Up against the wall like that will just kill us. We'll focus on assisting the other battalions."[32]

Lil'iek watched Queen, remembering her voice in Tolgrym moments before Fal'iek fell. Screaming to the motherwood, the huntress ran out, bow drawn. She shot up at the fake regent, landing a hit in her arm, before retreating back under the canvas.

32 I'm skeptical of much that follows. Evidence is scant either way, but it strikes me as the kind of embellished battle tales of heroes and loss. Warfare has always been more banal and void of meaning than its legends.

When she heard the call for retreat, she whirled on Tek'ouk. "No, we're not turning back. We just committed to this, we're moving in."

"I'm not sacrificing more lives for a cause not ours," he countered. "The others guard themselves while we fight out their conflict. We ought to stay back and watch for an opening to get the Chaos leaders, or the cult. The shadowmen could appear any moment, could be watching right now even."

He has a good point, she thought. *Except that I want their heads.* She grabbed a pair of climbing hooks and vine. "Retreat then. I'm going after what we came for while the risk is not too great."

She turned to the wall and heard Tek'ouk curse then call out, "Prepare the ascent. Six on hooks with her and the rest giving cover." She smiled.

Howling a warcry, she ran out, twirling the clawed vine. Arrows fell and bolts missed, but her throw was true. She pushed her mind into the vine, encouraging its momentum to go high and catch the crenelations at the top. The hooked claw caught, barely, but enough to hold her off the ground.

As Ka'shuar'iik and Yarok had caught up beside her, a stream of darkfire from King froze the area above them, then moved downward. They narrowly avoided it, but now the wall and parts of their ropes were frozen, as was their ability to advance.

Darkfire came again, this time straight at Ka'shuar'iik. He dodged but not fast enough. It enveloped him, and when the blackness of it was gone, a frozen figure hung there. A defiant scream escaped Lil'iek's lips. Yarok roared as his friend, nothing more than a icy corpse now, fell to break on the ground below.

With a snarl, Lil'iek pulled out one of her hand axes, and as King began another blast of darkfire, she swung herself toward him and threw the axe. The throw was better than she could've hoped, thumping into his mask and hopefully his head beneath. Axe in his face, he fell back, and soldiers crowded in to fill his spot as she descended down.

The sight of Ka'shuar'iik, frozen and broken, made her want to retch and weep and attack all at once. She entered their camp barrier and went to Tek'ouk, his normally stoic face reflected how she felt, a mixture of anger and sorrow.

"King is dead," Lil'iek said. "We achieved that part of our goal."

His eyes raged about losing Ka'shuar'iik but softened before blaming her outright.

"I am sorry about Ka'shuar'iik, you were right about that. But we knew this might happen, and will happen again. Yet we go on anyway."

"How many more will have to be avenged after the first is completed?" He sighed, nodding. "Mistakes I can forgive... If you can forgive me one of mine."

"What's that?" Her smile betrayed her unease.

"After granting our pact, the Quoarn'riik asked me to undermine our allies. Divide or deplete them when we see opportunities to do so."

She stared at him, then past him at the neighboring warcamps. "They want us to betray our allies instead of focus on our objective?"

"I agree, and I've not done more than pound their barriers with bulls. But if our allies do something to us, as I suspect they might, then I'll do what is necessary."

"I'm not here for those palemen." She waved her hand at the allies. "I'm here for the others."

He nodded. "Well, at least with King gone the attrition will work faster." He drank from his gourd, then wiped his mouth. "Great throw. We'll prepare Ka'shuar'iik's body while we wait."

She took comfort in his encouragement when he could've rebuked her instead. She went to him and put her arms around his waist, laying her head on his chest. Surprised at first, he held her. He cleared his throat. "I don't know any poetry or songs like Fal'iek did. But I could tell you all about my last reading on the transitional phases of dynal sentiments and how they affect the material elements."

She smiled. "Maybe later." But then her head popped back up to look into his eyes. "However, I'd be *mildly* interested to know what all these, er, *studies* say about spirits. That is, if you—"

The moment was broken by shouts at the western side of camp. They both grabbed their weapons and ran over to see a monster at the barrier. In spite of being full of arrows, the great Teyu'yaguak, a furacán malwolf with seven heads, continued tearing at the barrier. One head hung limp, as if dead, and another was panting and coughing blood from two arrows in its neck. The multi-wolf was enormous, an abnormal creature that was legendary among Kimoc tribes as a descendant of the eternals, although it didn't look so magnificent now.

Two heads were pulling the spike posts of the barrier out of the ground while one held a rat corpse, attempting to keep it from the other heads.

Roah'riik shot arrows into it and fire from Tek'ouk's dyne crackled around its head, only enraging it more.

Snarling, the two heads yanked free the posts, and it charged. One of its heads knocked Tek'ouk down, a maw knocking his crutch, and he fell beneath the claws. Cursing, Lil'iek ran and slashed at one of its necks with her hand-axe. That head yelped and the beast stumbled. The giant monstrosity thrashed in confusion and frustration, biting and clawing at everything around it, even at its own heads. In the chaos Lil'iek darted around its backside and saw Tek'ouk nimbly roll away from claws that raked at him. She grabbed him to help him up just as one of the claws reached out and grabbed his leg. But it wasn't a claw, it was a furry human hand.

For a split second, they both stared down at it in bizarre wonderment before Yarok ran up to hack at the arm and help them get away. As the rest of the Roah'riik made quick work of the furacán, Lil'iek and Tek'ouk stared at its twitching form, seeing what they'd not seen before. Black fur thinned out along the torso and limbs into black skin. Some of its legs were humanoid. There were tales that spoke of such oddities, but not quite like this. This Teyu'yaguak was a spectacular creature, but at the same time neither natural nor divine; a more sick, twisted, and crude thing.[33]

Once the beast was dead, all of it, they began the fire ceremony to purify its soul and destroy its body, alongside Ka'shuar'iik. Then they began questioning which of the Asturion camps had led it to their barrier.

---

[33] Friar Camu's studies have shown that Teyu'yaguak have always been the most common feldinal, the Asturion word for furacán. The Kimoo often viewed them as divine.

CHAPTER SEVEN
CHANGE IN THE HOUSE OF QOSKU

Based on *Writings of Qosku*, cc bastica 177;
The Nordvargor Testaments, cc bastica 896;
The Dark Fortress of Mephorash, cc bastica xx;

18th of Novumbre, 246

In prayer, Qosku tried to clear his mind and evade the surfacing werebeast, but all he found was memories. Old and painful. Five days before the execution ceremony in Chuqi'kirau, Qosku and Chaska crept out of their bedrolls in the Unakan-temple-turned-Deovan-monastery and headed up past the farm terraces to the smithy.

He paused when he saw a guard outside the granary. Chaska tugged on his tunic and he nodded and led on, winding up steep steps to the mountainside smithy. They needed to steal food today, being unable to get it at regular meal times, and Qosku had left a secret stash inside after scribing for the merchants that day.

Qosku crouched beneath a window and peeked in. All lay quiet and, as he'd hoped, Quspi wasn't there but off drinking chicha with his friends. Chaska held out her hands to lift him in.

Once in the dense room of tools and clutter, he reached behind a stack of shields into a small cavity where a single stone had been removed. Hidden there was the forbidden food offering to the eternals and apus. He fingered them, they were sacred and not really for him, and also gone stale. But he and Chaska were starving.

Then the slatted wood door flew open, and the boys entered, with Chaska in tow, a hand over her mouth. Qosku didn't dart forth and fight them off as he'd wanted to. Nor did he get pinned down with calm dignity as he'd hoped, either.

"No, please," he said, his voice and hands trembling as they grabbed him. "I don't—I'm just—please."

They tittered, small laughter in the little room. The older boys lifted him onto the central anvil. He used dyne to rip himself loose, but they held him firm, for he wasn't as deft in those days. Someone lit one of the lanterns, barely enough to provide visibility. There were six of them, most of them bigger than he. Except, of course, for Akualchac, the only of Qosku's age. Even in the dim smithy, Qosku could see that his former friend didn't want to be there. He avoided Qosku's eyes but acted like he was having as much fun as the older boys he followed. A hollow act.

"Open the cabinets," Alkapac, Akualchac's older brother and the ringleader of the group, whispered to his friends, who pulled an herb pouch out of the hiding place. "Let's see what we can make out of this thing we have here."

Chaska struggled, but Qosku begged her quiet with his eyes. So far, their attention had solely been on him; he didn't want that to change. After they tied Qosku's feet down with rags and pulled his tunic up, Alkapac moved in front of him, angular face cold as he sneered, "Aren't we supposed to oil him before the hammering."

"I think it's after," Pachultec said. "We'd better do it both ways just to be safe."

The group laughed, and Qosku felt cold fluids being dripped on his bare back. He said nothing, fearing that his voice would stumble again or otherwise encourage them. He fell into deep prayer. *At least none of this could be worse than my Takanaku training.*

"Hey, this forge is still hot," Pachultec said. "We can use it."

Qosku snapped out of his stillness, a cold pit in his stomach. *No, no.*

"Yeah, get those tongs and a fork," Alkapac said. "We'll fix him. Would you still like to be a woman now?"

Qosku thought of how to escape. He moved the sentiments through his body but felt too much fear. Fear could help one run, if used well. His feet vibrated, and he twisted, but not enough to break or slip out of his bonds. His arms stayed in the grips of four older boys. One shouted, "Oy, he's trying to do that monk thing."

They all set into twisting the skin of his limbs. Qosku thrashed hard, and something whacked the back of the head, causing his face to hit the table. Stars flashed behind his eyes.

"What?" Alkapac whispered right by his head. He grabbed Qosku by the ear and turned him so they were face to face. "You don't want our help, Qos? Well, you're my girl now, so you do what I say."

He gave a gentle slap to Qosku's face and moved away. Qosku's eyes met Akualchac's. Qosku held it, feeling true courage for a brief moment. Akualchac looked away. Pachultec said, "I think it's ready."

"All right, let's do this," Alkapac said. "I say on his dick or his bum. What do you think, Akualchac?"

"I—I don't know," Akualchac replied.

"What's wrong, little brother? You're not bored, are you?" Alkapac stood in front of him. "Pick a side, front or back."

Akualchac tried to shrug nonchalantly, but this act failed too. He did manage to keep any wavering out of his voice, but Qosku knew it would've been there. "Jus—whichever. The fron—back, I guess."

"Kual, you don't know what you want," Alkapac said. "Or you're just too afraid. Fine, I'll ask the material. Hey Qos-girl, where do you want your mark?"

Qosku didn't give him the dignity of a response, instead closing his eyes. His insides churned with shame and revulsion and fear. Yet a small part of him wondered if they castrated him, would he be she then? Could this be the answer?

"Fine. We'll do both front and back."

Searing hot pain burned him, and despite his best efforts, he failed to remain impassively still. He screamed as they held it to his right buttocks, pressed it in. He heard a hiss and wondered if that was from the cooking oil or his skin; he hoped the latter. The agony consumed him.

Then they pulled it off. Tulosk laughed and said, "You like that, Qos-girl?"

Qosku felt it again on his right cheek. This time he held back a growl. When it ended, someone snapped a rag painfully across his butt, and everyone laughed. Then they flipped him over, and Qosku felt, aside from the pain of the burns, the mixture smudging against the table. Alkapac looked down at Qosku's genitals and hesitated, then said, "Time to cut it off, make him like a eunuch. Or one of those circumcised."

"Hey," Akualchac said. "I thought we were just going to burn him?" This was it, and Qosku found that he wanted it done so bad he'd accept it from them. Maybe this was the Great Ones giving it to him. Or if not, he couldn't be blamed for it happening to him.

"Do it," he said. Not loud, but it could've been a thunderclap for the deafening silence it left them stunned in. "Go on, I want it. Do it for me and I'll stay away from you, or whatever it is you want."

"Well, I-uh," Alkapac looked away. "No I can't do that. Maybe we'll just brand you more."

"We should just go," Akualchac said.

"Shut up, Kual," Alkapac yelled.

"No," Qosku sat up, none had realized they'd released him. "Please cut me, I beg you."

Horror flashed across their faces. But why now? It was their idea. Alkapac shoved him down and said more forcefully, "I said no—"

He halted, and Tulosk moved away from Qosku. "What's going on?" Quspi stood at the door, an Asturion guard behind him.[34] They entered and both looked on in anger. Qosku felt unexpected hope rise in his chest mixed with loss of the opportunity. Maybe he was saved from further violence at least.

The guard, who was new to the yaqta, said to Quspi in Asturion, "Tell them to keep it down and stay out of here."

Quspi looked at him, swaying drunkenly, "No, you tell them!"

"I don't speak your stupid language." He forcefully turned the man toward them, a dirk pointing into the man's side. "Tell them."

Quspi looked on them coldly, stupidly. "Keep the noise down and clean up the mess."

Qosku's heart sank as the two men left. He felt another burn on his abdomen above his genitals, but not a cut. The boys hoisted him off the table and left him crumpled on the floor. *Is this it, Great Ones? Is your message actually that I cannot switch but am to keep my body as it was born and live with it thus?*

Alkapac said, "Yeah, we better clean off this table real good. Probably contaminated now."

When they left, he numbly picked himself up with Chaska's aid, her sobs the only sound in the room, and together they walked back to the monastery. Although hurting, they did get to eat the food.

Later, other memories haunted Qosku as he walked with Katti and Andras north, where the furthest army camp sat some distance away. Lights

---

34 *See Losnin Liberado Kani,* 13

of protection faded away as they walked through the dark wilderness. Leyta had told him that he would have to secrete himself away for his and others' protection. The isolation didn't sit well with him, especially in the outerwild, but the thought of hurting others sat even worse.

The only memories he had of the previous night, that of his infection, were brief but strong. Though the images caused him anxiety, he was more disturbed by what he couldn't remember. Half the night was gone to the savage beast within him. He feared what he'd done in that mental blackness. He both did and didn't want to know.

His training gave him a large measure of control over his body, but he feared above all the painful experience of beastly transformation. Lüg's medicine had helped calm him. The apothecary had wanted to come, but Qosku said no. All the touching the handsome boy's practice required reminded Qosku too much of his own crooked sexuality. Being away would be a reprieve. Behind Qosku, Andras looked around cautiously, as nervous as he at being so vulnerable in the dark with monsters near, and Katti hummed a hymn quietly. Her steady faith, or indifference to danger, impressed Qosku. But he really needed Chaska. She would've comforted him, carried him through this safe and sane. She'd never judged him, only supported.

A flashing memory of the previous night made him shiver. His falling on a large man, a soldier, and mauling him in front of his family. Screams. Blood.

He thought on a poem he'd written.

> *What is this change? Who is this change?*
> *This new monster takes me, a new maker makes me*
> *Who will save me? Who will have me?*
> *To make my suffering suffer, misery for my misery*
> *Am I your gloom?*
> *First gain my pain, then pain away my gain*
> *Who will kill me? Who will kill me?*
> *We are lost in asymmetry, only the kind are there for me*[35]

---

35 One of many of Qosku's poems found in his writings, all of them in the original Unakan were translated roughly to the present language, losing much of their original power.

They came to a grassy area that led into a ravine, not high enough to cage him in, but hopefully enough to get him to stay. Wind rustled the sweet-smelling evening grass. Ideally, they would chain him up but there was no such equipment available. Leyta had mentioned that she might be able to ground him with dyne but that they should first try for a peaceful seclusion and hope that it contented him.

Another flash of memory. He'd thrown a door at a group of kids. Screams. Blood.

He didn't want to remember these anymore, nor his older traumas, and didn't want to create new ones. The moon had risen over the mountains faintly shining through parted clouds, and he could feel it working on his body, a sickness that he'd resisted with his training. Now sweating, he feared he couldn't anymore. He held onto the hope Leyta and Katti had given him, that with the moon no longer full, his night would be easier and more controllable than the previous had been. A faint distant hope that paled before all of his fears.

"Katti," he said, his voice hoarse, wavering. "Will I still be me?"

"I don't know," she replied and sat down with him, putting her hand on his. "I know nothing about it except that the phases of the moon determine the completeness of the transformation. But we're here with you, at least for a little while. And I must say, I'm very impressed by your courage and fortitude. I'm sorry if I spoke rudely to you before, back when we first met."

Qosku barely heard her. His muscles rippled, skin itched, head ached, stomach churned. He'd never been so terrified. "Sh-sh-shhhouldn't you leavvve? D-d-don't want to h-hurt y-ouuu."

"We'll be fine," Katti said, smiling sweetly. "We can handle ourselves, and I think that you'll have more restraint than that. It's not full moon anymore. You'll have to learn to control it, which might be hard, but if anyone can, it's you."

"Don't fear for us," Andras said. Though his face and hand on his sword betrayed his words. "Focus on staying you."

The biggest pain was in the bones, his entire skeleton was on fire. He groaned. Qosku's whole body shook violently as he resisted the change within him. "C-can't—" He vomited.

"Qosku, don't fight it, just control it. Nobody's ever stopped it completely. Fight it mentally and spiritually, not physically."

At the last second, he ripped the gauntlets off his arms and greaves off of his legs to free his expanding limbs, so they wouldn't break, though he kept his tunic on. He battled his subconscious to permit the change, trying to trust in what Katti said. He felt his entire body expand. Thick dark fur covered him. His hearing and sense of smell sharpened. The most notable change was in the sheer power of his muscles. His fingers kneaded the rocky soil as claws extended from them, such power needed to be used. To climb or claw or bite. He reared up on his hind legs and roared at the moon, feeling giant.

"Qosku?" a white human girl at his side said.

He snapped his gaze at her and grunted. She looked familiar... but she was in his territory. Something in the back of his mind said she could be here. He stared at her, smelling and listening, the boy as well. She'd put a hand out to prevent him from walking forward. Wise move. He growled at the shiny boy, daring him to come closer, but the bright girl kept him back. He couldn't place her, but he decided she was not challenging. He used to like her somehow, the boy too, but that didn't matter.

And he could just kill them if he changed his mind.

Owls hooted nearby. He snorted and moved around the edges of the clearing, throwing up dirt and urinating in a few key spots while checking for food or danger. Some inhibition in the back of his mind wondered how he got there. He realized he didn't know. He paused, staring at the clearing. The two stood there watching him. Did they have something to do with this mystery?

Feeling troubled and confused, he took a random swipe at a thornbush and sat down.

Suddenly another girl appeared behind the two, and another boy with her. He jumped up and ran at them. They tensed, he could smell and see their fear, but to his surprise they didn't move, except for a twitch to their weapons. On a closer look, he recognized these two as well. Brown boy and stick girl, because of the stick she held. He somehow liked them even more. But they intruded. Were they a danger?

"Qosku, it's me, Leyta," noised stick girl.

"Do you remember me? I'm Syago, we're friends," noised the brown boy.

Why did the noise sound familiar? It felt wrong but right at the same time. So much confusion. The only thing he knew was that he had that other spot to hide and hunt from, and he'd left something there.

He stood tall again, roared, then ran off on all fours to his spot in the glowing place. The little ones noised some other things and suddenly the ground in front of him exploded. His thick furry hide protected him from the rocks that hit him, and he continued on at an enjoyably quick speed toward the big glowing place.

He didn't slow for the wall, aiming for the area in between bright explosions and easily scaling it with his claws. Several little people there cried out, but they didn't matter. He moved across rooftops like lightning, bowling over any in his way. It felt incredible, and he wondered why he hadn't done it before. He stopped on top of a familiar building to sniff about and immediately found a pack of items with his scent on them.

Why was it important? But it just was. He moved around to survey and mark the territory when he smelled another. With a growl, he spotted another beast that looked much as he did. It roared a challenge. He responded the same.

They slammed into each other, clawing and biting. He pushed, and it smashed into a building across the way. He followed it, and claws and teeth came in again. Though slightly smaller, he was much faster and better at this than the other monster. Fighting like this felt oddly natural to him.

Their thunderous pounding resounded throughout the city, punctuating the explosions in the background. He grabbed it and slammed it into the roof, then swung it into the window of another building. Again he followed it, lowering himself into the broken window area. As soon as he was through, it smashed into him. Bricks, wood splinters, and screams cascaded around them as he pounded the offender.

Something pulled him back from his opponent, slamming him into the street. He snapped to his feet, turning to see a giant armor-wearing corpse monster, bigger and with a large sword in hand. The other beast, now bloody, charged in and latched on to the corpse's sword arm, pulling him down. The metal giant thrust its sword into the other beast then retrieved it to turn back on him. He darted in quickly, rolled under the swing of the blade, and clawed at the rival beast. But it was already bleeding out.

The giant blade had stuck into a building. As the metal giant pulled out the sword, he climbed up the building and left the scene but saw the metal giant drag the dead beast away. Perhaps in the future he'd have to return to fight Metal Giant, now he needed a safe place to recover his wounds.[36] [37]

---

36 The entire account here displays an incredible amount of clarity for a beastspawn. We know from other accounts that fights like this were happening, but the telling here is likely invented.35

37 That these comments are made more often of Kimoc or Unakan accounts than Asturion should be telling to the reader.

CHAPTER EIGHT
BREAKING BARRIERS

Based on *Annals of Syago,* cc bastica 140;
The Dark Fortress of Mephorash, cc bastica x;

21st of Novumbre, 246

Dusk faded on the third day of the siege, following a light rain that washed away the camp stench. Syago looked forward to sundown for possibly the first time in his life. In a moment of calm as both sides collected themselves, he sat in the shadows, worn out and feeling the brunt of the assault weighing on his shoulders. The holy knight yearned for something to change the standstill. His skills with the Judgment Sword had improved, but only marginally. He'd gone from blocking dyne with just his shield to blocking it with Alexandre as well, a feat unique to soulweapons, but he still missed parries against other objects.[38] Harder than the occasional overeager swing was Alexandre's constant judgment. Even now, on a brief waterbreak, it chided him for not being at the front line. Its never-ending push for perfection was annoying and exhausting.

Although the sparkle of wielding Alexandre was gone, the charade of this spiritual duty continued. Syago worked at the warfront, giving out battle cries and cheers as Leyta had asked him to. To motivate the soldiers, she'd said. To act for them, he'd thought.

He looked up as Leyta approached him. "You know, if you used your shield, it would protect you more and you wouldn't have to work as hard."

"The sword—Alexandre—doesn't like it," he said, wiping his brow with a handkerchief. Alexandre had pressed that it was more effective with two

---

38 See *Schiltron of Magodeoz,* 54-56

hands, and he needed the conditioning anyways, which wasn't untrue. He'd been fit before, but the improvements surprised him. "We're still working all of that out. And in any case, I wield it better in two hands. My new armor has made up for anything lacking." Though his cheap plate armor would only do so much, he hadn't yet taken the offers to sponsor a newer set.

She nodded thoughtfully. "Well, your fighting today has been impressive. I got another message from Qosku, he's agreed to stay in the city and says it's madness in there. We're about to start working on the breach. If you want to join the battering ram, the allies will be joining the assault within the hour and so will give good cover."

When he didn't answer right away, she continued. "I can have some dynasts help you too. Most are needed to cover us and burrow under the wall, but I can have one or two cover you at the gate."

"We'll be fine," he said. "Whatever you think is necessary."

"All right." She nodded, clasping her hands nervously. Syago smiled inwardly; normally he was the awkward one unless he was purposefully making her blush... an activity he hadn't done in some time. "I'll have one help you, and if you need more, just call it out."

He nodded and his gaze moving up to the wall at the sight of movement. King appeared, fresh as ever with his darkfire and a crack in the mask where the axe had planted. Syago jumped to his feet. "He's alive?!"

"I thought they'd killed him?" Leyta asked.

"They did, I even saw the axe throw myself. It was an amazing shot. He must have a really good helmet there."

One gain not gained. And Syago wondered once again what they were doing in there.

Leaving Leyta behind, Syago stood and went to the battering ram. He had little faith in its capacity for breaking the gate, which was built to take constant hits from daemogs, trees, and worse.

Both the dynast's digging and his ramming the gates would take them into the under-stables area. Syago was sure it would be easier to break through and replace a door than to deal with the repercussions of digging underneath the city. For that reason he'd argued against the burrowing.

"You're to ram the gates then?" Lil'iek said, approaching from the barrier, her dark face ever unreadable.

"That's the order," he muttered.

"We'll help distract them then," she said. "And did you see that multi-wolf monster that attacked us?"

"No, is that what the shouting was about? Well, I'm glad you made it all right."

"Strange to me," she said after a brief moment, "that you haven't been attacked yet by anything like we have. Do you have any secret to it?"

"No," Syago said, standing to face her. "But believe me, if I had anything more significant that I could tell you, I would." He thought he dissembled masterfully, not a difficult task in low light and low mood. It was also not untrue; he knew some soldiers had scared something off, a tree he'd thought, though the feldinal sounded more like something Cantarchar might do. Syago held her eyes. "All things are possible with the Good Lady Deova Bondua."

"I don't doubt it," she said, nearly sarcastically. She paused then, seeming on the verge of asking something else, but then nodded. He guessed she felt the same awkward pull between being old friends, allies, and tentative enemies. "I wish you well with the ramming. I must return to my camp." As she turned to walk back with Yarok under darkening skies, Syago felt Alexandre hum in his mind in approval of his kindness, one of its more annoying habits, like getting a pat on the head for doing something he'd always done. At least it approved of *something* he did.

The horn sounded behind and the drums atop the wall rang out too. He and several soldiers gathered to heft the log, but all jumped back when a thumping noise came from the walltop. Syago's gaze shot up to see bodies, mutilated and dirty, hanging off the wall from ropes. He could only imagine what horror the tethered corpses would be when the darkness animated them. The goal was likely for effect, but it wouldn't stop the lifeless from trying to attack them.

Screams rent the air, and Syago recognized one elementist amongst those screaming, pointing at the bodies and shouting about the murder of his parents. Horrified, Syago realized that the Chaos had punished those inside for the appeal the allies had made earlier.

"When Leyta calls," Syago said to the young soldiers assembled for the battering ram, none taking their eyes off of the gently swaying corpses. "Go hard and don't stop."

Somewhere deeper in the camp, Tongu began a song of weeping, soothing and healing. Syago thought it strange to see the man, usually a children's fool making them laugh with tricks, in a battlefield driving violence or mourning. But he'd come to admire him for that genuineness.

The sound of braying caught his attention. He looked south at the Kimoc camp, the last vestiges of sunlight illuminating the herd of daemog. Tek'ouk stood atop a mound, with others on nearby mounds, all holding up horned skulls. Syago watched them, mesmerized as smoke mixed with dust in a dazzling sunset, and hoped he'd not offended Lil'iek in his response.

"Commence assault!" Leyta shouted as the sun fell beneath the Barbathor Mountains and the lifeless on the wall began to twitch.

Syago gripped the ram at the front position, checking quickly to see a dynast standing nearby with his staff at the ready. Together, the men shouldered the ram, aimed for the crack between the two gates, and charged.

On counts, they pounded the doors. Arrows fell far afield as crossbowmen and archers from below gave cover. Tongu's song fueled their limbs and hearts with courage and energy. As they pressed at the doors, the hanging lifeless reached for them helplessly. Fear of one of them falling on them added to the stress of muscles beginning to ache, skin sweating. The air rippled from the exchange of dyne and missile. The doors splintered and cracked, but its iron braces held firm.

It was when the full black of night fell that someone behind Syago screamed and a tug on the ram told him something was wrong. Another one, and they lost balance, dropping the ram to the ground. Syago turned to see two men at the back missing, except for a bloody arm on the ground. The dynast was also gone. Yet it wasn't the attacks from above, those had stopped. One soldier ran for the burrowing regimen; Syago felt to go with him but stayed with his remaining companion. Then right before his eyes, the last soldier in the back simply vanished. Syago had seen this before, defending the wall against a pack of malwolves. At night, they were near invisible.

"On your guard!" he yelled to the burrowing group as he drew Alexandre. "Malwolves are inside the barrier!" The remaining men stood together, sword hands trembling. They searched the dark field for those hollow yellow eyes, the only way to spot them in a night such as this. A pair appeared in a dark outline, coming fast, then disappearing and reappearing closer than it was before. He shouted for the men to form a circle, but they moved too slow. The eyes vanished as a soldier readied his sword. The man got taken, but this time Syago was able to follow the man being dragged around a knoll. Paces away, the large black beast shook the flailing soldier in his jaws, whipping his limbs about like rags, blood spraying everywhere. Hearing his approach, the wolf bounded back, but Syago leapt, Alexandre's speed aiding him, and he cut the monster's side with a flare of the shining sword.

The added momentum, however, caused Syago to stumble, and he panicked at the opening this offered the predator. He took another swing, the sword jerking his body back up and away. *Bomog shit, I'm trying to fight not fly!* It snarled once more and rebounded off of a mound before coming at him. Exposed again, Syago slashed, shifting to a thrust mid-swing. The huge black beast landed on the point of his sword, crashing Syago down in a mess of blood and fur. He wedged his way out from under its body and saw two more malwolves tearing a soldier in half. Arrows finished one malwolf while the other moved around to help his packmate. Syago ran at it, but it changed direction in a clever feint to leap at Syago's side. *Foding shit!* In a panic, he swung at it wildly, missed, and felt Alexandre lift him up and up as jaws snapped at his legs. He shifted the sword down, suddenly descending into the maw. Monster blood sprayed him in the landing. He looked around, noting the stillness that now settled with the malwolves dead, and saw that the other soldiers stood breathing heavily over their fallen.

When Leyta heard the screams, she feared that perhaps Knave had finally descended to attack. On looking, she saw only Syago waving Alexandre in the darkness. When soldiers cried out about malwolves, she moved to aid him, but it was done before she could join in.

How did the malwolves get in?

It couldn't have been the rebels, from inside the city. She wouldn't put it past the Chaos leaders, but the entire troupe was noticeable in all that they did. Leyta looked over at the Quoak camp, the Roah'riik still driving their daemogs. *Could they have let the malwolves in?*

She set fire to the now dead beasts and moved quickly, conscious of the enemy above and the need to maintain pressure on the gate. However, she noted that the soldiers of the wall had displayed the mercy, or common courtesy in warfare, to abstain from taking advantage of a human foe while he confronts a monster of the outside. *At least they've retained some sanity.*

It wasn't long before the assault from above resumed, missiles fell and then worse. Fire vials dropped, bursting and throwing up flames that caught on the grass and camp equipment. Leyta set a quarter of the elementists to control and eliminate the blazes.

As she led the work on the flames so the ramming could continue, Leyta saw Syago take an arrow in his thigh. He fell to his knee, clutching it. As he stumbled back to his feet, the field lit up as arrows tipped with fire arced through the air. So that's their new strategy, set the fields to hell with fire so they can't attack the wall. A risky move, as the city was also exposed to the flames.

Her thoughts returned to what could be a serious problem, sabotage from the allies. *We spoke of sabotaging them, could they have done so for us? Well, I suppose we now have a precedent. And if I don't assert my position, I risk losing it.*

Before she could think more on the possible intrigue, Syago stumbled toward her. She cleared the way for him, and Syago sat next to her, then snapped the arrowshaft, blood gushing. Luckily, it had not hit a vital area, nor was it deep. To her surprise, getting the arrow out appeared surprisingly easy. A painful expression covered Syago's face as he clutched the wound, and she realized that it was sealing up, slowly but noticeably, and the bleeding slowed to a stop. Alexandre was healing him with a warm glow. Once the process was done, taking only minutes for the small wound, he wiped his hands on the grass and stood up.

Leyta was dumbfounded. "The way that healed was incredible!"

"It surprised me too," he said, seeming pleased for once. "Though Qosku has been healing himself similarly for weeks now, so maybe it isn't that impressive. The healing does hurt more, though, which I suppose makes sense." He moved his leg, stretching it with a grimace.

"Yes, that was amazing," Katti said as she approached them. "When I get healing from a prayer, it's rarely that quick." He shrugged, but Leyta saw in him a solution. He could now fight well and even heal. He could handle hardship others could not and was trustworthy. Perhaps following the attack he, too, would want to figure out where the malwolves came from.

Syago ceased his stretching, awkwardly waiting as Katti blessed him for his noble service and Leyta stared at him.

"Listen," Leyta said, fidgeting with her dress. "I need you to do one more thing. Since the Kimoc trust you, and I'm fairly certain it was they who let the malwolves in, we need you to go to their camp and ask about it, or spy on them. And possibly break their fence as was done to us."

He stared at her, confused. *She can't really be asking me this.* But her firm gaze told him as much, and his stomach sunk. He'd suspected as much himself, but rather than treat with betrayal, he'd bet on trust. There was so little reason to believe that the people of Quoak, who'd rescued them before, would now sabotage them. His blood rose to a boil as he considered that even so, they should be the better people and not retaliate in kind. The request, or command, went against everything he and they stood for, and she knew it. He replied, "I'll speak with them but I'm not doing anything that would hurt them."

"What I'm really asking is," Leyta began, "if you learned that they were a danger to us, would you make an effort to protect us, if not avenge the wrong?"

"How can you ask this of me? We swore after that meeting that we would not attack our own allies," he said, his voice rising, hand clenching.

"I don't intend you to betray them," she said, her tone now defensive. "I only want us protected from them betraying us."

"I will defend my people, but I'll not deceive and betray allies that trust us. In particular Lil'iek, who still calls me friend." But his rage at the request was not yet finished. "I'll stay with them as liaison until I'm ready to come back. Goodbye."

And with that, he turned to leave for Lil'iek's camp.

CHAPTER NINE
WAKE

Based on *Writings of Qosku,* cc bastica 177;
The Hunter's Parchments, cc bastica 250;
The Dark Fortress of Mephorash, cc bastica xx;

27th–29th of Novumbre, 246

At the sounds of people fighting in the streets over food, Qosku slipped out of his bedroll on the old theater rooftop. Following his accidental return to Mantlgrym, he'd taken advantage of the re-positioning to continue as a spy inside. He'd woken up confused, back on his old abandoned rooftop spot, completely naked, with his lost pack. Disgusted at seeing his naked body, so wrong and not feminine, he quickly found a theater costume to wear while he cleared his mind and looked for a tunic. At first, he'd been unable to remember how he'd arrived there, but it came back to him.

After coming to terms with the situation, he stole some some new armor pieces that made a oversized fit. Having less time without clothes made him feel better, he loathed being naked even when alone. He spied in the day, and then at night prayed in preparation for a smooth transformation. Each successive night fared better, either because of the waning moon or because of increased practice, or both. He still harbored fear from not having total control and from the pain that it continued to bring him and others. But it was less of a danger.

What he had found in the eight days since his return was that there were a lot of werebeasts in Mantlgrym.[39] They hadn't been successfully exiled or killed and the disease had spread throughout the city. It became such a problem that Knight ordered the evening guard to hunt and

---

39 See *Losnin Liberado Kani,* 63

eliminate them. He remembered fighting many in self-defense and, last night, in defense of a family. The first good thing he remembered doing, though he'd also mauled another armored soldier. He remembered more and more, and retained more thought each night as well. This previous night, he recalled encountering a deepwraith, the shadowy shapeshifters who'd invaded Voium and killed Fal'iek. He only smelled that faint ashen scent before seeing its shadowy form looming over him. He tried to grab it, but it danced around him, toying with him. Probably identifying him too. Then it darted away to report to its masters what it had observed of the state of the city and the assaulting armies, he supposed.

Qosku still wondered at the absence of the leaders. He'd not seen Queen in two days, but King had just made an unexpected reappearance. He occasionally saw Knave fly above the city, usually at night. The demon never interacted in the battle. Jester appeared occasionally to sing to the mob-crowds, keep them riled up. He hadn't been seen for three days.

The people were beginning to notice too. Murmurings about being abandoned, some wanting to surrender the lost cause. The unending presence of Knight undoubtedly held their qualms in check. Bigger than any ukuku giant he'd heard of; he wondered what kind of being it had been in life. The demon Knave also haunted his thoughts following his discovery of its hideout. He'd debated going back there but understood a special weapon would be necessary to slay the demon. He would've felt more confident fighting as a wereozor than as Qosku, but the beast didn't have a mind to go look for Knave at night.

Then he found them.

It was not where he'd expected, not in any of the mansions, inns, or the city court. They hid in a garment shop. Through the boarded up windows, in between planks, he spied King and Queen one cloudy afternoon, sitting at a table. He listened carefully, trying to determine how many were inside and what plans they might be discussing. But all he heard was the clattering of plates as Jester cleared away the parchments strewn over the table to set up tea. Once all was ready, the two fake monarchs didn't touch it, didn't even move. Only Jester ate and drank, the belltails of his hood jingling, while the others sat there in silence.

"You know," Jester began, "sometimes I still miss the old haunt. More food, less gaunt." He gave a laugh-sob. But no comment came from the two regents.

Not even when Jester asked of King, "Oy, I'm not complaining. But if I'm the one to go out and inspect dangerous ruins in search of your treasures, I at least deserve extra dessert." His head swiveled to the untouched cakes in front of King. "You going to eat that? Thanks." As he took some of King's cakes, he hastily assured Queen that he'd not take hers, she didn't have to behead him like the last court fool. Still, neither offered a word.

Are they asleep? Or dead? What am I seeing?

"Ah, but the final platter is finally here," Jester said as he set down a plate of something burnt black. "And this time the wretch is already dead. But do we eat it because we're brave enough to eat what others will not in a starving city, or because all rulers, including non-ruler rulers, eventually eat their followers?"

With a start, Qosku realized that the platter held a human head and two arms. His jaw dropped as Jester drew up his mask to bite onto a crisp black arm. King and Queen seemed to lurch to life, soundlessly reaching for the head. Qosku backed away, feeling vomit rise in his throat. The sight of it was horrible on its own, but it was the memory it evoked—of that fateful day when he'd participated in a ritual sacrifice that turned out to be his sister—that made Qosku ill.

The clanging sounds of Knight's giant footsteps alerted him to the need to retreat and send a message to Leyta. Wanting more information first, he didn't yet mention his most poignant question: what treasure are they hunting? And why during a civil war?

When he later returned, the room was dark and empty. He paused, mulling over the foolish danger he was putting himself in. But he had to risk it. He pulled a board off the window and nimbly crawled through dust and cobweb. Inside, he found the dishes put away in haphazard order. Some sewing tools were left on the table around a toy doll, if it could be called that. Small sacks of dirt had been tied together in the shape of a human, with buttons for eyes and stitches for a mouth.

A horrible thought occurred to him, that the toys might be a way to lure the children into their snares. He looked to his left to see two doors side by side. It was hard to see much else in the gloom. A door creaked behind him, and he jumped. But no, it was just a rat searching for crumbs. Heart racing, he decided to hurry. If the Chaos leaders came back and found him there, he was doomed.

Qosku went to the door the rat had come through. A larger room, a work-shop, he supposed, but now lay empty save crates, tools, and other projects. Across the way was a few more doors, these closed. He repeatedly looked over his shoulder to ensure he wasn't about to be sprung on by something. There were several maps laid out on a table, all marked up. He considered taking them in case they indicated whatever odd search the demon was undertaking.

Creaking boards above made him jump. His heart pounded. *Any of those doors could open any second—*

The sounds of scratching made him whip his his head around. He saw nothing, but the scratching continued, even growing in frequency. Something screeched. It was the rat running across the kitchen floor. Heartbeat in his ears, Qosku backed away, unsure if the rat was coming for him or fleeing something bigger. He got his answer when a glob of darkness shot out from near the oven and caught the rat, snuffing its life. But it was just a black cat, now eating its disemboweled prey. Qosku gulped, thinking he'd had enough. He returned back to the theater rafters, worn and discouraged. About everything. Sounds of rats scratching along the floorboards below caught his attention. It was as if they were follow-ing him. Not wanting to hear them anymore, he went down to get rid of them. Stepping onto the floor below, he caught movement through a hole in the wall. It wasn't rats.

The agony Knave had followed him home.

Wings tucked back, tail swerving, it sauntered in with a predatory smirk on the girl's face. Qosku moved away from the hole, out of view and trem-bling. *I can't fight it, weapon or no, I can't.*

He retreated as silently as possible up the stairs. But he was trapped. Unless he could slip past it as it went up a different staircase. He stopped as he reached the top. There in the shadows was those eyes like two stars in the night sky. The deepwraith's unwavering stare froze him on the stair-case, vulnerable to the prowling demon. Or vulnerable to the deepwraith, which neared like a great black abyss opening up to drain his soul. The eyes were right in front of his dazed face; the deepwraith's head moved in, to eat. Qosku gave up all hope; this was the end. And not a courageous or honorable one, but to be lost in the appetites of the enemy. Tears streamed his face.

To his surprise, it backed away. Thinking it must be a trap, he stared at it. Then suddenly Qosku was on the floor, knocked down from behind as the demon flew over him at the deepwraith. He regained his sense of self and rose to his feet. The deepwraith danced around the demon as it pounced and lashed at it. *Did Knave come for me or that?*

Either way, he wouldn't run or hide anymore. With the deepwraith distracted, perhaps he could find an ally in the demon, or vice versa since he considered Knave's collection of heads to be the greater abomination. He ran up, grabbing a coat stand, and rammed it at Knave like a spear, pinning the creature against the wall. It hissed, but no blood spilled. The sickle-tail whipped around at him, gouging the wall and nearly catching his neck as it squirmed out of the hold. The deepwraith stabbed at Knave from the shadows, but the pricks had little effect either. Knave leapt at it, but it shifted out of the way.

Qosku's worst nightmares became realized as the deepwraith wrapped a long arm around him and threw him at Knave. He struggled to keep the bony demon's claws away while they both fumbled to their feet. The demon hissed, leaping for the deepwraith as it escaped through a window, and Qosku took the opportunity to run to the next room and grab an axe. The demon followed. Hiding behind a curtain, Qosku swung at the demon's smiling face, arms powered by all his rage. The eerie smile turned to a grimace as the blade thunked in. Qosku swung his gauntleted hand at its head in another dyne-powered hook and felt a sickening crack; anyone else would've died on the spot. For a second, it paused to halt the bleeding, but if that cut wasn't enough to kill it, then nothing was. He ran down the stairs to the tiring rooms behind the stage. The axe fell from its face, leaving a deep gash.

A girl's voice snickered, "Come out, come out, wherever you are. I just want to eat you and wear your head, little bitch."

Just as he thought of fleeing from his hiding spot or preparing a better attack, he heard it prowling nearby. This time, the face wasn't smiling, but gaping as if dead. Yet its nose clearly worked, for it came at him, bladed tail swishing, shearing the curtain down over him. He stumbled back, away from the child's deadpan expression, escaping the tangle of the curtain. Stumbling out onto the stage, Qosku threw a chair at it, then a coat hanger as he stumbled out onto the stage. Blood trickled from the orifices of its face, more than the gash, but it continued whipping its sickle-bladed tail as it stalked closer.

Then it stopped again, hunched over. It whimpered, grooming its face. Qosku considered trying another attack, but again knew he wasn't equipped for it. He'd made his best effort, it was time to leave it for another time. The agony didn't notice him slip out the back door into the hail.

CHAPTER TEN
Paying Hell's Due

Based on *A Chamand's Confessions*, cc bastica 308;
The Nordvargor Testaments, cc bastica 886;
The Dark Fortress of Mephorash, cc bastica xxx;

24th of Novumbre, 246

Hoyoche trembled inside. Outwardly, though, the summoner calmly worked with his five companions, four priestesses and a bishopess, to inscribe the design needed to call the meta gate Osmos.[40] He didn't know what was to be done with the gate, only that Davagis had commanded the lines be drawn. An ornate circle connected to a triangle, ancient writing filling in the margins. With all the benches pushed behind the pillars, the towering size of the room felt like his old home Thornwood, but this place crushed with its massive gloom.

The prelatas had courageously resisted the cultist's tortures at first, prepared for martyrdom, until Davagis mentioned that Osmos would be summoned in any case and their lack of cooperation would make them sacrifices. For his part, Hoyoche was enticed by promises that the cult would be able to revive his dead wife once they got their long dead powers.

Hoyoche wasn't sure which he feared more: the treacherous cultist or the gate Osmos and whatever came out of it. He did this not out of fear, but for love. If Davagis's plan worked, Hoyoche would be able to do more than just talk to her spirit; she could be resurrected. The Razhod had been able to do that, and though Davagis wasn't one, he needed a summoner like Hoyoche and promised with the aid of these devils to be summoned there'd be a way. It was a slim hope, Hoyoche knew, but at the edge of despair, it was this or suicide.

Hoyoche looked over the work of the priestesses, though his summoning ability was still blinded by the cult's grimshades, he knew the markings for summoning Osmos that the priestesses lacked. When the circle and triangle were finished, he turned to nod at Davagis and jumped on finding the man right behind him. A new ritual scar, still scabbing, marred the man's left cheek. Even though only a disciple and not an actual Razhod, the source of Hoyoche's nightmares, the man intimidated.

"It is done," Davagis said. "Seal the doors. Prepare the torches and begin the chant."[41]

Hoyoche tethered a young bomog to a pillar near the triangle to be the sacrifice of summoning, a pagan element that bothered the Deovans. Then he noticed that the other cultists were closing the doors from the outside, with the loud clank of a lock. His chest tightened, just the seven of them with the gate? He looked at Davagis, "They barred it from the outside?"

"No one leaves until Osmos finishes, though many will want to," Davagis said. "Now pray."

It began.

The priestesses, weak or wicked, obeyed. They prayed for knowledge in this time of ignorance. They prayed for strength to make effective decisions. They prayed for forgiveness for this evil. And they prayed for Osmos to come and open to them the many worlds it connected. The torchlights in the room flickered and dimmed as the air and floor shuddered deeply. They prayed, not really to their Lady Deova Bondua, who would rather curse them at this moment, but to whatever merciful powers that might listen.

Hoyoche prayed only to his dead wife, Heikewe.

Osmos answered their call.

A great marble gate materialized atop the pattern they'd drawn with a profound thud. Smaller statues of man, woman, and beast, agony and pleasure on their faces, stretched along the trapezoidal doorframe. The Door of Infinite Spaces groaned open to a black void and elongated human arms stretched out to grab the squealing infant bomog. Despite the bomog's feeble resistance, the arms dragged it into the void and the doors closed. At the top of the doors, an obsidian orb opened to reveal an eye. The voice of Osmos grated out of their mouths as one, "Osmos comes as beckoned. Now ask."

---

41 This happened. All of it.

"We, uh, desire—" Hoyoche's voice cracked, and he coughed to clear it. A glare from Davagis spurred him on. "We desire to speak with an agent of the Hellpits of the Inferno. We are prepared to pay the—the t-toll."

The eye closed, and a deep hum reverberated from within the door and stone ground on stone, though nothing visibly changed. No indication that Osmos accepted or understood.

"Hmmmm, the solute price is steep. You will pay much."

The entire gate expanded to almost double its original size, filling the chapel. The eye rolled in place as the doors parted to reveal a dark, hazy world.[42] Agonizing moments passed. The cloud stirred, something big moved within. This time, a long web shot out and caught one of the priestesses. It dragged her into the haze, and her screams pierced the space, until they suddenly cut off.

Stunned, Hoyoche turned to Davagis. "You promised that wouldn't happen!"

The tall man's eye, beneath the scar, turned to regard him. "Shut up or you're next."

Then a devil emerged out of the clouds. It had the head and torso of a large human, with gray skin and a deadpan face, and wore a necklace of human hands around a muscular neck, indicating high rank. Its dark eyes glinted. At the waist, its body was as an insect with six clawed legs and an armored carapace that scraped the stony ground. At the front of its lower body, multiple beady bulb-eyes gleamed and a giant maw full of razor mandibles foamed around the protruding limbs of a smaller furry devil it was consuming. The gigantic greed moved slowly. The drag of some of its clawed feet screeched gratingly on the stone floor. Hoyoche couldn't tell if the ill-fitting human torso on top meant it had once been a human or was merely wearing a corpse.

"Who called for us?" the human-devil voiced in deep monotone. "I require substantial payment before helping any mortal."

"Call forth your companions, mighty fiend," Davagis said. "I am a disciple of the Razhod, who paid with service. We seek to restore the former glory of the coven and subjugate the land with your aid. Break their villages and strengthen us."

---

42 See *Ornamentos del Miedon* and *Funeral Leech FvK,* if you can stomach such black.

"The Razhod... Very well, give what's due that more might pass."

"Take what you must, they are all for you."

The devil darted forward and grabbed another priestess with one of its large arms and threw her through the gate. Not even a scream escaped her petrified face. The others began to run as its bulk darted in quick strikes, using claws and arms to feed the gate. It finished with the three hostages Davagis had brought in from the now open chapel doors. Hoyoche watched the entire thing in horror, yet he forced himself to stay next to Davagis and act unconcerned. It was the only remotely safe place to flee to.

Once all but Hoyoche and Davagis had been thrown into the cosmic gate, the therein clouds shifted. From it crawled five of the most awful things Hoyoche could've imagined. The sequence of horrors that slithered and shambled past them were outside the words at his disposal. To call them monsters didn't capture it in Hoyoche's mind; they were plagues or nightmares to scourge a land of monsters. Each abomination titanic, fetid, and menacingly hungry, they barely fit into the high-vaulted chapel one at a time. Hoyoche trembled despite himself, nearly pissing himself as the large devils left through the open door.

My eternals and my love, what have I done?

CHAPTER ELEVEN

DANCES WITH DEVILS

Based on *The Hunter's Parchments*, cc bastica 247;
The Dark Fortress of Mephorash, cc bastica xx;

24th of Novumbre, 246

Daylight shone through clouds, and all armies now assaulted the rebel walls. Tek'ouk clenched a large horned skull to his head, routing the herd of fearsome daemogs to ram the wall, spitting fire at the top as they came in. The men atop the wall ducked back as the fire flashed across the parapet.

As the herd circumvented the Quoak field barrier, he lowered his skull to take stock of the progress.[43] Syago's appearance at his camp surprised him, and he took measure of the man he'd called friend.

Syago, grim-faced, ran up the mound to his side and said, "They need you to send the herd to ram the gate again. They've weakened it and Leyta got about halfway into the tunnel, but the fires are in our way now."

"Why can't you put it out?" he asked, looking over at the blaze.

"They've been trying, turning dirt over onto it. But the ground here is really rocky and has lots of grass, so it doesn't snuff well. No water in the area to use either. And they can't take control of the fires because the elementists on the wall have maintained dominance of it."

"You keep saying 'they' as if you're not one of them," Tek'ouk said, eyes narrowing. The young man shifted from one foot to another, eyes flickering to the ground.

"Well, I am, and I'm not. Either way, I'm still your ally and their subject."

Interesting, they're already splitting apart, and I barely had to do anything.

---

43 *See Sol Sistere de Selbst* by Himetuks Himi'n

"Are you? You've been with our camp for three days now. What of your duty to your people as they die there at the wall?"

"I'm best with a sword, which doesn't do much against the wall even with a special blade."

He stared at the boy a moment, still wondering what he might gain by spying on the Kimoc. He doubted Syago, whom Fal'iek had trusted completely, would agree to it. Yet Syago was of Tolgrym, the rival mastozon territory stolen from Quoak. Regardless, the evident feud was division among them and possible leverage for him. He replied, "If you say so. Virgow would call it desertion; only Fal'iek has gotten away with this among us, so at least you're following in his tracks. But it's up to you."

"Well, we do things differently. But they could really use that herd, which is the main reason I returned."

He nodded and shouted orders to the others. Raising his skull, he pressed the herd, causing them to reverse direction back to the wall by Cantlgrym's camp where they'd left. Daemogs were less intelligent than gurows but still bigger and more aggressive, making them harder to manipulate.[44]

Once beside the other camp, he diverted them through the fires, to which they were mostly impervious, and into the door.

When the sun went down and darkness reigned, the fires lit the field and wall with eerie glow. The hanging bodies on the wall again struggled mindlessly until burnt down by the elementists, same as with the lifeless prying in futility at the barriers.

Tek'ouk saw through the minds of the daemog that the gate doors were both now completely broken but that several braces of rock and wood sat behind. He stoked their fury, had them blow some fire into the stable, but only enough to smoke out the blockading foes. And with the other armies now joined in, that progress could only quicken. To the right, the camp of Voium, led by Count Cantarchar, threw heavy fire at the wall as dynasts burrowed.

A loud boom drew his attention. No, not a boom, a roar. He broke the connection to look for the source. Everything hushed. For some moments he saw nothing in the dark. The moon, now waning gibbous, provided some light in between clouds. Then another roar came as a massive shadow passed in front of the moon.

44 *See Reptilium Nimrod, 67*

Tek'ouk turned to his men and shouted, "Get the herd back behind the camps and take cover!"

A cloudy night hid the black beast well. His archers aimed into the air, waiting for the beast to appear. Suddenly it was right above them, coming down in a hard dive that slammed into the Roah'riik camp, shattering their tents. Something with leathery bat wings nine spans big and twisting horns stood with its back to him. His Roah'riik pressed it with spears. The unknown monstrosity thrashed its arms, fast and snarling, throwing up blood from what must've been several victims caught in the landing along with broken pieces of the barrier. Syago ran to it, and Tek'ouk raised his scepter-crutch, making lightning pop around its head. A tail whipped across and hit them onto their backs.

Others rolled to their feet and jumped back, but Tek'ouk could not and was all but pinned as it moved over him. Now clearly not a creature of the wild, but a devil from the pits. A furry mass of claws and teeth bore down on him in the dark while his own hands scrambled for his scepter-crutch. Then Syago's sword was there, blinding in its light as he slashed furiously.

This was no small fiend either and to fight that Tek'ouk would need Ravenger, the tribe's hellknife. While screaming and fighting surrounded him, he began crawling toward where his box had been as the terror thundered closer to him. Suddenly Lil'iek was there, pulling him away. "It should be over there," he said without needing to indicate what. She dragged him toward it. "No, leave me and take it! I can't use it, but you can."

For a second he thought she'd refuse, but she finally gave him the scepter and left him to rifle through the wreckage and bring him a bag with several wood and clay jars. He grabbed the one he knew to be the knife. He gently handed her the jagged red stone blade and bone handle, held together by black leather linings. A fiery gem shone from the hilt. *I didn't expect to ever use this, I'd hoped not.*

She grasped it and ran at the devil, Syago and Alexandre eerily nowhere to be seen. Tek'ouk raised his scepter to reissue lightning around its head while Lil'iek edged in cautiously. It snarled and shot back up into the sky, disappearing once more as its wings leveled a burst of wind. Arrows and stones followed it up uselessly. As they watched the skies, commotion at the barrier reminded him of the herd that nobody now controlled. He cursed as they burned and charged the barriers; of course he didn't care that they attacked Leyta's as well but the destruction of his had to be stopped yet he couldn't get control of them by himself and his camp was in disarray. He yelled for a focus on tracking the devil and turned to find Syago limping toward him. He pointed at the herd. "Can you scare them off with Alexandre? Or kill the ones that get close? Anything to contain this madness."

Syago looked as though he might pass out but nodded and went to the barrier. Tek'ouk began commanding a regrouping of the camp while, from the corner of his eye, he saw that familiar white flash of the blade and heard the pained baying of the beasts. Memories flickered of seeing his old friend Fal'iek fighting alongside Odiru, and the evils they confronted. He turned back to searching for the otherworlder, still no sign of the devil until he heard it howl over Cantarchar's camp. He turned and saw it spitting something black onto the battalion. They fired arrows and used dyne, but most had to take cover from what Tek'ouk guessed was acid. Ignoring the return assault, it dove and gore splashed as it tore through their ranks then shot up and flew over the wall began spitting onto buildings as it passed over the city. He understood this as making its presence known and feared. Intelligent or not, it had no side or stake in the civil war.

Reed'luk ran up to him and reported, "All accounted for except Boam'ikik."

"What do you mean? Where's his body?"

"We don't know. There's a lot of blood but nothing of him. Even his remains are not here." *So all that gore was from just one man being completely shredded? Golkaw, how many do we have to lose to this?!*

Shouting for any to follow, he grabbed his daemog skull and hobbled toward the field barrier holding out the infuriated monsters. Syago waved his sword in a dazzling series of haphazard swings, culminating in the clean decapitation of a bull that rammed the field barrier. Brown blood gushed from the neck and the others roared. Tek'ouk used the skull to move them away from the barrier and circle when something caught his attention through the daemogs' senses. *Something else comes.*

He yelled for everyone to back away as a massive insectoid human plowed through the herd, tossing some aside and snatching one in its mandibles, ripping it apart. The gigantic monstrosity nimbly crawled over the barrier and grabbed at people and objects, breaking and tearing as it went toward Leyta's camp, then to the city wall, wreaking damage along the way. Those on top quickly began firing down at it, then moved away as it easily crested the battlement and descended into the city.

Tek'ouk and his men quickly regained control of the wily herd and pushed them away. The Roah'riik returned to the camp center to tend to wounds and repairs. The battle among civilians went on hold as each side minded the new disaster. The screams from inside Mantlgrym diminished. *Must be on the other side now.* He sent scouts to the other camps to learn where the two otherworlders went and if they'd seen more. Mentally, he prepared for what came next. With more losses, was it still fitting to stay and fight?

"Go to Leyta for her report," he told Syago, who replied that he'd rather someone else do it. Both could see her talking to her soldiers in the torchlight of her wrecked camp, and so weren't worried about how she fared.

Irritation flared in him at the moodiness of the two youths, though considering all that Leyta had done, leveled her scepter at him, then broke their fence, perhaps Syago's dissociation was understandable. "You—never mind," he said as he saw that she now left the camp to approach them.

"Two devils, am I right?" she asked on arrival.

He nodded, "Probably let in by the cult, just as the coven did. And my bet is on there being more. I expect their strategy is to let the devils wreak havoc for a time and then they'll bring them to heel for a specific front. Or they'll try to reign them in and be devoured as soon as the otherworlders realize the disciples are more pushovers than the old witchlords were."

"How do we fight them off? That nearly ruined us." She looked tired now, for the first time he'd seen. She didn't say it, but it was obvious that he'd have to leave the siege in hunt of the otherworlders. The devils would pose a great threat to any Kimoc groups, particularly nearby Quoak, if left unchecked. On top of that, the Roah'riik were called hellhunters for a reason: they were the best at the task and equipped for it, whereas Asturions needed a whole army to clumsily invade the wild and conquer them.

The only problem was hunting the devils dragged them away from what they'd come for and against even deadlier foes. There was the chance they'd see the shadowmen too, or stop the cult in some other way, but it seemed a far chance. Leyta continued, "I suppose we could set up a trap and lure them into it."

"No, that has never worked," he said bitterly. Of course they needed to be hunted down. He felt it was the Asturions' fault, and therefore their responsibility, since both enemy groups had come from their societies and were more broadly their problem. But the Asturions only cared about their civil war at the moment. Their towns would repel most attacks, but smaller Quoak, missing most of its warriors, would be easier prey. Once again Quoak would be hit by devils from an Asturion born conflict. So it had always been. More frustrating still was that he couldn't ask their aid, for to ask for something you know will be denied loses face and he'd rather die than lose face to the palemen. He felt a faint smile betray his resentment. "We'll have to leave the siege and go after them. Something we might have had to do anyways considering our losses. But those otherworlders could be anywhere plaguing the land without obstacle. We have to track them while the trail is fresh and before they do more damage. I suppose it was too much to expect we'd not get stuck with this, but we'll take care of it as we always have."

"Or they'll destroy you instead," she said. "I'm glad you've the bravery for that initiative but I fear you'll be insufficient. We should try a trap first."

And she has the gall to misperceive me. "They won't come back, bait or no, and my people can't risk it. The cult will probably be content with letting us fight each other here while they and the fiends pillage and plague the land everywhere else. We'll have to go after them, and fast."

"But *we* cannot," Leyta said, looking southeast at the Voium camp as a soldier approached from there.

"And we will not," Captain Barascon de Santomas said. "We came for the siege. We're far along and will not be led astray into futile hunts. So Count Cantarchar has sent me to request the hellhunters pursue the fiends."

"Just as we've always done," Tek'ouk said quietly, barely quelling his anger. "Cleaning up your refuse while you take what we want. As you've always done."

But the man's expression only turned more smug. "It's up to you. Keep throwing yourselves on the wall while the otherworlders thrash your villages, or go do the one thing you're good at." He shrugged and walked off.

Tek'ouk ground his teeth, wishing he could walk up and hit the man. *Golkaw, the bastard is right.*

Leyta began, "Maybe they'll lead you to the grimshades—"

Tek'ouk snarled as he let out a small jet of anger through his crutch and into the ground, causing a tremor.

Leyta's face tightened at the taboo, hypocritically. He hadn't done it *at* her. Before she could retort with something she'd regret, Syago intervened. "Why don't we take a moment to finalize our decisions instead of bickering."

They glared each other down then consented. Syago held Leyta's eyes, continuing, "I'm going with them. I'll give a speech if you want, to show that I'm not abandoning Cantlgrym but am instead taking the fight to the enemy, preemptively. Alexandre can hurt the devils too, and I'll be more useful out there than here. I'll return but you'll have this won before then."

"That's fine," she said, voice flat. Spy or not, Syago was leaving them and bringing Alexandre with him, which would be a great boon to the devil hunt. *Being away from this pit of betrayal traps will be a relief if nothing else.*

"We'll keep you informed and return when we can," Tek'ouk said, doubting his own words.

She thanked him and embraced Syago briefly. A faint look on Syago's face made Tek'ouk wonder if there was something else between them. She left for her camp, and Syago followed to give them a farewell and commission. The Roah'riik prepared to leave.

CHAPTER TWELVE

HUNTING HELL

Based on *Annals of Syago*, cc bastica 160; *The Nordvargor Testaments*, cc bastica 886; *The Dark Fortress of Mephorash*, cc bastica x; *Scars of the Martyrs*, cc bastica 1026;

27th–28th of Novumbre, 246

Before the Roah'riik departed the siege, they walked Lolish'ith into the forest. His mad, bird-like movements made it difficult to get there. He twitched and pecked at the air, drooled at the mouth, and clawed at those around him. It'd have been easier to tie him up, but they respected him too much. Syago watched the whole thing in trepidation, knowing what was coming even though none spoke it.

In the dense woods, they circled around the man. Syago had gathered that in their lore, his soul and the bird's had switched bodies. But he saw in their uneasy eyes, behind painted faces, that they believed it less. Tek'ouk said a prayer in Kimoc, blowing leaves and thrush-smoke onto Lolish'ith, then nodded to the others. They raised their javelins, and in an instant, the man was dead, resting peacefully beneath a covering of flowers and leaves, pinned by the javelins to the spot where his body would feed the wild. Before they left, the Roah'riik shouted bird cries to the sky, almost celebratory and joyous.

The devil hunting party followed the trail of the greed up to the Troisack Mountains on the east side of Thornwood. Syago had hunted on the slopes, but not as far as this. In addition to Syago, Lil'iek, and Tek'ouk, the party included Yarok, Reed'luk, Kor'miir, Mour'ikik, and Qul'toq. The last being a brave young warrior, shorter than Syago with narrow eyes. Each wore their traditional Roah'riik hellhunting clothes of feathers, furs, and animal bones. Beads in their hair marked their ranks. Syago stood out among them in metal chestplate, shoulder pauldrons, and morion helm.

Syago had never seen a devil until the siege. Their power lived up to the frightening legends.[45] Worse than beasts, than feldinals even, they were similar to demons, but different in ways he wasn't clear on. Both came from the Otherworlds and could not slain like the monsters of this world. Only soulweapons or hellweapons would truly suffice in the end. Or the bindings of a priest or chamand, if available. He'd felt nervous at first; he'd always hated hunting even natural monsters but wanted to love it and be good at it. But he took comfort in having the Kimoc hellhunters as his companions, as well as having better use of Alexandre.

They climbed the steep rocky slopes of the fern—and vine-ridden mountainside. Vegetation was trampled along the trail and a small cave yawned open above them. Once they reached it, they saw it was more than a mere cave but what had been an old temple or cavern dwelling. Crumbling walls sat at its entrance, which led to a descending spiral staircase, brambles snaking into it from the the forest. He looked southwest to where he knew Tolgrym to be, obscured by the brambles. Fal'iek had scoffed at the idea, but Syago'd heard stories about ghosts haunting the mountains, yet no ghost was likely to be as bad as what they now hunted.[46]

Alexandre sensed something in the cave. Their communication had improved alongside their ability to fight and hunt together. He found that not just constant practice, but also living in line with the moral view of the sword brought them in closer harmony, though it wasn't easy with a perfectionist entity.

With night nearly upon them, they decided to camp outside and follow the trail down the cave at dawn rather than risk excavating it during the creeping hour. Their position gave them a height advantage, and the walls, as ruined as they were, could help shield them as well. If the devil came out and attacked them, which they thought a strong possibility, their watchmen would be ready.

Against the setting sun, he practiced forms and swings with Alexandre, still learning the enhanced speed of the blade. With enough experience, he hoped he would be able to control the flight Alexandre provided through its speed and weight reduction. To be able to fly, or rather jump and glide

45 That so much of this chapter would've embarrassed its author speaks to its reliability.

46 See *Sol Sistere de Selbst* by Himetuks Himi'n

on command, was something he'd only heard stories of though he knew he was far from achieving that control. Alexandre's unwieldy lifts during the malwolf battle proved that. At the very least, Syago improved on his timing and movements every day.

"You're better than he was at this time," Lil'iek said from behind him. "Odiru was an impressive swordsman, but you've caught up to him. Relatively speaking."

"You lie," Syago said in between hit-grunts, now slicing through a large stone.

"Only sometimes. Truth is, you're a faster learner than he was. Probably take from your mother, who could pick up another language in half the time anyone else did." Lil'iek stood next to him. "Did you ever learn your mother's language?"

She referred not to the language she'd spoken for most of her life, but the one she'd been raised in until she'd abandoned it. His skin prickled, but he continued the practice to hide any blush. "No. Well, I picked up some from Fal'iek."

"I could teach you," Lil'iek said. "I remember as little girls we'd sing together, she and I. She loved singing in our tongue. Would you like to learn one of the songs we sang together?"

He stopped and looked at her. What was he supposed to say? He loved his mother, but he wasn't her. He was his father if anybody, and there wasn't anything he could do to change it even if he'd wanted to. Not that he had anything against his mother, he was grateful to her, but the longing connection for her wasn't there the way it was for his father. Was that wrong? His mind turned to Alexandre briefly, as if it'd have answers, but there was no response. Even so, Alexandre and Odiru were his legacy, the other more pagan half was not. "That would be nice, but I, uh, think it best I focus on training right now."

She nodded and drew her hand-axes.

Wordlessly, they raised their weapons to each other in the challenger's salute and commenced sparring.

A fast but gentle flow, the warriors danced in fading golden sunlight the way he'd often done with Fal'iek. Most of the victory hits went to Lil'iek while Syago nearly landed two, but also nearly stumbled off the cliff's edge. Steady improvement, he noted, and a fun contest for the both of them. After, panting, Syago asked, "Did you hunt many fiends with them?"

They both sat down. "Only two. It was mostly Fal'iek, his specialty, and he usually went with the other three companions, or accompanied by groups of Roah'riik, but sometimes with me. The companionship of Odiru, Fal'iek, Amaruc, and Matias... well, those four eclipsed everything."[47] She folded her arms, looking out over the forest, reminiscent.

"I'd always wanted to be in one of those, a legendary companionship of warriors, even before we had our two enemies," Syago said. "After the rescue from Covadongar, I'd kind of hoped that me, Fal'iek, Leyta, and Qosku could become the next one."

She smiled. "Just do it before you're married or your wife will hate you. But really I put up with it because it was good, everyone liked them, and together they built up a lot of hope and unity in those dark times. But you don't need a special team to do that."

Syago sighed. "I did want to be the kind of monument my father was, but now it's so different than I expected. And it's made worse by this disconnect between me and Alexandre. We're doing better, but it's almost like we're still just tolerating each other rather than bonding. Getting Alexandre just made me realize how fake the hero legend would be for me."

"It's fake all around, Syago. It was a glorious day for us in many ways, and we enjoyed each other's company, but it was never nearly as fun or glamorous as it's told now. In truth, it was hell." Her voice dropped low, and her face took on a more serious note as she looked at Syago, or maybe past him.

A few moments passed, then Lil'iek said again in lighter tones, "I do think Leyta's a better leader than the other counts, with relation to us at least. But sometimes I can't tell how much we can trust her. How far would you say we can trust her?"

Syago didn't want to be there, in that moment, but there he was. "I trust her, and I think you should too." He thought of saying it goes both ways, as Alexandre wanted him to, but bit his tongue. She watched him closely, then looked back to the sunset.

"The only Asturion I trust is you, and if you trust her, that might be enough. But I worry you both might be played for fools by the rest, or used against us. Regardless, she might be off on some things, but you should

47 Amaruc was part of the companionship but died just before *The Nascendante* and so is often omitted when speaking of the legendary heroes, unfortunately. Matias de Sanyago died on the ship and so is similarly forgotten.

support her more against the others. Abandoning them for us isn't helping her. I'm happy you're here, but you have a duty."

"Maybe I will," he muttered, wondering if she'd have a different opinion if he'd told her Leyta'd directly asked him to betray her. If he bluntly told the truth as Alexandre now chastised him for not doing. "And maybe you should stay out of it."

He stood up and walked to his bedding. They planned for an early night and early morning, the most dangerous point yet. But surprisingly, the night passed uneventfully. The following morning, as the sky began to blue and dense fog blanketed the land below them, they gazed down into the hole. Stones were overturned and dead branches lay strewn about. The trail couldn't be more obvious, which made them expect a trap. But there was nothing else for it. They edged down the worn stone stairs, single file for its narrowness, holding onto thorny branches for support. Once they got to the spot the stairs had been broken away completely, Syago realized the trail came from a different creature. Alexandre buzzed in his mind, like anxiety but also eager.

"These are serpent tracks," Syago said quietly, crouching beside Yarok and Mour'ikik. "I thought we were chasing a giant bug?"

"We were," Mour'ikik said. "They could be hiding together. Or just crossed paths."

"Could it have changed forms?" Syago asked.

"No." Tek'ouk shook his head, leaning against the wall. "There's some speculation that they grow, slowly, in their home-worlds, but not here. Especially not cross species like that. Let's guard as if there's two."

He repeated his order in Kimoc for Reed'luk and Qul'toq, who didn't speak Asturion. Weapons drawn, they used the thick bramble to cross the broken section then continued the stairs down, deeper into the twisting cavern.

Once light left them, they lit torches. This would be a giveaway, but they weren't likely to surprise the devils even without it. Syago refused a torch, seeing that Alexandre glowed with increasing light. The sword's complete disregard for stealth and other tactics unnerved him. One other divide between the two. Syago pulled out his shield and informed Alexandre that it would have to accept it because of their vulnerability in the dark. It made its displeasure known but didn't appear to relent any of its assistance. It yearned for devil flesh more than anything he'd seen before.

Once at the bottom of the stairs, it was difficult to see where stone temple began and natural cavern ended. Syago began to wonder if it really was an old Kimoc or Unakan temple, or if only some of it was. The team moved through thick branches to map out the circular room and the many passages that branched off. They couldn't discern which way the serpent had gone.

After conversing in whispers and silent hand motions, they separated into twos, Syago following Yarok down one with his sword shining brighter than the hellhunter's torch. He turned to Yarok and said, "Alexandre senses something down this one."

Yarok gave no reply. Syago sensed the man didn't like him; he'd always been cold, but maybe only to him. The lights of their sword and torch only illuminated a stone tunnel that opened into a large cavern. They carefully walked through a series of thick branches, passing by the skeleton of a dae-mog. The strange slime covering it indicated it was recent. A crack in the wall, like a window, let in small sunlight that shone directly on a pagan shrine, or well and statue, he couldn't tell. The worn creature on it meant nothing to him, but Yarok stared at it, mouth slightly open, eyes awonder.

"What is it?" Syago asked. Instead of answering, Yarok moved around it and began climbing up a thornvine along another staircase to an alcove above, where the statue almost seemed to be pointing. He followed the Roah'riik up, glancing at the clogged doorway below.

Once at the top, the alcove led to another chamber, a warrior skeleton laying in the path. Yarok knelt to examine its leather armor, so worn it'd fallen off. Syago walked ahead to a thick vine that blocked another door-way. He began hacking at it with Alexandre, the Judgment Sword shining brighter than ever, cutting a path open to peek into the next chamber. Within Alexandre's illuminated area, he saw only more thick vines that twisted down by another staircase into another dark chamber. Beyond the edge of his light was only silent darkness. He turned back to Yarok.

But Yarok was gone.

Looking all around, he saw no sign of the warrior. Syago felt a pit in his stomach, and when he noticed Alexandre shaking in his hands, he breathed deep and went to the opening they'd climbed up. Nothing. His heart continued to race. The skeleton had been moved slightly, yet there was no sign of his companion. The trembling returned. *Don't panic, you fool. Handle it! Fortify.*

His skin prickled as he turned about to make sure nothing was sneaking up on him. *Did the devil get him? Or something else?* As another possibility passed through his mind, he calmed a bit. *Or did he take an opportunity to ditch me?* If eaten, he didn't want to give away his position, and if abandoned, he didn't want to retreat. Although everything in him screamed to go back, he decided he would at least check the next chamber, where he likely wouldn't find anything anyway. Alexandre, however, seemed to think they were close and exuded an absurd amount of confidence, encouraging him with blurry memories of his father fighting.

Making it down the stairs under thick vines wasn't hard, and the large room appeared to be a dead end, empty except for some broken stones and more old skeletons partially crushed. But Alexandre buzzed in his mind, bringing attention to a large diamond-shaped silhouette in the shadows. Confused at the excitement at first, Syago cautiously stepped closer allowing his swordlight to reach it. Hanging down from a thick branch, it looked like some kind of a plant. Until he noticed the bulge-like eyes. His stomach knotted at the sight, his heart thundering.

A giant snake head.

It didn't move, and the unwavering eyes appeared shut, as though it might be sleeping. It had strange skin that unnerved him, knotted instead of scaly. Since it showed no awareness of him, he pondered making a preemptive strike but knew better. He decided to slip past and bring the others.

"Odiru'ssson," a voice hissed from the head. "Recognizzze you. Remember him, we do."

Syago stopped. The head still hadn't moved, and the voice coming from it struck him as strangely human. He lifted shining Alexandre to illuminate it better. The serpent's head wore many heads, or rather the skin of human faces fitted together like scales. Two full heads of lighter skin acted as the eyes. They now seemed to look at him vacantly. Dead faces.

"Odiru warrior," the voice said. Then several other human voices joined in as a dull chorus. "Odiru holy knight."

All with a slight hiss, but still unmistakably human. That and the mention of Odiru felt eerie but somehow much less threatening. He asked quietly, "How know you my father? He put you away?"

"He sold us," the one voice began, and the others finished, "to be slaves to this devil."

"Sold you? What lie is this?"

"No lie!" they decanted dully, then one picked up alone. "For what purpossse would we choozzze to be ssskin to an envy? To be hide to a devil of the infernal pitsssssssssss?" He did feel some pity for them in their condition, nobody deserved that regardless of how dishonest they were.

"My father was a good man." Syago didn't want to stand there and argue, but he felt indignant. A sense Alexandre shared. He started to turn for the lower tunnel as he said, "I trust *that* more than I'll ever trust you."

"Know him you did not," they chanted, and he stopped. Then one said, "Like him, you are not. He sssacrificed usss to banishhh the devil. Paid a price to be hero. And you, young boy, with your new toy sssword walk azzz if nothing'sss wrong. Naivete is blisssssssssssssss."

"You didn't know him either," Syago growled and took a step toward it. Alexandre flared in agreement. He felt some satisfaction at their unity on this point. "But Alexandre did know him and would recognize if what you say were true."

"Sssword is not reliable. How would you know any better? How would you know thisss truth?" they stated, monotonous. "We knew him in Tolgrym before he betrayed usss, offered usss, and the envy took usss."

The great head shook, almost like a shiver. Seeing the head of faces rattle like that felt hypnotic. Another chill swept through Syago. "You're not the serpent's head, are you?"

"No," they replied, rattling again. "We're not."

Alexandre buzzed a warning, and he dived left just as the true serpent's head crashed in. A fang grazed his shoulder plate, shearing it, and the lower part of the jaw bumped him aside. Alexandre's speed was the only reason he avoided sure death. The head quickly retracted out of his light, and Syago rolled back onto his feet. The raw speed and stealth of something so big terrified him. He could see only the base of the serpent's coiled body as the head rose high out of his bubble of light. A deep hiss trailed its ascent, and Alexandre, sensing the attack that he could not, prompted him to dash right again. The head slammed into the ground where Syago'd been, clipping his shield and knocking him down again. A brief glimpse of it in the light revealed a slitted eye and a head plated with hard, ridged scales and horns.

As it moved back into the darkness, Syago turned for protection in the passageway and found a giant vine, no, a serpent coil sliding in front of him. Looking around in horror, he realized that what he thought were branches were actually the envy's coils, covered in human skins. He tried not to stare at the human quilt it wore in a twisted reversal of reptilian shedding. Ridged spikes protruded along its body, and the coils moved and shifted, closing in, tightening his fighting space.

The darkness hissed.

Suddenly the tail bulb swung in. He dive-rolled underneath it and bumped against a coil. With nowhere else to move, he brought his shield up just as its head struck forward. The impact jarred his arm, throwing him back. Alexandre slashed its jaw on the way, and the beast gave a deep hiss. But it was not daunted and rammed him again, shoving him back into the coil. Scale-pikes dug at Syago's back between armor, and the feel of that clammy human skin repulsed him. Fume-filled flames shot from the skin's mouths, burning his leg and arm.

"Lil'iek, HELP!" he screamed and the envy followed its hiss with a deep chuckle somewhere in the dark. Stumbling to the ground and resisting the urge to clutch at his burns, Alexandre already worked at healing them but the pain was nigh unbearable. Panic and doom welled in him; any second he'd get bit and the venom would do him in. Or maybe it would just swallow him whole. Hissing followed him, more drawn out now as if the thing was enjoying the game.

He hobbled as fast as he could. Barely escaping another lightning quick strike, Alexandre guiding him, he jumped onto a coil, trying to ignore its horrible human skin. He stabbed it with Alexandre, barely piercing. He tried stabbing at one of the fire pores, and this time, it hissed in pain.

He swung Alexandre around, letting the blade draw him backward, barely in time as the head smashed the wall in front of him. His leg began to throb, and he looked down, seeing a new gash and hoping to the heavens it was not from one of the fangs. He must not have gotten out of the way quickly enough. The head turned as if to continue snapping at him, and he waved his sword into a defensive point. The envy hissed low then withdrew from the light. Fires and noxious fumes continued to burst while he continued cutting at the coil's heat pores. His burn pains eased from Alexandre's healing, but too slowly. He coughed on the air.

He was dying. He could feel it. A prey cornered.

"SOMEBODY HELP ME!" he screamed again just as commotion near the door caught his attention. His companions struggled against the coil, trying to break into the room when suddenly the coil he stood on lifted, opening the passageway.

He saw them run in and shouted "No! Wait—" but it was too late. The coil dropped behind them, closing off the doorway, just as the snake head struck at them. They dove and scattered, some getting hit.

Frantic to buy them time, Syago plunged Alexandre into another fire pore, earning another angry hiss. A gleaming arrow plucked into the side of its head, earning a bigger hiss, and he realized it'd been tied to a black dagger that Syago recognized as the hellblade Ravenger,. Its head rose to Lil'iek on the upper ledge, standing with bow drawn, and whipped its tail up, smashing the edge as she retreated inside.

As Lil'iek distracted it, the other five Roah'riik joined Syago in attacking its pores. It swung its tail back around to hit them, the tail-faces forcing them back with its shooting flames. Putrid smoke began to fill the cavern, cloaking the massive devil and choking them.

The envy hissed in a voice different from the faces, stronger and more grating, bladelike, "Remember you I do, Lil'iek. Pity you'll die before I usher in the return of the infernal domination of theze landzzz. That isss... unlesss you join my collection."

Watching for the head, Syago and the others resumed stabbing the pores, and the coils flew into motion, wreaking chaos as the warriors struggled not to get crushed. The serpent head struck down, lightning quick, biting into one of the warriors and lifting him out of the light.

Its tail rose to meet Lil'iek's re-emergence and blasted fires at her. But the jets were blown away by winds sent from Tek'ouk in the lower tunnel. Distracted by the roiling coils, Syago didn't notice the head coming for him till the fangs flashed before him, he barely got his shield up. It caught him in its jaws, causing him to lose his grip on Alexandre. Too late to dodge, he held its fangs at bay with his shield while he grasped for Alexandre. His hand closed around the sword, bringing its tip up just as the giant maw pressed him against the wall.

With Alexandre pressed against the roof of its mouth, and the maw trying to clamp around him, they were in a stalemate. Syago's mind rushed, trying to figure a way out. If he pressed Alexandre up into its head, he'd get himself crushed in the process. Before he could think on what to do, the head slammed sideways into a wall, throwing him out and breaking the stalemate. The second he was free, Syago rolled backward, his heart racing. Coils thrashed and burned the area relentlessly. He moved under and over flying coils, tripping and getting smacked. Syago looked wildly around for help, but his companions were occupied, flying about in a desperate fight against the monster's tail.

He lost track of the head, a bad sign. Alexandre sensed it. Syago jumped onto a coil as it hit the floor and then leaped with the anticipated rise. Just as he lifted off, the head reappeared, coming down at him out of the darkness. Syago had only enough time to register its huge maw closing over him. With Alexandre aiding him, Syago twisted in the air, evading its fangs as it swallowed him. He held the sword out from him as the sword propelled his spin, shredding the serpent's throat during his descent.

After three spins inside the bleeding throatway, he felt the dead body falling. Quickly, he cut an opening on the side and pulled out, landing roughly on his back.

The blood covering him burned his skin, but he hurriedly brushed it off. Getting up, he saw only still coils amid the haze. He called out, "Lil'iek? Anyone there?"

He heard some muffled calls, and Mour'ikik appeared on top of a coil. The others soon appeared, all except Reed'luk.

At Lil'iek's questioning glance, Mour'ikik said, "He got hit by a coil. We helped him up, then the head just flew in and took him out, it blew us aside too. I didn't see where the body landed. He might've been swallowed."

A deep silence fell briefly on the group before Tek'ouk turned and examined the remains of the devil while Lil'iek pulled out her improvised Ravenger arrow. Syago and Lil'iek then began dismantling the serpent. They would have to destroy the entire corpse using Alexandre and the hellknife to ensure no parts regenerated. The spirit or spirits of the devil would then wander in search of a new body or a way back home to regenerate. Except for the ones trapped in Ravenger.

"That was an impressive maneuver," Tek'ouk said, clasping Syago on the shoulder in spite of the sadness in his eyes at losing their companion. "One of the most I've ever seen, and on one so big as this."

Pride surged in him. Alexandre responded with strong disapproval, but Syago ignored it. Before he thought he and Alexandre had a long ways to flying together, but now he felt capable of learning it. After finding and burning the remains of their friend in a Kimoc ceremony of purification, they set out to leave the area, mentioning to Syago that they'd found no signs of the other devil.

Later that day, at dinner break, Syago sat looking across the field of mounds at the distant Mantlgrym. A rare breathtaking scene to behold, he'd never had an elevated view such as this before. He saw signs of what was quickly becoming a three-front war as the devils had hit both sides of the conflict at the capital. Fires still raged at the city wall, signifying that it went in favor of the siege. Yarok came up to him and, in terse tone, said, "Syago, I sorry for leave you. It was not intention, but I fell into ancient trap of temple." He extended an arm for a stiff handshake.

Syago didn't know if he was telling the truth or not but took it regardless, thinking that the true apology would be in the man's future behavior. "Not a problem. It happens to the best of us."

Yarok nodded and walked away as Lil'iek sat down next to him. "You've come a long ways, both as a hunter and a warrior. Really, no lies... this time."

Syago snorted. "And you? Are you getting so old that I have to finish the job?" It struck him how much joking with her was like talking to Fal'iek.

"Probably, but I have you and the others to hide behind. Both Odiru and Fal'iek would be impressed though. However, for the record, it wasn't all you. My dagger arrow, and our other hits, did help destroy the body. At the very least, we distracted it for you."

"Ah, just when I thought I'd finally accomplished something." He set his empty tin down, scraped clean of their stew, a sort of early "celebration" of the victory. "Before I forget, the faces on the devil's tail, they spoke to me. Separate from the envy. They said they knew Odiru, lived with him in Tolgrym, and that he'd sacrificed them to the envy to banish it. What a lie."

Lil'iek merely grunted as they looked out at the city. An uneasy feeling set in Syago's gut, and he turned more fully toward her. "That is a lie, right? From the devil?"

Instead of responding with a quick "no," she sighed, and the feeling in his gut worsened. With a shake of her head, she said, "The devil was trying to lure you into a conversation so it could kill you. And it wanted to diminish your beliefs and ancestral pride as well. That's what they do. It's not enough for them to kill, they want to wear down the soul. Don't believe what you hear."

"I'm fully aware of that, but you didn't answer the question," he pressed, eyes narrowing. "In fighting devils and demons, did my father sacrifice anyone to them?"

An implicit question in this was did Fal'iek or she sacrifice anyone as well, but Syago kept it in check. Lil'iek lowered her eyes. Nearby Tek'ouk fingered Ravenger on his belt. She said softly, "We were at war with the Razhod, Syago. The bloodiest war we've ever known, lasting five generations and eventually taking Odiru's life. You have no idea what it's like to fight them, those stories you've read don't come close. We used criminals that would've been executed otherwise. We didn't enjoy it, we tried to avoid it, beat the things the normal way, the way we did today. But there was so many of them and we had so much against us."

Syago clutched his head, feeling dizzy, his world spinning. His heroes, how could they have done this? "Criminals? When we execute a criminal, we don't send him to slavery in hell as the skin of a devil! You don't even like *our* executions, how could you—How many were there?"

Lil'iek's expression remained calm. "Syago, I don't know. Believe me, what we had to do then still haunts me."

Syago looked at Tek'ouk. "Were you involved in this too? Why has nobody told me?"

Tek'ouk stared impassive.

Lil'iek continued, "It's easy to condemn it here and now, and I'm with you in part, but you can't imagine how desperate we were. You can't imagine the kind of enemy the Razhod was or what a world is like with that many devils released into it."

Syago's voice started to rise. "Can't I? What did we just do? I basically beat that thing by myself. But this experienced team of warriors had to descend to their level, to do the same thing the Razhod did, and *sacrifice* someone to slavery in hell?!"

Lil'iek's eyes flashed, her voice now rising too. "You're being an arrogant little child. Keep talking big and naive like that and it'll get you somewhere low real quick. You nearly died until we got there. This was only one fiend. Imagine if you had faced a group of fiends, as we did. We only went along with it to get your people to sacrifice criminals instead of Kimoc captives. Don't pretend you wouldn't do what had to be done in order to save your people from sure death."

"I'm arrogant? I didn't keep secrets from my friend and heir of a legacy built on lies. Maybe that's the real disappointment here, that everyone I've trusted has kept me in the dark about my father's—*my* own legacy. You know if you'd simply said it was all a lie, I would've believed you completely, never brought it up again. That's how much I trusted you, a trust misplaced."

"Syago," Tek'ouk said calmly, "we never told you something that was untrue. Well, I can't speak for the Asturions, but *we* never lied to you. He was still a great man."

"Do great men do that? Or does that make him not great, in spite of his other victories? Really, not telling me untrue things is only one small step back from withholding the whole truth. I'm surprised you even told me now if it's so easy to sidestep the truth, keep me in blissful ignorance. Purpose well served until now."

Tek'ouk snapped, "If you're so much more noble a hero, why don't you go out and destroy the rest of them by yourself? That'll show you truth."

"Fine," Syago said and began shoving his things into his travel sack. *Deova's bowls, what else don't I know?*

Lil'iek stood up. "Syago, what are you doing?"

"Leaving to destroy the rest of the devils as you said—alone and without sacrificing people. You're moving too slow for me anyways." He finished and stood tall, the sack over his shoulder.

"Syago, I wasn't..." Tek'ouk started, rising to his feet with effort.

"Wasn't what? Serious? You're always serious. You can't not be, it's what makes you so hard to work with sometimes. I was feeling done here anyway." He walked past a stunned Lil'iek, heading south.

She put a hand on his shoulder, but Syago brushed it off. "Syago, you can't do this. Traveling alone out here. Even we don't do it. Add to that the devils, the cult, the other enemies... this is suicide. Don't be ridiculous."

Syago merely raised his eyebrows at her. He turned away, snapped his hand in a goodbye wave, and walked on. The other Roah'riik stood as well, trying to call after him to come back, but he ignored them.

CHAPTER THIRTEEN
IMMORTAL WAR

Based on *Writings of Qosku*, cc bastica 177;
The Hunter's Parchments, cc bastica 250;
The Dark Fortress of Mephorash, cc bastica xx;

29th of Novumbre, 246

Qosku peered over the rooftop at some people running through the cobblestone streets. It was raining outside, not hard, but at least it wasn't hail or snow. He'd slept in somewhat, as every night had him up for most of it, but the commotion had awoken him. He couldn't tell what they were doing exactly until he realized they were running around a market area. He'd identified this area as the best place for Leyta's forces to surface from the understables and catacombs. The most obvious path was through the stable lift building, but the people knew this too and had put a strong defense around it. But the center of the open market area wasn't so fortified. The commotion signaled to him that Leyta's forces were now attempting this route.

He quickly rolled up his things and armored himself, then climbed to the top of the building. It would be difficult to fight in what he had, but he would adapt. Looking down at the frantic people, he wondered what to do. He preferred going after the Royal Chaos members instead of common cityfolk pretending to knighthood.

He felt a surprising amount of excitement for this. Not only did it keep his mind off his many troubles, but it also gave him something important to do. He felt needed, essential, and good at what lay before him. Although he enjoyed the mission, there was still a burning sadness in him that his new life, which had begun to feel stabilized in spite of the war, was falling apart. A werebeast curse by night, and plagues of depression, loneliness, and body dissociation by day.

He leaped to the roof of another building for a better look at the market clearing where people had closed up shop and even carried goods down the streets to safer plazas. Lines of people brought wood, bricks, and other supplies to the now cracking area. They'd ceased building something there and now just piled it on, though it wouldn't slow the siege much. Knight emerged from a main street to stand on the edge of the square. The giant armored corpse filled the space between two old buildings of white plaster and cruck supports. His helmeted head was almost level with the second story.

Holding a massive axe made of a guillotine blade tied to a branch, he, it, watched and waited.

Deciding he needed to occupy that foe for the allies' emergence into the city, Qosku moved out of sight, circling around closer to where Knight stood. Though the rain had stopped and sun peeked out, the wet roofs combined with Qosku's haste made him slip off the clay tiles, tumbling to the ground atop the tent covering of a stand.

He stood, disoriented and finding himself in clear view of Knight, everyone else more focused on the booms taking place underground. *Stupid! No matter, I'll still take him.* Mace and flail in hand, he ran straight at Knight. The giant hefted his large executioner axe and brought it down, but Qosku pushed a burst of rage through his limbs, dashing to the side as the blade crashed on cobblestone. He swung at the armored wrist, but Knight's steel gauntlet took the brunt of it and the other arm grabbed him, raising him up in clenched fist.

He twisted out of the vice grip and fell onto its shoulder. Seeing an opportunity, Qosku scrabbled up to slip under the helmet's chin, and found himself falling. He had expected flesh, but instead the giant was an empty carcass inside, one Qosku now tumbled down. For someone accustomed to entering mine shafts, this was a new kind of disgusting claustrophobia, squeezing into the ribcage of a desiccated corpse. The thing shook, unable to reach him, and knocked him about the slimy confines. The musty stench choked him, and he wondered briefly at how this lifeless was animated all the time. He prayed back into focus and began kicking out at ribs. Then the blade of a sword plunged in at him between armor plates, and again and again. He dodged this way and that, but the corpse managed to nick his shoulder and throw his balanced off. Qosku tumbled down again, this time falling out of the moldy gambeson and onto the ground.

Explosions drew his and Knight's brief attention to the center of the square. As Knight moved toward the hole that blasted open, Qosku grabbed its ankle like a hug and with all his hate, held the foot back, tripping up the stiff armored corpse.

After a brief stumble, Knight kicked him out into the square. He stood as several soldiers rushed past him. Knight held up his great blade for a horizontal swing and Qosku yelled for everyone to get down. But none listened and the guillotine axe whirred across, cutting down both the soldiers of both sides in bloody crunches of metal and body. A second swing came, passing over Qosku, felling a few others. As the giant plunged the blade down at the army below, Qosku sprang up, powered by hate energy, and kicked its chestplate, causing the giant to stumble back with a dull thrum. Qosku moved to knock the weapon out of his hand but he hefted it and turned away.

As his companion forces entered the market area, filling it and organizing, the enemy soldiers retreated to the square's edge. Knight withdrew behind a blockade of stacked furniture, shop stands, and benches. Qosku saw now that the haphazard construct stretched around this section of the city across cobblestone streets and in between the plastered wooden buildings.

Qosku started to run toward the blockade but a pair of arms stopped him, wrapping around him from behind gently, warmly. "Leyta!" he shouted louder than he'd intended.

"Qosku, you're my hero," she said with a big smile. "We couldn't have done this without your brilliant work. Truly your victory."

"I—well, you—" he stammered for a good response but, as always, found none. Modesty and ineptitude with the language held his tongue.

"Just accept the compliment," she said, still beaming, then straightened as Alfonsor walked up. "Captain."

"Castellan," he responded in kind. "I have to say you've surprised even me. Especially this informant of yours. My men tell me he held off the giant. Both of you've got the kind of metal I like."

"Your work was equally victorious here, Captain," she said.

"Well enough of that," he said as Cantarchar and Toriacus joined them. "It appears now that we're in the same position as the fight in Cantabryn. Inner-city struggle. Though the opposition here is close to surrender, if your soldier spy is to be believed. We can begin recriminations and executing any we capture to send a message."

"We can't execute them," she said. "Not today at least, or nobody'll believe the trial was fair. It's what the Chaos wants."

"We can't not do it," Alfonsor snapped. "To not punish them allows for others to follow suit in the lawlessness. We have to show a strong hand to those who spit on offers of clemency."

"But that's exactly what they planned for," Leyta said. "You know what the Chaos was doing, and my spy confirmed it. He implicated the entire city in the rebellion so that they'd have to fight or risk reprisals with us. The lyrics of Jester's songs talk about our executions, how unfair they are. If you do this, you'll be fueling that strategy as they take it to other cities. More effective is to give them slow and transparent trial and the opportunity to fight with us, give us information on the enemy. Or face reprisals. We need the soldiers anyway. At most, we can jail the leaders until a trial."

The captain said nothing for a moment, thinking it over and probably fighting against the admission that she had it right. The others looked the same. "Fine, but no bending on the offer," he said. "And any that turn again get cut. Perhaps you want to make this part of another stab at that plea before we press them. Two hours should be enough."

The captains looked at each other and agreed, then broke up to establish camps, assess the city, repair damages done, and prepare to move forward. Leyta turned back to Qosku as Katti ran up to them, giving him a hug and asking how he fared.

"I am really well. Very great," he responded, trying to sound more enthusiastic about his progress than he felt. "Every night is more better."

The negotiation plea offer didn't go well, or at all. They made the open plea, directed at the blockaded areas, but it was clear nobody listened. Qosku agreed it was important to demonstrate the effort at least.

They saw nobody beyond the makeshift fortifications save a handful of archers and heard only distant activity beyond the blockade. Archers and crossbowmen prevented them from getting deeper in. *At least they've not many elementists,* Qosku thought.

When the allotted two hours ended and no response had been given to their offer, the Asturions resumed their assault to find the blockade not only abandoned but rigged with dynal traps. Once through, they found a second barrier, less hastily built and full of pikes and more dynal traps; the first had only bought them time. A game of archers and crossbowmen began as the ranged attackers had the advantage of hiding in windows, around corners, and behind objects. Shield walls failed against elementist assaults. The warmachines remained forgotten outside.

Resuming his post as her personal guard, Qosku followed Leyta and her captains' small-scale strategizing. The Maolgon and Bokhor armies worked underground to find other spots to surface beneath the defending armies. But the defending armies weren't fighting back, they defended but never pressed an advantage, and the Chaos leaders were absent. A fact that puzzled everyone including Qosku. It made him think that the people were waiting for the Royal Chaos to come in and save their lost cause, but then where were they? They may have done well to start the rebellion but didn't appear too keen on sustaining it.

That night, as dusk turned to dark and the tense battle of patience wore on, Qosku was about to leave for his alcove when screams sounded from the rebellion side. Then a booming roar came, one familiar enough. The large winged devil had returned. Qosku saw the dark red beast flutter over the enemy territory but coming their way, spitting its acid breath and diving at people and devouring them. On the devil's back rode a human, as if commanding it.[48]

As he drew silent gratitude that it attacked their enemies, it turned toward them. He ran back to Leyta's command room as she emerged from the door. Soldiers, elementists, and archers ran everywhere. She spotted the devil then began barking out orders to take defensive positions in the windows of buildings. Other captains gave similar commands.

When she saw him standing next to her, she snapped, "Qosku! What are you doing here? You still have to go—"

The roar of the monster interrupted her as its shadow loomed nearer. "I'm not leaving you to this," he protested.

"Go now! That's an order," she shouted as she went back into her building. "I'm fine, we'll be fine. We just have to wait it out."

Refusing, he followed her as the winged devil, a wrath, arrived spraying its breath into the square. Once in the command room, enough people cloistered together that she didn't notice him slip in behind. But then he felt ridiculous. The room was packed with armed men and women. His standing there wouldn't protect her. He'd thought to try and resist the transformation. Given his experience with it and the waning moon, there might be a chance for his training to win out. But a nervousness reminded him that this was a long shot. A better chance might be to run to the rooftop of the building and hold it off first.

An idea took hold and he went, squeezing up the crowded stairs until he found the rooftop hatch in an empty room. Fear of losing himself to the beast had been replaced by appreciation for what it gave him, though he still trembled at the thought.

Ascending the building, he sought the animal inside himself and brought it out. The change began as he ascended and he released his armor and clothes to bring it on. The devil circled the town in the firelight, tearing it apart. He pushed hard for the change, to make himself as big and strong as he could, feeling confident in the progress he'd made with it. Once complete, he climbed out onto a buttress and challenged the devil with a roar. A slight spark of glee at being more cognizant of who he was, that he had a self and a history, and what he did the previous night gave him added purpose.

Not waiting, he barreled across rooftops to intercept the distracted fiend and rider. He came fast and they saw him at the last second. The rider, a man in cultish black garb, loosed an arrow, which Qosku ducked under in his charge. He leaped, crashing into the winged creature and locking with it in midair. Using his combat skills and his strength, Qosku wrestled the devil out of its aerial advantage. They flipped aside and the man fell off, landing on a rooftop.

He now got his first good look at it. A furry beast much like him, but with extra limbs on a lighter body. It wasn't without skill or capability, however, and managed to bring him from its side to the front using clawed arms and legs. They spun, the wrath trying to carry him upward, and he saw the true savagery of it. The real threat of the thing was not in its odious bat face of beady eyes or foaming snout of oversized fangs. Nor in its muscled arms with claws, or hook-ended tail, but in a second maw on its stomach, full of teeth and big enough to rip his head off. Putrid breath. The wings also served as a second pair of long clawed arms over the regular pair. These reached out and grabbed him, trying to pull him into the slobbering, fangorous mouth on its torso.

They tumbled through the evening sky, falling, city fires burning in the background. Arrows and bolts zipped past them. Nothing slowing their spite for each other.

They crashed into a rooftop, one already charred and broken from the fire bombings. As they smashed and rolled through smoldering wood, shattering everything in their path, Qosku grabbed the edge of a hole with one arm and threw the wrath at the wall with his other. Its claws raked him as it flew past and slammed into the wall, breaking through.

Standing up, he looked at his wounds. The cuts gradually began to seal up, slow and burning. He went to the hole in the wall but didn't see the wrath. As he turned, arms came around him and ripped him off the building. He fought the grip to avoid that fatal maw and got thrown down onto another rooftop. Shingles breaking beneath him, he slid and rolled back onto his paws. The wrath landed on the other end. The head jaws clenched and acid sprayed out at him, but he moved behind a chimney. The wrath broke a cross off its mount, bearing it as a weapon, then launched forward at him with a roar. He ducked under the cross, grabbed another cross from a different buttress, and they clashed. The wrath had every advantage. Bigger, stronger, faster even, and a more ferocious style. Outmatched.. Even shifting deeper into his primal fury, losing himself more to the transformation, only helped him keep speed. The crosses broke against each other and the two bore into each other with raw strength.

Qosku relied on his bigger arms to claw viciously at it while biting for its neck. But instead of returning blows, it barreled into him. They went over the roof, roiling through the air again, his focus turning to pushing away from that maw. He'd thought his bulk, skill, and ferocity sufficient to make up for the devil's advantages, but it matched, even surpassed, him on those as well.

They crashed into a pile of burning furniture on the street. He stood up, gaining renewed fury. The wrath rose from the flames as well. It beat its wings once, fanning the fires without getting burned. Qosku stood tall and roared, and several soldiers behind yelled. An arrow stuck in his shoulder and he turned to roar at them as more arrows flew past at the devil. He dashed at them, tossing some aside and nearly hitting two that looked familiar to him. He halted not, for they still interrupted his challenge. The wingbeats of the wrath brought his attention back as the devil shot into the air, then came back down on top of him in a savage crash. They tussled down the street, nearly rolling over more people. Pushing off of a building, he slammed the wrath into a wall, then climbed up, dragging the devil by the tail. But the devil flew up and yanked him over the rooftop toward its claws. Arrows whizzed at them and he rolled away from the wrath just as six people appeared on the roof, seemingly out of nowhere, with dark brown skin and smells of forest. At first, he felt grateful for the distraction, but anger took him over as they stole in to surround *his* enemy.

After Syago had stormed off, the Roah'riik had quickly packed up their belongings to follow. With Tek'ouk's inability to journey quickly, they were unable to keep up. Then they saw the wrath, with a rider astride it, flying toward Mantlgrym. Lil'iek made the decision that the devil took priority over Syago's idiocy. She regretted it but had to be realistic in war. To help them reach Mantlgrym sooner, they used quervosk skulls to control a murder as it flew by, and rode two birds to a man in an extremely risky move. Within an hour they landed atop the wall and immediately spied the winged beast and a werebeast beating each other into the roof, destroying parts of the city in the contest. She remembered its gory assault on their camp and fought the pit in her stomach.

The Roah'riik entered with flying arrows, leaving Tek'ouk on an adjacent building to cover with dyne while Mour'ikik got close with Ravenger. The group closed in around the two beasts, Lil'iek behind Mour'ikik, but the wrath's hooktail whipped back at the man, yanking him down. Lil'iek ran up to pull the tail off him and grabbed the hellknife from Mour'ikik's hand. In that brief moment, the hellknife exacted its toll, connecting devil and woman together in mind, body, and soul and plunging their minds into a vast abyss. It ravenously stole from the devil, physical, mental, and spiritual health, and fed it into Lil'iek's mortal frame as she gritted her teeth against the flow. The blade cut the fiend with an unhealable wound, draining its spirit while filling Lil'iek with a darkly addictive energy that she fought to resist. Her vision darkened into bloody hues, and savage hunger and spite filled her being. She began to fall into this new state, then realized the devil was pulling her in, changing her. She put up memories of family and friends, of holding her children and eating good food with her sister and making love to Fal'iek. The memories wavered before the power of the weapon and the old fiend, while her body accepted the energy hungrily, leeching it to heal her wounds.

Covered in blood, the devil howled, throwing her back and breaking the connection. Before she could fully recover from her shock, it threw the werebeast at her, but she rolled to the side of it, Ravenger still in hand. Not quick enough, the slavering devil was on her, picking her up. *Wormrot, it's fast!* She barely got one leg up to brace against its chest, keeping herself from the ravenous maw that opened on its stomach. The bat face was hideous enough, but the size of the abdominal maw told her what had happened to Boam'ikik at the camp, it'd eaten him whole.

With her whole body burning and losing strength, she tried to get out from its hold, but its inner arms were too tight around her and the wing-arms kept the rest at bay. Plunging Ravenger into the claw that held her, she felt herself in the bottom of a great black sea, cold and endless except for a flame feeding her body. For a moment, she couldn't even remember how she'd got there but something at the back of her mind said it was urgent to get out as soon as possible. She held something in her hand, a knife, and could hear an animal, but couldn't see it. As she began to numb, she pulled on the blade. They jolted out of the shared meld, and she howled before she made another thrust. Again the meld, again the shock of it being broken off. She was drooling profusely while her companions' attacks availed nothing.

Hook lines from the men latched onto the wrath, pulling its wings and arms, but still the arms edged her closer into salivating death. It wasn't until the werebeast plowed through the Roah'riik and grabbed the wings that she was released. The weremonster thew it back, trying to tear the wings off. But the wrath shook free, roared, and choked up some acid at them as it turned to claw the other beast. They scattered and two vineropes withered under the spit. It cut one more and came at them, bleeding and snarling. *Just end it, please Fathers and Mothers. It's taking too much.*

From the roof of a nearby building, the cultist rider shot an arrow at her. She pivoted, narrowly avoiding the arrow. She called for cover and got it as two Roah'riik fired back at the cultist, killing him. Lil'iek ran around the werebeast and slashed the back of the wrath's leg with Ravenger, a brief prick, but still drawing her and the devil together with a vicious fury. Her eyes rolled back in her head and mouth foamed, mind dark, until someone pulled her arm away. She snapped out of it and rolled back from its claw when, to her horror, it pulled one of the lines hard enough to yank Yarok flailing in headfirst.

Reacting quickly, Lil'iek stabbed it hard just as her companion entered the grinder of stomach teeth, followed by a fountain of blood that obscured their view and filled her mind; his gore thick on her tongue. She tasted Yarok's death. The indescribable horror in her brought up bile from her stomach.

The wounded werebeast reared up and slammed the wrath down, pummeling and raking it. Lil'iek snapped out of her daze and stood, yelling for Yarok, weeping.

Then the savagery of the werebeast turned her to wonderment and confusion and she called out. The werebeast smacked her backward with a snarl, causing her to tumble while the others moved to defend her. The werebeast roared at them too but their counter-attack faltered as it turned to finish off the wrath by biting its throat out. It roared at the moon and limped away in the burning night, covered in blood.

Lil'iek stood on shaking knees, looking over the monster's destruction. Qul'toq took Ravenger from her trembling hand to dismantle the wrath devil. She couldn't help but recall that this was her hunt. She'd demanded and directed it, so these losses were her fault. She accepted the support of the men as they led her down to get care for the wounds all over her body. They took her down to the streets where Tek'ouk hobbled up to her with a great hug and kiss. "I'm sorry for another loss of your men," she said, exhausted of all but sorrow.

That's not even what we came out to fight.

CHAPTER FOURTEEN
THE TAKING

Based on *Leyta's Journals*, cc bastica 187;
Writings of Qosku, cc bastica 180;
The Dark Fortress of Mephorash, cc bastica xx;

27th–30th of Novumbre, 246

"Prepare to move on the rebels," Leyta said to the crowded room of fearful soldiers. Sounds of thunderous violence echoed outside, confirmation the two monsters still battled. Virgow, she regretted, had holed up in a different building, so she would be on her own here. When she finished rebandaging her leg wound, she stood up. "The fight above will prove the distraction we need."[49]

"You want us to go out in that? At night?" Fernandeon said. "That's suicide."

"We can't go out there!" Milgalic de Culon, a friend of Fernandeon's, said. "You can't make us do that."

"We're no safer huddled in here than we are out there. Fear is the worst defense." The victory of her leading them into the city hadn't won them over, and she'd grown weary of their constant pushing against her orders. She'd wanted Fernandeon and his friends to stay behind at Cantlgrym, but the thought of leaving them there to wreak dissent without her present bore even worse. And they were good fighters. She looked each of them in the eye. "If you can't follow a simple order, then you can pack your way back home. Understood?"

"If you can't accept feedback, maybe you shouldn't lead," Fernandeon snapped.

---

49 It's going to hurt

More yelling crescendoed, and she grew frustrated at all the side-talking. She snapped her scepter at the table, throwing her wrath into the already angry wood. It burst into flames and everyone immediately quieted, staring at her in surprise. Truthfully, she'd surprised herself, and maybe not in a good way. Using dyne was rigidly reserved for enemies or special projects.[50] The flames raged until she swung her scepter again and the fires snuffed. Smoke filled the silent room, and people rushed to open the shuttered windows. Insubordination or desertion would normally be punished by whipping or execution, but these were children of wealthy families she couldn't afford to offend just yet. *Maybe extra cleaning duties later on.*

To break the frightened silence, she said, "Don't be weak. We can do this." She raised her scepter and walked to the door. "With me. Any coward that disobeys will never see the castle again."

With one last look at Fernandeon and his friends, she went outside. The battalion followed, the rest coming out of the other buildings. Roars and sounds of wood breaking resounded somewhere in the distance of the burning city. She signaled for the battalion to move in the nighttime shadows under the overhang jetties of the buildings toward the barriers. They shifted over to another street, one wider, where the blockade was weaker and the sounds of clashing rang closer.

Leyta felt fear. Not only did she fear for her soldiers in this most crucial moment, the only opportunity in days to break the stalemate, but she also feared for Qosku, who she knew to be the beast fighting the wrath devil. The brutal echoes of the fight only increased her worries.

But fear was the enemy of a dynast, the most uncontrollable sentiment. Taking a deep breath, she began dismissing her fears. She took heart in the sight of other armies, led by Counts Cantarchar and Toriacus, also moving forward toward the barrier. She brought to bear other negative emotions, tapping into her hate, that dark well she kept hidden. She hated this rebellion and its leaders.

When they were in range of the barrier, she motioned with her scepter to the dynasts who'd followed. They brought fire down on the wall of wooden furniture. Shouts called out from above, and she had to take cover behind her shield-bearing soldiers as arrows fell. She stepped out briefly to

---

further the fires and blow some of them apart. Dynasts behind her threw attacks at the rooftop crossbowmen, setting fire to the wooden buildings.

Then the two beasts crashed into the blazing barrier in front of her battalion. She recognized Qosku tumbling out of the fire as the wrath tore at the flaming remains of the blockade to get at him. *Hells, it's fast. And hideous.*

As the two monsters beat into each other, her soldiers shouted and began firing bolts. She called for them to focus on the wrath and avoid the werebeast but was too late. One struck Qosku, who turned with a roar and threw himself at them, pushing them aside and back, tossing two. Qosku then reared on her and Andras. They both froze, hearts stopping. Qosku hesitated as well but the wrath charged into the distracted werebeast and they blew past her battalion, bowling some over. The two beasts rolled down an alley, hitting each other before rising to the rooftops.

Leyta recovered quickly and ordered her men to move through the opening created in the barrier as enemy crossbowmen focused on the more frightening combatants. The other battalions also used the opportunity to press forward, storming the buildings and taking prisoners as they went. The monstrous fighting shifted back to the top of the city where it disappeared from view. The siege filled the city and took claim of it with surprisingly little resistance. The fighting and fires were soon quelled into a desolate peace, it was done. The allies had recaptured the city from the rebellion.

The following morning they learned why taking the rest of the city had been so free of fighting. The citizen leaders of the opposition had fled with the Royal Chaos. With all of the armies drawing into the city, they'd left the outside unguarded. All the rebellion heads had to do was slip out and flee.

This plan preoccupied Leyta's mind as she and her captains, along with the counts, searched what had been the enemy buildings for information. Scouts sent to follow the rebellion had not returned. What part of the enemy likely had escaped was a fraction of what it had been, broken and dispirited. The rest of her army helped restabilize the rest of the city against a surge of crime, rebuilding and administering supplies while investigating the remaining population for any traitors worthy of prosecution. A number of former rebels guided her through areas thought to be the residence of the Royal Chaos leaders during the occupation. She moved quickly, wanting to get back to Cantlgrym but feeling a need to be there for the next direction of the conflict.

The enemy survived, diminished and hiding, but still a threat. The Royal Chaos hadn't used any of the main government manors or forts as expected, not only because they were mostly burnt down in the riots but also because such places were a symbol to be hated. The churches and market areas also got ruled out, though Knave's chapel had been a horrific find it provided no leads. The hasty if planned retreat meant that the group was likely to have left some things behind. Some clues to guide the next stage of the war while the army scouts sought to track the location of the rebellion. They spent most of the day searching buildings and found nothing substantial other than remnants of a disordered society living in fear. She had to hand it to the group, though: everyone had food and shelter as well as protection from their self-created threats. Werebeast curses, plague, and criminality wrought havoc but they were never abandoned to it according to everyone she'd talked to. *But what was all this for then? What were they trying to achieve?*

Later that night she found what she'd sought. She'd been in the old garment shop Qosku had entered, where the Chaos leadership had been hiding most, surveying a city map with Andras, Alfonsor, Toriacus, Cantarchar, Catalana, Virgow, and others of lesser rank, in addition to some townsmen. The allies were marking on the city map where the enemy leaders had hid, as well as a couple sites in which the Cult of the Rippers, as they'd come to be called, had left some kind of ritual sacrifice. A body gored open on the cathedral steps, and another inside a smaller chapel. Both had been messy, sloppy in contrast to the precise, even artistic works of their dead masters the Razhod. At least these cultists remained amateurs in their butchery and subterfuge.

Weary and feeling that she might leave the following morning if the conflicts didn't end soon, she felt relief when a soldier called for her. She followed him to what appeared to be a roughly constructed study and workshop, with books and old maps of the outside strewn about in abandonment from the rebellion. It was to these that her soldier pointed.

She walked up, confused. "What's significant about these? They're just old tales and myths. The maps are really out of date."

"Yes, but look at the topics," he said. She recognized him as Emeric, a young boy of Voium squiring at Cantlgrym, with an interest in history and mythology. "The books are all about the origins of dyne. Religious texts here, Saints Casilda, Columbar, and Nubeiru; mythological works there, the epic maps of Lustmord de Gallowbraid and some Diabulus in Morda' Stigmata; and Vega's historical investigations over there.

"But wait," he said, holding up a finger to silence the annoyed objections from her and the other leaders who'd followed her. "The maps. All of these focus on the possible locations of the Tiakanawu Temple, portrayed in most of these books as either related to or directly being part of the dynal history. It's not marked, but the books do that for us."

Alfonsor and the others scoffed and went back downstairs, but Leyta waited. She felt a chill looking at the maps, not because she understood what he was getting at, but because the cult had taken, among other things, similar maps from Cantlgrym. In fact these were alternate copies, the originals mostly lost. One by Lustmord about the temple's stores of gold and powerful relics; gemstones that granted wishes and a scepter that gave dynasts unlimited power. If there ever had been such a temple, she doubted that relics as fantastically powerful as the various works described could ever be lost, but gold maybe. Emeric rambled on about the significance of his discovery, but she didn't pay attention, her mind swimming with what this could mean. Both her enemies chased after a lost myth, a treasure hunt? It sounded ridiculous, but she couldn't deny the correlation. At the very least, it was a clue to something about them.

"Gather it. All of it. We're going back to Cantlgrym immediately," she said abruptly. Her two men in the room looked stunned, then with a glare from her snapped into motion, collecting it all into stacks. She descended back to the table where the other generals stood talking.

"We're heading back to Cantlgrym. We'll regroup with you when more information is to be had."

They nodded, hardly considering her until her soldiers followed with the books and maps. Then they laughed. Virgow watched her steadily, probably not liking what she was doing. Countess Catalana quipped, "Are you going off on a little quest? A grand treasure hunt?"

"The maps and books resemble the items taken by the Razhod. A potential connection between the two enemy forces warrants investigation."

"So long as you share the spoils with us," Cantarchar sneered. She ignored him.

"Pushing your luck, Count," Virgow growled beside the man, who snapped his grin away. "Someone needs to remind you how diplomacy works."

"Castellan Leyta," Alfonsor began sternly. "This is most unwise. The hobby of some rebel performers is hardly even a lead. I'd thought better of you."

"Well, when you turn up a better lead warranting my attention, I'll start thinking better of you." She smiled sweetly.

"You don't mean to leave now?" Toriacus asked, gesturing to the darkness outside. "The lifeless and devils..."

She slowed, giving away her lack of foresight. *Good point.* "First thing tomorrow morning, of course." She left the building resolved and ready, with Virgow following behind.

"Too rash?" she asked, fully expecting more criticism—the only thing she'd received from him this entire campaign, the only thing she'd ever heard come out of the veteran's mouth.

"No, you're standing ground, being independent, being bold. Only way to gain respect from them," he grunted as he descended the stairs behind her on his cane. She slowed her normally fast pace and hid a smile. That was the closest thing to a compliment she'd ever gotten from him. And he went on, "Been thinking about telling you we ought to be going anyway. Tired of coddling their pampered arses just to get a little cooperation out of 'em. The only negotiation they respond to is money and flattery. They can have the rest of the war, good riddance."

Qosku'd recovered well in the two days since the slaying of the wrath, having taken most wounds as a werebeast, but was still vulnerable and in need of treatment. Lüg and Katti, with Andras's help, had bandaged him and snuck him down inside an abandoned home, where they made a makeshift infirmary. The small room was reserved only for him and the wounded Roah'riik, who now knew his secret. Transforming again that following night had done wonders for his healing, which seemed faster than he could achieve in prayer. One of many benefits he was discovering.

"Qosku," Lil'iek mumbled, sitting up in an adjacent bed, Mour'ikik sleeping on another. She'd been asleep the entire time that Qosku had seen through his waking spells. Lil'iek had fared much worse, surviving the fight only because of the hellknife's healing. She would carry many scars after this. Katti and that apothecary boy, Lüg, had been seeing to Lil'iek's wounds constantly, more worried about fiendish infections than anything else. Uncertainty about her survival had faded the previous night as her fever broke, giving relief to Tek'ouk in his unending vigilance, though he was absent now. Lil'iek winced and shifted to a sideways position that allowed her to look at Qosku and ask, "How long?"

"Two days," he replied. "And we leave this morning soon."

"That we do," Tek'ouk said as he limped into the room. She beamed at him, clearly wishing to shout and embrace him if not for her condition. "Of course you'd wake up the one moment I step away. But I *have* been watching and waiting."

"I'll take your word for it," she said as he stiffly dropped down next to her. They embraced and kissed, and Qosku watched not with a blush but jealousy inside. Seeing them do this awakened that old, buried yearning. It made him itch for his beast form, which had fixed his wrong-body problem he'd come to realize. When he was a beast, he never dwelt on what gender he was or who he loved. Lil'iek looked at her love. "We can't continue the hunt like this. We've lost too much and have too many wounded, and still haven't any of the heads we sought."

"We'd been thinking the same," Tek'ouk said, "to return to Quoak and recover—" They switched to Kimoc, and Qosku couldn't understand them. Qosku tried to look away, even lay down with the pillow plugging his ears. He yearned for a drink. Anything to block out the pain. Then Tek'ouk stood to leave and turned to Qosku. "Qosku, nice to see you alive and well, or mostly well."

"You also, Tek'ouk," Qosku said more stiffly than he'd intended. "I leave with you today?"

"No, you leave with me," Katti said as she entered with Lüg behind. Tek'ouk nodded at them, then hobbled out. "But you, Lil'iek, need to stay here a little longer. Mour'ikik also needs more time to recover. I would have Qosku stay too, a bumpy ride isn't good for those wounds, but with your other... condition, we can't."

Lüg saw to Lil'iek's bandages while Katti came to Qosku and asked, "Your healing is impressive; I don't think you even need a prayer for it today. How fare your transformations?"

"Better," he said, more enthusiastically than he intended. "I mean I'm still... it's hard. And I don't know what will happen during the, er... growing moon."

"You seem pleased by it?" Her voice sounded amused, but her expression looked concerned.

"It has fight advantages. And when in that way, all my other problems vanish." The half-lie didn't fall easy from his mouth, and he blushed speaking it. He noticed Lil'iek looking at him curiously while Lüg finished re-wrapping, the boy's face deep in concentration. *Stones but he is handsome.*

"Well don't let it take over. You did attack us during the fight, but it wasn't serious." She went over to Lil'iek as Lüg picked up his things and came to Qosku.

He promptly pulled off Qosku's blanket, leaving scant bandages as his only covering. Self-conscious, and uncomfortable around Lüg's treatments, Qosku blushed furiously.

Lüg took no notice, taking off his new bandages, cleaning his wounds, then putting on new ones quickly and efficiently. Though not so quick that Qosku didn't feel his warm hands tantalize his skin. Feeling embarrassed, Qosku struggled to look away and realized that Lil'iek, also mostly naked, was watching him past Katti's praying. His blush deepened and he looked the other way to hide it, fidgeting with his hands. Katti and Lüg finished at about the same time, and with a bid for Qosku to get ready to leave soon, they left.

Qosku's face started to cool though he still felt Lil'iek's eyes on him, causing him to blush again. He couldn't hide it, so he turned to face her, trying to act composed. She said, "You're different, aren't you? You're what they call a 'twist'? You're attracted to other boys, not girls."

Qosku looked down. He said "yes" though no sound came out, so he nodded. His hands trembled slightly. Before he could stop himself, more words spilled out. "I'm more. I like boys and inside, I'm girl, not boy. I don't know why, but it like this all my life, but mostly one year ago when I was in Chuqi'kirau with my twin sister. But now with her gone, I think my yanantin balance is gone and my female inside come back. I feel I have wrong body." *At least I'm not crying, not yet.* He looked back to see Lil'iek still appraising him.

"Interesting," she said quietly. "I've heard of people like you but never known one myself. I can't imagine how hard that must be. To live in a world like this, where your body determines everything."

"I—I don't want to be... that." Qosku's fingers toyed with the blanket, twisting it around and around. "I only want to focus on my training and finding my lost parents... and beating my enemies... and being good to my friends. And controlling my beast, it relieves me from the feelings. And being, er, twisted, is really hard. I mean to say is hard either way, but this way I don't have to hide what I'm doing."

"No. You just have to hide who you are. You should do what is natural for you. Live it."

Anger welled up inside him. "Stop telling me what to do! Everyone's always telling me what I should be. Be the normal, kiss the girls, or go be a twisted sex boy. Or go make moneys from it. Or don't be werebeast. I do what I want, not you!"

If Lil'iek was surprised or hurt by the sudden vehemence, she didn't show it, but gently nodded, still appraising him. Qosku saw this and softened his anger but remained resolute. "I—please don't tell others. Especially Syago, please."

"Of course," she said. Her calm and intense face showing a hint of gentleness. "Your identity belongs to you. You have nothing to fear from me." The motherly gleam of her face hurt, not just as a reminder of the mother he didn't have, but also as the kind of incredible woman he'd wished to be.

She said after a moment's pause, "Besides, we don't know where Syago is anyways." Leyta entered the room just as Lil'iek said it.

"Do you have any idea where he might've gone?" Leyta asked.

Lil'iek shook her head. "He's a capable warrior and hunter. He was heading in the direction of Tolgrym, so maybe he's still there. But him succeeding, finding the devils alone, is what I fear most."

"You've already killed two, truth?" Qosku asked. He thought of his own time traversing from his home in the outerwild until he landed at Cantlgrym. Long, lonely, and brutal his sojourn into self-exile had been. "Syago good enough. Syago do anything good."

"I hope you're right," Leyta said, genuine worry in her face. "We'll not hear of our friend for some time and can't wait here in any case. If you're ready, Qosku, we're leaving early in the morning. Lil'iek, I'll leave you to your men. And terribly sorry for your losses, Ka'shuar'iik, Yarok, Reed'luk, and Bo-er, Bo—"

"Boam'ikik," Lil'iek finished for her.

She nodded, blushing. "—and Boam'ikik did the Asturion peoples a great service. All of you have."

Lil'iek simply nodded in agreement. After Leyta left, Qosku collected his things, thinking on Lil'iek's reception of his secret. His experiences with this had never ended well. Perhaps in Lil'iek there was hope. Perhaps things would be different here. She'd pushed, but was mostly friendly. Better, she'd promised to keep his secret safe.

The last time he'd told someone his secret, it had not been safe. His best friend, Akualchac—who he had foolishly told his secret to, hoping Akualchac felt the same way—had responded with rejection. Rejection and a look of disgust so painful it would never heal, but it didn't stop there. He began telling everyone Qosku was bent crooked and perverted. Akualchac got laughs from them, but it really turned bad when Akualchac told his older brother, Alkapac. The jokes got meaner, bullying more brutal. The Unaka leaders turned a blind eye until Qosku began to fear for his life. He took Chaska and fled their home in Chuqi'kirau to Izquchaka where he'd had to flee again, though for different reasons. The second flight he'd left his twin sister behind, betrayed to marry an Asturion taskmaster, going out into the forbidden outerwild that they'd promised would eat him up. He braved the outerwild in search of something more. In search of escape and new beginnings from the memories and evil disease inside him. If not a way to cleanse it out of him, then a way to subdue it.

He now found that in the curse of the werebeast; the raw passion, hunger, and violence of it haunted him when uncontrolled, but now that he was better able to direct them away from innocents, he could enjoy it as a reprieve from the bigger curse of his mind-body problem, or as he'd come to think of it: the werewoman. The werebeast in contrast made him more *man*. That night, he studied and practiced more poetry.

Pain is my maker
And darkness my covering
Oft hated of heaven
Yet welcome in heaviest hell
Nurtured of Nightfall
And displeased of Day's light
From my blackest life
I am crowned rebel with name
Wrought-iron made will

Cast-iron forged of fury
Outcast yet survived
Courts of the misunderstood
Solitude solace
Delighted by the deep and dark
Now come, spit your spite
Tiny, it toucheth me not
For I am power
Thus is the metal in me
Unaffected by such as thee[51]

CHAPTER FIFTEEN

WELCOME TO INFERNO

Based on *Annals of Syago,* cc bastica 169;
Scars of the Martyrs, cc bastica 1029;
The Dark Fortress of Mephorash, cc bastica xx;

27th–28th of Novumbre, 246

Weary and scared out of his mind, Syago approached Tolgrym on foot through Thornwood's main road. Regrets filled him about leaving the group and his unending argument with Alexandre, who remained obscure about its own involvement in the darker side of Syago's family legacy and thought him overreacting. The soulsword had a vague idea that one fiend was north of them and another went by Thornwood, but after the hellhunters had abandoned following him to chase the wrath, Syago got confused by conflicting tracks. He thought Tolgrym would be a good post to rest and gather his wits, plus the urge to return to Grandfather Goidiberic nagged at him. He hadn't planned on going back, but questions about his past burned into him, and he deeply needed to talk to someone else about it. Owls hooted ominously everywhere while malwolves and gurows stalked him, a single, easy prey. He'd known that it would be dangerous going on foot alone, but Fal'iek had often done it, and having slain the envy, he felt ready. A day and a half and he now neared Tolgrym as night descended. He picked up to a jog; he wouldn't survive nighttime, being exhausted, and suspected the present quiet was mostly due to the nearness of the creeping hour when all life hides from the lifeless.[52]

He ran the path through Thornwood, cresting a small hill as the last tinges of light began to fade, and noticed smoke rising above the

---

52 See *Lambogod the Aviator,* 3

bramblewood. Thick, dark smoke too big for chimneys. His pace quickened in fear, then quickened more when he finally caught sight of the small town. The walls, the homes—everything burned. He screamed and ran ahead, ignoring the ache in his side. He halted at the gatehouse, which hung slightly ajar, but not enough for him to slip in. He drew Alexandre to cut through but decided against it—they might need the doors. Instead he looked up at the walltop around the gate and gripped Alexandre nervously before swinging a sideways slash, going up. It lifted him, but his aim was off and he slammed into the gatehouse wall, kicking off it while trying again. This time he made it over, stumbling into his old village. Looking around, he saw no one. *Why aren't they putting the fires out?* Few elementists lived here, but they ought to be enough. He ran deeper in, heading to the town square through to his home.

The square was riddled with the bodies of townsfolk. In spite of the blood covering them, and the encroaching black smoke, he recognized each person. Somewhere in the distance screams echoed through the sound of the blaze. He saw figures hiding in shadows. *Why aren't they fighting the flames?*

Tears and sweat streamed his face, and fear for his grandfather and cousin moved him on to their cottage. Just as it came into view, his home collapsed in flame. He cried out in despair, but saw Goidiberic lying in front on the stone pathway with Elisabet in his arms. Syago yelled, or tried to, coughing instead. The smoke and heat were unbearable, but he had greater burdens. He ran through the haze until he reached them, cradling them both in his arms while trying to wake them.

Elisabet's face was covered in soot, but her eyes flickered open and she clutched his hand before fading back out.

Goidiberic coughed, and his eyes opened on Syago. Called Goia by the villagers, he said something indistinguishable. Syago wiped the blood clean from his head. "I'm here, Grandfather," he whispered and pulled out Alexandre to rest it on Goia's lap, hoping it would, could, heal him. "What happened?"

The fires answered for him. Across from him, they churned as a large reptilian beast emerged from the flames. Walking eight feet tall on six muscular legs, a forked tongue flickered from an eyeless head of hard scales and ridged spikes and horns. Spiked frills ran across its back all the way down to a spiny tail. Flames jetted out from its skin all along its body and head. A devil, a sloth. Syago clutched Alexandre and rose to stand over

Goia as it walked up to him, slow and calm, stopping a pace away. Before Syago could leap at it in rage, the flames to his left seemed to part, and a dark figure strode confidently between them toward Syago, sword loosely in hand. Kask, the cult leader and old friend turned traitor.

"I'd hoped to meet you here," Kask began as Syago yelled and ran at him with Alexandre raised. Kask calmly deflected Syago's swing, stepping aside. "Though I didn't think you were already on your way." Syago whirled, spinning Alexandre in a dazzling blur. Lacking a soulblade, Kask struggled to keep up but had enough skill and fortitude to keep Syago at bay. Syago pressed him hard, indignation fueling both him and Alexandre in a rare moment of unity, not giving the cultist a moment to fight back. Syago felt a moment of triumph as he gained an offensive edge against the older man's fading upkeep.

Seeming to realize he would soon lose this fight, Kask circled to put himself closer to the devil pet. Moving quickly, Syago attacked harder, forcing Kask to back away from the devil. He shouted something at Syago, but it was moments before Syago heard the repetition, "The sloth with kill them if you don't stop."

Syago slowed a moment to look back at Goia, lying beneath the maw of the sloth, Elisabet right next to him. His own mistake, Syago realized with inward fury. He lowered his weapon, and Kask walked up to Goia, grabbed him by his hair, and pulled the old man to his knees.

"Why are you doing this?!" Syago yelled. "What do you want from me?!"

"From you? I want it all!" Kask smiled. He held out his swordhand and gestured to the raging fires and clouds of smoke around them. "Welcome to hell! For you do I burn this town. I want you in our ranks, but for now I'll settle with a family heirloom. This old fool didn't know where it is, but I gathered that you have it. A relic called the Horn of Barthandeon, perhaps crafted into something else. Give it me and I walk away."

"What—all of *this* for a stupid relic?!" Syago asked. "Your master is dead. Forever. You can't even summon him, nor any of the greater spirits, nor any of their weapons. And you never will. Move on with your life and worship something else."

"The relic, Syago," Kask said, resting his blade on Goia.

"I have no idea what you're talking about," Syago yelled, shaking his head in genuine confusion. "Forget that foding Barthandeon—"

"Do NOT speak the Great Lord's name!" Kask snarled, yanking on Goia's head and bringing his sword closer to Goia's neck. Passion intensified in his eyes, nostrils flaring. "Not with your mouth. You could never hold a candle up to him. Now if the relic is nothing to you, tell me enough that I need not return for your family's heads."

Syago racked his brain for what Kask could be speaking of and settled on the only possibility he could think of. "I have one old brooch, I believe it's sitting in my room in Cantlgrym, in the barracks. Last bedroll in the left corner," Syago said. Ugly little thing was supposed to be from his father, but he rarely wore it. "So good luck getting it. It won't give you any of the old powers, won't bring your dead masters back, or I'd refuse. Now leave."

Kask smiled again and released Goia. "Farewell until next time." Kask swung atop the sloth, flames and spiked back parting for him to sit, and Syago noticed what appeared to be a helldagger at his beltside. The otherworlder obeyed his commands without issue. *So Kask is a helltamer as well?* Syago thought. The disciple flashed a smile. "Take good care of him."

The sloth snorted fire onto Goia before running off. Crying out, Syago ran to him and brushed out the flames on his clothes. His grandfather stirred then, coughing hard. "Syago," he rasped. "Don't let—don't let it consume you. Save Elisabet."

"Grandfather, don't speak," Syago said, bringing Elisabet up with one arm. "Just breathe. Alexandre will help me heal you and we'll get you out of here. You and Elisabet." Alexandre appeared to be trying but was moving slow, or insufficiently. Needing a place clear of the heat and smoke, Syago whipped his head around, seeking a clear space. Then he saw it. The graveyard was free from flame. Syago, himself coughing but more worried of their fragile state, managed to carry first Elisabet, then Goia into the tight area of tombstones. Tired, he set Goia down to rest and regain a better hold, but when he looked down, he realized it was too late; his grandfather, the man who'd raised him, had gone. He tried to wake him again but knew it was hopeless. He screamed into the night, and Elisabet, waking at the noise, clutched them both and wept.

Syago didn't remember falling asleep, but he woke in the gray of morning, flakes of ash covering them in gray, Elisabet, and nearby tombstones, the snow of death. They had tied Goia's body to the fence, to prevent it waking and attacking them. Darkemorg or no, he couldn't bring himself to hack it up so soon, not in front of Elisabet. He shook himself clean, untied his grandfather's body, then woke her.

Sounds of village activity told him they were gathering. Sorrow filled him, but he forced himself to the town square with Elisabet beside him, quietly clutching his hand. She wasn't speaking. A few people worked, salvaging, treating, rescuing, handing out supplies, and moving bodies into where the chapel had been. Barons Milgalic and Roberochester, and Bishopess Myrian, all covered in bandages, directed the work, Count Toriacus still being at Mantlgrym. They didn't seem surprised that he was there. Normally they would burn the bodies, but given the fire that had just taken place, it seemed an odd task to undertake. Inside the husk of the church lay a pile of bodies, most hacked up to prevent a rise during the night. He asked someone for help with Goia's body, carrying it over and dismantling it. He looked on that face one more time, a goodbye, before they lit the pile on fire. He knew the sentiments would do him no good. It was now time to move on. It made sense to burn his body in the church remains, given that they were destroyed anyway and Goidiberic was so close to this chapel, close to the children and other elders that Syago spotted in the pile. Fire consumed them slow, silent, and full.

No room for sentiments, no more of them.

Except anger.

It grew in him now, burning out all regret. He angered at himself, but even more so at these enemies who trampled on the innocent and infirm of an already miserable world. Alexandre didn't like this stream of thought, and Syago told it to fode off. No more negotiating, no more daydreaming of heroisms, only action. Aggressive and victorious, a way that forced the world to be just. A wild rage burned in him, and he wondered if maybe his father's tactics had been necessary after all, but part of his rage insisted that it had not. A strong but still heroic hand could still prevail. He would prove it.

CHAPTER SIXTEEN
THE BAW'KOOK

Based on *The Hunter's Parchments,* cc bastica 207;
The Nordvargor Testaments, cc bastica 900;

6th of Decimosk, 246

Some days after waking, Tek'ouk and the Roah'riik escorted Lil'iek out of Mantlgrym and back to Quoak. The healers had advised her to stay longer, and although she'd assured Tek'ouk that she was fine, he saw her wince as they moved. But he couldn't be more glad to get out of that cramped, filthy place. All of them were sick of it and convinced she'd heal better in the arms of Motherwood Yoaom. Despite his gratitude of being out, he also feared being back in Quoak. Would they make him leave or sacrifice his life? Would he even want to stay? It was hard to know with all the land in turmoil.[53] He'd heard of the fall of Tolgrym from its refugees, who were almost denied entrance into Mantlgrym. Tek'ouk had heard from some of them that Syago had been sighted in the village. Relief had filled him that the boy had not come to any harm. He'd wavered between blaming himself and leaving the boy to his own foolishness, but since Syago had at least made it to Tolgrym and then back to Mantlgrym, Tek'ouk could dust his hands of that fate.[54]

The group felt some disquiet at leaving without achieving their goal. They'd not slain a shadowman much less any of the Royal Chaos, and had only barely diminished the Asturion might. But all came to agree with him that returning was necessary to fully recover, if nothing else.

---

53 See *Treha Sektori de Gojirak,* 43

54 See *Hail Waylander Cruachan!,* 63

Moving slow, they entered Thornwood late in the day, a light fog creeping into the forest from the sea. Shortly thereafter, two Roah'riik scouts galloped up to them through the towering brambletrunks. The party halted as Guara'upik approached. His dual hook knives were in hand and his long hair settled out of its braids on his shoulders from his flight. He began anxiously, "Another army marches. West of here, a group of barbarian Baw'kook coming up the river.[55] They've camped and not seen us yet but are clearly heading out of the forest."

"How many?" Tek'ouk asked.

Guara'upik dismounted. The other mewil'ishyuuks were also growing restless so he spoke quickly, "Hard to tell without getting closer, I'd say at least sixty. I can't determine their target either."

Tek'ouk looked at those around him, all looking back at him in shock. He barely remembered the fearsome humanoid beasts, being young when they'd last raided here, and knew his other Roah'riik would recall even less. Kor'miir said before he could, "You shouldn't go, Tek. You can't ride fast and are in no condition to fight. Nor she. Send us."

His struggle was already beginning again. *Not even returned to the village and they would restrict me as more a liability than asset.* He shook his head and began in the direction of the army. *Could this be related to the other conflicts? The timing is too bad to be a coincidence.* Lil'iek's eyes met his; he saw concern but not denial. She would want to go herself as well. He spoke to her more than them. "Only to survey. Thirty years since they came last, I must see it myself. With me!"

Relying on the gracefulness of the mewil'ishyuuks to ease the challenge of riding with one leg, Tek'ouk rode off. In actuality, he just was tired of being holed up and useless. Guara'upik led them south, off the main trail, toward the sea, whence they'd come. Few things served to strengthen the shoddy alliance of the Asturion and Kimoc peoples, and the Baw'kook giants were among them. They knew of two main groupings. Those of the northern mountains and the seafarers of the southwest, of which these probably were. The monstrous raiders cared not for the different folk of the lands, pillaging them equally. They would care little for the growing

---

55 The Kimoc would sometimes say Fomorion, but more often their equivalent Baw'kook. See *Sol Sistere de Selbst* by Himetuks Himi'n

conflict at hand and may even see it as an opportunity, unless someone had invited them here.[56]

Guara'upik slowed ahead then dismounted. Lil'iek led ahead as she always did, so fearless, and the rest followed, beckoning to the mewil'ishyuuks to stay as they moved through the brush toward sounds of activity.

Tek'ouk didn't go far from his mount. They stopped behind some ferns and a fallen log and pulled off their bird skulls. Easily finding nearby forest birds, Tek'ouk saw dimly in his mind's eye and felt the quervosk's cruel spite for anything not a quervosk. Tek'ouk pressed it with curiosity, moved it closer to the camp, careful not to draw attention. They too had hellhunters and would know what watched them. He could see them, they had a barrier set up and tents being erected, but he couldn't tell how big or what manner of raiding party they were. Tek'ouk exited the bird as the others did. He whispered, "I need to get closer."

"Too risky," Kor'miir countered.

Tek'ouk knew what Kor'miir said was true, but he refused to be seen as useless.

"The risk is already there, greater if I don't leave with a better estimate of the threat. Can one of you go? Or just get closer, then maybe go around for a different angle?" They looked at each other, then advanced closer through the fern-filled brush. He'd hoped to go with them, having asked insincerely, but they moved too quick. He again looked in on the camp through some other birds. Indeed, it was hard to miss the beastmen. They were often referred to as giants due to their height and bulk almost doubling that of an average man. They held no favor for stealth once on land. Their violence and raucous interactions, as well as the clamor of their armaments, stirred the forest. But what they lacked in stealth, they made up with force of presence.

Checking his immediate surroundings to ensure no dangers approached, and spotting Lil'iek far ahead closer to the camp, he re-entered through the skull. He finally got a blackbird to perch over them, its own odd appetites now paling in comparison with the fear it felt. He stoked the appetites, focusing on what it could gain by looking down on them. In that way, he saw them for the first time since he was a young boy.

They weren't human, not really. As he'd read once when he'd briefly

---

56 *Ibid*, 77

studied in Cantlgrym, Fomorion had originally referred to one specific humanoid, the cyclopean ohancanu, far kin of Balgor. Now there were other groups under the canopy: the ukuku, ozor-like men from the mountains; the wookalar, tall swine men with tusks; and the goatmen, foxmen, wolfmen, birdmen, and so on were smaller in number. It was thought that they were the offspring of the eternals, or of fiends. But Tek'ouk's experience in Mantlgrym made him wonder if the werebeasts were not connected.

He saw one better than the others, at the center of camp. Nine feet tall with gray fur, the wookalar had twisting horns atop its head, tusks along its elongated, flat-nosed snout, and the same heartless eyes that marked so many other creatures of the wild. It wore only a leather loincloth and a skull necklace but held an axe in one hand and a spiked flail hooked on its hip.

It was having a heated conversation with a shorter but bulkier ukuku barbarian with thick dark fur and a pale, hairless snout of fangs. The two talked in a guttural language, pointing at a wooden post with a crossbeam. A smaller goatman walked up to it, clawed arms out, and the other two whipped him on the front and back. But the Baw'kook wasn't chained; he appeared willing. He laid down on the post, furry genitals hanging out, and the other two began hammering nails into the goatman's limbs, into the wood. The hard clang-splat-thunk of their work grated on even Tek'ouk's ears, further away and through the quervosk. The shocking submission to such ritual violence was made more chilling by how the entire camp gathered around and roared and cawed and bleated in celebration as the goatman was raised up. Bleeding all over in the center of their sanctified camp.

As the monsters bowed in worship, a wolfman pointed upwards, right at Tek'ouk, or at the blackbird whose eyes he was using. An ohancanu cyclops threw a stone right into Tek'ouk's vision. The shock of the blackout, of being ripped from a killed connection, left him dazed and puking behind the log. He counted himself fortunate it hadn't taken his mind with it.

"Don't make a sound," a voice whispered in his ear. Feeling a metal blade against his throat, Tek'ouk froze, only his eyes moving as he took in the surroundings. A cultist dressed in black crouched behind him. A serpentine shadow creature, its star-pricked eyes watching him, slithered past soundlessly through the underbrush and toward the camp.

We finally catch up to our primary targets and we can't fight them because there's a golking giant army nearby. Well he's not getting away from me!

Brush snapped. A wookalar dragged a carcass through the forest, headed right for them. It must've come from the camp. Tek'ouk looked into the distance, searching for his men. Through the dense forest, he found them. Lil'iek's eyes were fixed on him as the cultist behind him cursed, releasing his hold. Tek'ouk took the opportunity and grabbed the man's knife arm, rolling with him under a rotting log. The Baw'kook continued in their direction. The cultist looked surprised at such a maneuver from a cripple, and Tek'ouk smirked, reaching for his own knife. *What is he doing here in the first place?*

The disciple smiled and punched out with his knife. Tek'ouk snapped his arm, pinning the man's knife hand against the log above them. They tensed as the snorting and grunting of the giant neared, smelling awful, then passed by. The steps halted and the wet cracking of a carcass being skewered on a post reached Tek'ouk's ears. He breathed a sigh of relief, resuming his struggle with the disciple beneath the log and ferns the disciple who brought the knife forward.

Tek'ouk twitched his hand and Ravenger's tip nicked the disciple, the sinister link pulling them both in. From that tiny breach of skin, the nightmare edge sapped the cultist's strength and gave it to Tek'ouk. Being bonded to that fervently devoted mind, one pledged to an eternity of servitude to beings he'd never seen, racked Tek'ouk with pity. But the link also provided opportunity for information, a trick he'd used before. The Cult of the Rippers was searching for something old. This one was here as a spy, believing the barbarians to be related to the Royal Chaos.

Before he could learn more, the connection broke. They both gasped for breath. The disciple was gaunt and white as snow, coughing. Something big had moved the log, and caused Ravenger to shift from the cultist's wrist.

The wookalar, snorting, moved it again and exposed the man's leg. It grabbed, tearing him out of the ditch and leaving Tek'ouk huddled in paralyzed fear about being discovered and dismembered or eaten. But it did not grab him, perhaps he'd remained hidden. After a tear, a crack, a splatter, the man's body fell on him. Blood showered all around. The wookalar snorted and gave a triumphal squeal.

Lil'iek watched the silhouette of her husband fumble with the cultist beneath the log, praying for him, reminding herself to trust that capable man. Going to him would only put her in open view. Then she saw the shadow creature slither through the ferns toward the Baw'kook camp. She snapped her axe at it, but it zipped around the attack. She thumped it again, hitting this time and pinning it. Careful of the noise she made, she held the creature down but it slipped out, shuddering as it lost a piece of itself.

Before she could reclaim it, it darted away into the camp. She huffed in frustration, torn between going after it and staying hidden. But her options ran out when she realized a wolfman stood over her, looking right down at her, its nostrils flaring. With a yell, she snapped her axe at its belly, but its claw caught her arm. She twisted and tried to bring her other axe up, but it grabbed that arm too as another wolfman punched her in the gut, doubling her over. Wildly, she looked around for the Roah'riik, seeing that they'd stayed safely hidden from the wolfmen. All except Mour'ikik, who was held by a wolfman nearby. She assumed he'd tried to come to her aid and was caught in the process.

With a glare from one of the wolfmen, a message that clearly said "don't resist," she was suddenly released and Mour'ikik was brought to her side. Three wolfmen surrounded them, taking the weapons and skulls from their persons. The first, who had the most scars beneath his dark fur, gestured for her to go into the camp.

As she entered the enemy barbarian camp, she shrank. The giants towered over her and even the wolfmen too, being bigger than her but still the smaller of the Baw'kook. They drew her up before the horrific crucifixion of the goatman whose bloody, hairy body still hung. The old wolfman went to a priestly deerman, sitting cross-legged in a cloth mantle, and spoke to him in a growling tongue she couldn't begin to understand.

The wolfman then pointed at at a log on the ground for her and Mour'ikik to sit on.

They did so, and the antlered one spoke in a lighter tone of the same language, its lithe arms making grand gestures.

She eyed possible escape routes; now that she was in the camp they'd given her a little more space. There was a cyclops to her left, an ukuku to her right, a wookalar behind her. She could dive between the wookalar's legs, but it'd be tight and an even closer chase. She only met his eyes.

Finally the deerman pointed at her, then out of the camp. She and Mour'ikik both nodded and stood. But the deerman made a low disapproving sound, and a thick hand fell on Mour'ikik's shoulder.

He shrugged off the wookalar's claw, but it looked more feeble than tough. Giant monsters around them laughed great hoots, howls, snorts, and grunts. Lil'iek searched for an opening or weapon to bear up. But for once she felt so small and out of options, out of fire inside with which to fight. *What of my husband and companions? Where are they?*

A fire popped above their heads and they turned to Tek'ouk'iek, who stood with the other Roah'riik just outside the camp, staring down the other wolfmen who'd stayed to guard. The rest of the giants laughed at them too, training their own arrows, much larger, on the Kimoc.

The wolfman shoved her forward as it barked, dismissing her mockingly. She hesitated between the groups, looking back at Mour'ikik, whose worried eyes gave her pause. But her fear was great too. The wolfmen herded her out to her beloved.

"Send him out too or incur the wrath of all Kimoc of the forest," Tek'ouk'iek said.

The deerman walked forward, holding up a wooden cross. Not an Asturion one with a circle around it or two letters hanging from the sides, just a cross held high. An owlman hooted at them several times like a chant, which made them uneasy, as if a spell was being cast.

She looked back at Mour'ikik, lifelong friend and companion. So far away from each other, so deep in their errors with no way out. She mouthed a promise to him. She knew they'd find a way to rescue him, if he didn't free himself first. They nodded and backed off, disappearing into the forest. Leaving him alone, tiny, among giants.

CHAPTER SEVENTEEN
BECOMING DEVILS

Based on *Annals of Syago* cc bastica 191; *Scars of the Martyrs*, cc bastica 1036;
The Nordvargor Testaments, cc bastica 906;
The Dark Fortress of Mephorash, cc bastica x;

unknown day, 246

Syago walked with Elisabet through the torn streets of Mantlgrym, grateful for its brokenness. It frustrated him that he'd just missed Leyta and the Cantlgrym group, and that nobody from Tolgrym would care for Elisabet, who was now mute and completely orphaned. It had even resulted in a shouting match with his own liege lord over it. And he couldn't care for her. She needed a warm relative to coddle her, not his own increasingly aloof and irritable self as he quested for revenge. *Of what use is swearing to a liege lord if they can just ignore their end of it? Count Toriacus and the barons could've fallen and we'd have fared little different. Maybe we are better off without them after all.*[57]

Around them people began the long process of rebuilding, sorting out any remaining disputes of property and damages. He took Elisabet's hand in his, only to withdraw it later. He would take her to her sister, Eliana, who he needed to check on regardless. Things had not ended well on the last visit and it could only have gotten worse after he'd stolen medicine from her wealthy husband.

Their manor was as broken and desolate as anything else, but not abandoned. What surprised him was the lack of hired hands repairing it. Even their serving lady, Slania, was not there anymore, only Eliana cleaning the yard and Theordoric boarding up broken windows. Eliana's hands flew to her mouth

---

57 See *Sol Sistere de Selbst* by Himetuks Himi'n

when she saw them, then she embraced Elisabet. "Oh, sister! I've missed you. I'm so glad to see you made it out of that illness alive. What's wrong, Syago?"

"She's mute, and Grandfather is dead." He wasn't sure how his words were supposed to sound coming out. Angry? Sad? He hadn't expected flat. She gasped but didn't seem as surprised as she should have.

"I'm so sorry," she said, embracing Elisabet again. "How—what happened there?"

"Let's go in and talk," he said, walking up to the door. Theordoric stopped his work. Syago met his eyes and entered without comment.

There was still furniture, though the nicest were gone. The front room was dusty and dark save the windows. Theordoric came in after Eliana's words with him outside.

As they sat, both eyes settled on Alexandre. Eliana began overly pleasant, "I heard you'd finally been chosen. Congratulations!"

He looked at Elisabet and back at them. "One of the cultists, formerly a vagrant named Kask who'd roamed here in Mantlgrym, took a demon to burn the village down. Even with Alexandre, I was not enough to stop it."

Shock filled their eyes. He resumed, "I need you to take in Elisabet while I hunt them down."

After a pause, Theordoric cleared his throat. "It would be our pleasure except we barely have food for ourselves—"

"We'll do it," Eliana interrupted with a look at her husband. "It'll be hard and none of us will eat well, but with faith in Deova Bondua, we'll find a way."

Theordoric frowned but nodded, patting her hand. He then leaned forward. "We will indeed. And my deepest sympathies for your loss. If I may make one request in exchange for taking her in—"

"You see, we lost everything in the rebellion," Eliana jumped in, smoothing over what she'd probably guessed would come next. Syago waited for the other hammer to drop, bored and bothered and wanting to get back to his hunt. She continued, "When it got serious, we had to pretend to be on their side. Then they took our medicines to treat the upsurge in illnesses. Then they took other objects of ours as—"

"We've lost everything," Theordoric cut back in, though he'd evidently not lost his nice vest. Syago might've been pleased to see them truly humbled in a change of heart, and they were some, but this had too much stench of opportunism. "As have many others here, but I can't run a business and treat the city's ill let alone a household—"

"Get to the point." Syago kept his face expressionless, trying to not make this worse than it already was.

"I need your support. Your leverage at court—"

"No." He stood to leave. "I serve the people, and the Lady Bondua, if I serve anyone. Now take good care of her while I'm gone; I'll know if you don't."

"B-but we can't without your help," he sputtered.

Syago let his disbelief show on his face. "I see around me enough wealth to feed for weeks. Still nice furniture, there a painting, plenty of space to rent to the refugees coming in. Elisabet already has nothing, so being here will leave her no worse off even if you skip meals."

"But you can't—"

"Can't let you eat the consequences of your role in this? Or could you tell me why it took so long for me and the Tolgrym refugees to enter the city? Or why family that has shunned us suddenly wants my help? No, I've no sympathy for someone who's known only the comforts of wealth to finally learn how the rest of us live. You're reaping the harvest you've sown. If you want me back as family in good graces, earn it."

He left without hugging either of his two cousins goodbye.

He later regretted how that had ended, but not as much as he ought to have. Alexandre rebuked him for it, and he in turn rebuked Alexandre for their earlier dispute about the legacy. The world was getting colder, more meaningless. There was no such thing as heroes anymore and nothing for him to rely on. Even the Lady Deova Bondua, who admittedly had been more of a casual presence in his life to begin with, somehow seemed more distant now.

Days later, he arrived at a rocky cliff overlooking Karuquoik valley, a small canyon in the Veinda Plains north of Maolgon, near the trail he'd abandoned. Impatience itched at him, a burning rage stronger than his sorrow, and his only motivation. Behind his caravan dragged a carcass he'd tied up, a large lizard called a xarampion with long claws. He'd never seen one before, had almost lost an eye to it, and hoped to trade it in the village but it was too hideous in appearance and smell to go in the wagon with him.

As the plains stretched toward the mountains, they dried and turned rocky, descending into valleys. Valleys where the Kimoc tribes of Deenuk lived.They carved homes into the sides of the steep limestone cliffs, finding it safer than living on top of the mesas or at the bottom of the valleys.

There he found they killed their own reptiles so took his xarampion for a cheap price. The valley also provided space for the migratory people to rotate farming, moving quarterly to the other homes as the forest people did. Syago had begun to appreciate the cultural tendency of the Kimoc to reside in difficult places. The amount of labor and accidental deaths was slightly higher than in regular cities, he believed, but the strategic advantages, not to mention sheer beauty of the civilizations, accounted for its worth. He also thought their farming risked less than the hunting and gathering Asturions did. If nothing else, the Kimoc had an incredible climbing ability and sense of balance from living literally on the edge.

The valley he overlooked descended some thirty paces and rose another twenty from the alcove he stood in. On the opposite cliff, square dwellings were etched into the wall. From his vantage point, they looked tiny but he knew they expanded inward. A cool desert wind blew the brown and green wool blanket that he wore as a makeshift cloak, having bartered his dented helmet for it with the local people, and he pulled it tight. The squeals of children playing brought his attention to a small boy running naked, gleefully, across a rickety wooden bridge as an old woman yelled at him. Syago smiled faintly, if anything could lessen his bitterness, it was the laughter of the innocents. But the grim thoughts didn't fade, the kids dashed about on the bridge while the lady went out after them. The devil he was tracking could swoop down any moment and take them, adult included. Even a large bird could come and take one of the little ones, so in the open.[58] He had work to do.

He turned to walk inside one of the sandstone brick buildings. A wooden ladder took him up to the door of one of the larger buildings. This particular building looked like any other home on the cliff face, save the ornate human skull decked with feathers and flowers that hung over the door, signifying an important political or religious center.

Did she ever come here? Or did my mother only ever know the people of Thornwood? It was a useless question, but he found himself thinking that side of his heritage more and more. Not embracing it by any means, just curious as frustration with his father's legacy grew.

Who am I?

---

58 *See Saint Casilda's arias on the iron pscylopean apocalypse.*

Syago sat down at the edge of a large dark room that served as the the village council room. Circular floors layered down as each of the three rows formed seats. The petitioner would stand in the center at the bottom. He wondered at their society, if their manner of rule and communal sharing of collective wealth would be a better alternative to the Asturions' uncaring hierarchy of inheritance. If a revolution was taking place, and he now felt one was needed, perhaps this would be a good arrival point. A more equal and fair replacement.

Normally foreigners would not be welcome in this remote area except as traders. Alexandre served as his ticket to entry, aided by his familiarity with Kimoc customs. Faw'kohk, one of the Quoarn'riik, let him stay the night. In his time here, he'd asked each of the Quoarn'riik about the devil he'd tracked to that region. They didn't want to talk about it, preferring that it was a problem of *his* people's wars, even though their fellow Kimoc of Quoak had been affected. But with the devil terrorizing their livestock and eating their men, he was able to get them to concede that it was there and they needed his help.

Unlike the Roah'riik of Thornwood, these hellhunters mainly trained in basic hunting and rarely of late, much preferring farm life. Being so removed from the conflicts of the rest of the region, they'd not needed as much study in the ways of hell, natural or otherworlder. *They've grown soft*, Syago thought, *and it will cost them if they don't let me help*. The one thing they did have, and the main reason he was still here, was a hellblade. A hand-axe made of bone like most, or so he'd heard. He'd not seen it yet and didn't think anyone living in this area had ever used it, being afraid of its curse.

Soft.

Alexandre disapproved strongly of his intent for the dark tool. Normally Syago would agree and acquiesce, but the disapproval now felt mutual. Weeks since leaving Tek'ouk and Lil'iek, and the soulsword still hadn't fessed up to its role in the fiendish sacrifices, or anything else Syago might be ignorant of, making him increasingly bitter and pessimistic. It didn't deny, nor did it affirm; it dodged his questions and self-righteously judged him for leaving. It had to at least know about what happened even if it had been unable to do anything at the time. How could it condemn his wanting a valuable weapon to fight a devil if it hadn't condemned his father for sacrificing people to do the same?

He stood once the Quoarn'riik began entering. A rare honor for him to even be allowed into the room, let alone hold council with them. Their need was great and they held some respect for him, though he suspected it was more a general hospitality. If he was in a better mood, he'd have respected them, instead he felt such ought to be earned. He looked over their fancy chieftain clothing and hair and wondered if these leaders were like Asturion ones. *Do they shun their duty to protect and care for their people like Count Toriacus does? Do they take privileges from their people while also making harsh demands of them like Theordoric and Gallegom did? Probably.*

Once they were seated, they conversed in words he didn't understand, knowing only conversational Quoakan Kimoc. Finally one motioned for him to stand in the center. "Take spot."

Syago walked down the small stairway to stand there. Another brought forth a leather bundle wherein he knew the axe to be. They laid it at his feet and opened it, revealing a bone handle and a single blade made of blue stone. Black feathers hung off the back by a spike. It had the same appearance as the throwing axes he'd seen them with, but slightly bigger and not for throwing. The way they clutched their necklaces in prayer to ancestral spirits reminded him this was no sacred relic. They viewed it as a curse and a blight on their village. A dark history they didn't like to remember. They'd named it merely Garkiask, *the Darkness.*

Faw'kohk stood on the top level and asked, "What can you do for us, warrior, against a devil?"

"I've fought and slain one already," Syago said. "I have Alexandre, the holy sword, to aid me but need more to ensure success. It's already taken two of your people. Surely, I won't make things worse by using your weapon."

"Greater warriors have come back worse," said the other chieftain who'd motioned to him.[59] "How do we know you won't slay one devil and become another?"

"Alexandre will protect me. I have the skills and the will to do good here. And you have no other option. But an accompanying group of hunters would be welcome." The room then fell into arguments all around, indecipherable to him. Though heated, their tone remained remarkably calm;

59 See *Gybiaaw Blackbraid: Born of Winter* and *Mutilated Tyrant,* both have a multitude of similar stories.

no shouting as was often found in Asturion courts. He supposed he didn't really need the hell-axe, but with the rift between him and Alexandre, it seemed an appropriate precaution. Besides, he was curious.

Finally the first said, "We can spare no hunters or room for you to stay here, but you may take Garkiask. Return it and return yourself whole, no less than you left. I plead of you this, in the name of the council and the Kimoc peoples of Deenuk."

The Quoarn'riik nodded, and Syago bowed as they rose. "You have my word." But he saw the pity in their eyes. *They think I'm leaving to my death, ridding them of the weapon as well.*

An hour later, he sat on the floor of Faw'kohk's residence, a tight room with rolled bedding and a food prep area. In a blink, he had a sense of how surreal the moment was. He was spiritually in a place contrary to where he'd wanted to be. He'd lost his family, his faith in his legacy, and even his love for his liege lords. A part of him agreed with the Royal Chaos, wanting to run down and overthrow the counts and barons, then the Cult, then the Chaos leaders themselves just for starting all of this.

He wept and turned to pondering what came next. Darkness and Alexandre lay side by side in front of him. Alexandre hated the thing. Darkness, like all hellblades he knew of, wasn't sentient. And while Alexandre could increase or develop new abilities in a bond with a wielder, hellweapons had only the narrow capabilities built into them. As he remembered it, bones connected living things symbolically, like black magic, depending on which parts were present. For a mental connection, a piece of skull had to be present at least partially. Darkness had a bone handle, showing that there would be some interaction of wielder and victim. A different piece of bone stuck near the top of the handle, which he guessed to be a skull piece. He wasn't sure what the blue edge meant, though it was very sharp, marked with the tenebrous scrawl hellweapons had. Ravenger had a blade of black and red, like blood, that drained life. What did blue do? And what did the feathers bring into effect? These uncertainties warranted caution. At most he guessed that it would bring a mental or physical connection to the devil, which could be dangerous. Perhaps that's why the pagan relics were banned by the Church; he wouldn't hesitate to destroy it if necessary.

"Oh shut up," he snapped at Alexandre, who'd been pestering him this whole time with thoughts of holy disappointment and corrupted warriors.

Hypocritically. "It's not as though you've never done anything wrong."

Alexandre pressed him on how petty and negative he was being about the legacy.

"And you're not? What would a sword know about people anyway?"

Alexandre reminded him of its age and extensive battle experience at the hands of great heroes.

"Great heroes like Odiru? When were you going to tell me the truth about my own father?"

It protested that he didn't know what he was talking about.

"Well, neither do you. Why am I talking to a sword anyway?"

Alexandre reminded him of their relationship as partners dependent on each other.

"Yes, but the relationship's always been about you. Me conceding to your whims and comforts, me taking the blame when things go wrong. Tell you what, you're taking a break on this one. Maybe I'll let you get in a few cuts in at the end but most of this fight's now for me and Darkness."

Darkness will destroy you.

"I'd sooner destroy it. It's nothing more than a temporary tool to me. Time to go," he said, standing, shield on his back. Ignoring its incessant protests, he sheathed Alexandre, then latched Darkness onto his belt. Its remaining mysteries would have to be discovered in the fight.

He walked until he reached the edge of the village crevice, then grabbed the rope ladder and climbed up, his blanket cloak blowing in the wind. Atop the mostly flat but rocky mesa, a herd of bomogs rustled slightly, but their watchers didn't even notice him. Their gaze was fixed ahead, on the cliff's edge. There stood a person shrouded in a ragged yellow blanket. Syago looked to the watchers, then back to the unmoving person.

"Who is that?" he called to the watchers.

For a moment they didn't answer, then one said, "We know not. But Wam'anzak wore that blanket when the devil took her."

"Take care, pale warrior," said the other. "The dead who walk never bring good tidings."

Well, I didn't come for good tidings.

He went up to the figure swathed in yellow, but as he approached, it began descending down a staircase cut into the cliff. He couldn't see anything of the person. Not a rotted hand or foot. He could tell, however, that the yellow blanket was more likely stained with blood than dirt. Darkness was already in hand, Syago feeling more nervous than he'd have liked to admit. Not sure what this was, he kept his distance, eyes alert.

For over an hour, he followed the slow, slow wandering of the yellow shroud. They crossed bridges and plateaus, all leading down into the shadows of the canyon's bottom. Exactly where Alexandre had sensed the devil earlier. The further they went, the more advantage he ceded to the devil.

He paused and called out to her, "Alo? Who are you? Where are you going?" But she continued her path, leading him to the devil. He supposed. When he stopped, she did too. As they walked into the late afternoon, the sun began to wane, shadows thickening. He'd seen large scratches and gouges on walls and ground. Bones and skulls littered the floor, broken and dry. Blood stained the rough walls, some old and fading and others more recent. The smell was corpse-rotten, but he couldn't tell if this was the figure or the terrain. The flies too were only getting worse. He grew weary of the ridiculously slow pace of whatever this was and his apprehension faded to frustration. With daylight on the wane, he had to slay the devil soon and return to the village. He walked ahead, catching up to her shortly. He repeated his questions, tapping her on the shoulder.

Still no response.

Finally he grabbed the hood and pulled it back. Instead of a person's head, there was a mass of large worms. The blanket fell away completely. Long and fat, the worms swarmed over each other in a giant coordinated mass that held the hunched shape of a human, clicking, sucking, and glistening in the grim sunlight. Heart pounding in disgusted horror, he backed away as the mass sank to the floor and spread out. He stomped on them as they moved toward him, but a rockslide on the crags above alerted him to a new presence. An insectoid greed, as it crawled from one side to the other. He moved away from the falling rocks and creeping carpet of leeches in front of him.

Drawing his shield out, he ran down the tight ravine. He told himself that fear wasn't getting the better of him, he just wanted a more strategic position, but the feeling of having walked into an obvious trap didn't help. The scratching above alerted him of another rockslide. He raised his shield above his head just as dust began to choke him. A rock hit his shoulder pauldron causing him to stumble. *Good thing you traded away your helmet, genius.*

A near total avalanche began to collapse over him and he ran blindly down a side crevice. Emerging from dustclouds, he turned the corner to find his path walled off by a large dead bomog, bloated beyond its original size. A large gurow pecked at it, then cawed at him but his eyes were on the canyon top where the devil lurked. Syago slipped between the wall and the dead bomog. But no, it wasn't dead after all. It moaned in pain and as he edged around it, the stomach throbbed, then burst. Gore flew everywhere, and he ducked, avoiding most of it. The bomog's shrieks and squeals quickly gave way to dying gurgles and sounds of slurping. Long insectoid claws, dripping with blood, reached out of the hole in its side. The gurow had raised into the air warily but the claws hooked it. Syago forgot about escaping, transfixed as the struggling creature was pulled into the carcass where its shrieks ended with a crunch. When he saw membranous wings sprout and beat a loud buzz, something bulbous rising out of the corpse, he recalled the need to flee.

But it was too late, the parent devil was already descending into the narrow ravine on long jagged legs. At its front was a mouth of tusks and razor mandibles and lidless eyes, too many of them; waist up it was human: naked, muscular, and pale. It held a Kimoc spear in one hand and a scepter in the other. "I've been waiting for you, squire," said the human-devil in a deep monotone voice. "Holy emblem of the realm you may be, but you're no holy knight."

"Maybe I don't conform," Syago said more for himself. In truth he fought to not panic at being cornered and held up his shield in the other hand. He backed up as the greed bore down on him until realizing the heavy buzzing behind was growing louder. He whipped around, swinging Darkness just as the newly hatched creature fell on him. The blade sheared through one of its legs and jolted him, leaving him dizzy and briefly delirious. *Only a vorpal blade would cut so efficiently, but that jolt is going ruin me.* The parent greed watched solemnly behind, waiting. Unfazed, the greedling reached for him again and he rolled under it, putting it between them, with another cut to a leg. The cut jolted him harder and his vision spun, oozed, and fumed as he stood and the wounded greedling turned. Then a wind from the devil blew back the creature, and the Kimoc spear flew into its chest, pinning it to the stone wall. "Patience, my offspring." The larger devil's back opened into great membranous wings that beat heavily as it lowered down further, stirring up dust clouds. "My prey must first sit for judgment and last rites."

It threw the scepter at the torn bomog corpse, which then burst into flames, putrid black smoke rising up into the sky. Syago made an impulsive leap at the devil, hell-axe swinging, but it backed up.

"You call me greed," it began, hands clasped reverently. "Then I already rule this world and am necessary. I dominate all as the life blood of the world, its very rust and decay. I starve nations—"

Syago choked on the haze, seeking counsel from Alexandre, but it refused him.

You told me to sit this out, the sword replied.

"Listen to me, squire." The devil-man's ire was monotone. Behind, the offspring rose from its pin, unbothered by the oozing hole in its chest. It buzzed toward him, long proboscis extending, sucking. "I said no," the parent reiterated. The larger devil charged through the flames, knocking Syago aside with a claw as it met its child. The two monsters struggled, and Syago swung Darkness at the parent, severing one of its legs easily. The jolt threw him back against the canyon wall and his mind filled with melting walls. This time the hallucinations solidified. In front of the walls stood Elisabet, Eliana, and Goia, smoke pouring from their mouths. He rolled to the side as a leg snapped out to cut him, punching a hole in the stone where he'd laid.

The devil rose and backed up, almost over him, and Syago noted the end rearing up as if ready to sting him. He swung at it in anticipation, and blackness pressed at his mind.

He woke up on the ground, acidic blood sizzling everywhere. Down the canyon, his family and friends stood with smoking mouths, standing in solemn vigil. But it was the agony in his left arm that drew his attention. Blood seeped from a hand wound. On the other side, the devil struggled, the rear of its abdomen and a leg gone. Syago ripped off his glove to find a large puncture wound, the skin around it black, in his palm. He couldn't move his arm, and the blackness, clearly poison from the stinger, was edging upward. Darkness lay on the ground in front of him.

The greed had returned to fighting the greedling, which curled up into a slimy ball. The parent tossed it aside. Syago grabbed Darkness off the ground, ran up the side of a boulder, and slashed down in a last bid for survival. As the hellblade lanced down, the devil moved, but not before Syago severed one of its human arms. The devil looked at him dispassionately then pushed off the wall. Syago began to slide off, but he wasted no time, striking at its neck. He braced against another shock as its head rolled clean off and he lost hold of Darkness. The devil's entire human half deflated as the writhing megadriles poured out like spilling guts. He slid off the carapace and, with extreme effort, he drew Alexandre to slash through two of its jagged limbs. When he was done, Syago fell to his knees. He was out of energy, the poison from the devil's claw having sapped everything from him as it spread up his arm to his elbow. The melting walls began to pulse as lingering effects beneath a heavy sun, his group held vigil.

He held Alexandre to his poison arm with his other hand, and begged Alexandre to hurry and heal the poison, but nothing happened. Alexandre did nothing. Did not heal him, did not save him. The hallucinations didn't even fade. He stared at Alexandre, never feeling so furious and frightened at the same time. He tried arguing for his plight, but Alexandre only reminded him that he'd made his choice with Darkness.

"But I did use you!" he shouted in protest.

But not as much as Darkness.

Nauseous with pain and despair, Syago threw the sword against the stone wall where it clattered to the floor, sticking upright. The poison had now reached his left bicep. There was only one option that he could see. Before he could give it thought, he grabbed Darkness, wiped it clean, and, with a roar, whacked the blade into his upper arm, near the shoulder. The power of the blade made a large cut, but not a complete severance as he'd hoped and needed. Its power would not work as well on himself. Blood sprayed but he barely saw it as the vigil group began singing in low chant. The melting canyon walls pulsed. He screamed in both physical and emotional agony. He hacked again, sweat beading with the effort and pain, until the rest was sawed off. The now all black arm fell to the ground. Thankfully no black shone on the small stump left behind. The cruel irony was that he was one of the few knights in the land who could heal wounds. And now he was a one-armed warrior because of a disagreement with a sword, the same that would heal. A damnable sword.

Finally the walls ceased melting and his choir changed to a higher tone then began to fade. Then he saw the true irony. His now dismembered arm had no poison line on it. The limb looked fine, as if he'd hallucinated the poison. There had been nothing to heal.

Syago screamed until his voice gave out.

Delirious with the pain and blood loss, he realized with horror that the devil wasn't dead yet. It struggled to rise on its remaining legs and he knew it would heal and rise again if he didn't destroy it soon. The greedling also uncurled and began feeding on its severed limbs, the child eating its father.

Another movement distracted Syago from his torment. The devil's human arm he'd cut off writhed on the ground, changing colors. It turned deep red and the human fingers developed sharp claws.

On a wild improvisation, perhaps in addled thought, Syago grabbed the devil arm he'd severed. It tried to claw at him, choke him, but he snarled at it and held the claws away even as he brought its stump to his. The devil arm latching on hungrily Again he yelled in pain as the stumps began to join tendons, bones, muscle. Skin.

His new arm pulsed with satisfaction. He removed the rest of his shirt to examine the binding. Red faded to light brown at the shoulder with veins bulging around the area. The arm was much more muscly than his other and he'd have to learn to balance it out. But he'd done it, he'd slain the devil and survived. He gasped in relief and rose to finish the greed.

CHAPTER EIGHTEEN
LINES IN THE DIRT

Based on *The Nordvargor Testaments*, cc bastica 907;
Leyta's Journals, cc bastica 190;
Writings of Qosku, cc bastica 198;

Decimosk-Febreron, 246-247
6th of Marza, 247

On one night sometime before the Deovanad Festival, the great hall clattered with sounds of wooden spoons on bowls and the clinking of goblets. Conversations flitted low throughout the hall. A notable change to Leyta, who now sat at the head of the table between Roza and Balgor. Qosku, her personal guard, sat nearby looking up at the tapestry of Otrantor as he drank. Clinking a glass for attention, she stood. "I appreciate your patience. Little progress has been made in the war these last two months, but nothing serious has happened since we retook Mantlgrym and for that we can be grateful."[60] The only strange occurrence they'd had in Cantlgrym was of a grimshade robbing Syago's vacant quarters. She didn't know what it'd taken but they moved the rest of his things into secured storage until he returned. Whenever that would be. "If you remember the horrors involved in that undertaking, you ought to consider this fortunate." She quieted as she heard some snickers from the back. Her eyes went to Fernandeon's table, but they were sitting quietly. So the dissension had spread beyond him.

The room went even more quiet under her glare, she realized. Still a hint of timidity after that night she'd burned the table to quiet them. She wasn't proud of it but at least it kept them from interrupting her.

"However, I recommend we extend our hunting and gathering expeditions

---

further to keep ourselves sharp. Perhaps it will also lead us to the enemy, so long as we're careful to not fall into their traps. In the meantime, train hard and we'll give information as it comes to us. Thank you." She nodded to those at her side, who watched the room silently, and exited the room with Qosku following.

At first, she'd thought it awkward and annoying that he followed her everywhere. But as her position further isolated her from others—even her friendship with the other masters felt more professional as they always talked of administrative matters—she enjoyed the one person she could talk to. It also made her miss Syago more, who she sometimes dreamed of making a return with heartfelt apology followed by a fervent validation of her dominion.

She'd heard a rumor of him being in Tolgrym when it burnt down but also in Mantlgrym shortly after. And then he'd vanished from public knowledge. Something was obviously going on with him, something more than the siege and the burning of Tolgrym. She could sympathize but tried not to care. He'd abandoned his charge with the Kimoc, with no word of what he was about, and to her, that desertion was reprehensible.

Shortly after the meal, Leyta walked down the stairs, headed to her class, and passed by Banesa, who'd been her friend both in Voium and at Cantlgrym. Banesa called out, "Oy Leyta—er Mastra Leyta," she corrected at a narrowing of Leyta's eyes then continued, "Sorry, I just—well, I wondered if you'd heard about Camila?" There were, of course, several Camilas, but she could only be referring to the girl that Leyta had been close friends with prior to keeping at Cantlgrym, then abandoned when Leyta became annoyed with discussing her marriage problems constantly. Leyta had been one of her few friends. Though she rarely thought of it anymore, she still felt a twinge of shame for such cruel pettiness.

"No, what of her?" Leyta asked. Qosku stood behind her, having learned to keep his distance during private interactions. Banesa's friends had learned to listen in on gossip and stayed close.

"Oh, it's sad. Really terrible, she killed herself not ten days ago. She hung herself in her bedroom."

Leyta's heart sank. She stared at Banesa, eyes unmoving, and the girl wrung her hands. Even the friends shifted in discomfort, all knew of Leyta's abrupt break from Camila. Perhaps had she stayed friends with her, Camila would've survived her marriage. It was too much to think of.

"Wonderful," Leyta snapped. "A woman killed herself because of me. Just what I needed for today. Inform me of something useful next time." She turned and walked out of the castle to her class, wiping her eyes so Qosku wouldn't see. *That was a shameful thing to say. But they have to see me as hard or everything we're building and protecting crumbles.*

Fortunately the class she was going to was for younger children, to learn letters, arithmetic, basics of combat, and principles of dyne. The youngest was ten, all of them from wealthy families, but still sweet children. Though they could be a handful, she loved working with youths. Their innocence and joy alleviated her own grief. Later she led a small but older class of dyne adepts in the bailey. Her response to Banesa continued to bother her, as well as the news itself, and she wondered if it was not possible to live without regretting every single thing. She'd always told herself that Camila hadn't wanted to be a burden to Leyta, who had her own issues to deal with, but knew deep down that this was only a self-assurance to avoid the consequences of her actions.[61]

Refocusing on her students, she cleared her mind, never forgetting what uncontrolled hatred had done to Gabriol at Covadongar. His terrified face flashed through her mind as he caught fire. She looked at the water in the bowls before them. Water wasn't so volatile. Working with water, they moved rows of wooden bowls around on the patchy grass and switched water from container to container. The challenge here being the need to push sentimental movement into tranquil substances. Water undisturbed lay calm and serene, it took sentiments easily and dissipated them just as quick. They manipulated it with hate, sorrow, and ambition, which the students felt in droves. Anger was too explosive and fear too difficult to control for the present exercise. There were positive sentiments they could use, love and joy, but these merely heated up an object. Only negative emotions served any purpose in battle. Together they repeated the elementist mantra, "Weakness is my enemy, anger my arrow, hate my sword, fear my armor, sorrow my balm, and joy my reward."

Leyta felt the hate, hatred about losing soldiers in the war and for what had happened to her former home of Voium. And for all those who disrespected or opposed her. And for what had happened to Camila. Some of it a self-hate but also a hatred for the real culprit, Camila's violent, drunkard of a husband.

---

61 *Best keep it in, don't want to the blood coming back to haunt*

With her staff, she used the hate to draw up water first out of the ground, then from all the bowls at the same time in an effort to impress the youths who weren't listening very well. Irritated by this and by the whisperings of dissent and disrespect among others, despising their spoiled lives, hate simmered within her. Drawing it out of the ground with dyne felt good, but insufficient. The students now appeared vaguely impressed by her dynal feats.

"No," she scolded one who'd made his water ripple. "You have to push sentiments into it suddenly. Subtlety won't be strong enough for this part. You have to throw the water around."

"Is there a point to learning the water?" Milgalic asked. "Nobody ever fights around water anyway."

"When either enemy returns to the castle and you're on wall duty," she said, meeting his eyes, "then you will be working with an entire lake to defend Castle Cantlgrym. But since you're continuing this disrespect, you can sit out the rest of this lesson as well as the next one." He stared, stunned, and mumbled an apology but she wasn't having it. "Go. Before I—"

"Mastra Leyta," a voice from behind interrupted her.

"What?!" she snapped.

Andras, the speaker, halted a little, shocked. "We have an urgent punitive matter that you need to see to." He pointed to a boy behind him who stood disheveled with his hands tied behind his back, held by another soldier, Maolcuim. Just about her age, the prisoner's long curly crimson hair draped in front of his bowed face.

"Name," she asked, brushing aside his hair so she could see his face.

"Colombar de Ourense. Of Mantlgrym," he said, looking up and smiling, just as Andras opened his mouth to say it. She noticed a purple swelling underneath one eye and looked at Andras with a raised eyebrow. Andras shifted uncomfortably, betraying the nonchalant shrug he offered.

"And the crime accused?" she asked, stepping away.

"He—uh, raped a… girl," Andras said. "Just a few moments ago. The girls came and told me, as I was heading for wall duty."

"Girl or girls?" she asked, a cold weariness of their endless conflicts settled in her.

"Well he raped one, but her friends saw it, or the end of it I think. Anyway they backed her up," he said. Maolcuim nodded in agreement, also armored for wall duty.

"And where are they? I can't try him if they don't bring the accusations." She looked around and back at the castle doors.

"She didn't really want to come forward. I tried to convince her, but she's a little shaken right now and, well, embarrassed by it too."

"Well, tell her to fortify and accuse, I can do nothing until she comes out."

Andras fidgeted again and looked at the group of students behind now watching the mini-trial. "Please, Mastra. Not in front of them."

The concern surprised her. Did he carry affections for the victim? Who had she seen him with? Sabela! That sweet girl from Voium studying archemy. For some reason, this also bothered her; the connection made him less objective and kept this at the feud she'd suspected it was. Leyta stepped closer to Andras so only he could hear. "Would you have brought this to me if you had no feelings for her?"

A mixed look of horror and anger twisted his face. "What?! How can you—"

"Never mind, sorry. Where can I find her?" she asked, regretting the comment and taking a deep breath.

His face eased a bit. "When we walked out, she was with a friend in the entrance hall. She may've gone to her room."

"Thank you, wait here," she said and began walking to the front doors. Still walking, she turned to the students. "I didn't say stop training. We still have half the hour remaining. Focus!"

She found the three girls holding each other tightly, past crying and now sitting in silence. Sabela sat in the middle, a shell of sorrow that had emptied herself out in heavy sobs. Leyta stood over them and asked what happened, starting with the victim's account. Sabela told of how she'd been studying with Colombar when he switched from practicing the dynal operations to trying to kiss her. When she'd refused, he pushed her against the wall, smiling like it was a game. She said no several times, but he told her to shut up and let him finish as he tore open her dress. She'd been too afraid to scream or fight back, and he completed the vile act and was telling her not to say anything to anyone before her two friends came in. The friends verified their end of the story, hearing him threaten her and seeing her a wreck of torn dress and tears, both still evident, Leyta could see. They'd been smart enough to retain that part of the evidence. He'd also threatened the friends. Hearing the experience, seeing her emptiness and pain as she recounted it, eyes dried out from crying, reached beneath Leyta's layers of irritation and touched something dark.

Gripping her staff tightly, she returned to the field where they stood. The students asked if they could leave now, it being time nearly to end the class. She'd thought of dismissing them but instead said, "No, I want you to see this."

They looked at each other, worried. *They should be*, she thought as she turned to Colombar, no longer held by the soldiers. "Their accusations line up. What have you to say?"

"She wanted it," he said, trying to smile past his fattening lip.

Her eyebrows rose at his words. "Wanted it? The torn dress too?" she growled.

"Well, she started it, actually. Coming hard then changing her mind, but you can't switch after starting me like that, right? So I kept going, and she still liked it anyway. Didn't fight me at all."

The complete lack of sympathy and remorse, not to mention the lie, awakened a monster in Leyta never before known.

"You confess your guilt then?" she asked, her voice dangerously quiet.

"Yes, I—what? No—" he said, trying to fix his witty response. Like so many children of wealthy noble families, he'd looked as though he'd gotten away with too many things in life and now that he wasn't, he didn't know how to act.

"And we have two witnesses, and two guards in addition to myself having heard the accounts, correct?" she asked, looking at Andras and Maolcuim, who both affirmed grimly.

"But she was asking for it," he protested. "Meeting me alone in that dress. She made me do—"

A large clump of dirt shot from the ground in front of him, at her push. In a brown flash, it hit him in the stomach and he doubled over. "Really?" she said in high sarcasm. "Well, you were asking for that. Your stupidity made me do it. And it's asking me to continue." She brought the dirt to trap his legs and snarled, "Execution by water... you took from her what is necessary for life, now I take from you the same."

Lying crumpled on the ground, gasping for air, he groaned. She pointed her staff at him, focusing more forcefully. Any traumatic thoughts of what she'd done to Gabriol were gone. In the vision, she saw the dark reds of anger and hate in the dirt, but that didn't feel enough to her. She looked at his body harder. Dynasts never targeted a person or creature directly because dyne never did much that way. It was thought that the dense complex network of organs, or the generation of its own sentiments, blocked out intrusions by sentiments from outside except when conveyed to the senses like in a song or through dynfist practices. But as Eume the Wise had shown, sentiments did affect living bodies directly just at a far smaller degree.

By seeing all of the water within him, she knew somehow she could use it, and she pressed her hate into it. For a second nothing happened, but the power raged in her, a frightening dark torrent that she almost feared but embraced instead. It was born of those she knew who'd been hurt, born also of the recent memory of Sabela's sobs. As she pressed the water out of him, sweat glistened on Colombar's skin, then dripped, watering the ground as steam rose off of him in the cool air. His body started squirming in pain, he'd been trying to say "sorry," and someone said something to her, but she was far past hearing. His body withered as if starved, shriveling past the point of death, until all of the hate-filled water left him a gaunt, dried husk of a man. When she stopped, breathing heavily, all that remained was the skin flaking away, crumbling over a skeleton and leathery organs on a wet patch of grass. She reentered the vision and turned the dirt over them, burying the remains until the bailey was flat again. Chest heaving, she faded out of the vision to see everyone around looking at her, horrified. Even Andras, the least disturbed of everyone watching, didn't seem to approve. That'd been only slightly more brutal than usual executions, but she knew the closer proximity and the power she'd pushed into it, not to mention the raw difficulty, had made this more disturbing.

She'd done it, though: the first recorded draining. And for a brief moment, she felt alive.

She calmed her breathing and turned to the students. If they didn't respect her before, they would now. "Class dismissed." And with that she walked off to the castle doors, leaving behind a patch of disturbed dirt and torn grass. The entire area was still wet.

In spite of her elation, the sight of the desiccated husk imprinted in her mind. *If I acted correctly, why is the memory of it catching and hurting me so?*

Later that night, candles lit her small table as she studied in the master's corner of the library. She pored over the documents and maps they'd taken from Mantlgrym for what must've been the thousandth time, sorting through all the relevant transcripts she could find. She'd studied the language of the Tiakanawu, the probable ancestors of Kimoc and Unaka, though they could only understand fragments and even then it was much a guess. More interesting was the Asturion writings about Tiakanawu, but they gave her nothing she'd sought. At least the maps and books pointed her to what the Royal Chaos and the cult seemed obsessed with. The mythical story of the dydatris, the True Scepter. One of the old pagan creation myths.

Many days after the eternals made the world, they'd accidentally made people. Depending on the version, the people soon began to disrespect them. Seeing their mistake, the eternals released monsters into the world. Living in caves and mountaintops provided some protection for people, but not enough. They requested aid and one eternal told them of a secret power. A ruler called Pagutec was brave enough to learn control of the power, with staves given to him by the eternals. He then taught the others who were willing. This became dyne.

This story contradicted the greater number of other writings that claimed the Kimoc, Unaka, and Amoyara didn't have dyne before the Asturions brought it and set up the colonies, except for one source that said the Unka, or One Ruler, had been a dynast. That those accounts were all written down by Asturions raised some suspicion in Leyta.

Regardless, this power created conflict among Pagutec's people. To settle the matter, the Sun came down and commanded order, giving a piece of itself for them to command how the power should function. That piece hardened into a fine gold scepter, whereon written were laws on the proper uses of dyne, or the laws were dyne. They contradicted here, or went multiple ways, but in all they mounted the piece in the golden temple of a golden city. Peace came, for a time, until different factions wanted access to the True Scepter, which allowed a ruler to govern the use of dyne, whatever that means. On the brink of total destruction, immortal Pagutec went to the temple and buried it, with himself alone inside, never to be heard of again and reported only by his scribes. Fantastical tales of searching for this golden city abounded in folklore.

Of course it was all false. The Church taught that Deova Bondua had come after creation to bestow dyne as a gift, the only way to survive in a world of monsters into which people had been damned and exiled as punishment into the first of the hells, more natural and gentle than the underworlds, for their crimes in the First Garden. Leyta had found many old documents supporting the Church's claims, if with great variation. What she sought now wasn't even the hidden truth behind these old myths, but what the cult and the rebel group thought they were finding in them. Qosku had backed this up when confirming that this Cult of the Rippers was known in the mountains as Zupayk's or Saqra's cult, who'd obsessed over finding ancient relics and ruins. The Royal Chaos wasn't the only group chasing fantasies.

Then she noticed something peculiar. One book, written by Saint Culon, mentioned that the Kimoc gave their sacrifices directly to the biggest mewil'ishyuuks of each herd and that the biggest one ever seen was as tall as a man. But that wouldn't be very tall. She wasn't a naturalist, but even she knew most adult mewil'ishyuuks would be a head taller than an average person. Were people shorter now? Or were mewil'ishyuuks then?

She stood and went to a bookshelf that had a bestiary by Ourense de Balbathon from only a decade ago. She found the current average height of men at five feet and a half, with women just a little shorter. Mewil'ishyuuks were average heights of seven feet now to Culon's six hands. Culon didn't use the same measurement system and in this case only made relative statements anyway. She rifled through pages until he got to daemogs. She found Ourense saying that daemogs, ten years ago, were larger than Culon's daemogs, maybe three centuries ago, and with larger horns and more fire. She found the same with ozors, rabbits, blackbirds, everything. Culon even described blackbirds as mostly docile and daemogs as being violent only when provoked. Had they changed or was the old saint just holed up in his sanctuary too much?

I must be reading it wrong. She needed to ask Katti, who was more of a naturalist, but with Katti gone on a gathering expedition, she wasn't sure what to do. Few others knew much more than what they saw on hunts. She felt she ought to be going on more of those than she was but her studies had kept her inside. And maybe a small fear of the hell outside.

Ourense wrote his just under a decade ago, and Leyta agreed with his measurements. Culon was hundreds of years ago, at least three hundred but possibly more. All they really knew was that he'd been before the conquest of Pelagiod and so dates weren't consistent. On top of that, a number of his writings had been lost in fires. Roza insisted that this document wasn't an original but a copy of a copy as were most old texts. If that were the case, she could envision a slow and subtle change of the texts overtime. But why would the original authors have written their monsters at a smaller size, only to be grown to their actual size by later copyists? Or if the reverse, why shrink the animals to incorrect sizes in the older texts?

Or the authors wrote actual sizes, which collectively changed over time. But why would the creatures change in size? She stared at the open books in front of her as if they'd just tell her. It was peculiar that not only had the monster descriptions gotten bigger, but also more fierce. More violent in temperament and more hellish in appearance. She yawned and stretched, her eyes falling on her staff, which leaned against the table. The Criod created everything, bestowed the hell outside as a punishment from which Deova Bondua will rescue them. What if it was an increase in penalty? But the scriptures would've said so. Instead, the Criod allowed them dyne to fight for redemption. Indeed, one of Culon's main conclusions was that dyne had changed considerably over the years with the expansion of their faith. Something clear to every advanced student of dyne. From its pagan origins to being adopted by the Church as Heaven's gift, to now where it built cities and conquered the hell outside, people had improved on their power. She'd even seen advancements in her five years of practice. One thing seemed certain, dyne and natural monsters had grown together over the years. But a correlation didn't mean the two were related. Still, Leyta wondered if they could be. *If our continued pushing of negative sentiments into the outside through dyne has transformed beasts into monsters, then.*

.our main weapon to fight the outside is twisting it into the very curse we must fight?

The heretical idea struck her so suddenly she slammed the book shut, stood up, and backed away from the table, hands wringing. "No, no, no—that's not true," she said to herself, breathlessly. "No, can't be true." The Church taught that their hell was made by the Criod, not by humans, and dyne a gift to fight it. A dark but sacred duty. Neither could humans alter creation except in the moment. This was heresy. *But what if the flow of sentimental energy is mostly outwards, and mostly negative—no, I can't think about it. I have to be wrong, somehow.* Intellectual curiosity compelled her to pursue the line of thought, but her faithful upbringing and fear of easy reprisals to her precarious position held her back. It was best to not look into it. Leave it behind.

Noise in the stairwell startled her and she resumed her seat, closing books to get back to the maps. Balgor entered with a soft knock, ducking under a beam to allow his bulk through. He went directly to a large chair made specifically for him, and sat down. "Greetings, Mastra Leyta! How fares the studies tonight?" he said joyfully in the quiet expanse.

"As unproductive as used candles," she said. "I've learned nothing."

"No, you've learned. Even if it's only that this is becoming a dead end. You're always learning even if you don't know it."

"What of the report from Quoak? On the—the Fomorions that came..." she trailed off, always feeling uncomfortable discussing them with Balgor, who'd been left behind as a child in the last raid over thirty years ago to be raised at Cantlgrym.

He shrugged. "The report you ask of has nothing new. They're edging close to Cantlgrym but not toward it. I suspect they most definitely are here for the Chaos as Tek'ouk feared. They've passed several good raiding opportunities on the western Kimoc tribes and with a slowness that makes them restless but methodical.[62] It also makes them easier for the Roah'riik to follow. Hopefully it provides a stronger lead than this," he said, tapping the map.

She looked forlornly at the map. "It was a mistake to leave Mantlgrym on such a loose lead. I should've started working on it in secret there."

"We all make mistakes, m'lady. But if mistake that was, it was one of the more reasonable ones. You had to return soon regardless. Let us worry about what comes next and the past will die its own death. Now the execution you did earlier..."

She sighed as he trailed off. "It was too far, wasn't it?"

"Yes, it was, but more so of an immediate and unceremonious act. Not becoming of the leader they need to trust. And I suppose banishment or exile might've been a better action. We'll also have to dig up the remains and send them to the family, which I did today. The real concern to me is you. Every elementist, particularly dynasts, has a wall beyond which they lose control and reason. Some lose themselves completely in it, and those we strip of dynal authority. I'd hate to have this happen to you, especially as Castellan." His deep green eye bore into her with wisdom and kind intensity. "And if you would win the hearts of your subjects, shock and awe will not be the best way. Some will not be won without it and so may not be ones worth winning."

Silence fell on the room as she nodded her understanding. She didn't feel remorse for what she'd done and wondered at the implications of that. What was she becoming? And how would it affect her dyne? "Balgor, what do the ohancanus believe is the origin of dyne?"

"Hmm," he mused, fingering his braided beard, one of the few cultural trademarks he'd retained from his old people. "As best I remember, which is very little of them, they saw the world more akin to the Kimoc than anyone else, but by no means the same. You know, a wild land born of the eternals. Although I think some now believe in a single supreme eternal similar to our own."

"And what do you think?"

"I think large scale history is impossible for us to understand beyond the reign of Pelagiod when he unified the cities into a kingdom. Just think of the vanishings, entire armies that have disappeared in one campaign. No, we haven't the faintest clue as to the origin of dyne or of anything. At least not beyond the scriptures."

She didn't think it was that impossible to know the truth. With thorough investigation and critical thinking, they could figure out a great deal. She hesitated, then said, "What would you think of a theory stating that dyne has shaped the natural world."

"What do you mean?" He stroked his beard again, eye staring off into the distance as she summarized her hypothesis. Eventually he interrupted, "No, that's not correct. It—our dyne is too small to change this world, made by the Criod and not man or woman, and so we can't change creation. And in any case the scriptures teach us it's impossible, and that we're responsible for ourselves and not for all that."

"But if it was proven to you that wildlife has changed along with dyne—"

"The scriptures clearly state that such a thing is impossible and—and I grew up a barbarian living in the outside before coming here where Deova's sacred knowledge converted me to the truth, so I know what you said is wrong. And you'd be better off not thinking of it again."

Leyta hid her surprise at Balgor's uncharacteristic reaction. He'd never closed up like that before.

Still, what he said rang true. "I suppose you're right, this is a waste of time then. Well, anyway, these myths don't matter so much as the actual plans and whereabouts of the Royal Chaos and that Cult of the Rippers. Maybe if we follow the path of the Fomorions?"

He drew up the current map and marked the path of the raiding party. From the sea somewhere just west of Quoak, going along the border of Thornwood, then exiting north of the western tribes, nearing Cantlgrym, then past the trail into the mountains. He marked just at the edge of the Barbathor Mountains where they were last reported. "Now, they could hide easily in there, but it's worth noting that before they disappeared into the Barbathors, they didn't attack anybody. So they clearly believe these ruins to be somewhere in the mountains. What know you about the Tiakanawu ruins? Or of those mountains?"

"Nothing, but I believe Roza knows about both," she said, rising.

His eye glinted with pride and amusement. "Indeed, though she usually forbids visitors this late."

She waved his concern away. "Oh, I'm sure she won't mind a quick question, she can at least think on it and respond on the morrow." As she went for the door, she noticed his eye narrow and smile flatten, that look he always had when he wanted to disagree but couldn't bring his good-natured self to do it. "It'll be fine. I'm the Castellan; she'll understand."

She left the room and made her way to Roza's private quarters, one of the few it was tucked into a gloomy corridor between library and greathall. She'd never seen inside and wondered if she might find the opportunity this night. Knocking at the door hard, she heard what sounded like painful squealing. "Mastra Roza? Are you well? This is Leyta."

She heard a faint, "Yes, I'm fine, goodnight." Then another squeal that got cut short. It reminded Leyta of hearing her friends getting hurt by their parents after they'd climbed onto the city roofs to explore. "That doesn't sound good, may we talk?"

"I'M FINE!" she shouted. "It's past my curfew, goodnight."

Leyta heard a clatter as a number of things fell to the floor. More screeching, but fainter this time, and it too stopped abruptly.

Leyta's concern deepened. "As Castellan, I invoke my right to talk and know what you're up to. I'm coming in." Her scepter slashed at the door hinges, yanking the metals off the wall. The door fell inward with a kick from her foot as she ascended the last steps.

The tiny room was dimly lit by candles, a lot of them, everywhere. In the middle sat a tiny table with a crane and stretcher over it. In between was a large rat, almost as big as Leyta's torso, and freshly dead. Blood leaked from it into a small vase on the table below. Mouth open in shock, Leyta looked around and saw bloody tracks running from a pool of blood by an open cage. Unable to fathom what this might be, Leyta held her scepter tight. "Mastra Roza, you have some explaining to do."

"I can do that," her deeper than normal voice said from the closet alcove, too dark to see into. "I was—"

Leyta interrupted, "No, come out and talk to me."

"As you will." Mastra Gretal Roza emerged from the room, stiffer, paler, and more serious than Leyta had ever seen her. Blood lined her mouth where she'd failed to wipe clean. Any hint of the kind and encouraging mentor Leyta had known in her years at Cantlgrym disappeared. Standing before her was a moving corpse. But not a lifeless, Leyta reminded herself, as it had spoke and now stood calmly, presenting herself for Leyta to see in all terrible glory. The white icy eyes, above all, were unbearable, different. She wanted to flee but wasn't sure if that was necessary or even wise. *Stay, so you can understand this first.*

Silence filled the room, choking Leyta until she could stand it no longer. "What are you?"

"I don't know," she said. That deep voice, inhuman, chilled Leyta to the bone as much as the eyes. "I call it gravespawn, or a type of one. I am not lifeless, nor am I a living human. During the day I can resemble who I once was, if I'm careful. At night, I turn more myself and must hide. Sunlight hurts me, and I must eat fresh hearts to survive as my dead body only thrives on the weight of sentiments found in hearts. They power my body else I perish, slow and miserable."

"And the cup of blood?" Leyta asked, trying to keep the tremor away.

"Blood is merely a byproduct. I don't need it, but being the only thing I can actually taste or feel..." Her eyes shifted to the table, a slight longing in the whites. "...sometimes it's too much to resist."

Leyta hoped her disgust wasn't showing on her face, she didn't want to threaten or antagonize the undead woman. Resisting the urge to cross herself, she said, "How long..."

"I was changed... so long ago, infected or cursed while in a hunting party." She bent down and grabbed the door with one hand to lift it back into its place. The ease with which she lifted the massive wooden door bespoke incredible strength. "I know that only because I found the party looking for my body after I woke. Whatever it is, it takes most of your memories. I woke with nothing. I almost killed them when they found me, they tried to burn me, thought me to be some aberration of lifeless. I fled, came to terms with it, re-entered society in another town, and began my life as a scholar. Always in search of what I am and never learning it, never finding others like me though I'm certain they exist."

Leyta knew full well how debilitating that sort of uncertainty was. She'd felt it every day since becoming Castellan. Perhaps even before. She could feel her fear ebbing as compassion took over. "Why haven't you told me? You needn't hide it from me."

"I might've eventually, Alkant and Davagis knew. I have been considering leaving, perhaps faking a death... Perhaps revealing... I've learned much here, and the good I do with the children gives a sense of purpose. But that's been fading as I feel less and less emotion in my diminishing humanity. The soul, not the body, decays. I suspect my moral preference of animal hearts has that effect. And these eyes... they see things in people, especially at night. You don't know a person until you've seen them the way I do. Living with so many people becomes difficult after all these years. All these years... almost fifty now."

Leyta was speechless. She'd had no idea of the turmoil Roza has been living with. Roza turned to her from the door, flat expression haunting. Leyta suddenly became aware that her only exit had been blocked, and the fear returned. "Why have you come to disturb me in my evil hour when I've asked you not to?"

Leyta cleared her throat, regretting the intrusion. "We—Balgor and I— wondered at the maps. He believes the rebels are somewhere in the mountains to the north, we think seeking some temple ruins called Tiakanawu. Said you might know about it. I thought it urgent. I'm sorry I didn't think to wait till the morrow."

Roza paused too long for Leyta's comfort, eyes searing into her. "I'll see what I can find. I know much but some things cannot be obtained from study or exploration. Lost in the cold, cruel darkness of time does truth die. The hour is drawing nigh when we'll need to consult the angels."

This was another danger Leyta didn't like approaching. "Working with the angels is not an easy task, and Osmos is dangerous. If we can avoid it... or any help you can give us—"

This time Roza cut her off. "I cannot approach them with you. They would destroy me. Or try to. But advise I can. We'll discuss this on the morrow. Do not reveal my secret, and do not seek me at night again. Now leave."

Leyta went to the door faster than she'd intended, then spent a long moment struggling to open it. Reaching around her in a breathless, heart-pounding moment, Roza grabbed it and slid the door open enough for Leyta to slip through. It closed behind her, and she forced herself to walk, not run, back to the study.

Qosku punched out at the sack of cotton and loose dirt that hung from the rafters of the monastery training room. He needed mastery over his body. So he trained late. Following a long prayer, he entered the pure motion of being, working himself for hours. It helped him avert the three things he feared: turning into a beast, his femininity, and his growing attraction to Lügos.

Despite his best efforts, the two had become friends. Qosku's silence and reservation availed nothing. The boy would sit by him, talk to him, compliment him even. All melting Qosku's heart, a heart that couldn't trust. A heart that knew better. He did wonder if maybe Lüg held the same secret, but his being friends with most girls of the castle made it hard to imagine. He was good to Qosku even when Qosku didn't respond or tried to push away. But not too hard; Qosku now liked him too much to hurt him and secretly wanted more to happen. So why not?

The heart knew better. Kindness, admiration, general friendship, sympathy for his condition, any of these things could explain the affection being displayed. The kindness being shown by all his friends here was the greatest thing to ever have happened to him, he couldn't let it fall to ruin. He couldn't see living past that if it did.

He punched the bag hard and fast, moving through all those sentiments, but he lacked focus. Fighting on a troubled, confused, and conflicted heart never lent focus. After a lightning fast beating from his fists, the bag finally exploded, throwing up dirt on his heaving, sweating body. He saw through the settling dust that the candles burned low, almost out. *How long have I been here, two hours?*

A hand fell on his shoulder. "I think that enough for now, young one." It was Master Constantin and with the kindest expression Qosku had ever seen on him. Leyta had wanted to tell the master of his beast affliction, but Qosku refused it, scared. Constantin continued, "I'll even clean up the mess, but for you I recommend sleeping off the rest of whatever it is that troubles you." Qosku nodded but wasn't sure what to do. He knew that sleeping would just allow the beast to come, although he didn't think even being awake and training would've kept it off much longer. And the truth was he still kind of wanted the beast because it held off the woman. In fact, the comfort he'd come to feel in it was what scared him. When training and prayer didn't evade his femininity, the beastly transformation did, but with other dangers.

The dust washed away under the water basin that he tipped over himself. Ice cold on his sweltering body, but the chill was nothing to the pervading thoughts of Lüg. He felt as though he could like him more than he ever did Akualchac. And Lüg was more kind than that jokester. Qosku speculated—no! He shook the water off, watching it run down his legs and into the mud. He couldn't shake it largely because part of him didn't want to. If there was a chance for happiness with Lüg, he didn't want it to disappear, though he knew that even if the chance presented, he would have to turn it down. Or would he? He already had one secret dangerously pressing the doors of public knowledge. Ah, the agony of the unrequited, impossible love. How could they make it work in the world today? But it wasn't just that, his twisted fantasy was a crime against nature and humanity. His ancestors would be severely disappointed and not accept him into their homes of the next life, let alone assist him in this, which was a thought he couldn't bear. And the diseases or curses he'd incur with it, in addition to his werebeast curse. His preference for men, a filthy curse, was a greater monster than his night turning.

If only his twin sister had been here to balance him out. Now lacking her, his feminine side surged. Or if only he could fall in love with a woman, but he liked none more than a friend and repulsed at the idea of kissing one. Not like kissing Lüg. Alone in the bailey, he slapped himself. Punishing hurt but didn't work for very long.

Though painful and dangerous, the beast allowed him to be man enough, to keep his ancestors' favor instead of being shunned at death. He'd do what he had to do. *There's no other way.* He slipped out a window, moved behind the monastery and along the wall to one of the castle's niches. And there he let his monster on. It came quick, painful as always, but a relieving pain this time. His mind faded, a sense that he resisted at first, but saw that with it went thoughts of love. So he allowed his mind to fade, letting the monster take over.

Once transformed, he moved fast, ascending the castle walls with the help of flying buttresses, gargoyles, and pointed ledges. He rose to one of the towers at the back and crawled along the roof. He felt dimly aware that this wasn't the first time he'd ever done this but couldn't remember. It was the perfect place to climb. And it provided a perfect view in every direction, making it the perfect territory. If it wasn't already someone's territory. If so, he'd find out and challenge them for it.

He stood on the tallest spire, and before he could roar and search for food, a figure emerged from the window, amazingly graceful as it slipped out to stand there on the crenellated roof. It didn't come to him or make any sounds, so he descended to the pointed roof and crawled toward the being. The figure looked more like those little humans walking the wall below than he, but something about it made his skin crawl and itch. He heard no breathing or pulse and smelled only a sour odor, faint but undeniable. It watched him coolly, eyes gleaming white in the moonlight, unnerving him more. But he was bigger, and so he growled threateningly.

It did nothing; perhaps it wasn't claiming this territory or stealing his food. Then it need get off his. He reared up, bearing claws and fangs, and roared. When the pale face didn't even flinch, he lumbered at it with a great swipe. It raised an arm that stopped his paw. A dull thud resounded, but it did not move. It held a power in that little body greater than he'd expected. He hooked from the left, harder, and it stopped him with another arm. With a snarl, he threw several swipes and punches, fast and strong. It stopped them all.

He roared again, and humans called out from the wall below, but he barely took notice. The figure, a woman, surprised him by jumping down to the pointed roof, lower than he. Her finger went to her mouth, and she made a "*shh*" sound. Her hand beckoned him. He understood her gesture, and as two arrows whizzed past him, he followed. They dropped down to the roof's edge that connected both keeps, and sat in a corner. Still wanting to fight but curious about this new rival, he decided to watch it first. He clung to a cleft just above her and sat.

"I am not your enemy," she said. "You may have this territory if you'd like. Though I think you'll regret it. It doesn't give you the freedom you're thinking of. Those archers will be looking; attack them and more will come until there's enough to take you down... though I could help you... Or I could take you down..."

He snarled, "Try then!"

Even in the night, he could tell she was as surprised by his speaking as he was. It seemed like he'd done it before, but he didn't like it, and yet, it felt right. Like eating a forgotten food.

"No," she said. Something about the flatness of her voice bothered him. "I tired of fighting quickly after becoming gravespawn. Between resisting all the gore I caused, and the pointless ease at which I created it, I stopped caring. The long years of hiding with so much power hasn't helped. It's getting harder for me to care for anything anymore, especially at night."

"Caring," he said. Something about the word filled him with contempt. "Caring is burden."

"A burden that was good and gave meaning," she said. "Meaning, the energy of life. For a beast or a human, maybe you can make do on mere pleasure. Without it, I'm little different than the corpses in the ground. And it's been getting worse, I don't know how your curse gets worse, but for me it's the slow fade into nothing. Physically immortal but losing my mortal soul... don't know how much longer I can bear it.

"What is your name?" she asked.

"Name? What is name?"

"What do you call yourself?"

"I don't know," he said, searching inward. "Champion... no, Monster."

He felt like a laugh should follow, one seemed to pop inside him in silence, but nothing came from her. He continued, "I had other name. Don't remember."

"I'm not talking about your human name, werebeast." She turned stiffly to look up at him, eyes shining at him from the cloud-covered moon. "I know who you are anyway. I saw you in Qosku once, just before retiring for the night. I see truths in people. But you have fled that person, hiding from her even during the day. You hide much, I see that too. You're something else now, trading a good self for a lesser one. If I had my self, my sentiments,

I'd probably say you're both hiding in a bad state, but the beast is worse than the boy, or girl. I'd say this beast escape to is more dangerous to you and everyone else than a feminine Qosku is. A false refuge."

He struggled to follow her line of reasoning. "What say now?" All he could think of was that he didn't like this Qosku she spoke of but didn't know why. Something was horribly wrong with him and he was weak. He snarled in disagreement.

"More and more terrible things will happen while the beast is in control. I don't doubt that eventually it will destroy you... as mine does me... I suppose I still have enough in me to see that... there's still something left in me then..."

The moon peeked out of the clouds, illuminating her pale skin under the black cloak. She rose to her feet. "I go now, for I must feed again. I might not come back." And then she was gone with a jump that shot her far over the wall and even the lake. He heard her land on the other side. Men ran the wall with torches but he didn't move for the rest of the night.

When the black dogs come for me—
I shall follow willingly
And embrace my time of dead
Enter unknown chillingly
I do not my ending dread
When the black dogs come for me—
Lament long and dear I might
Tremble not in death rattle
Weep as I fade into night
With worse have I done battle
When the black dogs come for me—
Ends not too early my life
We ought not fear cold death's call
Dark days of unceasing strife
Lit up by blaze of my fall
When the black dogs come for me—
With a final dreamless sleep
Or per'lous adventure more
I bid long farewell my keep
And yet fight for many more

CHAPTER NINETEEN

THE COLD HAND OF DEATH

Based on *Annals of Syago*, cc bastica 202;
The Nordvargor Testaments, cc bastica 913;
The Dark Fortress of Mephorash, cc bastica x;

unknown day, 247

Syago sat in the back of the large cart, bundled up tightly against the cold, as it wobbled through the snow-laden mountains to Killfrost Town, so called by the Asturion trappers. An apt name if uninventive but he couldn't remember the name in its original language. The town of the northern Amoyara would not be welcoming to him. The Amoyara had stayed, un-mapped, just out of the Nevermore domain, which they openly despised. Even now, he rode hidden behind stacks of wood, wool, and a sack of fish caught from a lake. Three months of hunting devils, going from town to town, had consisted of lonely travels, with the occasional ride from cara-vans passing by. He prided himself on being able to go alone in the wild, beating old fears of the outside time and again, though the truth was it remained a miserable, dangerous, and fearful experience. He rather felt now that he could do anything, even die a slow, miserable, and lonely death if it came to. He didn't care.

The principal devil that he'd sought, the flaming sloth and its cultist master Kask, had eluded him. His frustration and anger had only contin-ued to simmer and grow. He'd even contemplated joining the Royal Chaos, thinking how much he'd come to agree with them and hate his own liege lords. Not Leyta so much, but all the wealthy and powerful who'd let this world rot. From his initial disquiet and frustration surrounding the poi-soning incident before he first left Tolgrym in the beginning, to the current feud with Toriacus and the aristocrats of Mantlgrym, he now saw problems everywhere but no solutions. *Maybe we have to burn everything down and search through the ashes for a better way. Can't go wrong with a new start.*

Alexandre remained on his back, out of the way and out of mind except the occasional argument. It burned his hand when he touched it, his human hand. He dare not touch it with the fiend arm, which felt bigger and stronger every week as he got more accustomed to it. Alexandre hated it but remained with him instead of trying to return to its grove. He took that to mean it hadn't given up on him, not that he cared anymore.

Once he saw through the boards that they'd entered the gates to Killfrost, named Kalaspunku according to the sign, he hopped out of the back onto a stony street cleared of the recent ice and snow.[63] The snow was thicker than anything Thornwood ever got; it covered the stony Amoyaran buildings. He shivered, feeling colder than ever before in his life and regretted the reptilian devil arm, which sapped more heat from the rest of his body. So far the strength had been worth it. Alexandre only judged. He looked around at the small dark huts of stone and thatched roofing peeked out of the snow. Homes and taverns were packed with brown people in woolen clothes and rags, and on closer look he realized how different everything actually was. Everything from the blankets to the pottery to the weapons might've been more similar to the Unaka than the Asturions or even Kimoc, but it wasn't the same. The lake's edge went right up to the town and calm waters held small canoe-like boats. Out on the water, he saw a small island aglow with lights. He guessed that to be the famous floating city of Orus.

From the buildings, small windows emitted the glow of promised warmth—as long as they didn't kill him as a lone Asturion spy. A couple passersby in the mostly barren street regarded him suspiciously in the fading daylight. It wasn't forbidden for him to be there, but it was dangerous. There hadn't been any wars with the Amoyara; high mountains, heavy snows, and perhaps too few warriors kept them to fishing. But he'd also heard that Kalaspunku was effectively cut off, not just geographically but also politically. High in the mountains, they were too isolated for alliances and trade connections, edged out of areas they *could* farm or hunt by everyone else. All they had was the lake.

But it was of no import to him whichever struggle kept them in rags,

---

63 Recall that in *Atrium Carceri*, Darko finds the ukuku living in a town of this name. But he might've been confusing the region's locales. It's undeniable that the Amoyara have had dealings, friendly and not, with the ukuku of the mountains.

crowded into buildings where they watched him, unless it be his missing devil. He'd concluded recently that this was not the sloth he neared, but some unknown type. Too late to turn back, he'd slay this companion of the sloth and servant of the cult all the same. The Unakan colony had described it as a shadow that took any who sought it, be it army or small hunting party, and it had gone north near this area where Kalaspunku possessed a legendary hellweapon. A large mace called Tigawu that he expected to find in the town chief's throne room or temple. It would be a useful tool, since he'd left Darkness at Deenuk and was still in dispute with Alexandre.

The tallest building, centrally located, was a stout tower with statues about the door. The large stone bricks were impressively tight-fitting. No mortar or cracks in between. The door was a slat of wood with squared designs etched into its face and some kind of pagan eternal carved into the bust above.

He considered knocking, but then just pushed his way in. The room was small, it was no cathedral, but it was resplendent with gold statues, decadent pottery, and intricate rugs. On the golden platform a man sat cross-legged, with men to either side of him. A brazier in the middle filled the space with warmth. The chieftain, or high priest, or whoever he was, stared at Syago dispassionately, though indignant surprise flashed across the others' faces. The leader raised a hand to halt the guards who'd stepped toward Syago. *Another aristocrat who thinks himself better and privileges himself accordingly? How many people suffer for his comfort?*

Syago stared back, then dropped to one knee, though it stung him to do so. He looked up and said, "I am Syago, son of Odiru, Holy Knight of Nevermore and hunter of devils. I've slain two and tracked a third here and ask your aid in finding and killing it with the legendary Tigawu."

They glared at him, not dissembling enough to hide their spite. The chieftain muttered something to the one on Syago's right who'd been about to draw weapon. The man instead disappeared up a set of stairs, then returned with one of their slaves. A pretty mastozan girl of age indeterminable due to being so unkempt. When she saw Syago, she straightened and asked, "My master wish to know why you enter their domain?"

Feeling slightly unnerved, though not surprised, at the mastozan slave, Syago repeated himself, and she translated it. It sounded odd coming from her tiny mouth. They laughed and she gave their reply, "They are supreme warrior and can deal with any devil they do not want."

"And what of this devil, the shadow that takes?" Syago asked.

"It rules here," she said, following her master's words. "Our master rule by day and this devil rule by night. It stopped the ukuku attack and now we are safe. Shemonkuru bring us peace."

Syago was taken aback. He'd never seen or heard of this set up before. No wonder it came so far north. "Forgive me, but it seems a dishonor to his Lordship before me that he should demure to another, especially of another world so gross as the infernal pits. Why have you ceded?"

"The great one is mighty and make us strong again. We not afraid of him—her, as you little... *palebottom*," she emphasized where the leader did, making clear their opinion of him.

"What does it take from you?" Syago asked.

"We give much," she said after he did, heavily, almost sadly. "But that is why we are strong and you are weak."

"And do you have a weapon with which to defeat it should you need to?"

"Our sacrifices are enough. We are enough. Perhaps we give you next."

"Perhaps not." He nodded one more bow of his head before respectfully backing out, seeing no hint of the hellweapon or even a chest where it might be kept. The men on the side looked as though they might draw their weapons or reach for him but, on looking at their leader, made no movement. He hadn't done anything to provoke them, yet. He also realized how formidable he must've looked to them with steel armor and weapons to theirs of wood, bronze, and stone. Or perhaps they didn't want to kill what they wanted to deliver to their new master alive. As he backed out, the girl sat on the leader's lap, smiling up at him.

After leaving that poor excuse of a throne room, and not seeing the hellweapon anywhere, he went to what he determined to be a religious temple on a hill, or ruin of one. He'd heard of it in the legend of the mace. Climbing out the village wall wasn't difficult, it wasn't as large as the city walls he came from nor was it well guarded, and in any case, his devil arm aided him. Trudging over snowy ground, he found the crumbling stone pillars on the side of a mountain just as the sun began to set. There were no weapons or treasures to be seen, but a number of bodies, all frozen over, littered the area. Beneath their frost was some kind of slime or sticky substance that stuck to his glove.

He did marvel at the impressive ruins. Like the mountain cave, they hinted at lost civilizations, their endless cycles of rise and fall across the world. On his way back down, Syago pondered the decline of his own society and if a theocratic, single rule like the Amoyara would be better at meeting the needs of its people. Or perhaps another monarchy, if it could stay with benevolent and incorruptible leaders who focused on feeding and protecting the people instead of leeching them. Or the collectivist Kimoc societies, where all benefited. But the way the tribes squabbled and stumbled to half-hearted decisions, for this or that urgent conflict, didn't look better. They weren't notably happier or richer, either. And turning to a different system only happened with violent revolution which never settled into peaceful liberty when completed. *Perhaps we humans can't rule or be ruled, can't barely cooperate well for long,* he thought. Syago recalled a conversation with Goia after trying to re-arrange things in the cramped hut he'd grown up in, so that everyone had enough room to happily live and work. "You can rearrange the furniture all you want," his grandfather had said, "but it'll never solve the problem of too many people in too small a space. And one of those people, you, has a head too big to even be alone in here. Even building a bigger home might only delay the squeeze because we'd only just grow with it. The problem is this: no matter how you organize us, we're still human."

Deova's blood, I miss him!

There may be no point to revolution, Syago considered, but there was to revenge.

He returned to the town wet and freezing and tried to push his way into the huts, but they barred his passage. He considered forcing his way in, but then noticed the island again. He went to the lakeshore and stepped onto one of the small boats made of woven reeds. With the weather calm, it didn't take him long to approach the island, which wasn't far to begin with. As the light faded above him, he realized he was easy prey to the denizens of the lake, including possibly the devil. Yet the eerie peace allowed him safe passage.

The island was small, but he saw that the stories were true. The island was a manmade island village, made of reeds and wood, all woven and packed densely enough to float and hold people and wood huts atop it. Even in foul mood, he felt impressed. Docking and tying up the boat was a simple enough matter. Walking along the island's straw floor, he found the largest building to be some kind of meal hall. The men inside wore burly fur coats, cloaks, and bone armor. None prevented his entrance, but the fish and odd drink they reluctantly gave inside was hard to swallow. He hated this place, he decided, Killfrost fit it perfectly. He hated a lot of things at that moment: this place, this people. This *chicha*. Alexandre. His family legacy, a lie he'd been living obsessively up until three months ago. Everyone he knew, though with Leyta it was more the situation.

The bitterness twisted inside him. He felt so different now than that bright and hopeful squire he'd been half a year ago when he'd left home. He took a swig out of his wooden mug.

As he set it down, a group of Amoyaran men at a nearby table burst into laughter, some looking at him. He drank again, as if he didn't notice or care. Did he? Can an effort of not caring really count as not caring? One of them slammed his mug down on the table with a loud curse in Asturion, then said, "I'll be damned if I let the palemen conquer this place. We're already dealing with ukuku invasions, one foding overlord, and don't need another." Acting indifferent to the surprisingly good Asturion, Syago drank. The men were large for Amoyarans. He heard the man's chair fall back on to the wood floor. The heavy man approached from behind. His husky voice continued, "Time to pay up and get out, gogger."

Syago finished one last sip as the hand fell on his shoulder. In a flash, Syago twisted the hand around, breaking it, and threw the man onto the table. The drunk Amoyara squirmed as Syago pinned him but couldn't get out of the hold without hurting his arm more. The rest of the room had risen from their seats, ten men total, which suddenly struck him as odd that there'd be so few. Then he realized they were all armed and bigger than he, bulky trappers, traders, and fishermen. *But why are they out here instead of the town?* Syago turned his focus back to his main aggressor. "You want payment? I deal in pain."

The man snarled. Syago noticed the men looking at his devil's arm, which had become partially exposed above his glove in the tussle. He kicked his assailant's leg, sending him face down into the collapsing table. Syago walked around the wreckage, throwing open his blankets to reveal the entirety of his devil's arm, in addition to the weapons hanging from his belt and back. He opened his arms, inviting, "Anyone else want a turn? I'm ready. Come at me."

They stopped their angry advance and glared warily.

"No? Then help me. I'm here to slay the devil. I understand it rules your keeps. Are you cowards or fighters?"

"You dare call coward?!" roared the one on the floor, rising to his feet to stand over Syago.

"If you do not fight by my side, you make it true. I need your mace, the legendary Tigawu. Devils are frightening, true, but can be easily defeated with a hellweapon such as that." The lie rolled easily enough, half-true and justified by his quest. "Where is it?"

None moved again; the ones that spoke Asturion looked confused. Syago pressed, "You have it somewhere, don't you? Or have you lost it?" He looked around he room at each of them, growing frustrated. Then he saw it. Behind them on the wall of religious idols, fearsome relics of their divinities, hung an ornate spear. He almost missed it, due to it not being bone, or even a mace. His information had been wrong, but the dark coloring of it, along with a sudden itching in his devil arm, guaranteed its identity.

Its history and power must have been lost on them, or why hang it there? The man he'd pinned attempted another grab at him, but Syago turned and snapped a light punch, stunning him for the moment. "There," he said, pointing and walking toward the mantle, in between two angry warriors. "This will destroy what afflicts you. With this, you retake your safety and dignity. After slaying the devil and bringing its head back as a trophy, you can overthrow your lord with it."

Before his fingers could touch it, a large hand snapped onto the crude handle. "Stranger no take weapon," a different one said, disdain clear in the man's eyes. "We fight our battles, we kill killer. Not little boy."

"Then do it," Syago said, meeting the fisherman's hard eyes. *Let them discover how hard it really is, teach them the lessons I've already had to learn as I rescue them.* "And I will come to make sure it is done right."

"You be bait while we trap."

Shrugging, he said, "Whatever you want."

The fisherman took the spear and said some things in Amoyara that Syago guessed to be a call to arms, or an explanation of what they'd said. Either way, they roared in their language, preparing to march out. The woman cook merely scowled at Syago and the new leader. He ignored her and walked past to a privy, which actually had a mirror, an old cracked one that had probably belonged to some noblewoman living at an Unakan colony. After making use of the pot, he looked in the dirty mirror to see a face he barely recognized, not having seen it in over three months. Thinner, more worn, with dark stubble around his chin, and a cold, hard edge that ran deeper than skin. At first, the change surprised him, but it was a good look for how he felt. The red scaly arm caught his eye in the dim candlelight. He removed his shirt and armor to see the connection and gasped. He hadn't looked at it since entering the Barbathors. It had grown. The connection no longer stopped at his shoulder, but now half his chest was of red scales, veins still visible at the border, changing more of his body than just the arm. It was somewhat impressive, looking more muscly than his more human side, but the growth deeply disturbed him.

What am I becoming? Maybe Alexandre was right after all.

Sounds of the group leaving drew his attention. Deciding to think on it more after, he covered up. For now, fighting had to be done, even if it meant following, or leading, these unwary savages to their deaths. Maybe they hunted and fought well, but they'd no idea what they were up against. Well, if they didn't learn quick, the devil would teach them, or perhaps Syago would teach them by example. Whatever, he just wanted to hack the thing to pieces. Of course he knew this would likely be as miserable a battle as the previous ones had been, but he was better now and not alone.

The war party of seven, plus Syago, emerged from the long house ready for the cold night. They saw him as tagging along, and he saw them the same. As they walked across the isle, Syago's thoughts turned to the chieftain, safe on the mainland. The man was a pathetic leader for these fearsome savages. He would not last long after this.

Syago had no idea where this devil might be, but the men seemed to. He got into his boat, they in theirs, and followed them. To his surprise, they spread out, heading farther into the lake. The leader, named Muerenka, paddled next to him, and Syago asked, "We're not going back to land? Where is it?"

"It is at Orus," he replied.

"Wait, that wasn't Orus back there?"

"No, that Punchuku. Shemonkuru walk on water, is why we not at Orus. Is why Orus dead. Is why Kalaspunku full."

"Walks on water..." Syago shook his head, his eyes never leaving the opaque waters they glided through. How many other abilities did it have that he didn't know of? Unease began to creep up his spine. "So what kind of devil are we hunting here, anyway?"

"None of us see it. Nobody see it and live. We know only those things. Now go in front so you see her first. That way." He gestured ahead with his paddle.

He hesitated, not wanting to be out front when this unknown fiend water-walked up to them. But he didn't want the man to just knock him into the water either.

The stars gleamed above as the town lights faded away behind them. Syago's eyes moved side to side, searching for any small movement, his hand gripping his oar so tightly his knuckles had turned white. Even just the water itself unsettled him; all it would take is for him to lose balance on the tiny craft and he'd sink into freezing obscurity. Behind him, the Amoyara had earned Syago's begrudging admiration—they'd welcomed him into their party, even if as bait. Hells, he was trying to do the same to them. At least he could credit them for defying their leader in marching against the horror that had subjugated their community. His eyes strained against the night for that horror, but all he saw was vast tenebrous water with no land in sight. He felt himself tense as a light fog graced the surface. *A shadow that takes, walking on water. What does that?*

Then the floating city emerged out of darkness, suddenly closer than gave him comfort. There was the same raft-like floor of woven reeds and wooden stakes and huts on top. But this was much bigger and grander than Punchuku had been—or it would've been grander but for the haunting emptiness. The entire isle town was unlit, all gloom and abandonment. All the buildings lay dark. Desolate. He'd slowed in his approach, but the others behind didn't wait. They passed him, boarded the floating city of Orus, and he followed.

As they entered, a torch was lit and passed to him. This gave him comfort, but the pitying, sad look from them made him swallow. His mix of tough bravery and apathy was fading now. As if he'd gained nothing in all his victories. This devil seemed somehow worse than the previous two he'd encountered, but at least this time he wouldn't be alone. The thought of a repeat of his last fight with a devil, the one whose arm he now wore, instilled a fear in him that he didn't dare admit. At least he didn't have to wield the hellweapon, for which he found himself immensely grateful.

They pushed him forward to the front. He considered taking out Alexandre and laughed inwardly at the irony and their impending doom. Holding the torch at an angle with one hand and grabbing his hand-axe with his other, he proceeded deeper into the floating village. A cloudy night hid much from their eyes, only their sphere of good torchlight helped. He noticed that parts of the huts were broken with holes, like something had punched into them. Other areas were covered in more of the same slime-like substance he'd seen back at the temple. He peered inside one hut, found it all a disarray, but no bodies. The group behind him looked about warily. In spite of their earlier bravado, they too looked frightened, which terrified him even further. *What could've emptied an entire village and scared off its hardiest warriors?*

They came to a kind of central square, but the middle had collapsed and sunken down into the water, leaving a large hole in the center. Around the central pit was a number of shriveled corpses. Kneeling next to one, Syago saw it was covered in a thick layer of slime, like a webbing, but shiny in its freshness. Another man, this one alive, was held up against the wall. Syago didn't understand the words he spoke, but as the others ran up to him, trying to pull or cut him loose, his words became more urgent. Syago guessed that he was saying to run. He looked about, watching for the trap to spring on them, but the place remained still. Suddenly the man screamed in pain and lurched in his wall cocoon, making Syago jump. Syago's eyes widened as something bulged out of the man's chest. He yelled for the others to get back, but when the chest exploded open in a splash of dark blood, and the spear-like arms reached out, Muerenka wasted no time in stabbing it with the hellspear. It screeched in pain. The man was dead. Behind them, another warrior pointed at another corpse. This one seemed to float in the air, not touching the ground.

The warrior stopped with a grunt of frustration. He began what looked like a dance, then dropped his torch to pull on his leg. As the torch fell, the light glistened off of what looked like a thin string. Syago raised his torch slightly, the light falling on the mottled corpse of a blackhound, its fanged mouth agape in death. It was covered in white webbing. Suddenly, the one who'd dropped the torch disappeared into the dark. Not even a scream or warcry to follow save from the others as they raised their weapons. Understanding dawned, and Syago yelled, "Spider web, don't move!"

But if they understood, they heeded not. Spreading out, one, two, three got caught in more webbing. Syago cursed, his battle-axe trembling in his hand. He hadn't anticipated this happening, and now he'd gotten his companions stuck. He'd wanted them to help him out of a bind with this devil, not get bound with him.

He thought of using his devil's arm, but all he could see happening was it getting stuck trying to cut the web. He moved his torch around looking for the strands and saw them faintly in front, above, and to the sides. He dared not move until he was certain he had space to. The others had either been caught already or barely walked through. They thought less calmly, hacking and fighting the strands, which were too strong even for them. Even if not yet caught, they were trapped.

He looked up to see the entirety of the web as it descended on them, something pulling or pushing it down on the yelling warriors to catch the rest of them. Syago tried to duck and roll out of the square but was caught by the sticky material and lifted back up into the air and over the waterhole in the middle. All struggle became useless and the return of the web to its resting place above tugged painfully at his twisted body. His heart pounded away in his chest and he fought to calm his breath.

Then it came, the predator in the darkness.

Syago watched in horror as long black arms reached into the light from the side and wove white webbing around one man in an extended hiss, suffocating his cry.

The spider devil was still out of sight.

Feeling time was running out, Syago pushed the torchflame at one strand to see if it burned. It did, but far too slowly. He held it there while trying to saw through another strand with his axe. The blade got stuck.

Syago heard a roar of triumph as the warrior above, who'd been fully spun up, somehow punched out of his containment and gasped for air.

Syago looked up at the warrior just as a giant shadow descended. Before he could register what had happened, the sickening sound of a bite echoed. He immediately went limp.

Another man was enveloped then yanked out of sight. Syago breathed in dismay. The bite had come from the opposite side of this webbing; the devil either moved really fast or had a partner. Or both. His stomach was in knots and body would've been trembling more if not for the web.

Syago saw the horrified eyes of another nearby as the webbing first closed around his mouth, then flailing arms, and finally the man's legs.

He saw its lidless bulb eyes first, the torchlight glinting off their glassy surface. Then came the rest of its bristled head, its large mouth open to expose its extending mandibles. The fanged mandibles reached out and stabbed the man repeatedly, quick and vicious, then slurped fluids from the warrior, draining him and turning him gaunt right before Syago's eyes.

Then the devil was gone. The man's torch fell from his hand and caught on a web strand and hung. The light shone briefly on a crawling devil. It moved fast. Then another passed through the light just as quickly. *So there is more than one. Wonderful.*

A movement below caught his eye. Syago's gaze went to the sunken pit of water in the center of the room and saw the shadow within the shadow, long black hair floating from a white head beneath the surface. On the head were dark eyes and great fanged mandibles. Larger than the first two. The original, the parent. A pride. *Rood's blood, I've been stupid. Holy Deova, please help me out of this.*

"I'm so glad you've come out to play," one of the pride children said. "Motherrr will be so happy forrr us."

Nearby, Muerenka had stopped his struggle. Instead of tugging or cutting the strands frantically, he and the man next to him tugged gently and waited. One of the children descended from above, but the companion saw it too late. A clawed human hand hit him in the back of the head, spraying blood. He yelped and swung up with his axe but the thing only chuckled, croaking and inhuman, then pulled the axe from his hand and speared the man through the chest.

Quick as lightning, another of its claws slashed at Muerenka, but Muerenka was ready. He snapped the hellspear up into the creature's underbelly. With a gargling screech, it pulled back into the darkness as its acidic blood rained down. Muerenka thrust at the second pride child as it descended on another man, but a hairy arm knocked his spear away. The devilspawn drew a claw across the Amoyaran's chest. "You will wait yourrr turrrn." It then pounced on its victim, tearing him apart and sucking on each of the pieces before dropping them.

The hellspear had fallen and caught in the web just in front of Syago. Acidic blood dripped from the spear onto the web, breaking the strands.

He'd already burned through one strand with his torch, partially freeing an arm. He burned his axe free and threw it hard at the devil child, miraculously hitting it in one of the eyes. It screeched in pain and retreated into the dark.

Above, Syago saw the wounded spawn on its back, legs twitching. The one Syago had hit came at him, and he threw the torch at it, a throw it easily deflected with a hairy arm. Syago braced himself, but it didn't come.

Instead, the parent emerged from the water-hole, human hands on inhumanly long violet arms lifting itself out of the water. It was so silent, Syago almost missed it. *Alexandre, I'm sorry about everything. I need you now. Please!* The soulsword at his side gave no response.

The pride stood to its full height—its bulbous body over twice as large as its devil children, and just as terrifying—its long black hair veiling its pale face.

Oh Deova, please no! Syago asked Alexandre again but instead of waiting, he chanced a touch. The sword didn't burn him, so he drew the glowing Alexandre with his gloved hand and began cutting the strands around him. The web jerked him, and his grip fumbled. Alexandre fell, glowing uselessly on the floor, though it'd at least let him briefly use it. With fewer strands to restrict him now, he tugged on the web, bringing the hellspear closer until he could grasp it.

Then he saw the reason for the jerking: the mother had reared up and was using its many human arm-legs to pull the entire web in. She reached out and grabbed one of her children first. Syago watched in confusion, wondering what it was doing. At first the devil child didn't react, but as the mother pulled it toward the mane of black hair, the child screeched, scrambling in obvious terror to get away. Syago flinched as a sickening pop sounded. She had bit her own spawn in its bulbous abdomen. Gushing and munching echoed as she ate her young, quickly finishing one before the next. She ate her children whole, dead and alive.

The horror Syago felt caused him to all but forget his escape efforts. Gritting his teeth, he threw the hellspear. She swiftly dodged it, backing into the darkness, then reemerging the other side. She ignored Syago, pulling in another warrior, one of the last. Syago yelled, hoping to draw her attention away from the warrior, but she paid him no mind. One of her long arms reached out and batted aside the man's axe. She grabbed the man's head and crushed it with a sickening crunch before folding the warrior's body into its mouth beneath its wet tangle of human hair. Again, Syago flinched, this time from guilt. All of them dead. Though he felt no love for them nor they for him, he was the reason this had happened. He'd pushed them to their deaths.

Syago looked down to see Muerenka, covered in acid burns and bleeding along his chest and head, but alive and free of web, though it seemed like he might fall over soon. The Amoyaran looked warily at Alexandre. Syago considered calling Alexandre up to his hand, or asking the man to pass it to him, but instead said, "Take it, ask it to heal you... and be really polite to it."

Maybe he could at least save one of them, and die with a clean conscience, having failed in all else.

As the devil pulled Syago closer in, he saw a once human face through the tangled hair, though the skin had stretched to hold four shiny black lidless eyes and fanged mandibles out of its mouth. He struggled futilely as the arrogance wrapped him up; even his devil arm availed naught as it pulled him up, tightly, into the dark. Powerless in its sticky swath, Syago managed the one thing he had. As one of the devil's arms passed right in front of his face, he bit into it. Hairy, wet, and cold, everything bad filled his mouth then but he held on. It gave a deep chuckle, its mandibles extending as it brought Syago up to its hideous mouth. Something pricked his abdomen, and Syago screamed as the prick seared as though he were being burned alive. The pride hissed as the hellspear flew into its torso. Muerenka had thrown it perfectly, having fully healed. The devil turned on him but hissed as he and Alexandre cut away one of the legs, then another. In another blinding flash, the soulsword sliced into the devil's face. It gave no sound as it fell back into the sunken pit of water, dead.

Muerenka cut away the webbing. Bending down over him with Alexandre in hand, he said, "Here, heal."

"Won't heal me," Syago mumbled before passing out again into the frightful dark.[64] [65]

---

64 The nature of the otherworlder in this account as taking residence in a cold region and underwater makes one wonder if it's a demon instead of devil. Lore places the Hellpits as subterranean and hot, unlike the arctic seas of the Abyss. Some wonder if it was a demon let in elsewhere and the cult's devil is still here.

65 Or it's just a devil that changed and adapted.

He woke days later, full of nightmares of being eaten, in a giant bed. The massive blankets over him felt good except for the difficulty breathing under those sweltering furs. He pushed them off, weak, and rolled onto the floor. He wanted to puke and realized he already had nights before. That poison—had Alexandre healed him finally? It leaned against the wall and gleamed knowingly.

"What, you finally come 'round?" Syago asked.

No response, so Syago responded for himself, "Well, I am sorry for what it's worth, not as though I'm the only one to make mistakes." But the miserable thoughts of his need during the fight reminded him of the fool he'd been. He noticed again the red scales that covered almost half his chest. He thought grimly on the implications of it, then crawled to take his things, putting Alexandre into its scabbard wordlessly before donning his tunic. Muerenka, who must've treated him, entered the room.

"No," he said gruffly. "We keep you, we sell you. Prisoner and slave."

The man clasped a manacle around Syago's wrists. Syago looked up, stupefied, and said, "I just helped you slay the devil. And saved your life."

"Yes, after leading us all to die," he said, sorrow and rage in his eyes. "You knew all and told nothing. We sell you to Unaka who your people make slaves. Now you see how it is." Then he left, taking Syago's weapons with him. Syago tested the manacles, trying to break free, but they were solid and tight, and in his weakened condition, unarmed, he saw no way to make a safe escape.

He'd won the fight and lost the war. And now he was sick, scarred in his head, and imprisoned. Instead of going on toward another devil or rejoining Leyta as he'd been thinking, he'd go toil in some mine somewhere while his grandfather's murderers continued their rampage across the land.

He'd not only failed at revenge, he'd failed everyone else in the process.

CHAPTER TWENTY
HEAVEN'S FURY AND NIGHT'S REVENGE

Based on *The Nordvargor Testaments*, cc bastica 913;
Writings of Qosku, cc bastica 200;
Leyta's Journals, cc bastica 220;

16th of Marza, 247
17th of Marza, 246

Write me a book I can read forever
Sing me a song to change how I listen
Kiss me a kiss that will heal all my wounds
Show me enough kindness to change the world
Give me the world and I will change it in myself
Returning it better than before
And I will be better than my past
Give me your self and I'll give you mine
My and your treasure, forevermore[66]

Lügos had invited Qosku to play games with some of the boys before bed
call. He both did and didn't want to go; he did and didn't want to reveal his
true feelings. It was torture. Most of his days, he followed Leyta around as
her personal guard but wasn't needed at the present hour. All that time of
standing around left him to his thoughts too much, dwelling on fantasies
about a different curse that would turn him into a girl at night where they
could meet and fall in love. But the fantasy distraction only made it worse.
He couldn't go drink, training wasn't helping, and the beast was not yet due.
It was rude to not go, and what if Lüg was interested in him in the same

---

66 *Whether the author was Qosku or Cavalera, they clearly drew inspiration from* Thy Light, Therion!, *22*

way? Qosku would lose him if he kept pushing him away like this, but wasn't that the point? A part of him ached to act bold and put on a dress, any kind, though he preferred the traditional Unakan ones, and present himself to his friends, revealing his true self. He slapped himself several times. *Idiot! See? That's why you can't go.*

He trained, but poorly and without success of distraction. He had to watch the time; it wasn't dark yet but would be fairly soon and he'd begun turning early, finding solace in the painful transformation. He couldn't decide what he wanted out of this. *A true warrior would be able to go and not be affected. I can conquer and dominate myself.* So he made his way to their spot, hating himself and everything about the situation. In a small alcove near the library, the boys sat on the floor playing cards. Qosku watched from behind the door post, still debating about joining until finally one of them saw him and called him in.

Lügos sat with Milgalic and Emeric in a circle, the room dark but for the candle lanterns. Qosku entered and sat in the furthest spot from Lüg, who looked really good in his double breasted tunic. "All right, we're dealing vivieral now," Lüg said, handing Qosku his set of cards. "In vivieral, you want all of your cards to line up in a perfect order, with no extras or missing cards."

Qosku rifled through his and noticed that the designs were mostly of Asturion royalty, similar to the Royal Chaos costumes. All except for a cloaked skeleton card. Lüg explained the rules, looking him in the eye, and when he finished, Qosku felt he still had no idea how to play. Part of it was being new to the language. Even with Lüg talking slower and simpler for him, the extensive list of complex rules he had to follow made it difficult to understand. Unakan games were more straightforward, used more skill, and relied less on chance. And judging by his understanding of what Lüg said, Qosku had been dealt a terrible hand. The cloaked skeleton would ruin everything if he couldn't get rid of it. He had a lot of royals but nothing else, including an extra knave and jester card that he'd have to sort out.

"You got the rules then, Qos?" Lüg asked.

Qosku didn't want to look stupid, or delay the game, so he mumbled a "yes" and planned how to best appear that he did understand. "We'd better get it moving then," Lüg said, eyeing Qosku. "I don't like staying up long past dark."

The game had no turns. They went as fast as they dared, watching each other's card trades or draws. Qosku's tenuous grasp of the rules made him slower than the others. He watched them go, then made a similar action, trading a knave for a king, which he later had to give up because of the skeleton. He felt coming to play a mistake, because in playing, he only went through the motions, which gave him plenty of time to watch Lüg. "Don't like staying past dark, you afraid of the dark, Lüg?" Milgalic asked.

"Only when you're in it," he muttered, absorbed in his cards. He looked beautiful even in such seriousness. Qosku yanked his eyes back to his cards, a terrible hand. *You won't win, you just have to not look stupid,* he thought. *Good luck with that. I should just leave now.*

As each player exchanged cards between each other and the two piles in the middle, the give and take of the game let Qosku figure out the rules the hard way. After accidentally giving away his crown and throne card in exchange for a hairy monster, he almost threw his cards in frustration. Training and fighting was his skillset, not negotiating over cards or chancing decks.

"Say, Qos," Milgalic said. "I'll give you a crown and throne card if you take my worst with it."

"Come on, Milgalic," Lüg said. "Don't play him so hard, he don't know words that well." Milgalic's eyes scrunched in annoyance, but he shrugged. Lüg turned to Qosku. "Here, trade me your jester for my crown and throne alongside a worst for worst—yeah switch me your skeleton for my demon. That's how you do it."

The demon card perturbed Qosku. Not only could he not remember what it did, but the artwork depicted a disturbing mix of tentacles, eyes, and fins. Milgalic and Emeric exchanged, and Qosku watched Lüg's frown, burning it into his mind. They played for several more minutes, Qosku still unable to get rid of his demon, until Milgalic chuckled in glee, then lay his cards down in victory. One of each royal and none of the black cards, a perfectly ordered straight. Emeric and Lügos tossed their cards into the center. "You won last time," Emeric said.

"Of course. I'm the best," Milgalic said, gathering up the cards.

"And you had the new kid to play off, that's like cheating," Emeric said.

"Knock it off," Lüg said. "I helped him more than Qosku did. Anyway, I think I'm finished for the night," he said with a hard look at Qosku, who could feel the beast itching at him. This night was the full moon, and he doubted he would be able to stave it off long. The monster waited for him, his one true escape.

Qosku sighed, then stood and walked to the door when Milgalic called to him, "Hey, Qosku, thanks for coming." Emeric and Lüg echoed his words, then Lüg followed Qosku out. Qosku wasn't sure how he felt about the evening, but when Lüg walked down the stairs behind him, a shiver tickled the back of his head.

"Oy, Qos, you all right for the night? It's full moon," Lüg said.

Qosku turned on the stairs. They were alone together in a dark stairwell... He wanted to do so many things in that moment, but the memory of his old rejection still hurt. "Yes, I'm past being afraid now. I have more control."

Lüg looked at him a long moment, which only made Qosku's torment more pronounced. Finally, Lüg said, "Well, be careful and don't strain yourself. We want you to be well. Anytime you want to talk about it, you can come to me."

"Lüg, you think... what you think of me?"

A mixture of surprise and confusion crossed his face. "I—I really care about you. I don't know, that's a strange question. I know you don't have a lot of friends here, but I and some of the others love you at least, having you around, I mean. You've nothing to worry about from us. Is something bothering you?"

Qosku's stomach leaped at that, but he quickly dismissed it as nothing. "Something always bothering me." He turned to go back down the stairs. "I see you tomorrow."

"Tomorrow. Be safe tonight, Qosku."

Bells tolled in the church tower for the late hour prayers, ringing Qosku's ears. Leyta had already retired to prepare for her early rise the following morning, to summon Osmos. He would join her for that if he felt well enough but now sat beneath the bell atop the chapel, preparing for the full moon to take him. Tonight the beast would consume him fully, a sweet respite from being in a male body that he hated.

The transformation would be most complete, lacking his will and bearing a contagious bite. He wanted to believe it still felt preferable to his other affliction, but no, this time again he felt terrified. The bell tolled and he stood, feeling the deep sound thrum through his itching and trembling body as fur sprouted and muscles grew. He was supposed to have already left the island, such carelessness would earn him a reprimand later. He removed the clothing and jumped down onto the roof, ran to the wall, and when all guards' eyes averted away, he jumped to the top. He leaped off toward the small island to the north. Isolating himself for their protection, and his. Most nights, hiding on the castle towers sufficed, but with a contagious bite and lack of self, they couldn't risk it on a full moon. An island with some bushes and rocks would do.

He landed in the cold, dark water. None of the guards would be able to see him out there in the dark as Qosku, though they might spot his larger and louder beast form. The dark swept the sky and the silvery moon glowered over him as he crawled out of the water and onto the island, fully beast.

He reviewed his body, something bigger, hairier, and stronger. His mind vanished along with Lügos, leaving him only with a sense of relief from pain. Gone. He rose on his feet, stretched, and roared triumphantly at the moon.

Calls on the wall caught his attention as they gathered to watch him. He moved to confront them, those pitiful challengers. No, but the water! How to cross the lake?

Suddenly, something landed right in front of him, cracking rocks from the impact of a heavy landing. A woman of pale skin, she looked familiar... Her cold body stared at him, blankly. Was he on her island? Then he would challenge her for it. The fury of the night built up in him; he had to fight her. He had to fight something, had to bite something too.

He roared in her face and she was gone, a single leap carrying her across the water to the shore. The jump impressed him. Taking a running start, he tried to beat it but only got most of the way, crashing into the rocky water then barreling up to the shore. Once out, he shook his fur and grabbed a large fish that had bit onto his leg, he broke it and ate it. He wasn't hungry but needed to rub something on his itching jaws that now foamed. He sniffed for her foul smell and saw her atop a large bush. He chased her, but she only jumped away. He moved after her, through rocky hills and large bushes, pursuing as she led him along. His frustration turned into relaxation as the night wore on, occasionally taking a branch to gnaw on and expunge the foam. This sufficed for the itch, but he needed something soft, something flesh; even her stench of death would be better than wood. They went far from the castle, flying over tall rocks, bushes, and fungi. A tree attacked him and he threw it down, but before he could bite it, the woman jumped in and killed it, then pulled something out of it to bite on. She ran away before he could grab her. Eventually the woman let him catch up, and a small thrill rose in him at the thought of finally catching his challenger.

Down the hill to a vale, the strangely familiar clamor of battle drew his attention. Forces of tall men, even bigger than he, fought with weapons against waves of rotted bodies that smelled worse than she did. The battle raged intensely, and he hungered to claw them, to bite them. He looked at his chase. Her calmness made her less interesting than what passed below.

"Come," she said and, to his surprise, jumped down into the fray. He roared and charged down the hill, falling into them right behind her. She slammed into a giant cyclops man, then a swineman, and he crashed through several corpses, smashing, scattering, and throwing them as they crawled over him in a frenzy. Eventually he came up to a large ozorman like he but with an axe who swept it through the bodies. The tumult increased into pure chaos. Lifeless flew everywhere, beast and giant slammed into each other. The woman brought the terror of the night thundering down on giant and body alike. The madness ebbed, the werebeast bit and thrashed body pieces, beating them against others just to let out his energy. The woman gorged herself on fresh hearts, covered in blood. What remained of the armies dispersed, and the two crawled back up the hill, wounded and worn, but more alive for it. The beast felt so free and true and complete; he was unstoppable.

Whomever summons devils is in danger of their hellfires. And whomever summons angels is in danger of their judgments.[67]

Leyta entered the chapel after the priests. Early morning rays beamed through the stained glass windows, hopefully endowing needed hope. The unbearable silence bore witness to the unease amongst the pious in this endeavor.

Osmos.

Dealing with the enigmatic sentient gate rarely fared well for any involved; legends and fables always resulted in tragedy. Yet Leyta had done her research and knew how to avoid such catastrophes. In the likely event

---

67 *Of the many sayings attributed to Saint Casilda, Archive iii, 3; unknown date.*

that one would happen anyways, she'd made careful plans. This gateway summoning would call upon the celestial Halls of Celos, The Kingdom in Heaven, for angelic aid.[68]

The priestesses laid out the floor symbols, intricate patterns of chalk, that would bring up the enigmatic gate. Once called, they would be able to do little to control the gate or its passengers. It would be Bishopess Gladys Yanet, Katti, and five more priestesses. And Leyta, at her own insistence, and Qosku, at his own insistence, to protect her. Two male priests accompanied, standing on the side anxiously. The Kingdom Republic couldn't afford anymore waiting. The Royal Chaos gathered a large army of barbarian raiders and dissenting rebels from the towns while the cultists continued to work from the shadows, taking lives in the process. The kingdom needed specific information, which at this point only an angel could give, if it could be given at all. This would've been the perfect time to have Syago present; angels enjoyed conversing with men of holy weapons, so say the legends. But lacking any word of him for months forced her to consider him dead, taking some self-blame for it. But she couldn't afford regrets now in a time for focus.

Yanet was examining the lines when Katti led the infant bomog offering to the circle. "No, not yet," Yanet snapped at her. "We have to finish the circle first. Everything in its order." Katti nodded sweetly and backed away to the corner of the room with the beast. It bothered Leyta the way Yanet snapped at them the way she did, a little too much like Leyta when herself in a dark mood. Especially Katti, who Leyta now felt a close friend and considered much too submissive to criticism.

The priestesses finished and stood in place. Yanet reminded everyone for the fourth time that she would do the talking. Leyta nodded impatiently. The prelata knew the angels better. Though she'd only ever summoned one, it was yet one more than Leyta had. She understood the hierarchies, divisions, and symbols but little else. The priestesses stood, examining the circle, then looked to the bishopess, who motioned for Katti to bring the bomog over.

It began.

The holy sisters prayed. They prayed for wisdom in this time of ignorance. They prayed for strength to make the right decisions. They prayed for forgiveness to be worthy of this blessing. And they called for Osmos, the

---

68 See Lustmord de Gallowbraid's commentary on the rotting crisis section in *Heavenly Batushqa*.

Door of Infinite Spaces, to come and exchange. The candles in the room flickered and dimmed, and the air and floor shuddered deeply.

Osmos materialized in the center of the pattern with a profound thud. On the bust, its marble eye rolled its gaze on them. The great stone doors ground open, and human arms immediately stretched out, excessively long, from a black void. Leyta looked away as they grabbed the young bomog. Her stomach churned as its squeals pierced the air and faded into the dark, shrinking to nothing. Then the doors boomed shut, and all was silent. The young bomog had been accepted. The statues' expressions remained fixed but the voice of Osmos grated out of their mouths as one, "Ask."

"We desire—erm," Yanet swallowed, betraying nervousness. "We desire to speak with the Kingdom in Heaven, with an agent of the Halls of Celos."

The eye closed and a deep hum reverberated from the gate, though nothing visibly changed. They waited.

"It will be done without charge," Osmos decanted, and everyone blinked in surprise. Leyta wasn't so sure this was a good thing. While others relaxed, she yearned for her staff or scepter. The eye spun in place as the doors unlocked then parted, flooding the hall with brilliant light. The group shielded their eyes until something came through and the doors closed shut. They looked up to see what looked like a ball of white feathered wings, a diligence, also called an Archon Sentinel of Devotion. Its feathers radiated glorious light.

A diligence was the last thing Leyta had wanted to see come out to them, had Yanet remembered to request a kindness or charity as Leyta recommended to her, they might've fared better before heaven. Only a chastity could have been worse.

Leyta's grasp of angelology extended only as far as being able to identify it; most texts intentionally left many mysteries, too full of awe to complete them. Watching this lump of shining white feathers grow, Leyta didn't feel awe. It made her think of strange birds more than the glorious beings described in scripture, its flawless radiance notwithstanding. It landed gracefully on the floor, seeming to stand on its feathers, its many wings wrapped around itself. That it appeared to be concealing itself sent chills up her spine. If the wings hid a body, head, or limbs, she couldn't see it. For a moment all stared at the dazzling glory of holy purity emanating from the wings before having to avert from the brightness that filled the chapel. But when it didn't speak, Leyta became confused. Then Katti tugged her dress. All others had fallen to the floor, bowing deeper than the angel.

Leyta hastened to comply.

"Good." His voice was deep and rough, but clean and warm. His two top-wings spanned out, and two small eyes on the crook of the wings gazed down at them. Leyta choked down a scream as its brilliance became painful. "Now that we've paid sufficient homage to our Lady of Redemption, let us begin."

Immediately, one of the priests cried out, and Leyta saw that his robes had caught fire. Before she could run to his aid, Katti clutched her dress, a warning in her eyes. Leyta stayed down. The angel too waited.

The priest's screams echoed in the chapel. "Somebody help me, please!" He nearly tripped over a priestess who shied away from his begging hands. "I'M BEGGING YOU, PLEASE!" Not one person moved to help him. The flames consumed him as if stoked by dyne. The young man collapsed in a heap of putrid black smoke. Burned bodies flashed through her mind and she suppressed an urge to vomit.

As the fire died down, the angel said, "Only the faithful shall be accepted of Heaven. Only true faith, unfeigned, will make the weak strong and pure that they may withstand my glory, a glory that burneth the wicked."

"Amen!" the priestesses said in unison.

With him all wings, spread just so, Leyta felt like she was looking on a hairy spider more than an angel. As if her fears confirmed, she noticed one, two... more than four eyes peeking out between the feathers, as if shy. But as soon as she saw them, they disappeared, winking shut. She imagined it pouncing on her, devouring her. Forcing herself not to shudder, she recited scripture to purify her mind.

"I am Eleleth of Sacred City Batushka. Who is it that leads this calling and why?" asked the angel in thickly accented Asturion.

Yanet rose and stepped forward. "I—I do, sire. I am Bishopess Gladys Yanet. We have need of your assistance. Our situation—"

Eleleth cut her off. "That is thy qualification, but what of worthiness? I must judge before proceeding. Sing the praise of the ninth canton. All of you." They looked at each other in worry, and Leyta felt a pang of fear. She didn't know it. They rose and started singing, off-tune at first and tremoring in timidity, then it picked up and Leyta joined in to follow their lead. As the haunting mantra filled the hall, Eleleth opened more eyes along the arms of its wings, though still concealing its core. Its eyes zeroed in on each person in such a way that was both mesmerizing and terrifying.

As they finished the song, the diligence said, "Thou art pure but some of thine assistants have evil eyes." It was then that the smoke reached Leyta's nose. She looked to the side to see the remaining priest and a priestess curled up on the floor, clutching at their faces as smoke poured from their eyes. "They watch with lust and not with light or truth, yearning for flesh. My natural aura is blinding them for this wrong, that they might learn and repent. May they learn purity from this trial."

"Amen," Leyta muttered with them.

His wings spanned open as he moved in front of Sister Amarias. "And this priestess allowed a heresy to persist. For this, she now receives a disease that will take her life in a month unless she practices the gauntlet of devotional prayers, then she only loses the use of her legs. May this trial teach her greater diligence in the faith."

"Amen." The word was bitter in Leyta's mouth.

The girl wailed and fell to her knees, crying into her hands. Again Leyta resisted the urge to help and pushed away anger at the girl's lack of responsibility for not mentioning this before the summoning. Eleleth moved to Leyta, who trembled in fear. She'd had a heresy, but not entertained it. The angel said, "I give thee no trials yet, for thou art dutiful in all things, although I sense thy commitment lacking." She nearly gasped in relief.

"Amen."

"And thy small warrior attendant here," he said of Qosku, almost forgotten and overlooked. Qosku straightened slightly. "A pagan, thou hast no favor for our power but respect it, I see. I would bind thee tighter, but I see thy sacrifice for purity. A deeper purge is needed and may follow conversion to the true knowledge, with faith, which in turn may convert thy soul to its correct design." Leyta noticed with curiosity that Qosku's attention intensified at this, in place of fear. "But more sacrifice will be good for thee. We cure thee not in this moment that thou mayest give more through suffering, learning what thou canst through this trial."

Qosku's face fell again, despondent. The diligence moved to Yanet. "And as for you, Bishopess, you have been involved in improper use of holy funds. Further, you did a good deed today, but not yesterday nor many days before, indicating a selfish heart. Your trial will be the crippling of your hands until you learn proper deeds. Then as they're done to thee, so do thou to others."

"What?! But, sire, I—"

"And for arguing with me, I give thee silence. That thou mayest learn thy place in the conduct of heaven. Now whom is to speak in her place?" Yanet visibly tried to speak, but no sound came out. Her second, Ariende, who stood next to her, looked terrified.

Katti stood quietly behind everyone, agonizingly remaining in her place, so Leyta stepped forward. "I am Leyta, archdynast and Castellan of Cantlgrym. I seek assistance for we are at conflict with enemies powerful and sinister. They seek an old legend, an artifact called the dydatris. We—"

The angel's voice drowned out hers. "It is not good for one without the ordinances to speak to an angel. Though thou art in the fellowship of Deova Bondua, thou hast not yet authority." She about threw her hands up in the air, but its sudden quietude gave her pause. She turned to look pointedly at Katti, who stepped forward.

Voice sweeter than ever, Katti said, "We need help with our enemies and their infernal powers."

"Thou hast conflict? We grant thee the free will to advance solutions thineselves." He hovered in front of the priestess, almost too close. Qosku moved to intervene, but Leyta gripped his shoulder, nearly yanking him back. Eleleth's eyes glanced from Qosku back to Katti, who, to her credit, didn't flinch from the proximity or glare of his shining brilliance. The diligence continued, "We deal only in conflicts against the Otherworlds and let thee to thine other unrelated conflicts, as fitting thy mortal punishments of this world."

"If it pleases your holiness," Katti said. "One of such foes wants to bring back the Crimson Covenant and has summoned several devils into our lands to this end. The dyd—"

"Of course," Eleleth said thoughtfully, looking off past them. "Devils could help them find the relic, and if they obtain it, they could change everything, ushering in many more. They'd have this world before we could bring to bear enough to stem it. Very well, I shall return and report to my lords. Summon for us in three days' time and we shall return with a mighty conquering army."

This was the opposite of what Leyta wanted. A cosmic war on their land, even if in quick victory against the fiends, wouldn't end well for them, but at least he'd implied that the angels believed the relic to be real instead of just a myth. Katti also understood this and pressed him. "Please, sire. We have need only of information. What is this artifact and where is it that we may stop them?"

Eleleth stared at her. "Thou art most honest of those I've met. Noble, competent, and good. Yet I cannot trust thee with it, for it contains great power over dyne, which may corrupt or easily fall into wicked hands."

"If you give us not the relic," Katti said gently, "then tell us where to go that we may protect it from them while we wait on you, before we summon you once more." *Good girl,* Leyta thought.

"Hmm, it is wise. Thou shalt guard it in the ruined place where pagan kings built legacies out of bones and where humanity made its claim to the powers of Nevermore, in a vale of the mountain-lands northeast of us by two of thy marching days. When thou obtainest this temple of ancient wisdom, guard it until an angel may aid thee. It is dangerous.

"Until then, I bid you farewell. I must return and report." And with that, the doors of Osmos opened, full of shining glory, and the diligence floated back from whence he came, the doors disappearing the moment he was gone.

Leyta was certain none in their group held intentions to open it again.

CHAPTER TWENTY-ONE

IN SEARCH OF PARADISE, PAIN

Based on *The Hunter's Parchments,* cc bastica 270;
The Nordvargor Testaments, cc bastica 916;

21st of Marza, 247

It had been a quiet night when Klamuth'olk woke, alone in her bed bundle. She left the woshik to see Wiq'olk, her husband and love of thirty years, standing on the edge of a small platform. She asked what he was looking at, but he gave no reply. Peering into the darkness that he faced, she saw two glowing points, like eyes of dying embers. She called for him again, more nervously. Then he raised his arms from his sides and fell forward off the platform. Her scream blocked out the sound of his landing. It wasn't a far fall, not unsurvivable, but for the log he landed on face down. Her screams shattered the stillness of the night. The eyes moved closer, a moving darkness twice her height, lithely bypassing her to enter their home. Only when it emerged with two of their children wrapped in its shadow arms did she break out of the shock. She ran at it, shouting, but had no weapons or way to stop it as it lifted into the canopy and disappeared with her little ones.[69]

She'd told all this to Lil'iek, who sat comforting her over some tea. "In some ways, it's almost worse than the Razhod," the woman sobbed, wiping her face. "Instead of a massacre, they're just gone. Who knows what those things are doing to them."

The words stung Lil'iek a little, whose own dead husband was somewhere in the cosmos. But she held off from counseling the woman, only offering sympathy. "It is terrible; I can't imagine."

---

[69] See *Sol Sistere de Selbst* by Himetuks Himi'n

A horn interrupted them, indicating the return of the hunting party.[70] Lil'iek hugged Klamuth'olk and went to her own woshik where Tek'ouk would meet her. To pass the agonizing wait, she began preparing dinner.

"What did you find?" Lil'iek asked as he entered the woshik and kissed her. "The children asked our guardians of the forest to help you find the body of a dead grimshade so you could use it to find the live ones."

"Thank you, but we found nothing except more reason to go further out," he said, sitting down as she took his hunting sack. "I'm not sure that would work anyway; they don't seem to have bones." They hadn't made any progress on the Baw'kook either. After leaving Mour'ikik to be their captive, they'd returned with more Roah'riik to find the barbarians had already left. In trying to follow the tracks, they were savagely attacked by a large mabin'guarik and had to return. She'd noticed Tek'ouk become increasingly despondent and reluctant to go out. Visibly frustrated by his disability. She worried for him.

"Would you like rainbow bird for dinner?" Lil'iek asked. When he said yes, she walked to a wooden cage hanging outside the woshik. The plump birds fluttered their wings nervously. She continued, "What comes next then? Because if we don't know how to stop this, it will continue. And our previous losses remain unavenged." She stabbed one through the cage and it went limp while the others squawked.

"Well, more pressing word from Cantlgrym found me. They've discovered the intentions of the enemies, both of them. Everyone is gathering at an ancient temple northeast of Cantlgrym. They think it will give them more power, or just more gold. It holds nothing for us and draws the fighting away from Quoak, so other than rescuing Mour'ikik, I think this is not our hunt."

Taking the dead bird from the cage, Lil'iek asked, "And would going bring us what we seek or more death for our people?"

"I don't know. But probably there is no justice without more death. Such is the way."

She placed the dead bird down on her table and wiped his knife clean, then knelt and lifted the dead bird in her hands. After he slid his hands beneath hers, she led the prayer:

---

70 Gybiaaw Blackbraid often spoke of Kimoc hunts, though it is known that they farmed more than hunted. It makes me wonder if there was a shift in their way of life not long ago.

"Gratitude to Motherwood, World of Violence and Life. We thank you for giving us of your children as nourishment. Thank you for your sustenance. Thank you for everything. And thank you, bird, for your body to feed us. We shall not waste any part of you."

They lowered the body in silence, and she began to pluck the feathers off, slowly at first.

"We have to go," Lil'iek said quietly.

"I know." He sighed. "But only to bring back Mour'ikik."

"We lose people here or we lose them there, and I'll not wait on the Asturions to ensure the war doesn't affect us." She said this as deliberately as she plucked feathers off the bleeding bird. Blood dripped down the funnel in the center, draining into a large bowl.

"And the children?"

"Same as before. They'll have my sister and mother to care for them while we're gone."

"Vengeance was only barely achieved before, while we lost several Roah'riik. At that pace we'd lose them all while the enemy remains. Are you sure it wouldn't be better to stay?"

"I *am*." She turned to him, pointing a bloody finger. "I will not pale in the face of our losses, nor will I let the conflict pass us by. I have to fight again, and I'll do it with you or I'll do it alone. The children will be safe here, and you'll be safe with me or with them. But I am *not* done."

"If you're serious about this," he said after a pause, looking at her hard, "then we must marry tonight."

"Yes," she responded. Now done with the feathers, she took a knife and began gutting the bird, pulling its intestines out. Inwardly she blossomed with warmth and excitement she'd all but forgotten. And not just for a wedding, but a man supporting her in her search for justice. He smiled and kissed her on the side of her head. "Then I shall tell the others and enjoy your company in the hunt."

Later that evening, the woshik swayed as their families filed in. He'd not bothered to send word to Yaoh, where he'd originally come from to marry his first wife in Quoak. They wouldn't have sent any dowry or even attendees, making it a half marriage instead of a full one, but which Lil'iek didn't mind.

Minutes later, Tek'ouk and Lil'iek knelt in front of Quoarn'riik Chtoam'luk, Kurak'iek and Link'ouk beside them. They'd debated the wisdom of having the wedding so soon after the Shuolk family losses, but in light of the other pressing matters, it was quickly agreed on.

Reams of feathers covered Lil'iek's whole body, a wooden mask over her face. Tek'ouk also wore a wooden mask, but with furs and beads covering him rather than feathers. Some Kimoc tribes skipped marriage ceremonies altogether; Quoak enjoyed them but also kept them short. The couple clasped hands, Chief Chtoam'luk handed them a cup with a blessing from the ancestors and eternals. They drank from it and he raised his arms in the air, proclaiming him Tek'ouk'iek, now part of the Quoiek family. Raising each others' masks, they kissed deeply, then connected their foreheads and joined minds, meeting each others' souls in a sweeter fashion than how a Roah'riik joins his mind to an animal.

"You should go to the war council," her mind said to his. *"But I'll be waiting for you when you're done, husband."*

"Whatever you want," was his reply. *"In any way you want it."* She laughed.

They broke the connection and kissed again, this time with tongue. She winked slyly at him before moving away. The Quoarn'riik prepared the woshik for the council.

Quoarn'riik Tok'olk placed the bandolier, with flute and pipe, on the central staff, then sat, completing the circle. Tek'ouk'iek hid weariness and trepidation beneath a stoic face. He couldn't try and fail at another hunt. They'd not let him continue. Numerous Quoarn'riik smoked chash straws or leaves for insight, and Chief Yuq'ikik, the oldest of them all, sat in a corner taking the Shor'une'natim drink, seeking the wisdom of the eternals and spirits. Now the hearing on the war would begin.

Oh Eternals, please make me strong and able for this. For I am being choked out of other options.

"Spirits of our fathers and mothers," Tok'olk began, "come to us, guide us, and fill us with your lights. Mamak Yoaom, sacred forest, motherwood to our family, keep us well. And care for your son, Wiq'olk, whom we've lost."

Then the whispers, then silence. Finally Kurak'iek stood, "Our brother and war leader Tek'ouk'iek is invited to speak with the circle."

Tek'ouk'iek stepped forward, standing inside it. "Respected leaders, our searches have brought nothing but more clues that the war moves out of the forest and toward the mountains to the north. I need permission to attack the Baw'kook and rescue our captive Roah'riik."

"You would not continue the war or the hunt?" Yano'creeh asked.

"Of course, if we see an opportunity of revenge, we'll take it," Tek'ouk'iek said, though he secretly wished to not do even that. However, Lil'iek would never accept it, and he couldn't appear to be as weak as they'd feared he'd become. "But I don't believe it's any longer in our interest. In a conflict that is moving away from us, it has already taken too much while giving too little back. If the eternals smile on us, the palemen will stop it and themselves be wasted in the process. If the legends of this temple are true, then it will offer gold we don't need or a relic of dynal power enough to wipe us out completely. We're better off with our warriors here to protect us, and our children."

"But it's a hunt left unfinished," Chief Qil'kor said. "An oath unfulfilled. We've been here protecting and it hasn't stopped, and more to the point, if you'd accomplished what you'd set out to do before, this might not have happened."

"Were you expecting this to be without sacrifice?" Com'anch'iik asked.

"Do not speak to me of sacrifice," Tek'ouk'iek growled back. The leaders sat comfortably before him, each with both legs. "I know it better than any of you."

"True," Chief Com'anch'iik said after a long pause. "But we've avoided the kinds of losses the palemen faced because we mostly stayed out of their way while involved. We sent you to collapse the pale forces while on that quest, which you also failed to do. Opportunist involvement fits us best in this. Why should we quit so soon?"

Link'ouk interceded, "We only worry that in light of your new injured state, you're seeking escape and turning away from the oaths we swore to the ancestors and the eternals, oaths which they'll hold us to."

"Bomok shit!" he snapped, leaning on his crutch, his hackles raised. "My disability has forced me to fight harder and smarter than any of you ever have. The *only* reason I do this is for our people. We have no peace and those eternals have not helped us in this."

Link'ouk held up his hands, more conciliatory. "We all recognize and appreciate your valor, Tek'ouk'iek. But the source of our discontent is not here but out there. The enemy is not yet insurmountable, they are not the Razhod. We committed to the hunt and now we must finish it. We'll petition Yaoh and Koah to join us, and I think they'll listen this time. If you wish to sit this out then perhaps that would be best after all..."

"If we are to war, then I am not sitting it out!" If the barbs were intended to change his mind, they were working. *I'm like to die proving I'm not useless, but so be it.*

Chief Yuq'ikik broke the silence with a tremulous voice. "The sun will riiise!"

The sage rose from his seat, an empty Shor'une'natim cup rolling away, chash smoke billowing from his three leaf-wraps. Tek'ouk had shared Fal'iek's skepticism that even one chash leaf was useful for spiritual revelation, much less the visionary drink. The senior Quoarn'riik walked into the circle without cane beneath his trembling limbs but none moved to support him.

"The Sun, it comes," the ancient's eyes were glazed over, almost rolled back in his head. He raised a hand to Tek'ouk'iek's face, placing a palm to it, and Tek'ouk'iek resisted the urge to back away. "It comes and you will fight for it. There, in the mountains where the Sun will rise once more."

The man then withdrew his hand and wandered out of the woshik, mumbling to himself in the night. Somebody soon followed him out, to watch over him.

The Quoarn'riik, surrounded in their own smoke of insight, exploded into conversation about the meaning. Tek'ouk'iek was more reminded of when he'd been a child, his father and grandfather had misused such plants to avoid nightmares and depression, causing him shame and difficulty with their stupors. The circle quieted and Com'anch'iik said, loud and firm, "It is agreed in unanimity, you will go. Take everything you need, and may the eternals be with you."

"Bring us back their skulls," Link'ouk said.

Bewildered, Tek'ouk'iek stood, half-tempted to point out the ridiculousness of Yuq'ikik's display, to which he had no clue of its meaning.[71] Of a sudden he felt he could breathe, for the eternals in their strange way had heeded his plea.

---

71 It's worth noting that Tek'ouk'iek recorded something *against* his beliefs. That he's skeptical of their visions but still includes this indicates the account is likely accurate. The same is true of the failed miracles noted in priestess accounts, including material that's an embarrassment to their views shows that they can't deny its reality.

CHAPTER TWENTY-TWO
LORDS OF MISERY

Based on *Annals of Syago,* cc bastica 227;
The Nordvargor Testaments, cc bastica 920;
The Dark Fortress of Mephorash, cc bastica x;

End of Marza, 247

Clouds swirled through the Barbathor Mountains, partially obscuring jagged peaks and forested inclines, the surrounding peaks glistening with snow.[72] The stony titans that housed the Unaka empire held many secrets and things foreign to Syago. As night fell, Unakan soldiers marched him up the mountain. The steep and narrow stairway led to a citadel, a cluster of stone buildings positioned on a small plain in between two peaks; stone farming terraces scaled along the ridge. A line of soldiers, with him shackled in the middle, entered the Unaka mountain colony of Izkuchaqa.

The Amoyara had sold him to the Unaka, who happened to be in the midst of a rebellion against their Asturion lords. The Unaka of the region had, for whatever reason, taken advantage of the struggles in the lowlands and overthrown their governors, some barons and a count whose names he couldn't remember. Even the local mastozons would tell him very little, but he suspected that they believed him to be a spy sent to quell the uprising. Far from his true quest, he'd complained to deaf ears as they marched him up the winding stone path. The Unaka impressed him, building on tall mountains that he struggled to climb. They could conquer far if they wanted, and had of the mountains.

Word had reached him in Mantlgrym that six devils had left Voium. He believed only two devils remained, the infernal sloth and something else

---

72 *Saqra's Cult* details the Yana Raymi and general indoraza ceremonies of mountain worship.

that had sparked the rebellion by killing a regimen of Asturion soldiers and leaders, terrorizing the Barbathors. Syago tried to remember which colony Qosku was from, thinking he'd mentioned this one and a couple others. He realized how little he knew of the Unaka or the region and how no lord from the Barbathors had been present at the war council in Voium. Both seemed telling of how neglected the region had become in spite of it being the source of so much metal to the Kingdom Republic. He knew only that a powerful but savage empire had once been here, but it'd since been tamed and provided the minerals to the rest of Nevermore.

Well, that had been the history he'd grown up with. *But what if that was a lie too? What if we didn't free them from cruel rulers so much as replace them with our own? Or why else rebel?*

They brought him up to a pile of chains, a pile of whips, an execution-er's block and axe, a pillory, a Fool's Box, and other similar instruments of imprisonment or torture. For a moment he thought this was for him, but the disordered pile spoke of abandonment. To his confusion, it was then set on fire, and they led him away from the pyre of Asturion cruelty. His relief was shadowed by a heart-sinking realization: these were hallmarks of oppression indicating that their life here had been different than what he'd understood. And so too did the evidence vanish in the fires of their revolution, but some traces would remain in scars and songs.

Then he passed a gallows whence hung three Asturion noblemen in their bloody breeches. They swayed in the gentle breeze, soft sunlight peering at them through the clouds. He mused again on the futility of revolution, a cycle of mobs. A pendulum of violence that swings back and forth, harder and further each time from the momentum given it by the previous swing. After what the Asturions had done to the Unaka, Amoyara, and Kimoc, what would they do in return?

This made him rethink his mother, Camila, originally named Kam'ilek. He'd always viewed her as a pagan girl turned faithful Deovan woman, but living in the shadow of her more legendary husband Odiru. It pained Syago that he'd neglected her memory. He looked at his human arm, and the brown skin there. He'd once worried about its shade, trying to keep out of the sun to stay light, to be paler. Since then his mind had been preoccupied with other, more important things, and he found himself glad to be relieved of that mental burden, though he felt the nagging still there, waiting.

He could break out of the chain holding his hands if he wanted; they had his weapons, including the hunting knife he hid in his boot, but didn't know the reason behind the larger plates on his left arm. An arm that might be able to snap the metal. But he needed information on the devil and any hellweapons they might possess. Most regions had at least one. Alexandre was warming up to him again but remained distant. Syago still didn't trust it, not fully. And he wasn't likely to survive an escape surrounded by soldiers. The deaths at the lake crushed him, smothering his motivation.

They didn't take him far into the fortified mountain city; it made sense to locate the prison on the outer edge. The city was small, more of a village, and with buildings not especially tall, but no less impressive for it. They pushed him into a small stone building with straw laced together on wooden beams for a roof and a dirt floor. They undid the chain that bound his hands while passing a wood-barred cell. He was thinking how easy it would be to break them when suddenly they pushed him into a pit. He tucked and rolled, landing painfully. He looked up as the bars closed over the small hole, ten feet above. A pit... breaking a cage was one thing, but a pit was different. The walls were steep, climbing inward toward a gate above, unscalable. *Wonderful,* he thought. *Always underestimate the situation.*

After he moved to a wall, a brazier was lowered to the center, giving low illumination. Sharing the cell with him was a pile of rags and a couple Asturion soldiers who, strangely, had armor on. Syago too had all his armor on. *Didn't they want the armor? Why let us keep it?*

That night, he had a nightmare of the pride. Caught in the webs, he struggled in desperation as its children mocked him somewhere in the dark. Then it emerged, drawing him and the surrounding desiccated bodies in. The children sucked them dry, but the parent ate them whole. It drew nearer to him, reaching with those long human arms, then Syago saw Kask's head instead of the one that had been. Fear turned to rage in him.

He woke with a jolt and sat up against the wall. His wool blanket tangled about his legs, like the webs had. He'd dreamed of the greed and envy as well, but the pride was most recent. He wiped sweat from his brow and peered around, but the soldiers slept. "Welcome to my humble home," the man next to him said, old age revealed in his wispy voice. His clothes almost resembled a pile of blankets—indeed that's what he thought the man was before falling asleep. "I am called Kranium. Kranium the Wanderer by our local friends here, or if you prefer, Kranium the Deserter by the chamand coven of Bokhor."

"You're a summoner?" Syago's eyebrows raised. "How did they catch you?"

"They didn't, rather I caught them, aha!" He pulled his cord out of the pile of blankets he wore. The bell tingled and his carved symbol hung above it. "And I managed to hide this from them."

Syago scoffed at the absurdity. "What, then why are you still here? You could escape any time you wish, or are you blinded from the True Night like the rest of them?"

"No, I wasn't there for it, see? I was up here in the mountains. And now I got my own little room here, that is, my own before you and the others came."

"Then get us out of here."

"Why would I do that?" he said, stuffing it back out of sight. "Here I have regular meals, a safe place to sleep. I was tired of so much traveling, and with a war building up and that cult on the rise, I preferred to weather it out in a safe place. I'm safe enough right here in my prison cell."

"You have to be joking," Syago said, halfway between amused and angry. "You're tired and want to hide? Tell me that's not real."

"Well, see, I was unfairly excommunicated from the coven, which was a terrible ordeal—"

"In the name of all weakeners," Syago said, anger rising and left arm beginning to pulse. "People are dying and you have such power to help, but you're hiding? That's the most craven thing I've ever heard."

The man stirred in his bundle and Syago briefly wondered if the man looked as wimpy as he sounded.

"Now look, I've good reason. The way the coven kicked me out was really painful. It was so intolerable I just had to get away for my own health. And my sympathies for your people, but the coven brought this on themselves by how they treated me."

Syago recognized that he'd done some of this too, but this man embraced the softness. "But you walked all over these mountains! Alone! If you were wounded or traumatized, that'd be different. For one as powerful as you, they and their dumb rules are nothing. Fode them. Stop accepting weakness you don't need."

"Stop saying that!" The outburst actually startled Syago.

"Then stop proving it true."

"You should be thanking me for letting you use my—"

210

"Would you two knock it off," one of the other soldiers growled.

"What? You don't want to get out either?" Syago quipped.

He scoffed, "No, not with what they've planned for when we do. Now let off 'im."

Syago tilted his head. "And what's that?" But the man rolled over to face away.

Talking in the building above broke the silence, preceding the shuddering of the gate. A rope ladder dropped down as a guard looked in and beckoned them in his harsh tongue to come up. Syago climbed out, thinking to see what they wanted first and then make his run. But where to go? He could still faintly sense Alexandre, in the center of the citadel. That surprised him, that they were still connected. *Would it come if I called?*

The soulsword gave no response. The guards, all shorter than he and the other Asturions, fidgeted while they waited for Kranium to ascend, taking his time. Syago wondered if his size advantage made them nervous. Kranium arrived, and Syago noticed for the first time his half-Unaka features; in the dark it'd been difficult to tell. Thin and in his sixties, Syago guessed, but with a wiry and fit body.

The guards surrounded them and they marched back outside. All around them, in the shadows of doors and tunnels, eyes watched them. Some raised a hand of three leaves in prayer. Eerie silence portended bad things. Syago decided he didn't want to go with them to what was increasingly looking like an execution, but Alexandre again couldn't or wouldn't come to his hand. He revised his thoughts of escape. Surrounded by armed men on a mountain top at night, he saw no path of flight that did not end in death. The stars and moon watched on.

The guards turned him onto a winding path, up a staircase, one of the larger ones. Always more climbing. Their walls amazed him, large stones cut perfectly flat and fitting together without mortar. Up and up they went, to a white monument that glowed on the mountain peak. Tiers went all the way up the monument like a fat tower, sconces lined the tiers, casting flickering blue and green lights on the open air gathering. Above them a clear sky opened to the moon and stars, and around them tightly bricked walls formed a perfect circle. And no tool for self defense that Syago could see.

"Oh, it can't be!" Kranium said in awed exasperation. "Spirits and eternals, is it so?" The guards sat him and Kranium down, the other soldiers around them, then sat themselves around them. More came in, filling the room.

"What? What is happening?" Syago asked.

Kranium's eyes never left the altar. "The Unka's waka. An altar carved out of a special marble, never moved from its place here. This is where the Unka made sacrifices and has his visions that lead the people. Normally only priests came here and on rare occasions the citizens, usually just the upper classes or ones with connections, can come. They certainly never let an outsider up here, well not willingly. It appears they've removed the Deovan decorations that had taken it over for the ritual. Oooh, we're in for a real treat!"

"I'm sure we are," Syago said, eyeing the axes and spears each of the guards carried. The monument looked much like he imagined a sacrificial altar to be, and he recalled all the stories he'd heard. Apparently they'd not forgotten their old ways.

The quietness of the room grew heavy, and from a door on the other side entered an entourage. Two royal guards, two high priests, and the new Unka, Tapuc the Rebel. Or so Kranium told him was the new Unka. Each dressed in elaborate gold jewelry in addition to woolen cloth, except the Unka. It looked to Syago as though he wore a whole tapestry with golden trimmings and headdress. Behind him came the torch bearers, bringing more light to the room. A woman in silver against the wall could only be his wife. The entourage parted in front of the Unka, who continued on until the waka, where he dropped the colorful stone crown and cloth covering to reveal his naked body, save for the gold jewelry. His skin, Syago now realized, was covered in blood. Not from wounds, but from a blood bath. *So the sacrifices have already been made?*

With the flickering light of the flames, and the dark-skinned faces watching solemnly, the scene was beautiful, but in a haunting way. The lights reflected off the Unka's jewelry, making it seem as though he glowed like the Sun as he arrived at the top of the altar. He stretched out his arms, face upturned, then turned to a high priest, who brought a large wooden bowl to him. The king took it and drank deeply of a thick black fluid before sitting crossed legged on the dais and placing the bowl in front of him.

Syago turned to Kranium and tugged on his rag of a shirt. Keeping his eyes on the Unka, Kranium leaned over and said, "Agamosk, the drink of vision made from the vines of the dead. If this is anything like it used to be, only the Unka is allowed to drink it, and afterward he vomits the evil out of him. Any vision he receives while in its spell becomes eternal scripture. Any edict, irrefutable law. If he survives, that is, for it is a lethal drink. We must pray with them."[73]

So sacrifice is still on the books then, he thought. He remembered hearing of something similar among the Kimoc and wondered if it was the same thing. He then realized the audience all around hummed a gentle rhythm. He couldn't pick out the words, and wouldn't understand them anyway, but found it both eerie and calming. They swayed with the shifting tune. Kranium prayed beside him and, feeling out of place, Syago chanced the ridiculousness of their prayer to sitting still and quiet.

Suddenly, the Unka leaned forward, grasped the bowl, and heaved into it a sickening black spray. The vomit gushed out of his nose and mouth like muddy water. When liquid stopped erupting from his orifices, he heaved empty a couple times before lying down, panting. The praying continued, and Syago found himself humming louder and swaying more than intended. The prayer was hypnotic. Feeling uneasy about the setup, Syago reached out for Alexandre; he could still feel it, though it still didn't respond. He sensed it shared his disquiet.

The Unka began twitching, then undulating on the waka in full thrall of Agamosk, muttering things Syago suspected nobody understood. The torches flickered. The praying intensified. He found that he couldn't look away, couldn't even stop swaying and humming, so hypnotic was the spell of the dark ceremony. He hated it.

This continued for far too long—hours it felt. The dark paganness of it made Syago wonder if he'd been right after all to forget his mother's heritage. But when he looked at the faces of the Unaka around him, most of them humble farmers and miners, tears streaming from their closed eyes, the profound meaning they took from the ceremony surprised him.

Syago yearned for Alexandre. The sword was annoying, burdensome, and dangerous even, but it never took anything from him except commitment and even healed or provided light when needed. He called for it and asked for forgiveness, but felt only its distant presence. Finally the Unka slowed

---

73 Syago's relation of Kranium's explanation is consistent with our documentation of Unakan traditions at that time when only Agamosk, usually done in secret, was said to produce Unakan scripture, or the equivalent. The account then is likely true as it fits its time period and not earlier or later ones, other incorrect notions notwithstanding.

to a rest and the people quieted, simmering off as the vision did. As the Unka stood, Syago saw that most of the blood had dripped off his body.

The old but muscled man looked over his people, embodying the apocalyptic power of Agamosk, magnificent, and spoke in native tongue. Syago nudged Kranium, who translated, "I have seen many terrible things. The devil comes for us next. His new army, our... er, captive family down the valley at Chuqi'kirau, prepare to march on us. We must strike now, attack pre—er, hit them before they come on us. Er, something about preparing. Sorry, I'm not—"

"Just tell me what you can," Syago snapped.

The Unka turned to them, looking down. Kranium translated, "The prisoners, great warriors, will be the vanguard. A sacrifice or a shield, or a weapon. They deserve mercy, having minimal part in our oppression, but in this time we must follow necessity. Their lives and freedoms depend on how well they serve. All ours do."

"And if we refuse?" Syago asked loudly, then turned to Kranium with a hard nudge. He sputtered out a translation then reiterated the Unka's response to them. Guards moved to silence him from blasphemously speaking to the Unka.

But the visionary leader was beyond the old pretense and stopped them with a hand. Kranium kept pace but not the booming tone. "You refuse, you die. We all live or die on this fight, perhaps we'll sacrifice you for more power from the Apus or the Great Ones. We'll not bow to this devil like our brothers have and they'll not let us refuse. We are done trading one master for another. You will take your weapons and er—lead the vanguard. March!"

Syago was about to ask after any hellweapons, but the guards hoisted him to his feet and pushed him out the building before he could say anything else. A guard brought Syago his weapons and shield, including Alexandre, and he quickly latched them into place as the guards shoved him into motion down the stairs. Once the other Asturion soldiers had been given their weapons, they followed. Kranium trembled behind him, and behind them both was the army with their torches and spears. Instead of going back to the citadel proper, they turned away up a stone path until they crested a ridge and began descending into a thick night fog.

As they pounded down the rocky slope of grass and bush, Syago's mind went to the last group he'd marched with. He'd led those men to their deaths. Well, they led him, but he felt that he'd tricked them. Perhaps it had been their will, but Syago couldn't but forget the horrible way each of them died barely understanding their mistake. He would never do that again, not with these Unaka, even though they held him prisoner. He'd been bitter then, and it had almost cost him his own life as well, not to mention aggravating the devil arm.

A thought occurred to Syago, and he turned to Kranium. "Listen, if I asked a favor of you when we're done, would you give it me?"

Amusement lined the man's response. "You would have words with a deceased? Your lost love, perhaps?"

He winced at the words—a pain forgotten then returned. Seeing the near slavery of the Unaka, desolation of the Amoyara and Kimoc, made him realize that these were people not unlike him. And Kranium's evident humility, love for the people, and interest in all of his heritage made Syago want to talk to his mother and apologize to her, or at least learn more of her. That, and get answers from his father. "Something like that. It's really important."

"Well, the covens don't approve of that sort of séance, but I'm not exactly in with them anymore, now am I? I suppose we can consider it. For a certain price."

Syago nodded. He would pay what he had to in order to make things right and learn what he could.

It wasn't long before the Sun began to rise and the fog thinned.

Kranium walked beside him, humming the prayer tune in a quicker tempo. Abruptly, he stopped. Syago turned to him. "What's wrong?"

Kranium stared ahead. "It's true then. The mountain is gone."

"What? What are you talking about?" Syago looked out, seeing only more mountains. "Wait, do you mean the devil collapsed a mountain?"

The chamand pointed ahead. "There used to be a mountain there, a small one with a sun gate on its side, but it was an Apu they'd worshiped. Now it's not there. I'd heard about this but not believed it. Such power, I can't imagine."

They continued, and Syago asked, "Why aren't you escaping? The fog would've been perfect for it."

"You made a good point; I've been running and hiding long enough. I let those bastards win that way, gave them power over me even in their absence. Besides, these people need me. This devil, I'd heard stories about the destruction it's wrought but paid them no heed... until now. Collapsed by just this one otherworlder." The chamand shook his head. "They'll need me and more."

"Glad to see you've finally come around," Syago muttered. "Do you know of any hellweapons we can use?"

"I have heard tell of them, powerful and destructive ones, but I know only rumor. Though my spirits and your sword should be enough."

"My sword is... having problems. Do you know what kind of devil we're up against?"

He nodded. "Something big. But none here know. The spirits tell me it's a hate, but they're too afraid of it to go nearer." Syago vaguely remembered in the diagrams he'd read hates as some type of rodent but couldn't imagine what that would look like in combat.

He saw the bottom of the gorge through the fading haze and it would've been a beautiful morning if not for the rotting smell. Around the stream, the rocky, grassy landscape offered hiding places both for him and enemy soldiers. And all about lay corpses, human and beast, rotting in the morning air. Syago noticed numerous corpses were crushed, either half buried under rock and dirt or splattered across a boulder. Then he saw it: a hellflail in the hand of a smashed soldier. It sat as if presented to him, a red and brown head of large thick spikes with lines running up the ridges, on the end of a dark leather weave chain. Alexandre didn't like it, though it was less repulsed than by previous hellweapons.

The cautious movements of the soldiers behind and the stream below were faint sounds in overall silence. Off in the distance, a deep thud broke the silence, followed by gentle rumbling. Some soldiers filed out behind him. Syago followed their gazes to see Unakan soldiers making their way toward them over dead bodies. They wore upside down sun crosses, as well as masks of skull and stone, a fact Kranium claimed was part of their allegiance to the devil, who had pretended to be one of their eternals.[74]

Another deep thud sounded, followed by more rumblings. *What is that?*

The field of broken dead was a grim reminder of what he was about to encounter. A full battle of two armies colliding, and a devil in the middle of it all. The thought made him queasy, like he might be better off running

---

74 *See Ornamentos del Miedon,* 26-66

to hide it out while the Unaka resolved their own dispute. Except for the devil, it wasn't his fight, but he didn't want a repeat of the lake either. In truth, if not for this otherworlder that his people had let in, this battle would not be happening in the first place.

Somewhere in the haze below, sounds of battle reached him. Syago and those behind him broke into a run, weaving between rocks and dead bodies. Syago grabbed the hellflail as javelins and rocks flew in. He ducked behind a boulder to examine the weapon. He had no idea what this one did. He'd trained some with flails; they were difficult, chaotic and dangerous to the wielder but effective if done right. He'd wield it in his human arm, to be safe. Memories of induced insanity returned to him with a sudden panic, but he couldn't defeat the devil without it. He'd just use wiser hands.

He drew his knife in the other hand and ran on with a war cry for Cantlgrym and Tolgrym, until he abruptly came face to face with an enemy Unaka. Syago reacted quicker, moving his already spinning flailhead into the chest of the surprised warrior. Syago felt a small jolt of energy in the hellflail's handle just before the soldier's chest exploded in a blast of blood, flesh, and bone. Gore showered onto Syago, causing his stomach to churn, and he turned and retched on a nearby rock. *You're shitting me. A concussive flail.*

He wiped his face then moved around a boulder to find three frightened men, startled but standing their ground. Syago didn't want to approach their spears or hit them directly with the hellflail, so he swung it into a pile of rocks, hoping to spray them at the group. The pile exploded, throwing him sideways and rocks everywhere, but mainly at them. He recovered quickly, bruised, and dashed toward one of the men, missing with his knife but landing a downward swipe of the hellflail. Harder and faster than he'd intended, he saw the man's face swell then burst. The body blew bigger than the first had, plastering Syago. Again, he felt the need to retch, but he pushed it down, instead determined not to use the flail until he absolutely needed to. But he couldn't stop as one of the two soldiers left rose with a spiked mace that glanced off Syago's chestplate. Syago parried with his knife and snapped his flail up with the smallest of movements. The soldier screamed as his arm blew out and clutched the bleeding stump in agony. The last man standing threw his axe then ran. Syago ducked beneath the axe, feeling sick of the bloodbaths, and stabbed the man in the ribs before moving past. As he ran, Syago minded well the location of that flailhead, not wanting to find out the nature of a simple bump against his leg.

Another deep thud made him jump, this one more of a boom in its proximity, followed by heavy rumbling that faded. *Whatever that is, it can't be good.*

He turned another rocky bend, crossing into soldiers from both sides. The rivals backed against the rocks and began stomping the ground. From beneath their skull and stone masks, they chanted. Syago thought they looked terrified. He looked at the other soldiers and charged in with them.

The thuds picked up to a steady rhythm, like a heartbeat underground.

Syago's devil arm tingled at this nearing presence. It frightened him that he didn't know exactly what was coming other than it had tremendous power. Ground shaking, gierra breaking, mountain sinking power. The dirt shuddered, then trembled, making standing difficult.

The enemy soldiers fought through it, throwing a bolas that wrapped around his arms, but it was no effort for his devil arm to break the leather cord. He lay into the men, the hellflail making quick work of their maces, axes, and javelins, then moving on to the men themselves as they all stumbled about over the tremors. Two more blew apart, such that Syago became dizzy from the carnage he;d created. Now dripping in blood that gleamed in daylight, he retched again. Unable to bear it anymore, his trembling hand put down the hellflail. He drew Alexandre and gripped it in both hands, hoping they could work together again. Anything but the hellflail. The explosions had blocked out the thudding, which was now constant, shaking gierra with a violence that incapacitated any movement. He fell over.

The devil burst from the ground in an explosion of dirt, stone, and surprised soldiers. Syago was thrown in the chaos by a giant claw. The long nail scratched through his chest plate and nicked into his gambeson beneath, barely missing skin. The wind left him as he slammed into a rock. The remaining swarm of soldiers fell on the large beast and were crushed or tossed away. But it ended as quickly as it began. The hate burrowed, leaving behind a wreckage of land and army. Syago regained his footing, noting the enemy soldiers had been blown away too.

Again the ground shook. Syago saw an emaion flying through the air, a large polyform being like a patchwork of animal parts. The mischievous, snarling foxhead, ozor arms, and a humanoid torso with birdlegs was unmistakable even to someone with only a surface knowledge of emaions.

Syago called out to Kranium, who he could see on top of a boulder. "Is that—You called Saqra?! How's he going to help us?"

"All things in their way, boy," he shouted back. Syago actually knew very little of the emaion other than its dark tricks. The quaking increased, and Syago turned and saw boulders flying or rolling as a lump in the ground moved. It found a group of soldiers, the ground tossing them, then it turned and raced toward him. Cursing, Syago picked up the hellflail and ran, leaping off a boulder to a nearby one. The charge found him anyway. Rocks slammed him as he tumbled, catching himself with his big arm on another rock. The hate surfaced, shearing the rock into pieces with a massive claw. It was a large beast with an elongated snout that ended in feelers reminiscent of human fingers—no, they actually were large fingers. The rest of the beast was animal, hairless white with beady black eyes and twisting, jagged fangs.

The fingered nose shifted around, smelling him as he slid around the rock. His wounds were too serious to fight a monster of that size, but he knew he couldn't hide from that nose. Alexandre healed him but as always, much too slow. The hate dug down once more and charged while submerged. Out of desperation, Syago slammed the hellflail at the ground as it approached, blocking his face and chest with his devil arm. He was thrown high and far, taking the hellflail out of his hand, though judging by the secondary blast it landed not far away. He crunched on a pile of dirt, breathless again. The beast made a sound halfway between a screech and a roar, then snorted. It spoke with a gravelly growl, "Mmmmnnn. You have valuable rrrelicz. And valuable blOODDD. I will grrrrrRRRACK FOT SHOTHELRRRECKZZZALAS!"

This time it charged above land, no slower or less destructive. As it pushed boulders aside, Syago saw that his blind attack with the hellflail had timed well: a fleshy hole burned at the side of its head where black blood oozed. It paid no notice and issued violence on through the land. Suddenly Kranium landed on its back, perched with a spiked mace, which he repeatedly beat the devil with. It couldn't shake him free and tried rolling, but the surprisingly agile old man jumped off onto a nearby boulder. Claws reached but couldn't catch. Finally Saqra came down, falling over him either as protection or as part of the attack. Blue flames danced around the greater spirit. Syago couldn't tell what it was doing, but the hate screeched in pain and struggled harder, throwing up boulders in thunderous crashes. Large rocks cracked and smashed around him. Syago tried to move away but couldn't, and images of exploding bodies burned into his mind. He pleaded with Alexandre to be of more help.

Disappointment ran through him when Alexandre gave no response. He watched in horror as the hate finally knocked the chamand off. Large jaws clamped down on the man in midair. Saqra, who'd tried to catch him, vanished. Syago screamed as the hate's jaws crushed and pierced the man, squirting blood everywhere. The devil turned back onto its belly and looked straight at Syago with those beady eyes as it bit again. While the shredded body slid down into its throat, Syago gripped Alexandre, hoping beyond hope the sword would help him, and rose.

Smacking lips with its tongue, the hate growled out more indecipherable words. Syago made as if to run at it but instead rolled to the side as the hate thundered in. He picked up the hellflail and threw it at the turning hate, just as a distraction, he told the sword. The side of the beast exploded, and Syago rushed in as Alexandre began to shine bright. He could feel the sword's desire to cut the hate, but also its decision to be softer on Syago, and more flexible. A moment of joy burst inside him at the rebuilt connection. Slashing hard and fast with glowing Alexandre, he sliced through a boulder and into the devil's arm.

A giant claw swept back and knocked Syago down, but he was already healing. The hate began to burrow down deep, causing the ground to quake so hard, the mountainside above them began to crack and fall. Syago dashed to the hole and jumped in, sword leading the way down. It planted into the hind flesh of the devil, burning bright as he pulled it out and stabbed the hate repeatedly. When it finally stopped struggling, he slashed again, making certain its death was permanent. Sighing in relief, Syago sat on the ichorous mass, clutching Alexandre, catching breath. He began to weep.

CHAPTER TWENTY-THREE
A WAR OF THREE

Based on *Leyta's Journals,* cc bastica 230;
The Nordvargor Testaments, cc bastica 926;
The Dark Fortress of Mephorash, cc bastica xxx;

1st of Akril, 247

The Cantlgrym war party arrived at the valley just before sundown, weary and nervous, their bodies sweaty and dusty beneath layers of leather and metal armor. The masters, commanders, and captains all rode on the supply wagons pulled by bomogs, while soldiers took turns walking. All eyes warily traced the rocky ledges around them. Bats and blackbirds had stalked them, occasionally picking at those along the ends, but for the most part, the group passed unhindered. They crossed over several ruins, walls broken and faded into the ground and undergrowth, confirming their ancient route.[75]

The Kimoc Quoak tribe, again led by Tek'ouk'iek, marched not far behind, having caught up just before and even somehow convinced a group of warriors from Koah to come as well, totaling well over sixty warriors. They and the Asturions tread carefully around each other, suspicious and resentful of what they believed the other group had done during the siege.

A smaller group of warrior chamands, around thirty-six, met them from the east, following a message she'd sent them. Leyta had sent urgent messages to Voium for bigger military assistance but worried that they wouldn't hasten sufficiently. Archamand Bartolina, leading the Bokhor group, said that when they passed north of Voium, it appeared to be confronted by a herd of daemog and so might be delayed.[76] During the trek, the chamands had done the most

---

75 *Moonspell Hell Light de Lostregos,* and note Lustmord's Hyades commentary.

76 Somewhat telling that they didn't go and aid Voium before continuing on. It's then no wonder Voium delayed.

to fight off the bats and quervosks. Although the strange summoners still lacked their spirit calling abilities, they remained astute fighters. The spry Bartolina especially. However, their interest was more in ending the affliction that had blinded their powers than winning any war.

Total, the allies numbered around three hundred, less than the siege but more of the most experienced in the region. Leyta didn't know what to expect, but sensed that what came next would be big. It made her nervous. They could be walking into a trap. They could find the Tiakanawu temple ruins with a real relic of power. She'd been doubtful of this, but the angel seemed to give credit to it. At most, this was likely to be a bigger battle than any previously fought in the war. Either way, too much rode on this fight and too much uncertainty flew in the air, which frightened her. She took comfort that she was less alone this time than in the siege. All of the masters had come save Seumas, Yanet, and enough guards to watch the wall in full. Even Roza had come, with several stipulations to help her maintain her secret. Balgor drove the first wagon and Qosku sat beside Leyta as her stomach churned from thoughts of what they might find at the end of the valley trail.

She hoped that having their armies together would ward off any threats. Stories of vanishing armies also haunted her; it'd been so long since more than a scouting party had gone and not returned, it'd seemed impossible. Maybe the size of their war party would guarantee against it, yet they now wandered far away from their walls to enemies unknown in lands eulogized and forgotten.

Overhead the sky was cloudy, with a large swathe of gurows circling above, and a faint breeze winding through the canyon which opened up into a broad vale. Between sloping mountainsides was a field of grass, boulders, and mud, and at the far end sat a raised platform surrounded by crumbling stone wall and gate. To the left of the enclosure camped a conglomerate of war parties, mostly consisting of Fomorion raiding camps and the central Royal Chaos leadership with their attendants. The Asturion rebels camped behind the Fomorions, away from the temple. Their army's size gave Leyta pause; they had a large number, and the Fomorions were large and more than ferocious. She could only hope that help arrived from Voium soon. On the other side of the ruins sat the much smaller cult encampment, a single large tent with equipment around it and strange shadows moving inside.

Around the outside, several cloaked cultists bowed in prayer. She wondered what tricks they'd brought to even the playing field, and how they kept their newer converts from fleeing in the face of two larger armies.

The Fomorion army could easily destroy the cultists, so it seemed odd to find them there as contenders for the temple. *Perhaps their tent meeting was about picking a side to ally with.* Leyta and her commanders halted at the edge to survey the landscape before marching down into the lower bowl. A straight march to it would be necessary, as the two enemies held either side, unless she wanted to take out the cult while they lurked in their tent. *No, we may need their help against the barbarian giants. We'll need everything available against that terrible force.*

Activity at the temple caught her eye. In the center of the platform, she saw statues leading up to a large stone-carved block. As she drew nearer, it became clear that the block itself was only a door to an underground chamber. Several men, mainly Fomorion giants, pried at the large stone slab serving as a rolling door. Leyta guessed that they were trying to open it, but then realized this was wrong. They were trying to close it. The giants fought to close it against a surging swarm of lifeless, mummies and skeletons, all brown with age, that were trying to get out. Though the sun was almost down, the lifeless had stopped their nightly risings as the season of darkemorg had turned to darkelan. This meant that the bodies had risen for some other reason, probably an old curse set to protect the temple.[77]

Some of the myths even claimed Pagutec had mummified himself inside, though they all said he'd done it alone. As she marched closer, she saw that the barbarians had succeeded in rolling the stone back, but not all the way as some of the mummies and skeletons had fallen in its path and blocked the door. The giants' roars echoed eerily through the vale as they fought to contain the mess they'd opened.

Shouts from her men snapped her attention away. Qosku, riding in front of her, clapped his hands and pointed to the ledge of a tall boulder, part of it hewn out. Up on that shadowy ledge glowed a sword held by a man. Syago. Her hands flew to her mouth, and she gasped in surprised joy. He wasn't dead as she'd thought—as she'd blamed herself for. He said nothing, but pointed with his other arm to just behind the rock, marking a place for

---

77 Now comes the pain. Now you can let it out. Final breath

her to set the camp. Yes, in front of the rock would be good, a good vantage and a little bit of high ground not far from the temple's front gate.

As she brought everyone around and gave orders for captains to organize the battle-ready setup, she looked again to Syago. Finally he spoke, yelling out to her soldiers, "My friends, I have traveled far and slain the devils that attacked us outside Mantlgrym, at Leyta's command. I come now to win this fight with you against our enemies. It looks dire, but I've watched them... and our leaders are well prepared. Together we can do this. We *will* come out right in the sight of Our Lady Deova Bondua!"

The army cheered. Syago lowered his sword and walked down the rock. Leyta saw Lil'iek running to meet him, Tek'ouk'iek fast hobbling behind, and Leyta walked there as well. As she rounded the large rock, she saw that he was removing his breastplate when Lil'iek caught him in a hug. She paused to let them have their moment. They laughed together, and Leyta resumed her stride, noticing Qosku walking anxiously behind her. As she neared, Lil'iek looked at her, then said, "Oh yeah, I almost forgot." Then she punched Syago in the face. Not hard, but Leyta heard it hit. Syago staggered from the blow. As he touched his lip for blood, Leyta found herself running up to him and slapping him on the cheek, too.

"Fair enough." He nodded, still managing a boyish smile. Without thought, she embraced him tightly and for longer than Lil'iek had. It ended more abruptly too, straightening her gloves and awkwardly meeting eyes.

"We thought you'd died," she said accusingly, shifting from warmth to shaming. "And took blame for ourselves."

"Well, that I can't help you with," he said. "I didn't aim for that, though you *did* push me to leave, all of you, except Qosku!" He laughed as he embraced Qosku in what appeared to be a very awkward hug, as if the young Unakan didn't know where to put his arms. Once it broke, Qosku looked at her, then swept a leg out and deftly dropped Syago to his back. "Stupid deserter," the monk muttered.

"All right, I get the point!" he said as he brought himself to sit against a boulder, pulling off more of his plates, clearly tired from his journey here. Then a thought struck her, and she looked around the area.

"Syago, how did you get here?" she asked.

He stood up and moved over to a small stream, part of what made this an ideal encampment, and removed his shirt. Numerous large scars lined his back and chest, more than when she'd seen him shirtless in the training grounds, but that wasn't what surprised her. All four of them gasped at the sight of his left arm—large, red, and inhuman. The scaly, veiny red skin abruptly faded into the light brown of his torso. "How did I get here? It's been a very long and rough few months, I'll put it that way. Glad to have it behind me." He knelt at the stream to wash his face and splash water on his arms and chest.

"What happened to your arm?" Tek'ouk'iek asked, crouching to sit on a boulder and inspect it as he unstrapped his own fur and leather vest. He too slid into the stream and rinsed.

"You remember that devil with the human torso? That happened to my arm. The... situation was such that I had no choice to replace mine with his. It's been a real treasure ever since." Further upstream, the rest of the army followed his example, with much needed washing in the water, trampling and dirtying it beyond recognition. *So much for drinking the stream, but at least we won't be needing it, within a day we'll all be dead or fleeing.*

"The devils are all destroyed then?" Leyta asked.

"All except one, an infernal sloth, and it is here," he said. "Up by their tent. The rest are gone."

"How can you be sure they're all gone?" she asked, slipping her sore, bare feet into the cold water, swishing them clean with her arms before pulling out and rebooting, refreshed.

"I can't be, but in my search I heard rumors of each of them, found and killed each of them except for this last one, which I saw when I arrived. I destroyed enough of the other fiends to prevent resurgence. I've not heard of any more, though nothing's really to stop them from just doing it again 'cept maybe a lack in sacrificial supply."

"These other scars are really bad, and it's so many." She found herself wanting to touch them, run her fingers gently over his back.

"Yeah, they are," he said quietly, looking past the stream to whatever terrible memories gave those scars.

"You impress me, Syago," Qosku said, fidgeting more and more as the stream filled with bare bodies, and Syago turned to face him while drying his arms with a rag. Syago also looked leaner, likely the months of traveling and fighting. "Very happy you returned and well enough to fight. And maybe new arm stronger."

"Yes, it is. And thank you, it is good to be back among people I can talk to and who aren't considering killing me. I intend to do it," he nodded at Alexandre, laying sheathed on a rock, "right this time."

"Then you'll report for tactics duty in half the hour," she said, noting his face was more calm, more pleasant than before he'd left. She turned back to her tent and slipped into commander mode for the pressing matters as Lil'iek assisted Tek'ouk'iek back to their camp. The sun now fell beneath the mountain ridgeline in the west, bringing on the dark. If there were any feldinals in the area, themselves much like devils, they would come to the vale for easy feeding.

She was about to enter her newly erected commander tent when she noticed that the tide of lifeless seemed to draw strength from the dimming of the sun and the army pushing the door shut gave up. They moved back to their side of the temple, or more appropriate perhaps, tomb. The stone door, unhindered, fell over with a loud boom, and the mummies swarmed out. At first they moved in confusion. Leyta heard Jester's song trying to control them, but it seemed to affect them less than the swarm he'd gathered at Quoak. Perhaps the curse that guided them made it difficult. Some attacked the barbarians, who slew them down, while most streamed out toward the cult camp. Leyta assumed that was Jester pushing them to attack the cult, but the song stopped, and she soon realized what he must have. Three faint bell chimes rang throughout the valley, unnaturally strong for a tiny hand bell, and she recognized it as a summoner's call. But none of the chamands could summon...

Everything had gone quiet at those chimes. The lifeless all stopped, now following a stronger command than the curse that empowered them. Leyta searched until she saw a lone cultist standing in front of the tent, holding a staff up in the air. And a bell. This was the summoner then. People behind Leyta gasped.

Though she couldn't make out who the cultist was, she could see, even from a distance, inside the cowl of that hooded robe: black eyes with irises that glowed red in the darkness. Eyes that burned like the inferno they worshiped. This was not a mere disciple or cultist of the Razhod, but a full Razhod, the first in nearly two decades.

Then Leyta noticed a great shadow looming over that camp, growing stronger. A strange fire burned inside their tent, smoke rising out the top.

However as shadows within the tent began to dance, she realized they resembled silhouettes of little children dancing, not in play or to music, but to a solemn ritual around flame's glow. Missing children dancing willingly in the obscured confines of that abominable tent.

As more disciples joined the lone witchlord, bowing at his feet, the air above him darkened and shimmered. A phantom formed fully into view, appearing over the cultists. The greater spirit that could only be Bophormothul the Necromancer beckoned to the moving corpses below as it swung a glowing pendulum from one furry, clawed hand, while the other held a large tome. Leyta watched, speechless, as the lifeless poured out of the temple, no longer bothering to attack the barbarians as they fell full under the Necromancer's spell, congregating beneath him.

Just when she didn't think it could get any worse, it did. Leyta noticed Roza stumbling through the army, away from her camp and toward the call of the grave. Up north, Knight also could be seen abandoning his army to the emaion's call as his team attempted to keep him. The halting clumsiness of Roza's normally graceful gait indicated her will to fight it, an insufficiently powerful will. Balgor shouted after her, "Gretal, what are you doing?! Come back!" He tried to grab her and suddenly Qosku was there helping him drag on her.

Leyta heard Roza respond to them, "HELP ME! Please don't let it take me!" For a moment, it looked as they might succeed at holding her. But she trembled, then threw them like dolls, tossing them aside before running and stumbling across the field to her new home and masters. She screamed, "NO! NO! PLEASE, NOOOOO!"

Pendulum swinging, Bophormothul opened his clenched jaw and an ultra-deep whisper swept the valley, "*OBEY*." Large, black, leathery wings extended from behind to cover himself like a shield beneath the evening sky, a sizable army of lifeless standing motionless, in ordered rows, beneath the ledge of cultists where the summoner raised his staff. As he lowered it, five others moved to stand by him inside the circle of bowing disciples. Drawn cowls obscured the six summoner's faces, but the red eyes shone unmistakably. The Cult of the Rippers had finally done it; they had somehow finally achieved the Crimson Covenant and elevated themselves, at least six of them, from mere disciples to full witchlords akin to their long dead masters, along with the old powers.

The Razhod were back.

Cries of fear filled Leyta's camp, some shrieking in confusion, demanding answers. Many crossing themselves, others forgetting completely. Leyta didn't understand how the Razhod could have come back, and she saw every member of the barbarian camps also motionless in bewilderment.

"NO, NO,not *them!* Anything but *them,*" Bartolina screamed behind Leyta, clutching her face in abject terror. "Not the Razhod, I can't fight them again. I can't, I can't!"

Someone put an arm around her as she trembled, sobbing. Balgor's mouth hung open. Even Tek'ouk'iek and Lil'iek looked as horror-struck as everyone else. Leyta's shock at the ease with which they'd taken control of all the lifeless, including Roza and Knight, turned to a deep pit in her gut.

Hoyoche had come with the allies to either die or confront the cult on their promise to restore his wife. When Hoyoche saw the Necromancer appear, the old fear had welled up in him, he'd been a boy during the terror of the Razhod and heard the stories. He'd not have approached if not for desperation, and now it was his time. He'd given up hope on the cult's promise to restore his wife, prepared to die fighting them. But that all changed now with the witchlords back. For a moment, his fear paralyzed him until he saw the Necromancer fading away, losing him his chance.

Running across the field, he neared the gathered group of lifeless. But they didn't scare him, only the gigantic phantom and its Razhod summoner did. "Restore me my dead wife as you promised," he called out. The Razhod looked down at him with those old, inhuman eyes. But he withstood and shouted again, "You promised!"

The Necromancer pointed a claw at one of the lifeless. It lurched and stiffened, then began shambling toward him. Hoyoche put a hand on his weapon, prepared to strike it down. "I am owed and—"

"Hussssband?" the zombi whispered through broken teeth and leather head covering.

"No," he gasped. "Is it you? How do I know it's really you?"

"Hoyo, my sssweet. I missed you," she'd spoken like that. The horror that welled in him began to vanish as she continued, "Being dead isss ssso terrible. I need you. Please save me."

"Of course." He was breathless. She approached him, arms outstretched, and pity found him. He gently took the dead hands that had received her soul. Her hesitance seemed borne out of fear of her own rotted state. He choked on his grief, "I've missed you so. I'm so, so sorry for your pain. Agh—"

He couldn't take it any more and embraced the fetid corpse whispering, "I accept you. Our love is eternal and not bound to the flesh. We are still one."

"Thhhankk you—" and she bit him in the neck. The teeth made jagged in their brokenness tore out the side of his neck as he stumbled back in shock. A hand swiped up an slashed his throat.

"Why—" he gurgled, drowning in his own blood.

The shocking drama of the lone chamand played out beneath the great shadow that they didn't notice had even vanished until the Razhod returned to their tent. Leyta could only guess that this summoner had been the one to facilitate the devils' entry in Voium. They'd suspected the Bokhor community for involvement in it. Leyta snapped back to attention and yelled, "Back to your posts, now! Fortify! Captains and commanders, tactics meeting in my tent, immediately."

The pace quickened, and she entered her tent with the other leaders close behind. As they entered, Tek'ouk'iek grabbed her arm and whispered in harsh tones, "What is she?"

He meant Roza. "Uh, we don't know. Gravespawn," she replied, pulling her arm free.

"And you didn't think that important enough to at least tell the other commanders?"

"It was her decision; a secret she wanted silent. It hasn't been a problem until now."

"There's always an 'until now' with secrets like those." He turned to Balgor, who stood by, observing with uncharacteristically serious expression, arms folded. "Did you know? Or any of Cantlgrym?"

"No, but it seems so obvious now. I don't know how I missed it."

"Perhaps you'll enlighten us on, what's his name... Hoyoche?" she retorted to Tek'ouk'iek.

"He's not of us anymore." With a glare, he said, "Keeping Roza's secret endangered us all."

"Stop telling me how to lead my people," she hissed. "I do mine, and you do yours." She turned to see that all the allied leaders, most of them masters of Cantlgrym, had gathered in the tent around a small table with a roughly drawn map of the battlefield sketched out it. The single lantern hanging above provided little light, casting shadows. Leyta addressed their questioning gazes, "Mastra Roza doesn't exactly know what she is, but she calls herself a graves-pawn. She's been this way for decades, and since there had been no problems thus far, we kept it a secret. I hadn't planned on her being abducted by the enemy in this way because I'd never seen... Well, it didn't seem possible."

"The Razhod are back, how do we fight them?" Captain Andras asked of their more pressing concern.

The room went quiet, silent in its void of hope. Syago spoke up. "I know I wasn't there in the old war. I and many others are new to this. But one thing I know is that you, we, did this before, and if we did it before, we can do it again. Now how do we do it?"

"We don't," Master Constantin said, his old wiry form belied the powerful dynfist that he was. "We can't. This army has trained for a great deal but not for this. Not enough. We need to get the Royal Chaos into mixing it up with them for us."

"And they'll do that willingly?" Virgow said. "That's the trick, a three-way field is no battle at all. As soon as one moves on the other, they become vulnerable to the third, allowing the third to either run away with the loot untouched, or to move on the exposed foe of their choosing. None of us are stupid enough to make the first move, and we all know that the others know it. We're at a stalemate."

"But the armies are not equal," Syago said. "The Royal Chaos has the most in number and raw force. The Razhod are strong, but they're only six plus thirteen disciples with a lesser devil and maybe the grimshades. But their army is merely a swarm of lifeless smaller than even our group. The bodies will only be fodder—"

"If you think the Razhod are the weaker army out there, son, you got a new lesson coming," Virgow said. "If they're anything like the older Hellfaces, then they're not just powerful summoners. They'll be more war-rior than witch and have access to any number of soulweapons on top of their emaions. Any three of those Razhod is enough to tear us apart. Even just one or two could be too much."

"Normally, I would agree the Razhod are our most dangerous foe," Tek'ouk'iek said carefully. "But the Royal Chaos have proven themselves capable of pulling a lot of big surprises on us, and they've quite an army. We could try to bring them to our side for a temporary alliance to quash the Razhod now, but expect every dirty trick in doing so. Our best hope might be to rely on the tri-fight deterrent, if we fight, all three of us do it at the same time. That'll be a chaotic mess, so we have to plan how to navigate it well or make it not happen in the first place."

"I'm not sure how well that will work," Balgor said. "They both have a history of wanton recklessness. And they want the temple more than we do."

"Do they?" Leyta asked. "Supposing there is a relic in there, we don't really know what they want of it. I suspect we're here to keep it away from them more than for the relic itself."

"And we'd best hope they don't make a deal with each other against us," Virgow said.

"Against the smaller, least intimidating army?" Constantin said. "Not likely. They're more concerned about each other, they'd sooner ask us for help, which they won't, and we shouldn't either. Who knows what trick they'd pull over our eyes if we allied."

"That gets us back to square one," Balgor said. "As it stands, we'll never leave this vale unless we get reinforcements. Even retreating is no good, we'd never make it through that small vale entrance; that bottleneck leaves an army wide open to attack and guarantees the victor is not you."

"Damn them all," Virgow growled. "We walked into a trap, one that all three armies created accidentally by showing up. If we'd gotten here sooner, we might've set a better position."

"What's done is done," Constantin said. "We have only to move forward now. Signaling for a negotiation is typically the next step, really the only viable one."

Virgow snorted. "Be my guest."

"I don't see either group agreeing to meet," Tek'ouk'iek said. "They're both uncompromising and treacherous. They'd sooner string up the messenger than sit and talk."

"I suppose that might depend on the strength of the tri-army deterrent," Balgor speculated, stroking his beard thoughtfully. "Obviously, none of them are the types to agree to that approach, but the situation is less than ideal for them as well. They'll see us as the lesser threat to pit against each other. They've no reason to join against us, but need us, which gives us some leverage. And consider what this battle will mean; the vale, including the temple, will not survive. Not with the the kind of power we'll be throwing around. They need to at least get the relic out of there first, if their goal is to take and use it, and I think it is, else their recklessness would've already manifested. No, I believe they'll agree to something, maybe a ceasefire or truce, just to guarantee the safety of the relic. They'll hate doing so, but they've no choice."

"Yes, in that case, I don't see a battle preceding the negotiation," Tek'ouk'iek said.

"So… how do we start a negotiation with them?" Andras asked. "What do we even negotiate?"

The room fell silent. Leyta looked at everyone, many present hadn't said a single word. Katti stood solemnly, unreadable. Bartolina, still looked drawn and weary from her breakdown. The bard Tongunabiagüs stroked his chin, thoughtfully, while writing on his scrolls. Andras looked worried, out of his game among the older commanders who had experience fighting Razhod in contrast to his childhood of horror stories. Syago looked more confident, but Leyta read him the same as Andras. Lil'iek and Tek'ouk'iek also returned stoic. *Well, at least the Razhod have united Asturion and Kimoc. Neither will think on more betrayal antics like before.*

Against all her deeper fears, she cleared her throat and said, "I'll go."

"You'll go? What do you mean?" Balgor said.

"If I walk out there alone, up to the temple door, that will present a clear signal of intent." She managed to keep the tremor out of her voice, nothing more dangerous had ever been proposed. "I could even just go in myself, and if they want to come, they will."

"It'd be safer to send messengers to each group," Syago said. "We shouldn't risk our leader that way."

"They'd assassinate or kidnap you, Mastra," Andras said, looking directly at her. "I can't let that happen to you."

"I don't think the messengers would work," Constantin said. "It never did with Razhod, I don't know about the other."

"I'd rather not sacrifice one of my men on a failed attempt at appeasement," Leyta said.

"Walking out there like that, it's bold," Virgow said with a faint smile, the first she'd seen him do in a long time. War seemed to energize him more than a hunt ever had. "I like that, and they would too. Impress the bastards, and you'll get their ear."

"But the threat on her..." Andras said. "Especially inside the temple out of our sight where there'll be traps and other dangers."

"They won't do anything to her," Constantin said. "It'd be akin to attacking an army, setting us on each other and giving the advantage to the third. But I do think someone else should go since Leyta is one of our more valued leaders and, well, newer and younger. Someone with more experience in dealing with the Hellfaces, more versed in entering uncharted areas. I'll go."

"No, this is a dynal relic, and you're not an elementist," Leyta said. "That might not matter, or it might mean everything. I should also point out that I'm more than capable of fighting and defending myself."

"Balgor then, might be a better option," Virgow said. "He'll be intimidating too."

"But less impressive than a little girl walking out there," she said with a glare.

"I don't have the kind of training and education Leyta does," Balgor muttered, still stroking his long braid. "The relic and temple walls will be written in old Tiakanawu glyphs, I can read many other old scripts in Nevermore, but not that one, which she can. Same with Tek'ouk'iek. And it would give her an edge to watching for the traps laid in there, at least an edge over the others who probably don't read any scripts."

This was mostly true, her grasp of Tiakanawu was very tenuous as little was known to begin with. It hardly even functioned as a regular language, working more in numbers and symbols than a narrative. She'd undertaken it specifically because nobody else at Cantlgrym had. Of course, Roza had also picked it up, even giving Leyta key insights to the interpretation, but her sad predicament ruled her out. If Leyta remembered enough to understand the temple and its relics, this could change everything for them. That is, if the ruins held this as a fundamental component. They knew so little about what lie inside there.

"I suppose you're right," Tek'ouk'iek said after a long pause. "Leyta is the best choice, perhaps we could have a single guard attend her up to the temple."

"No. Again, I can defend myself just fine. It won't be necessary, and it'll hurt the impression I'm supposed to make. At the very least I'm sure a number of you will be ready to rush to my rescue should anything happen, but it won't. For once, the Royal Chaos and the Razhod will have to listen to me."

"So you go in there," Tek'ouk'iek began, "and verify that it's real or not. Then sell out our support to the one best assuring peace? Have you forgotten that the witchlords may have some of our children?"

"They might have some of ours as well," Leyta said. "So no. Nor will we let them use those children as a shield, assuming it really is the children and not a trick. Some of our family may be in the Royal Chaos group as well."

Balgor responded, "I think it obvious we'd rather eliminate the Hellfaces now, while they're smaller in number and with a single devil, assuming we could get the Royal Chaos to agree to it. But like all negotiations, this could take several meetings. First we gather information, then see what we can get out of the others. Get their terms and state ours, then come back and consult and return to meeting them."

"Or on the inevitability that any plans will fall apart," Virgow countered, "we take what we can and run with it."

Leyta looked around. "Are we agreed then?"

They all nodded their agreement and set into battle and contingency plans.

It was past midnight when they'd finished and nothing had changed, as far as they could see, among the enemy camps. They agreed not to wait for morning when Leyta would take her walk to the temple; she wanted the sleep but couldn't afford the enemies taking first action. Anxiety kept her more than awake as she strapped on her leather-padded gambeson in the tent. Elementists rarely donned metal armor due to the odd way it interacted with dyne, sometimes catching lightning on themselves or just heating up. But she didn't appreciate the semi-gown that was custom. Like a tunic that stretched down to her knees, it maintained the standard of chaste modesty while supposedly giving extra protection in battle, but it still hindered her mobility and made her an easier object to target. Had she been a mere soldier, she might've gotten away without it, but not as archdynast and commander.

Syago and Qosku sat on a trunk of equipment as Lügos brewed a special tea that'd supposedly help her nerves. When she finished, they stood. Syago said, "You look good, and you'll do fine. Just be careful, be calm. Don't let them see you afraid. Act the part even if you don't feel it."

She nodded, taking the tea and drinking from it with a biscuit. "I know, thank you."

"I trust you, Leyta," Qosku said.

It'd taken some talking to get him to understand he couldn't come or even run out if something looked suspicious. They had plans for when to intervene and rescue, but anything more meant inviting the attack they didn't want. He'd managed to end his transformation early to be with her before she went, an act that took considerable effort for him but was achievable in the waxing moon. Her worry over his curse had faded, but seeing how others had reacted to Roza's secret, Leyta knew a day of reckoning would come for Qosku too. She placed a hand on his cheek. "Thank you, Qos. I trust you too."

Katti came in and said a prayer over her before she exited the tent. The sun remained yet hours away and the sky above was remarkably clear, allowing the bright half-moon and field of stars to give light to the landscape. As Leyta walked around the camp, people looked at her, some stopping to make the sign of the sun-wheel cross. Even Fernandeon and his cronies stood by respectfully. *Well, at least I won them over, for the moment, if nothing else.*

Finally she reached the camp's edge and lit her torch, staff in the other hand. All of the masters and commanders stood there, giving her the warrior's salute as she walked confidently to the temple door. Out of the corner of her eye, she saw commotion in the barbarian camp. Were they preparing to move on her? The lifeless on the other side stood eerily still beneath the small rock overhang, watching. As she passed beneath the haunting stone gate, up the steps, and onto the platform, she saw that she no longer approached it alone. From the left came King and on the right she recognized Kask, who'd led the attack on Cantlgrym. She achieved the small platform and waited quietly for the other two, the tomb yawning musty darkness. When they arrived, they stared at each other for a moment. King wore his usual costume, his gloves ready to ignite darkfire at a moment's notice, his face inscrutable behind the regal mask. Kask seemed even more unreadable. His glowing eyes glinted dispassionately, making the scars on his face seem even more stark. The old taunt-name 'Hellface' was fitting for him, his expression its own mask. He wore an old chainmail hauberk without the typical cloak most Razhod wore. King gestured toward the door, inviting them to go first. Moving out of sight of her army down into the dark, she relied on the same tri-part deterrent as the armies above, but now in three individuals rather than three armies. Having Kask and King at her back made her skin crawl. She could defend herself well enough, but knowing the power King brought and that Kask supposedly had, she wasn't so sure about standing her ground successfully.

Etchings lined the walls, mainly geometric designs more than any kind of writing. She walked slow, watching for any writing she could use but without looking close enough to give away that she could read them.

The stairs stopped at a short tunnel that opened into a large chamber. Lifting her torch higher, she moved forward, taking as much in as she could. Pieces of mummies littered the room, mostly arms. She saw no evidence of traps, though that only worried her more.

Eventually they came to the end of the chamber and a tall cylindrical dais with stairs leading up to the top. As they ascended, they passed several shadowed doorways. Leyta hoped that when this was all over, that something explorable would remain of this place, and that they'd be alive enough to do so. She did note the lack of piles of gold some had expected.

Arriving wordlessly at the top, they found a small stone altar. On it sat what could only be the dydatris: a small pyramid of gold, with intricate designs marking every side. It gleamed in the torchlight.

They surrounded the small table it sat on, three opposing rulers staring at an ancient relic of power. Leyta could read the basic fundamentals of elementist studies etched onto the relic. She reached out to twist the dydatris to the side she couldn't see when King cleared his throat, though it somehow sounded different. Metallic, almost.

"If you don't mind, I'm only trying to read it," she said in a carefully annoyed voice.

"This script is old," King said. "You don't know it."

"Then would you like to try?" she snapped. "I'm merely figuring out if this is a real relic of power or just a piece of jewelry."

"Oh, it has power," Kask said, almost breathless as his burning red eyes fixated on it.

"What does it do then?" she asked.

Kask didn't respond, as if it were beneath him. King spoke, "It is said to be that which governs power, young lady. It's the rule book of dyne, a charter. Control this, and you control the power. The jewel of a true ruler, the True Scepter." His mask also unnerved her, the paint reflected torchlight but also amplified shadows, making the small eyeholes darker than ever as if the entire costume were hollow.

Unease slithered its way down her spine. She'd read extensively on this, and they still seemed to know more about it than she. But she noticed one thing: it was three pieces fitted together.

"Well, what do we do then?" she asked, then gave a test of their information. "We can't all have it at once, not without destroying it. So we'll have to truce."

They both laughed. "We'll do no such thing," King said. "No, there *will* be battle, young lady. We've only to manage when."

So they don't know about its components.

"I should just kill them both and take it now," Kask muttered. "It's my right."

"Think that you could do us both in, young fool?" King mused.

"The instant you step out of this temple without us," Leyta said. "You and your friends die by both our armies."

This drew his eyes to hers, and she suppressed a shiver at his burning gaze. He looked both of them up and snarled, "Some things are worth dying for."

"I agree. Shall I help you?" King said.

"Children, stop bickering and work for a compromise, or we'll never leave here," Leyta said.

"The only other way, young bitch, is to seal it in here," King said. "In a way that will protect it while we fight it out above. The victor returns here for the spoils, succeed or die, the stakes are high. A most superior plan."

Kask countered, "Better that we fight down here and the winner then has the power of the relic to fend off the two armies above."

"That risks destroying it even more," Leyta said. "The remaining armies would rather destroy it than let the other have it. This gold doesn't have any protections on it the way soulblades do. I also find it unlikely that either of you understand how to use its power. If you were to even get out of here alive and with it intact, Kask, you might find a disappointing battle erupting up there."

"You have a plan that surpasses ours, young bitch?" King asked.

"Yes I do," she said. Inwardly relieved that Kask didn't just enact his plan of attack. "This isn't a single relic, but three pieces hooked together. We break them apart, each one to his piece, and go our separate ways."

"What makes you think it's three? I don't see any lines," Kask said.

"I happen to read Tiakanawu," she said, and wondered if Kask really could read Tiakanawu too.

"You can't read Tiakanawu," said King.

"I can too," she said. "I've been reading the hieroglyphs on the walls as well. Before coming, I read extensively on it, but these marks of three along the creases indicate it can separate but all three parts are necessary for full control."

"How do we know you're not lying?" King asked. "Who reads Tiakanawu anyway? It's dead, deader than Kask's army."

"People that value education and culture," she said. "And I think we can all at least agree I'm the most trustworthy person here. Anyway, all we need do is see if it pulls apart or not."

"She's not lying," Kask said, his coal eyes glinted in the torchlight as he gazed at the relic. *He does know some of it then. Or his spirits told him.*

"Then you propose we each take a piece and return above to fight over each others'." King stroked his fake beard as he spoke. "It's not winner take all, but I might make that concession to please your pretty little face."

She looked from one to another. "And we begin the fight by splitting armies to fight at each of our two fronts simultaneously? Starting at the crack of dawn?"

"Oh but we prefer to fight in the dark," King said with a low roughness to his voice. "It's when we feel most at home. Or is our young miss afraid of the dark?"

Leyta noticed Kask's eyes fixate on King. *Is that respect in his eyes?* It faded, and he said, "Night benefits the lifeless, an advantage I'll not give up. If you can't handle it, then you don't deserve your piece or place against us."

"I'm not afraid of either you or darkness itself. I only ask for my soldiers and my own wish of sleep. We can beat you in the night."

"Then don't play weak," King said. "We here are lords of hell. The dawn waits on me, not I on he. I'll concede that we start within the hour of leaving here, splitting as you said."

"Is that agreed then, Kask?" Leyta asked.

Evil eyes flickered, the scarred face gave nothing away before he spoke. "It is agreed."

There was a moment of silence as they stared at the relic, then Kask reached out. Leyta raised her scepter at him. He stopped and glared at her with such loathing and anger, she thought he might strike her down right then. "All three of us at the same time," she said. "How often must we remind you you're not alone in here."

The glare held, then he looked back at the relic. King and Leyta stretched out their hands and, together, all grabbed the relic and pulled, it resisted until Kask twisted his free, then Leyta and King did the same. They stood there, each holding a piece. For a moment, Leyta feared they would go back on their word and attack, and she knew they thought about it. Then Kask walked past her to descend the stairs. She followed and King went behind.

Once Leyta emerged from the door, she resisted the urge to run back to her camp. As she arrived, she heard King give a loud speech to his armies, and they roared and cheered. Her soldiers cheered when she entered, clapping her on the back, hugging her, and examining the relic fragment. They then returned to their posts when she told them the outcome. A full three-side battle for the other two pieces.

CHAPTER TWENTY-FOUR

The Battle of Tiakanawu

Based on *The Hunter's Parchments*, cc bastica 300;
Writings of Qosku, cc bastica 279; *Leyta's Journals,* cc bastica 233;
Annals of Syago, cc bastica 227; *The Nordvargor Testaments,* cc bastica 926;
The Dark Fortress of Mephorash, cc bastica xxx;

2nd of Akril, 247

The field kept quiet, not a whisper save the wind. The lull before the tempest. The last quiet moment alive so many of them would have. Anxious air swept the field, flapping tents and banners. He had to remind himself to breathe deep and steady. The camps rustled with nervous activity as troops closed up tents and bedrolls, sharpened weapons and oiled armor, then took up stations along the two split fronts. Mounted torches and clear skies provided visibility, but the evening still gave advantage to any enemies that could see in the dark, enemies like the Razhod. Hellfaces.[78] [79]

Tek'ouk'iek thought about Mour'ikik. They'd not been able to see him among the Baw'kook giants, and though he felt certain the veteran would handle anything with dignity and bravery, he still feared for their Brother of Bone. A great void opened in Tek'ouk'iek, unable to escape thoughts of the return of his worst fear. He'd fought alongside Fal'iek a fair deal more than Lil'iek had and feared the witchlords more than the devils and beasts, more than swarms of lifeless. Now, he would receive new memories to haunt his life and allow less sleep. Perhaps this newer restored coven wouldn't be quite as bad as their predecessors. They certainly lacked their old leader, the Dark Sage of the Inferno, who wouldn't have missed this fight for anything had he been alive.

---

[78] See *Arch Enemy Slayer,* 99

[79] And *Blood Magick Necromance* by Lustmord, 55

Lil'iek put an arm around him, noticing his dark expression, knowing what fears weighed him down. Highly competent with her spear and dual battle-axes, fighting beside her would normally be fun, but this fight would not be. Add to that the danger his immobility imposed, and he knew he'd hate every minute of it.

Self-preservation remained their primary strategy here. Let the enemies savage each other. Most of the planning had focused on logistics, as their own army consisted of several smaller ones: summoners, Roah'riik, elementists, dynfist monks, and Cantlgrym soldiers. They'd found a functioning setup that protected archers and elementists who provided cover for the foot soldiers and monks in front. The Roah'riik were the most out of place, but they knew Asturion tactics well enough to adapt and meld in, which they agreed would be preferable to separating.

Tek'ouk'iek and Lil'iek would lead the Kimoc on the Razhod front, where their experience was most needed, along with a large unit of monks, soldiers, and chamands led by Constantin and elementists led by Balgor. Chipo'maguak of Koah would lead against the Royal Chaos on the left, with Bartolina leading another unit of soldiers and chamands, and Leyta leading the elementists there. Syago and Andras would serve as sub-captains for Constantin and Bartolina. Qosku insisted on staying behind the lines as inner-guard. Katti's priestesses also would stay behind the fray, healing, treating, and praying against the enemies or keeping the braziers of fire and darkfire lit for the elementists. Tongu's minstrels would sing and support as needed. Virgow took the role of central commander in the back, up on the rock. The greatest difficulty would be managing two fronts. The watch of the commanders would be to ensure that solid defense lines held out and adapted with the flow of the fight.

Whatever way this battle went, it would be very long and take a heavy toll. They intended to retreat as soon as the enemy armies distracted or weakened sufficiently, a strategy they could do out of the cleverness of Leyta, who'd secured one of the relic's pieces, ensuring that so long as their portion remained separate from the others, neither enemy would win. He'd attempted to propose they just go ahead and destroy this piece now so that there'd be no possibility of the enemies gaining all three. This was quickly shut down for the typical reason that they might need the piece to destroy the enemies. It terrified Tek'ouk'iek that even if his side won, they'd still lose many of their people. He knew all of his men by name, yet most of these would likely be gone by the end of the day. A heavy cost, but there existed no other option, he prayed fervently to the eternals and ancestors. Aid from Voium wouldn't come until after dawn, if it did at all. So much to hope for and so much to lose. He absolutely hated large-scale battles even with more benign enemies. The total chaos, gore, and destruction left trauma as among the worst nightmares.

One thing he was grateful for, there'd be no question about loyalty or treachery among the allies. The emergence of the Razhod especially had given them that. They needed each other to be strong now more than ever, and the divisive, detrimental efforts earlier would ensure their doom if employed now.

Loud war drums and howls from the barbarians drew his attention. Fire and darkfire shot into the air as the Royal Chaos leaders, all except Knight, riled their troops in the night air. Baw'kook barbarian giants beat weapons on bone-laden shields and chest plates, punching each other in harmony with the drums, in proud display of their savagery. Tek'ouk'iek could already see a large wooden cross raised up, this time empty. A giant trumpeted a large hollowed horn. The few human troops they had seemed to stand by nervously before giving into their own war calls. The army moved to their two fronts, one facing the Razhod and one facing the allies. The Razhod camp stood in silence. No war calls or drums, save the faint sounds of unified chanting that echoed from inside that infernal tent. Tek'ouk'iek felt Lil'iek stiffen beside him. Both searched the area for signs of the shadowmen but saw nothing. And it worried him more. Her bravery was usually so boundless, but even she appeared unsettled. He felt glad that at least he would die with her.

Then they saw him. Mour'ikik was pushed and driven out of the giants' camp. Whipped once by a howling wolfman before letting Mour'ikik simply return to his camp. He received a hero's welcome to make his ancestors proud.

"No, they never hurt me," he answered to their questions. "Well, except for the lashings at the end there. Sleeping and eating among them was terrifying, but they never mistreated me except to push their crosses at me. I was surprised."

The Eternals have smiled on us in this at least, Tek'ouk'iek thought with some relief. *Let's see how they keep up the rest of the night.*

Leyta could see the nerves on each of her men's faces. Projecting the courage she was forcing herself to feel inside, she yelled, "Fortify and strong forth! We will survive this! We will beat them down and come out alive. Don't let up or bend down, but stand together. We fight for our right to live, our right to follow Deova's anointed leaders and laws, our right of worship and thought. They cannot take that from us. They may destroy our bodies, but they'll never destroy our dignity or our will to live and thrive. We will have the coming dawn, and we will give it the honor and glory we paid for in the blood and tears of our land! Fortify!" They cheered as new roars issued from the barbarians. Virgow even gave a nod of approval. Her trumpeters blew hard; soldiers beat weapons and shouted.

The barbarians charged, thundering across the field around the temple walls.

Leyta's heart pounded with each enemy footfall. She could see the rebel Asturions staying behind to guard Chaos leadership while the barbarian Fomorion monstrosities charged ahead. Like a tempest, they rampaged across the field at the allies' left flank. Qosku stood tense behind her.

"Blast and trench on three," Leyta shouted to her dynasts, walking up and down their rows, Tongu's song an empowering backdrop to the thundering terror ahead.

She counted out loud and on three, the dynasts thrust their staves at the ground before the charging giants. She felt the ground tremble just before a massive explosion of dirt and stone blew at the stampede of giants. She watched in satisfaction as a deep trench with jutting stones tore across the front line, and many of the chargers fell injured to the blast. Seeing such power erupt in front of her felt incredible, giving a surge of optimistic sentiments. Yet through the ensuing dust clouds, the Fomorions still came with a roar, fewer and injured but just as quick as before. Two came on so fast that they sprung over the trench and crashed into the soldiers before Leyta could even call for darkfire. Soldiers fell on the ohancanu with spear and sword, only to be knocked off or grabbed and broken. In the frenzy, two more made it over as a boar-faced wookalar bulled his way up the hill through the archers and elementists toward Leyta.

Qosku ran at the giant wookalar, slingstone spinning. Leyta led a churning of mud and dirt at the titan's legs, burying its hooves. The Fomorion swept aside fleeing elementists with a large flail, chopping one in half with an axe. It pulled one leg out as Leyta raised up a boulder at the beast but missed. Dropping its axe, the wookalar grabbed a spearman and rammed him into its tusked mouth. The spear and body fell as it turned to Leyta. Qosku ran to stand in front of her, picking up the spear and throwing it into the wookalar's belly. It squealed, pulling the spear out as quickly as it entered. Leyta didn't lose the situation, moving fire at it. The wookalar grunted and brushed the fire from his face then swept its flail wide. Her fire distracted it, and Qosku darted behind the wookalar to kick the back of the giant's knee, dropping it down to all fours. Then Bartolina ran in and jumped up with a slash to the throat.

She watched Qosku jump on the wookalar's back, but another wookalar appeared with two battle-axes and swung at him then her. Leyta hit its face with fire. Yet more giants appeared, and Leyta frantically backed away, lifting stones toward them only to have them knocked aside. Dirt in her eyes and mouth from all the dust her dyne was kicking up and blinding her, though the giants did not escape the dust clouds either.

The wookalar lost her as the line fell into disarray, giving her a moment to catch her breath. Qosku and Bartolina retreating with her. The order she'd commanded that the lines hold had faded, and it struck her how fickle her previous grip on control had been. Meaningless and unprepared for when the madness of the world took over, and she regretted her cold hand in trying to keep it. She joined several elementists in putting lightning to the wookalar's head. But as they finished him, an ukuku ozorman and ohancanu cyclops broke through, bashing at their scattered ranks with abandon.

All was chaos on the battlefield, screams and smoke filled the air, carnage covered the ground. *But I will adapt to this, if I can't stop the storm I will use it.* As the giants smashed and slaughtered, Leyta went into a frenzy of dyne just to protect her soldiers, which she realized with unexpected clarity that she wanted more than to defeat the enemy. She focused on shielding them and the elementists enough to regroup. She expended more energy doing this than ever before, feeling a dangerous threshold of her sentimental stores approach but having no other option. It drained her insides and burned beneath the skin, but she continued. She felt cornered by the madness, near exhaustion, until Bartolina appeared with another chamand, dashing in between giant legs with her short sword and decorated shield, pricking at their leg tendons, Syago also not far off. With these giants dead, they were able to return to managing the front. A short respite.

Lil'iek had longed to face these enemies that murdered Fal'iek, but now wished to be far away. Still watching dispassionately on the charging Baw'kook, the mummies of the Razhod camp turned to the two fronts and began to move out. The Razhod themselves formed a circle outside their tent. Pushing away her doubt, she mounted a tall boulder and, with axe raised high, issued her wailing warcall. She would not cower before their summoning. The rest of the Roah'riik joined in, then the rest of the army. She pumped her arm, shouting to the Stars and Moon, and the others followed. The ritual began regardless, but they were now less afraid.

Beside her, Tek'ouk'iek commanded the men to move closer, ahead of the soldier front, and begin firing arrows at the summoners just as Balgor's elementists rained havoc on the ritual. But the circle was too far. The arrows, fire, and lightning all fell short. A towering silhouette began to solidify above the circle. Lil'iek's heart was pounding through her chest, her mind again blank in paralyzed anticipation. *Which nightmare spirit will they call upon now?*

The giant shadow, some twenty feet tall, materialized into a skeleton with the skull of a bird. A shredded black and brown cloak covered it, and long clawed arms held up a large hourglass. A deep chuckle reverberated from the greater spirit. Grekiask the Slayer, old stalker of her trauma. Tek'ouk'iek ordered the Roah'riik into defensive formations. That old sensation of helplessness and fear Lil'iek had felt the one time she'd faced the Slayer came rushing back to her.

Grekiask hovered above the coven, emaion emblems faintly shifting along its tattered cloak and the hourglass draining as the circle of Razhod broke up. Three went to the Royal Chaos and three to the allied forces, each bearing tenebrous soulblades: a greatsword, a battle-axe, and a war scythe came to the allies. As sand fell in the hourglass, black smoky shrouds came up from the ground, enclosing each of the six Razhod in a darkness more pure than the night sky. Lil'iek had heard of this before.

Their wicked blades extended out of the shrouds just before they vanished, reappearing among the allied soldiers. They shot up out of the ground, slashing at the screaming soldiers before vanishing again and reappearing by other soldiers, too fast and vicious to escape or defend against, each time gone before the bloody soldier pieces even touched the ground. The only sound was the wind of their soulblades cutting through flesh. The three shrouded Razhod broke up the front line, sometimes slaying two at a time with a single steel whisper.

Further up, on the north side of the temple complex, Lil'iek saw the other three shearing through the barbarian giants. Lightning fast shadows turning giants into fountains of blood. Lil'iek watched in horror as they effortlessly tore apart both garrisons, breaking their positions as they retreated in terror.

She gripped her axe and shield while watching the hourglass and eyeing the ground around them. *Any time now, they'll get to us.* Constantin ran out with several monks to distract or assist in holding off while they retrenched, but where to strike? Even their crossbowmen had no viable targets.

Constantin called again to fortify down as he herded scattered groups. The ones remaining ran back and stood tight together, bearing their weapons in a solid barricade. One shrouded Razhod appeared behind them, and they backed away but not before a soldier fell to the ground, cut in half. The black shroud vanished before they could even see its weapon. Balgor called for wind, and the dynasts pushed forward with a fury to blow away the vapor shrouds.

The sands of the hourglass neared halfway. Though the shrouds struggled against the wind, they held. The hopeless slaughter continued, and Lil'iek saw that the Razhod pushed their attacks inward, the lifeless following in a shambling charge behind their phantom masters. Quicker than a blink, here, there, just a dark hush then blood and death.

"They come for the commanders!" Tek'ouk'iek shouted. Lil'iek moved closer to him while others jumped up to the boulder where Virgow barked orders while shooting bolts. Virgow yelled, "Bartolina, corner the giants so the elementists—"

Before he could finish his sentence, a Razhod materialized in front of him, a warscythe with a vorpal blade swiping at him. Lil'iek recognized it as Mordios the Reaver. Luckily, Virgow had already anticipated the attack, falling back as he brought his crossbow up to block the staff of the scythe. The vorpal blade shuddered and a slice appeared on the boulder behind Virgow, just above his head. The black shroud vanished, reappearing for a split second, ghostly except for scythe that cut through a Roah'riik. Again he vanished and came up on the other side, the invisible force of the blade slicing open a soldier's chest who'd shielded Virgow. Tek'ouk'iek sparked lightning and Lil'iek ran at the shroud, but he faded too quick even for the dynal spark. Nearby a third soldier screamed bloody death, and a hush behind told her the reaper reappeared behind Lil'iek, Mordios already cutting.

She jumped away from him, shield up, but the scythe blade halved her shield and gashed her arm. She cursed as the shroud vanished, again reappearing behind her, but she was already rolling behind a boulder. He was quicker than they could fight, appearing in a moment to slash and disappearing just as quickly.

She saw the shroud appear behind Tek'ouk'iek, but Tek'ouk'iek was already diving while making the ground explode. She couldn't tell if the burst of dirt and rock hit or not, but the shroud stayed this time. She ran at it, hoping to catch the shroud unaware, but he slashed at Lil'iek in a fury. She backpedaled frantically, dodging the swings by split seconds. The Razhod would kill her if nothing changed.

Fighting panic as the shroud pressed her, popping in and out of her range, Lil'iek only barely kept the slashes from her, dodging them entirely or blocking the pole with her axe and broken shield. Dirt flew as the swinging, swerving scythe cut up everything around as it didn't need to touch to cut. Any rock or soldier that happened to be behind her took a cut, though these shivering cuts weakened with distance. One severed her axe. Bolts and arrows from others nearby plucked into the protective shroud. As the shroud vanished to cut the others, Lil'iek returned to Tek'ouk'iek, both gasping for breath and trembling. She chucked the remains of her shield and axe stump, drew her second axe and picked up another, then bandaged her bleeding arm.

Lil'iek searched her memory for how Fal'iek, or anybody, had dealt with this. Far to the left, a shroud with a great-axe savaged the elementists and the soldiers that tried to protect them while avoiding the dynal attacks and chamand soldiers. No arrow or blade could touch it, too fast and protected. She watched in horror as three black shrouds ghosted and gored the allies.

The nightmare shroud returned, but this time she was more ready. Darting inside the weapon's range, she chopped hard with her axes. But the blades were caught by the shroud and the pole of the scythe knocked her down. The shroud raised its weapon, a finishing kill, but fire from Tek'ouk'iek swirled around the Razhod's head, hurting visibility if not the person.

Then Qosku was there too, mace and flail in hand. As Lil'iek and Qosku flanked the shroud, Tek'ouk'iek trapped the Razhod's legs in the ground, finally giving Lil'iek enough time to land an axe-swing in its side, but it was without blood. The shroud vanished then returned with an attack on Qosku he barely avoided. Lil'iek spun about, tripping up trying to keep up with its darting movements until Qosku sprung in with a quick kick to the back and a swinging mace to the front. But the Razhod vanished, causing Qosku to stumble in his miss. Lil'iek growled in frustration. They may as well fight the air. She needed to go on the offensive: attack the shroud while it was busy focusing on another.

Screams of terror filled the air, but it was Balgor's roar that caught Lil'iek's ear. Taking a moment to catch her breath and for her legs to stop trembling, Lil'iek looked down to see Balgor and Constantin, both gravely wounded, backing from a shroud and his large dark red flambard, Grievore the Violator. She approached low. Dynasts launched rocks and fire bursts that got evaded. The Grievore shroud sliced a monk in half just as both she and Syago arrived to attack. It vanished, then slashed at them both from behind. They narrowly ducked, the wavy blade clipping her shoulder in a jolting cut, and spun with a counter, but it was gone, Balgor's lightning nearly hitting them instead. She checked her shoulder, bone armor had mitigated it to a superficial cut but the jolt of the soulblade as it entered her skin then drained her lifeforce still rang her mind. It was the same as before. There was nothing to do but try to survive until the emaion left.

The hourglass sands fell, almost finished. They need only survive that long.

"Qosku, to me!"

The panic he heard in Leyta's voice spurred Qosku to run. He had power jumped to Lil'iek and Tek'ouk'iek when he'd seen what could only be described as a vanishing black cloud attacking them. He didn't want to abandon them, but at least he'd helped them enough to allow Lil'iek time to breathe.

Qosku ran up just as a shroud with the warscythe slashed through a soldier that stood in Leyta's defense. It shaded away as Qosku came in, only to reappear behind and slash at him in the back. Qosku dove under the blade, felt it cut his armor. The shroud was back at Leyta, who shot a stone at him. Missed. The shroud vanished again, back to Qosku with a broad cut he jumped over but got clipped by the staff of it. Then behind Leyta but her stumbling narrowly saved her, reducing the slash to a small cut through her gambeson dress. They both rolled to their feet but it had gone.

Before they could catch their breaths, another shroud, this one with a red wavy-sword, materialized and nearly slashed Leyta in half. Qosku shoved her out of the way and swung his axe at the Razhod, but it vanished. He saw it reappear next to Bartolina, who switched her attack to a dodge and a parry, narrowly avoiding death. The wavy blade ignited then, wreathed in yellow flames. Like something from his worst nightmare. Bartolina showed the same fear on her face as it shifted around her.

Qosku fought the fear, powering his body with anger. He jumped into the air, punching at the shroud, but his fist hit only air. The shroud moved around Bartolina, who brought her sword up in a perfect block, but the flame-blade burned right through it, continuing its arc until it split her in half completely in a burst of embers. Her body fell apart and blood gushed as Qosku screamed. He bolted in, but it vanished at the last second then reappeared behind with a flaming cut across his back, the heat searing over his cut armor as the blade cut across his skin. He twisted and spun out and back in desperation, it disappeared again. The cut was long, he felt, had even drained his life and burned his back in that split second to feed the Razhod. He began a healing prayer and saw with relief that all the Razhod witchlords had shrouded behind their lifeless swarm. As the giant hourglass behind them finished, their smoky black coverings faded away revealing Kask with the wavy sword, Davagis with the scythe, and an unknown woman with the axe. His vision became hazy, he bled too fast for his healing prayers. That nightmare had finished but he was fading.

Katti and a priest suddenly grabbed Qosku under his armpits to carry him away. An ohancanu charged them, pounding up after them as they dragged him into the large halo that surrounded Leyta, several wounded, and praying clerics. The circle's power rebuffed the giant, shielding them with light, and began sealing Qosku's wound, increasing the hot ache across his back. Lügos also tended to several wounded, himself covered in blood. Tongu and his minstrels sang a just rage that energized him. The miracle circle was the most incredible thing Qosku had ever seen, white light encircled them, protecting from the enraged cyclops who now pounded at the circle with his club and claw but couldn't breach it. Qosku felt the gash at his side ache as it began to seal up along with general pain of his body, also the work of Katti's holy sanctuary. He pulled himself into meditation to speed it up, for he understood the circle could not last. Qosku's loose clothing and plated limbs stuck to him under thick layers of sweat and blood from the intense battle made it difficult to focus, but focus inside himself he did. As the ohancanu focused on him, a group of soldiers snuck up behind and slashed his legs then neck.

"Holy Deova above," Katti yelled. "We thank thee for this sanctuary."

The lights faded and Qosku wasn't fully healed, but ready nevertheless.

Shouts down at the giant's front drew Qosku's attention. The battle had become a frenzy. As he watched, one ohancanu fell dead and another swung a massive axe at monks, chamands, and soldiers all at once. Then Qosku noticed Jester walking among the giants, all standing in front of the barrier of ice crystals from the darkfire. He walked in between them with a song stronger and harsher than Tongu's causing the giants to roar and bleat a warcall. Jester pulled out a small leather pouch and handed it to a goatman, who tossed it at the opposing pike barrier over the trench in an explosion of fire.

Barbarian giants jumped at the smoldering opening. They got a few swings in before the front soldiers gutted them. Jester continued to throw his fire bombs while avoiding arrows. Qosku yearned to jump across and confront him but knew the importance of his orders, maintain the front. Stay within and guard.

Then Queen appeared, riding the shoulder of a particularly big ohancanu, and from her came fire. She looked directly at Leyta and expanded the fires, pushing the line up the hill. Qosku started in panic, he couldn't block fire. Leyta whipped her staff up and a large boulder rose out of the dirt in front of her and deflected most of the flames. She growled and increased the push to throw the boulder over the trench and into some giants. With a wave of her staff, hundreds of smaller rocks tore out of the ground, they hovered briefly in the air, then shot forward, exploding on contact as they hit the army of giants. Qosku had never seen this type of speed or power from Leyta before. She looked and sounded as though she were in great pain, moving her hate and rage into the land around her with jaw clenched and eyes focused. And more importantly, her example impressed her dynasts who followed her lead.

None of this affected enough, however, as Jester and Queen refocused their attacks on not only the elementists but the crossbowmen and spearmen as well.

Something had to be done against Queen's fire. Qosku slipped through the front ranks, which shifted to avoid another of Jester's fire bomb vials. An idea coming to him, Qosku power jumped forward to catch it. Gently cradling the symbol-etched glass in his gauntleted hands, he rose, then rolled to avoid a thrown rock. As he retreated, Jester's masked head tilted, watching him. They did already have these, Balgor threw similar bombs, but Jester's were better. Qosku ran up to Andras, who shot arrows with the archers. "Andras, we have weapon for Queen," he said, holding the vial up to an arrow.

Andras looked briefly at it, puzzled, then understanding dawned. He put his crossbow down, saying, "An arrow won't work. It's too small, but a javelin could if we tie it right."

He grabbed one from a corpse, and Andras tied it so that it would fall correctly. "Come on," he said, motioning for Qosku to follow him to the front. Andras hid the weapon as he notched it in the javelin thrower, then ran up to the ditch and launched it at Queen and the ohancanu she sat upon. A very good throw, Qosku estimated. The javelin slowed early, then dove toward the target. The ohancanu's arm reached up to catch the spear, but still the vial burst on the shaft, throwing fire all over his upper body. Queen, dress burning, hopped off to another ohancanu giant. The burning ohancanu clawed at the fire consuming him, but the fire only spread further. As they watched, another ohancanu beheaded him, then kicked the burning body into the trench.

Qosku and Andras congratulated each other as they ran back to the front line. Qosku reached it first and turned to Andras. His breath left him as he saw Jester's vial descending on Andras. Qosku leaped forward, but the vial had already hit. Darkflames enveloped Andras and scattered around him, even catching on the pants of nearby soldiers who brushed theirs out. The flames burned with unleashed fury, and all hope fled as Andras fell to his knees: a stiff, smoldering darkpyre that left ice all around. Qosku thought he heard a scream. He certainly felt one inside. He looked past the darkfire to see Jester, hollow mask turned to them, clapping his hands and spinning in delight. Qosku felt his limbs move toward Jester but someone pulled him back behind the ranks as rocks, javelins, and arrows descended.

Syago had left his post. His soulblade was needed everywhere and the mayhem was not fixed in any one area, but once a semblance of order was restored, he returned to the right. In the wake of the summoning's end, the right flank's dynasts used the belated opportunity to blast and trench just as the slow swarm of lifeless arrived. Balgor led the count and the ground erupted beneath the swarm of bodies. It tossed them but hardly stopped most, only slowing the crawl. Worse, grimshades emerged from the enemy tent and flew down in winged form to swipe at soldiers or drop rocks or lifeless. They were more a distraction, like the swarm of bodies, allowing the real threat of the Razhod to flourish.

The front ranks struggled to regroup and tighten; soldiers fled in fear as something tore through the lifeless ahead and into the vanguard, unhindered by the spiked trench. The flaming reptile that had burnt Tolgrym came through, a woman atop it. She was Unakan in black leather and cloth that bore red markings. Her long dark hair whipped behind her, showing a face of scars and those same nightmarish eyes like smoldering coals. Hellface.

The devil she rode obeyed her completely as she cracked a soulwhip, Penaga the Slaver. Long, black, and covered in small barbs, she snapped it above a group of retreating soldiers, and small thorns shot out at them. With a spiked shield in the other hand, she maneuvered the eyeless sloth, torching the ground from the various pores along its head and sides, and lurched forward at the soldiers.

"FEAR ME!" she screamed. "Ye lovers of pleasure. The Lady of Pain rules here." The sloth charged, biting and jetting flames while she snapped Penaga.

Syago ran for them beside Lil'iek, and the Hellface charged in, lashing the soulwhip side to side. As the cord flicked, it ripped open armor and skin. Not deep cuts, but bloody and painful. With the fire and whip, the Razhod routed the soldiers and prevented them from closing ranks around the archers. Weaving between soldiers, Syago ran for her, but the witchlord lashed her whip out. Syago felt a barb bite through the leather of his glove and he hoped it wasn't poisoned. She snapped the whip again and, with the sloth's fire, disposed of most of the archers' weapons. As she terrorized the armies, the archers drew melee weapons and formed a schiltron around her at Tek'ouk'iek's command. But she would not be contained. Two soldiers fell immolated in flames; another's throat gushed blood from the whip.

Syago's devil arm twitched, and in a rush of anger, he nearly muscled his way through his own soldiers, but caught himself first, taking a deep breath. He swung Alexandre up and leaped over the men's schiltron wall, landing in the ring with the Hellface and sloth. Fire rushed toward him but stopped just shy of Alexandre, held in the air by the sword's power. His devil hand also repelled flames, deflecting them back to the devil. While it was distracted, Syago jumped forward to cut at the sloth's neck, but she reared it up, and thorns from the whip bit his flesh as the devil's front claws descended. Syago retreated slightly, coming forward to attack its side, but each time he got close, the devil would shoot flames, a whip would crack, and it moved away. Lil'iek, Ravenger in hand, darted in but halted as spurts of fire flared or the whip lashed. Their only hope was to distract it enough on one side to give the other an opening.

As Tek'ouk'iek commanded the sides close in to protect Syago and Lil'iek, the whip wound around Alexandre, which now blazed furiously, and the Razhod yanked the sword out of his hand. Syago called for it and it flew up to return, but the dark whip pulled it back. The whip barely able to contain its divine wrath, Alexandre flew every which way to return to him. In chasing it, he held their attention while Lil'iek darted forward with Ravenger, cutting the tail before retreating.

More fire short forth, forcing everyone back except Syago, who swept the fires aside with his devil arm. Anger at the devil, at the Razhod, burned through him, and he pushed through more fires and thrust the same fist up into the head of the sloth, grabbing and pulling back through with a yell. It shivered and fell, and Syago swiped his claw at its chest, feeling joy at tearing up the carcass until Alexandre returned to his hand with a rebuke.

It is not good that you rage so. Be still and grateful. The words were the most positive communication from the sword he'd experienced. He didn't want to break their harmony and so replied nothing.

Lil'iek ran up the back tail toward the woman, cutting as she went, and he prepared to flank her. The woman cracked the soulwhip in a way that propelled her up and over their reach, landing her in the throng of lifeless. Syago felt an impulse to pursue her there, but checked it when he saw Kask near the front of the lifeless swarm.

"KASK!" he roared as he ran. He sliced through the lifeless until he was near and brought Alexandre down on Grievore. There was a brief moment when Kask looked at him, no surprise, no anger, no jests. The scarred face was dispassionate save for the venom in those helleyes. Then it began, the two soulswords whirled around each other in such a heavy blur, Syago could barely follow it. He'd beaten Kask only months ago, or would have if not interrupted, so it was a shock when the blinding frenzy of steel clashes abruptly ended with Syago disarmed on the ground and Grievore piercing his chestplate.

Once the tip of the wavy blade drew blood, the agony started. Red wounds on Kask sealed up as Syago was racked, immobile and trembling on the ground as lifeless closed in and Kask coolly drained him. Then Kask let off, leaving him to die beneath the crowd of lifeless. Calling Alexandre back to him, Syago punched and slashed his way to his feet, then cut through to the front line. Worn and wounded but alive enough, he looked around for Kask, confused why the old nemesis hadn't finished him personally. The old acquaintance hadn't even taunted him. *It may be more in my head than his now,* he thought, *but I'll see it finished someday, rendering a judgment he and the others deserve.* Both Alexandre and his devil's arm approved of his thought, a rare moment of agreement.

Lil'iek finished carving up the devil, holding her nose against the rank odor of it. Her eyes searched the field for the elusive shadowmen but they seemed to have retreated to the tent, or the other fronts. The lifeless came in, their old and rusted weapons clumsily held as the wounded soldiers were pulled back and replaced by a new front line.

But the lady Hellface was not done and emerged in front, not following safely behind her zombi fodder but leading it and this time bearing the double-bladed battleax Lil'iek recognized as Zurrogiath the Desolator. Tek'ouk'iek called for a section of archers to focus on her and Balgor commanded the dynasts who brought a large pillar of flame down on her. She looked up at it before briefly disappearing under the fire blast, Lil'iek saw her spinning Zurrogiath above her head and deflecting the fire until it faded. Flames smoldered on the ashen ground around her but she stood unharmed, chest heaving, hellish face hungry. As other soldiers formed up, Lil'iek studied her prey. The black soulaxe with rusted head appeared too big for her lean figure to wield but she hefted it effortlessly in two hands. The ground bulged and moved at her from the dynasts' push and she chopped into it with a shriek, splitting the coming upheaval away from her, the ground rolled outward and knocked Lil'iek to the ground. A large crack in the ground yawned open from the cut and soldiers scrambled to not fall in. Tek'ouk'iek shouted pointing, "Stop her!"

Rocks flew up out of the ground and a wave of arrows fell on her but the Hellface swung Zurrogiath overhead and leaped thirty feet into the morning air twirling it as she went past the missiles. She cleared forty feet over the wreckage of bodies and rocks, landing lithely in the middle of the battalion. She dashed forward, shrieking, with a wide swing of the large axe in a fury that cut through the first row of five soldiers. She jumped back, away from a surge of arrows and spears, then forward again to cut down the next wave of defensive men, slicing through them as if nothing were there. They had armor, shields, and weapons to defend with, but these rusted and withered under the powerful soulblade and the heretofore unseen ferocity of the Razhod. The idea of approaching scared Lil'iek who sought a way to get at the woman. Her perfect dark lighting agility kept her from getting hit, screaming as she slashed. Metal rusting and wood leather rotting rapidly from the blade's touch.

Not ready but not willing to wait any longer, Lil'iek ran in, mustering her own ferocity in the face of her fears, axes in both hands. Armored soldiers fell in front of her and she nearly tripped over the piles of bodies. Bloody limbs and shredded armor were everywhere but she kept up her undulating warcry to match the Hellface's shrieks. Then the men in front fell apart in a grating splash of blood and the Hellface was on her, the Huntress's ferocity failing as the unstoppable greataxe swung in. She could only dive under it, the blade missing her shoulder, then she rolled back. The blade swung back so fast Lil'iek panicked, momentarily forgetting that the woman was more preoccupied with mowing down the armored soldiers than her specifically. The Huntress kicked the Hellface in the abdomen then the knee, pushing her back. The woman snarled and raised the axe to bring it down on Lil'iek but the Huntress snapped a handaxe into the Hellface's gut, through her gambeson. Exposed, Lil'iek didn't wait to see if the throw was even successful, but rolled back and out, hoping to at least have given the others some time, and herself some breath. Her attack stunned the woman long enough for the lightning to finish her from the dynasts. She fell to her knees, bleeding nose, and tried to rise again with a growl before she was hit again. After all that death, this one Razhod fell.

CHAPTER TWENTY-FIVE
THE BETRAYAL OF TIAKANAWU

Based on *The Hunter's Parchments*, cc bastica 300; *Writings of Qosku*, cc bastica 279; *Leyta's Journals*, cc bastica 233; *The Nordvargor Testaments*, cc bastica 926; *The Dark Fortress of Mephorash*, cc bastica xxx;

2nd of Akril, 247

Balgor boomed out commands on closing ranks after the slay of the woman Razhod. Tek'ouk'iek's dyne was beginning to wear thin in emotional exhaustion. He breathed in relief when Lil'iek ran up to him, panting. Virgow hobbled up next to Tek'ouk'iek and fired a crossbow bolt in sync with him and Lil'iek at the woman. "Need more marksmen." Virgow barked. "A bolt through the eye'd finish her quicker if we can keep from panic. Bodies are building up on your frontline, best we pull back and burn them."

The swarm of lifeless moved past her to fall on the scattered front line, which scrambled to form up and meet them. Tek'ouk'iek ordered his archers to prepare the fire arrows; they would burn the lifeless with their new dead.

To the left, the swarm encroached under the lead of Kask, though he'd lost sight of Davagis. The darkness of night hadn't been a huge impediment, even less as it now faded, but it did limit vision further afield, possibly hiding other doings of the witchlords. The rest were hopefully fighting the Chaos to the north, which appeared far more intense than it did here; a tempest of ice, stone, and fire.

Another figure appeared.

Tek'ouk'iek barely knew Roza, but even he recognized the imposing figure lost to the Necromancer's power, walking through the ranks of bodies, pale and dispassionate. Behind her, Kask cracked a faint smile. Roza quickened her pace and plowed into the front ranks, and lifeless poured into the opening behind her.

Tek'ouk'iek raised his scepter-crutch to stun the woman. Balgor got to her first, yet with unprecedented speed and strength, she tossed archers and overturned braziers. The two locked arms, giant and gravespawn, and Balgor yelled at her, "Gretal, waken and cease fighting! We are your friends!"

Tek'ouk'iek lowered his scepter; he didn't want to hit them both. Of the non-Kimoc allies, he liked Balgor best. She snapped an arm forward to grab Balgor's beard and shirt before lifting him in the air and heaving him at Lil'iek, who darted aside. "Balgor, she's too far under their spell," Lil'iek shouted. "We can't waken her like this."

Balgor opened his mouth to respond, but Roza moved in on them. Lil'iek kicked her knees, but may as well have kicked a thorntrunk. Tek'ouk'iek seized the moment by launching a rock into her face. The lifeless woman ignored it, shoving Balgor and Lil'iek aside. The gravespawn picked up a boulder and threw it at Virgow, who narrowly avoided getting smashed. Amidst this, Tek'ouk'iek switched to his bow and released an arrow into her eye. With the arrow protruding out of her eye, she darted to him. He was helpless as she ripped the bow from his hands and picked him up. Dirt cracked at her feet from his dyne, and she ripped his scepter-crutch from him. Lil'iek was there in an instant, axes cutting her arms. Roza slammed him into her, and they tumbled.

Calling for dynasts to aid him, Balgor rushed over and wrapped Roza in a great hug from the back. She pried his arms open and threw her head back into his face. Stunned, Balgor stumbled back a step, then punched her in the face with a thunderous right hook. The punch turned her head with a crack of bone, but when she faced him, neck bent, arrow in eye, he backed away, hands up apologetically. "Roza... are you in there at all?"

She spoke, a voice more hollow but still hers, "I'm s-so s-sorry. You have to bury me. Water or dirt will make a grave that binds."

"Like the lifeless," Tek'ouk'iek shouted. "It must be complete."

Balgor shouted to his dynasts, "Stay clear and bury her with dirt, using a hole like the trench, on three."

She freed a foot as they counted three, then the dirt around her heaved, preventing her the footing she needed to leap free. It swallowed her up to the thighs. She clawed at it, eroding her new grave quickly but not fast enough. Balgor and Tek'ouk'iek watched as another surge of dirt closed up to her neck, slowly consuming her. Balgor approached, looking sadly at her impassive corpse face. "I am sorry, Gretal," he muttered. "We hold none of this against you and at the nearest opportunity, I'll return and aid you in whatever way I can." The dirt covered her face and all movement immediately stopped. Balgor rolled a rock over the location of her head and marked it.

Lil'iek ran to Tek'ouk'iek, who now felt the pain of a dislocated shoulder. She helped him put it back into place. When he stood again, he realized it was hailing. Not hard, but the battle had kept his attention off of it. As they held each other in the pelting weather, they felt gratitude for another moment together in the face of death, beneath the growing dawn.

Loud booms drew his attention to the left. Flamebursts, flying rocks, and freezing darkfire held off the giants. Feeling movement, he looked up to see a herd of daemog on the eastern ledge. Drawn by the smell or noise, they watched the battle and stirred restlessly. He grabbed a daemog skull to bring the herd into the vale but when pressed, they turned and fled, and he marveled. Quervosks circled far off to the side instead of overhead, and a pack of malwolves paced anxiously on the opposite ridge before also running off. They weren't coming down; the torrent of blasts and metallic clashes had scared them. He knew then that this would from be known as the day the world broke. Infernos and blizzards raged side by side, humans slaughtered each other in the open, and the beasts of the wild feared humans for the first time in known history.[80] Stranger still, in Tek'ouk'iek's mind, was how the rocks along the mountainsides had jutted out more, becoming twisted. Even the dirt along the ground swirled into odd knots and green grass turned brown from all of the dyne being thrown around. His attention returned the swarm of lifeless that encircled them. The Asturions had held the line but now needed to regroup; he ordered his men to hold the front for them.

Dawn finally grew, and as the sky brightened, each of the allies felt a new hope through the weariness that weighed them down. Pushing aside the exhaustion, Qosku watched the enemy leaders. Their ranks had slowed down,

---

80 This is obviously exaggerated, but some of it was likely true. Noise attracts predators, but the amount probably had been too much for them to countenance.

weaker. Qosku figured it was only a matter of time until the battle ended, one way or another. His eyes went to the Razhod tent, where children sat watching the battle. He froze, unable to believe in his eyes. He rubbed them, looking again, and this time couldn't help his gasp of shock. His twin sister, Chaska, was among the children there. It was difficult to see at that distance, but he was sure it was her. He'd recognize her anywhere. Then she was gone, the children running inside the tent. Qosku wondered if he'd really seen her at all. He wondered briefly if her fleeting presence was why his internal feminine struggle had resurged. Or if he was merely projecting it onto her, even imagining her there. *Did I not kill her then? Why would they keep her captive? Or am I just still feeling guilty for what I did to her? What is happening?*

Looking over the greater field, he saw the shift happening. Leyta had continued throwing stones and fire at the enemies until she ran out of sentimental energy, a visibly weakened shell of a dynast, and switched from dyne to a crank-loading crossbow. The Fomorion giants began trying to move around the trench, spreading out in their impatience. On the right, the lifeless clamored against the tight ranks, also spilling over in their mindless assault at the behest of Kask, who herded them with a staff. The front lines had vanished. Now, the fighting was everywhere, truly filling the vale with no space and no barriers in between. The northern area was an tempest of darkfire from King, with ice crystals covering even the temple, now collapsing beneath its ice casing. The ally front lines tried to hold defensive positions and let the enemies wear themselves out on each other, but the enemy captains ensured that they too got attacked and drawn in such that the madness of what followed overwhelmed their reservations.

Qosku stood agape at the raw storm of violence, no longer able to follow its course. The two fronts of the allies blended together. Screams filled the air as never before. The lifeless mummies did well only in greater number, bodily fortitude, and with the aid of the Razhod, but they'd noticeably weakened under the ascending sun. The allied ranks began to scatter under the weight of the destructive tide; commanders everywhere called for them to pull back and tighten but forces could barely move without getting hit by foe or by friend. The allies had more wounded from the Royal Chaos side but more dead from the Razhod.

Qosku now felt grateful for his post on the inside, fighting in that incomprehensible mayhem would've been impossible even for him. Even the barbarian giants struggled to navigate the chaos, and the Razhod simply slashed apart everything in their way, including their own disciples and lifeless. Giants died under mummies simply by being overwhelmed. To the north, a Hellface was frozen by King, then shattered by a wookalar. Another traded blows with Knave. Knight swung distractedly at his own army, resisting the control. The greatest asset of the allies, that of a diverse army skillfully working together in coordinated units, faded away in the tiring frenzy.

In all his days of traveling and fighting, Qosku had never seen anything so brutal and bloody. Not just from a first encounter with the Crimson Coven, but the savagery of the Royal Chaos and how his own companions fought back. Shocking him and bringing on great despair, a sense that nothing in the world was truly good, nothing could be. All reason and order eventually bowed to the animal inside each of them, on the altar of survival, and although the emptiness of the world was not worth the horrid battle, violence remained unavoidable and inevitable. The kind of sight that permanently changes people by taking something out and putting it back in far worse than before. Just watching it horrified him in a way that would scar his dreams for years to come, but he struggled to look away or ignore the sounds. Even the competing songs of Jester and Tongu's group blended to form an awful mix of cacophonous sentiments that reverberated throughout everyone's core, an echo of the evil they experienced on each other.

Like a mirror, this reflection made him think on his own secret darkness. *What am I doing? Punishing myself for wanting to feel good? For having a unique sense of pleasure and identity? I've added pain and loneliness to myself on top of all this, and gained what for it? How dare I.*

Daylight grew and the fights petered out, even the Hellfaces needing rest for their yet mortal frames, though not letting off on what remained of the fighting. The allies' defensive efforts had accomplished something after all. They'd lasted surprisingly long, held up well. But time was up.

They were losing.

Then up on the ridge behind them, sunlight reflected off the shining armor of another army like hope's banner.

Having lasted till dawn, the army stationed at Voium had finally arrived. The allies' reinforcements had made it.

Qosku grabbed Leyta's arm and pointed at the new arrivals. When she finally turned to look up at the ridge, she gasped and tears sprang to her eyes. Arrived and now gathered at the top but hesitating to come down, other than a lone messenger. And why wouldn't they? The chaos of the scene before them must be confusing. She yelled at Virgow, who didn't hear over his own hoarse yelling. Qosku ran up to him and got him to look at the ridge. He cackled with glee. "I knew they'd come through eventually, ha ha!

"But the worst part is yet to come," Virgow said as he limped down the large stone with Qosku's aid. "They're smart not to come down to us, and we'd be stupid not to help them help us out of here. Just have to get to 'em." Then he looked at Leyta, Balgor, and Constantin. Most of the chamands and all of the Kimoc were further down in the thick of the fighting, courageously holding the brunt of the assault so the Asturions could get brief respite until their rotation. "We have to leave the ones in the fray."

Leyta gasped, but the other leaders seemed unsurprised and undeterred. "But they're trapped in there. If we just focus our efforts we can pull them out—"

Virgow held up a hand. "It's not about fighting them out of there. We have to get the rest of the army and your relic piece to safety. We need as much a head start on the Razhod as we can get. The only way to do that is to leave them occupied. Now stop wasting time and obey the chain of command."

She opened her mouth to object, but the other commanders had already moved to complete it, withdrawing those already free of the fray. All of her elementists were free, most of her soldiers too were just at the edge. But the Kimoc were near completely surrounded, and the summoners as well were scattered about, both groups trapped. She watched in awe as both groups held the front line with such ferocity in the thickest heat of it. The two groups couldn't possibly break out now without help and the Asturion treachery the Kimoc often spoke of, or the neglectful estrangement of the summoners, never seemed as validated as it did now.

Syago stood beside her and looked out. "Is this all there is?" His distant eyes seemed to speak more of the world at large than the battle. "No plan or purpose. Just chaos." And he was right, she felt a deep void as the rest of the allies already moved past them up the hill. The decision was already made, she just had to comply.

"We have to do it," she said. Syago nodded and ran down to them for a last second warning. She looked back at Virgow.

"Leyta, you have the relic piece, you above all can't linger!" Virgow yelled. "Where's your steel?"

She charged up the hill to him, snarling in his face, "We don't leave people behind. I will at least warn them."

"You think I don't know what we're doing to them?" His voice was as cold and hard as his eye. The scars on his dark brown face never looked brighter, more real. "I've been where they're at." He tapped his cane against his bad leg, then pointed it at them. "And if they've got the mettle I do, they can take it. Some might even survive. So don't lecture me from your comfortable past about sacrifice. I've paid it out more than you." He turned then to hobble up to the cart that'd carry them out. "At least better them than ours. Just make sure you also tell the counts so you can get credit for finally getting rid of 'em. Use the deed what's done."

Once on the cart with the rest of the soldiers, he pulled out his horn, only just now sounding the retreat, a belated alarm to the abandoned troops.

She turned to blast the lifeless as she retreated, but nothing came out. She'd used up her sentiments, all reserves drained out.

Syago ran up from the front line toward her, having warned them personally, and cut down a small opening for all the good it would do. He had the same grim look in his eyes she knew must be in hers. Just behind him lifeless clawed after him and a handful of Roah'riik that struggled out, though the majority of their group were still left behind. Leyta didn't see a single Asturion soldier or elementist in the fray. Once again they'd see this as the palemen murdering the brown and black and not be wrong. That it was commanded by an Unakan only confused her more, but the historical semblance remained.

Leyta took a deep breath, straightening her spine. She told herself that this was what being a leader was. Making hard decisions. The Kimoc understood sacrifice; they'd even defended it to her face. This was no different. Turning away, she wished she could believe that.

Before she could change her mind, Leyta fled up the slope, weeping.

The betrayal hit Tek'ouk'iek like a boulder. Lil'iek pointed out to him their flight and he gaped in horror at the troops, all of them. All of them retreating up the hill, away to the valley entrance. He raised his scepter to push back some lifeless from toppling over on top of his Roah'riik when he was suddenly pulled back. Lil'iek was dragging him up the hill, arms hooked under his armpits, through a tight opening Syago had left them. Below, Mour'ikik worked in a fury, not even noticing that behind him, an opening was being filled by more lifeless. They shouted warnings to him and the others, but the calls were lost in the frenzy.

Tek'ouk'iek threw wave after wave of rage back at the lifeless swarm, making a wall of fire and exploding the ground to free up the last of their companions. Protect Mour'ikik at least, but it wasn't long before he could no longer see them. He wanted Mour'ikik, the man they'd just rescued from a previous abandonment, to turn and see what was happening, to see Tek'ouk'iek trying to help him. *Will he know that he's been betrayed? Will he think I left him? Or will he die thinking we all lost?* Buried memories of being taken up by the mob in Mantlgrym resurfaced, and he shouted for Lil'iek to drop him and let him defend his people. He struggled against her grip. "Let me go!"

"We can't save them, Tek," Lil'iek replied, panting. "At most we could delay their deaths, but they'd much rather some of us escape than none of us. We're not betraying them, we're being betrayed." Tek'ouk'iek knew she was right but couldn't help himself. He struggled to get his dyne out, continued to raise stones until his sentiments were too weak to damage them. Once out of the fray, he couldn't tell how many had been left in the snare. He could see that some summoners were swallowed up in it as well while others had gotten out. To the left, the group led by Chipo'maguak was mostly lost from sight, not escaping either, not even the leaders. Of his own Roah'riik, he had but four fleeing with him: Klom'oth, Dar'miir, Machi'guenk, and Guaran'upik. Just the four and his wife, with the rest being left behind to be slaughtered. And the ones that made it did so only barely, fleeing together and fighting off the encroachment, all were wounded. He gasped in relief as they escaped the battle below, and wept for it. Sorrow turned to bitter rage at what had been done to them.[81]

81 *See Sol Sistere de Selbst by Himetuks Himi'n and Gyibaaw Blackbraid: Born of Winter, Mutilated Tyrant*

CHAPTER TWENTY-SIX
TAKE REFUGE

Based on *Leyta's Journals*, cc bastica 301; *The Hunter's Parchments*, cc bastica 300; *Scars of the Martyrs*, cc bastica 1000; *The Nordvargor Testaments*, cc bastica 930;

3rd of Akril, 247

The allies arrived at Voium only with the assistance of the Voium army. Just over a third had survived, the biggest loss being the Kimoc and ch-amand groups. It weighed Leyta down. Scenes of blood and destruction flashed through her mind. Scars that she knew would have to be factored into her dynal commanding, for it would deeply affect her sentimental control. Already she felt completely drained, like she'd never be able to use dyne again.[82]

And they weren't even done.

She still held a piece of the relic, which guaranteed that neither enemy could attain the power of all three and that she would face them again. She didn't know if she had the strength for this; she certainly didn't now and saw no way of gaining it. Not after seeing firsthand what the Razhod were truly capable of, nor after the increasingly virulent unpredictability of the Royal Chaos.

She wandered so deep in these ruminations that she hardly noticed Voium's gates open for her. The city she'd spent most of her life in, where her adoptive parents had raised her, and where she'd developed a love for learning that now seemed so lost. The city now felt alien in a world she couldn't understand and didn't want to be in.

But she was in it, nonetheless.

---

82 See *Thy Light, Therion!*, 93

On the wall and along the streets, people waited, cheering their return. They threw tassels and confetti, an unnatural burst of color against the drab of the four-story buildings. The excitement died somewhat, though not completely, when the arriving army didn't join in. All around Leyta, the forlorn soldiers tried to wave back with fake appreciation. Syago and Qosku were empty shells beside her. Balgor looked more grim than ever, hollow almost. Katti and the priestesses no longer prayed, but walked along the wagons in silence. Dirt, sweat, and blood covered all, and none made a sound or smiled at the big welcome. Were they as scarred as she or merely as tired? It had to be both; those eyes and slumped shoulders knew the same violence, and the betrayal. But she did wonder if the foul but necessary act weighed on their consciences the way it did hers. She looked back at Tek'ouk'iek and Lil'iek at the rear, perhaps the only two that held off the weariness with raging fires in their eyes. She wouldn't exactly blame them if they avenged themselves on her then and there, but she did worry about what would happen next. Surely the six of them who remained wouldn't try anything so drastic, not now. The disquiet deadened the welcome parade, but the people of Voium cheered in good intention nonetheless. She supposed celebration was warranted, they'd lost much but in the end came out mostly alive and with their primary objective accomplished.

Moving through Voium brought back memories, including that of Camila, the young woman Leyta had abandoned to a hellish marriage that'd eventually driven her to suicide. There had been others too. Tomas de Lucos had been an annoying boy Leyta had grown up with then later avoided, now said to be a drunken vagrant groveling in alleyways. Her one cousin, Guilliom de Syagon, she'd eventually shunned completely, he too had killed himself in lonely despair. Just as with the Kimoc, she'd abandoned them to fight their battles alone at a time they'd needed her. She knew she wasn't solely or directly responsible for any of these, but she couldn't deny that she'd contributed to their pain and isolation, to the communal void. And these were just those she knew of, what of the others she didn't? On realizing her fate, Camila had given Leyta parting words, "You put pain into the world, Leyta, and it doesn't just disappear when you're done."

No, it doesn't. The pain she'd given them now came back to her and many others. She had just witnessed some of that in the vale. Putting pain into circulation can return or it can continue on to others just as at the battle dyne had reverberated outward, warping the ground all the way up to the valley cliffs and scaring the animals, browning the grass. *The heresy is true then. Our powers press our sentiments on the world, and mostly negative sentiments at that.* Elementists fought with hate, anger, and fear because joy and love were harder to sustain, especially in battle. And these mostly flowed outward. Every elementist knew sentiments didn't just dissipate. But Leyta alone seemed to have figured out they go on to pollute and corrupt everything else, turning animals into monsters. *Of course we affect the condition of the world, we can't not given how much power we have.* It was people that made the world their hell, not the underworlders or the Criod as the Church taught. Of course she couldn't tell anyone this, she'd be lucky to only lose her position after a revelation like that. She was a heretic.

The armies were led to inns and homes with available space to immediately fall asleep. Sleeping all day, they regained what they could. The following eve fell the vigil held for those lost. Though clouds darkened the sky, candles filled the city streets and windows with light. Leyta stood on her family's balcony with Syago, Qosku, and Katti, all there at her request, in addition to her adoptive parents. She'd never been especially close to them, but they'd been more happy to see each other this time than ever before. Across the street, Lil'iek and Tek'ouk'iek stood in their own guest balcony with the remainder of their companions. So few of them, and those of Koah were completely gone. Leyta didn't know what would now happen with either group, but the dark, ominous gazes from across the way were not comforting.

Leyta always felt moved by the sight of the candles, but now it haunted her. Joining the battle had been necessary, but still she felt responsible for all the death. She knew she didn't kill them, that there was more to it than that. But she felt it all. Her mind ran through other things she might've done better, being quicker, more decisive. But it would've ultimately changed nothing. All of it because of her. Her investigation into the relic and the chase of it, convincing the allies to go after them, including inviting the Kimoc, and then splitting the relic instead of letting the two enemies fight over it. She wondered what would've happened if she'd let them fight each other while she and her army just left, and then perhaps returned shortly after to finish the two off and take the relic. She now felt as though this had been the best option, the one she should've done. But how to know? It ate at her, needing to know she'd made the best decision if not the right one, for she saw no right decision.

She shivered as the people of Voium sang the prayers, a harmonious wailing that filled the open streets. Memories of her people being dismembered played in her head. She again saw the Razhod come at her, obscured in darkness, bearing weapons of terrible power, and moving too fast for her to stop them.

Syago put an arm around her shoulders, drawing her close in comfort, obviously sensing the scars she now bore and some of which he already held. "Survive," he whispered in her ear. "We did it, we survived and you guided us out of it. You have nothing to fear from the past."

She melted into his chest and sobbed. He embraced her fully and simply held her. The prayer song rose in volume and pitch as the wailing cries of widows, daughters, sisters, and mothers let their grief sing. "It's all right," he whispered, his face glowed beautifully from the candles. So kind and gentle, she could've kissed him if not for these stupid tears. She wiped them away, shaking her head. He whispered, "I cried when... the last devil. Before I decided to come back to you. A human reaction that isn't allowed but maybe should be."

"No," she said, trying to pull away and wipe off the tears. "I have to be strong for them. I have to lead. To fortify."

"Fortify later," he said, his eyes meeting hers. "No one will blame you for being weak now, not when you have to be. We all have to be... sometimes. You have to heal. You only can't *stay* weak. Others need you and *you* have to survive. Take some time to recover, then fortify. Survive."

"But all my mistakes," she said. "So many in that battle, little ones even, not being quick enough. Risking too much. I could've prevented more deaths. We shouldn't have even been there. And all the other things I've done."

"We all make mistakes," he said. "All the time. I made a mistake leaving you. I made mistakes even before in Tolgrym, some of the pranks I pulled on other boys I didn't like. But I accepted the responsibility, and we all moved on. I made worse ones when fighting the devils, I used people. Maybe we have no excuse for the betrayal, I don't know. What matters is that we tried, you tried. And you can't be held to a high standard for working under extreme pressure. If it was a hero that willfully did something bad... well that's different. This isn't the angel's court. This is humanity living in hell. Justice will have to cut us a break in the end. We didn't choose to be in this world, but we did enter that battle of our own choice, you only helped us within it."

She couldn't say anything to that, but she felt it. She needed it, just to hear it. She looked at Qosku, who stood closer to the railing watching the candles calmly, listening to the men's prayer as it was now the father's, brothers, and son's turns to wail in harmony. Seeing the shining gleam of tear streaks on his face, she left Syago and went to him, bending slightly to embrace the Unakan monk. His arms came around her. Not awkward this time, but fierce. He sobbed too, and it made her do so again. Crying into each other, it felt strangely good the same way venting anger did, pushing sorrow out of themselves. The release. Though she couldn't help think again of where that sorrow would go.

As his people, the Unaka, talked about releasing evil in their rituals, eschewing the negative energy, she felt that she and he did that. The normally calm, even dispassionate, little monk surprised her in a way that reminded her of just how young he was. Over three years her junior and he'd seen everything she had in addition to his curse and whatever else he was dealing with. The sobbing ended, and they held for a brief moment before she stood straight and wiped the tears as Katti came to embrace her. The priestess put a hand to Leyta's cheek in a wordless gesture that promised forgiveness, support, and hope.

Leyta turned and saw her adoptive parents looking at her. The Eliots thought little of her life's work except for occasional pride. She wasn't the beautiful daughter-heir they'd sought, but she was accomplished. Their smiles were more warm than she'd ever seen them wear before and a brief hug from each felt the same. She returned to watch the ceremony finish into silence.

She would survive, for the others, for her friends and responsibilities if not for herself. Syago clasped her hand and she felt safe in the moment, for the moment that was then so precious, somehow, in spite of the horrors inside her.

"I can't do this anymore," Lil'iek turned from the balcony to storm away, inside. That woman's tears were too much. Tek'ouk'iek started following, and she turned to him. "What the golkaw does she have to be so sad about?!

She wasn't condemned to die by people she trusted. She didn't lose her entire army. She abandoned us."

"She did send Syago to warn us," Tek'ouk'iek supplied, leaning against the unlit wooden hall.

"After getting herself out! THOSE TEARS ARE FAKE!"

"She did experience terrible things there too, Lil'iek. All of us did."

"Are you really going to defend her?" Lil'iek growled.

"No," he said after a pause, rubbing his face. "Sorry, I'm just... still so tired. I'm just trying to find some peace out of this, to just be glad that we at least got out. You were right to drag me out like that; I wasn't thinking clearly."

They'd switched. In the escape she'd retained control while he fell apart, now it was her turn, so she appreciated his hearing her frustration as she aired it out. She breathed, running hands through her mane of hair.

They'd gone with forty-six Quoakans total plus up to twenty from Koah. Other than a handful who'd stayed behind, this constituted most of their warriors in total. Now, because of the betrayal, they were down to just six, and each wounded. But the Asturions had at least half their army left from the battle, and then some. The other four Kimoc had come into the hallway but stood quietly behind, digesting their own traumas in their own ways. "What do we do?" She turned, somewhat pacing. Outside the wailing became unbearable.

"Well, I can't mourn with them either," Tek'ouk'iek said, hobbling past in search of a chair. "Not without firing on them."

"No, I'm talking about generally. They have to recompense us for this. I'm not leaving without blood. We can't leave yet anyway." The dead faces of their lost companions flashed through her mind, and she prayed to each of them. *Stars and moon, I'm so sorry.*

"I don't know. Right now I just need sleep." As she followed him into an antechamber, they found an Asturion guard standing at the door to the stairs. Another one emerged to stand at another, leaving only their own room unguarded.

"What's the meaning of this?" she snapped. Tek'ouk'iek too looked dumbfounded. She raised her voice further still. "Why are you guarding those doors?"

"It is dangerous times m'lady," one said, stiffly. "We must raise our guard to meet it."

"Here? We're not fools."

270

"Also," began the other guard, gulping, then continuing, "Our guests will be escorted on all errands outside their quarters. Courtesy of the—"

"Shut the golkaw up," Lil'iek whipped her words at them as Tek'ouk'iek trembled beside her. "If any of you come near me, I'll shred you like a fish. Do *not* enter our rooms, you hear me?!"

"To what extent you benefit from what happened to us," Tek'ouk'iek began, "you have blood on your hands. We might not avenge it, but the eternals will never forget. The wild knows."

The guards gave no response, and the Kimoc went to their cramped room, having nowhere else to go.

DEFINING OUR TERMS

ANDREW WROTE THIS PART

Angels: Beings of the overworld Kingdom in Heaven, Halls of Celos, embodied in various forms. They come from the classes of Seven Virtues: Chastity, Temperance, Charity, Diligence (Devotion), Patience, Kindness, Humility. These parallel similar classes of Seven Blessings by the lesser known Celestians, neither which are as safe and innocent as they sound.

Alerhas: Plants with pollen that infects lifeforms' wounds to germinate, then grow roots in the body, usually killing it. The alerha then drives the body to infect more and spread its pollen.

Apus: A type of eternal or "god" for the Unaka, based on specific mountains in the Apugakas, their name for the Barbathors.

Archemist: Using dyne and alchemy to manipulate the elements, the needed symbol is etched into an appropriate object which then activates when touched. The person touching use their sentiments to power it.

Archdynast: A dynast at the top of the dynal hierarchy, including elementists who are not dynasts such as archemists. Like all dynasts, they require a foci, usually a scepter or staff, that lets them aim and direct their sentiments into the elements. *See Dyne*

Asturions: Called the palemen by the Kimoc for their whiter skin, came from overseas several hundred years ago. They brought castles, swords, and more monsters according to the Kimoc. According to the Asturions they brought peace and prosperity.

Bards: Minstrels, musicians, poets, story performers, dancers, jesters, fools, and the like. They specialized in using music and/or art to convey sentiments into people and animals. Dyne puts the sentiments into the art that then seeps into human bodies through perception.

Barons: Minor lords within towns or cities, generally under a count with the absence of kings. They're responsible to fund expeditions and defend the domains.

Baw'kook: Fomorion in Asturion, these half-human half-animal were giants and usually only seen raiding. Included the ukuku, ohancanu, wookalar, goatmen, wolfmen, and so forth.

Bolas: Stones on the end of a cord that when thrown wrap around the target, binding them.

Bomogs: Bomok in Kimoc. Burly bulls with thick fur and curling horns used for meat, wool, fertilizer in the outside, and pulling warwagons.

Canker: Unakan word for the Seeping. A blight corruption caused by the Razhod soulstaff Vilekor, seems to emanate from the metallic rock on its top getting heated.

Chamands: Summoners and necromancers accepted of the covens in Bokhor, they summon spirits with a bell but can also be warriors. Shunned summoners were witches, or witchlords in the case of the Razhod.

Claymore: A type of two-handed sword.

Counts: The lord of a town or city by male birthright. Wife would be countess until husband dies. They're usually over barons, like lower level lords. The count typically must be an archdynast to lead the defense of his domain and fund the expeditions.

Crenellations: The blocky, peggy lining that runs along the ramparts/ battlements of a city or castle wally wall.

Culicida: Legendary carnivorous fungi that exhales poison gas.

Daemogs: Thinner bulls that run in bigger herds and snort fire. Their farts also are flammable.

Deepwraiths: Grimshades or shadowmen in other languages. An odd shapeshifting shadowy creature of stealth and death.

Demons: Otherworlder monsters like devils but from The Vast Abyss, an arctic oceanic underworld. They're classified by the Seven Afflictions: Agony, Terror, Despair, Violation, Sorrow, Bondage (Slavery), Destitution (Starvation), and Insanity.

Deova Bondua: The Sanator, The Holy One, Our Blessed Lady in Heaven, Sofia the Savior, The One True Path, and the Eternal of the Palemen (Kimoc wording).

Devils: Underworld monsters like demons but from The Infernal Hellpits, apparently a mostly subterranean otherworld. Classified by the Seven Deadly Temptations: Greed, Gluttony, Lust, Wrath, Pride (Arrogance), Envy, Sloth, and Hate and Apathy.

Duende: Urisg brownies or the Kourii are other names for them, not to be confused with the Xanas. This tiny people are said to be dangerous and live in the marshes.

Dyne: Originally the power to move the elements, like a ruler over them as dynast or but also through archemist and bards. The real power is through sentiments identified in the Vision: Red is anger, hate is brown, fear bright green, anxiety less bright green, sorrow is blue, joy is yellow, pride is orange. But note that only some are used while others have less useful effects or are just not as explosive, common, or sustainable.

Dynfist Monk/Friar: Like a dynast or bard, they use dyne to shoot their sentiments into something. In this case the careful practice of putting it through their own body for greater bursts of speed and strength. Deleterious health effects may follow. It's more distinctly religious, called Takanaku among the Unaka.

Elementist: Anyone that can use dyne.

Emaions: Greater spirits with specific but broad powers, such as a Belfegor the Behemoth or Nimrød the Reptilium, that can be summoned. Spirits of fire, lightning, shadow.

Eternals: The Great Ones "gods" of the Kimoc, Unaka, and Amoyara pagans. But each group views theirs differently. Often associated with natural features.

Feldinal: Furacán in Kimoc, Amoyaran, and Unakan. They're oversized animals often with strange humanoid mutations, similar to demons and devils but less lethal.

Flambard: Two-handed sword with a wavy blade, like flames.

Foci: Usually a scepter or staff serving as the tool of a dynast to guide their sentiments in the practice called dyne. For archemists the foci would be the object they write on, for bards and dynfists it's their bodies.

Fomorions: Baw'kook in Asturion, these barbarian giants were half-human half-animal and usually only seen raiding by humans. Tribal collective that included the ukuku, ohancanu, wookalar, goatmen, wolfmen, and so forth.

Gierra: What the Asturions call their earth.

Grievore the Violator: A flambard soulweapon greatsword, maybe just short of a greatsword. But two-handed life-draining soulweapon wielded by the Razhod.

Grim'iik: Gigantic blackbird that stalks Thornwood and mountain valleys and is worshiped as an eternal.

Grimshades: Deepwraith or shadowmen in other languages. An odd shape-shifting shadowy creature of stealth and death.

Gurows: Large, vicious crow-like animals.

Hellfaces: Tauntname for the Razhod who'd had black eyes with red irises that glowed in the dark, these helleyes along with scars earned them it. Barthandeon, their leader, had one more unique: Old Devilface.

Hellweapons: Handcrafted by shamanic, necromancer figures specifically to slay otherworlders. Different materials grant narrow but spectacular abilities, usually at a dark tradeoff. Not to be confused with Soulweapons.

Kimoc: The tribal peoples of the land of Nevermore. Even though the desert canyon peoples and the forest peoples are quite different, the Asturions call them all Kimoc to simplify things.

Lifeless: Undead, animated by forces of one religious narrative or another. Or by forbidden magics. Oft called zombi by the Bokhor summoners.

Mabin'guarik: Fearsome forest beast with a vertical maw on its chest, bulky clawed arms, and a cycloptic eye on its head.

Machicolations: The extensions of the wall battlements that enable soldiers to shoot down through a small hole at siege assaults or battering rams while staying covered. If in a shooting mood.

Malwolves: Large wolves with tusk-like teeth, yellow eyes, and either thick black fur or no fur at all but hairless black skin. There's probably some reason for this.

Mastozon: Mastozan for women specifically, who'd be second class of an already second-class word meaning mixed blood/skin. Of both Asturion and Unakan/Kimoc ancestry.

Mewil'ishyuuks: Basically a huge sacred deer with wicked antlers. For some reason they let the Roah'riik ride them and worship them.

Mordios The Reaver: A soulweapon warscythe used by the Razhod. Said to kill instantly on touching blood. Had been a favorite weapon of Barthandeon.

Morion Helmet: Openfaced helm made to go with armor that has a collar. Morions have a rim around the edge and a small crest or fin along the top.

Morwolf Hounds: Smaller wolves that somehow cooperate as pets and hunting companions.

Mother/Mamak Yoaom: The motherwood, or eternal "goddess" of the forest, but like she is the forest.

Muru'unkuy: Massive boar-like animal with tusks and extra bad smells.

Nevermore: The Kingdom Republic of Nevermore is the undisputed(?) name for the largely unmapped realm herein which we find ourselves.

Ohancanu: Barbarian giants who are the most human of the Fomorion/Baw'kook collective, would be human except for their size and cycloptic eye. Balgor is sole proof they can be intelligent and peaceful, not that you've given them a chance.

Osmos: A mystic cosmic gate that connects gierra to the otherworlds (overworlds and underworlds), for a price. The osmosis of the cosmos. Do NOT summon unless prepared to pay a toll.

Otherworlder: Any being from the otherworlds, typically broken down to overworlds and underworlds, though gierra is sort of considered an underworld as well by the Church. Either way, better just not summon Osmos at all.

Ozor: Even if you think you can pay, or have nothing to lose, don't summon Osmos. Oh and ozors are just extra large angry bears.

Pauldron: Basic medieval terminology you really could've looked up on your internets. But guess I shouldn't complain you're here instead. Pauldrons are shoulder plates of armor.

Penaga the Slaver: Penaga the Punishment, as well. A barbed warwhip soulweapon wielded by the Razhod.

Pillory: Same, but medieval arm and neck brace to punish criminals, expose them for public mockery.

Piory/Abbey/Monastery/Convent: Sorry I'm not doing four of these, even if there are minute differences between them. They had monks, friars, abbots/abbesses, and sometimes priests and bishops. Religious communities wouldn't be so isolated in Nevermore anyways, but cloistered in some corner of a town or maybe on a mountaintop fortress.

Quelk: Like an elk, but with a q and more sinister.

Quervosks: Like big ravens with extra temper and razor beaks.

Quoarn'riik: Like a chieftain among the Kimoc, but also shamanic and usually elected by the women. This varied by people and tribe.

Razhod: Witchlords, the Crimson Coven who held the Crimson Covenant. When alive, they were called Hellfaces as well due to their hellish eyes. Not to be confused with their followers in the cult.

Roah'riik: Hellhunters and helltamers among the Kimoc, more so the forest tribes, who use bones as a telepathic medium.

Saqra: An eternal of the Unaka, but one that can be summoned and so also emaion or greater spirit. Known for dark tricks, he also had a mysterious cult.

Seeping: The Asturion word for Canker, or blighting corruption. It causes the body to ulcerate and seep blood as if from burns, caused by the metallic rock on the soulstaff Vilekor.

Soulweapons: Weapons with greater spirit emaions in them. The powers of the spirit are then embedded into the weapon pending good relations between wielder and weapon spirit. Not to be confused with hellweapons, these are sentient, durable, and select who can wield them. They also have extra sharp blades, control over weight and balance, and can fly. The Razhod destroyed all but Alexandre who in turn destroyed them.